A MOST IMPETUOUS UNION

Jared, earl of Hawkesly, needed to wed immediately, and the fact that he barely knew his beautiful, desperate bride Kathryn mattered not a whit. The instant their vows were spoken, the dashing rogue sailed off to seek his fortune—leaving his marriage unconsummated and his new wife behind as the mistress of his estate.

Now, two years later, Jared has returned, ready to perform his much neglected husbandly duties. But to his shock, not only has his bride transformed his once tranquil home into a thriving business enterprise overrun with strangers, Kate doesn't recognize her errant husband! Even as he vows *that* will change, Jared realizes he may have met his match in this spirited woman who enchants him more by the hour. And to win his own wife's heart, it will take a very special seduction indeed . . .

"Linda Needham has the ability to mix laughter with tears to touch a reader's heart."
Romantic Times

D0187537

Books by
Linda Needham

THE PLEASURE OF HER KISS
THE BRIDE BED
MY WICKED EARL
WEDDING NIGHT
HER SECRET GUARDIAN
EVER HIS BRIDE
FOR MY LADY'S KISS

If You've Enjoyed This Book,
Be Sure to Read Those Other
AVON ROMANTIC TREASURES

LOVE WITH A SCANDALOUS LORD *by Lorraine Heath*
STEALING THE BRIDE *by Elizabeth Boyle*
TAMING THE SCOTSMAN *by Kinley MacGregor*
TO LOVE A SCOTTISH LORD: BOOK FOUR OF
THE HIGHLAND LORDS *by Karen Ranney*
A WEDDING STORY *by Susan Kay Law*

Coming Soon

HOW TO TREAT A LADY *by Karen Hawkins*

LINDA NEEDHAM

The Pleasure of Her Kiss

An Avon Romantic Treasure

AVON BOOKS
An Imprint of HarperCollinsPublishers

This is a work of fiction. Names, characters, places, and incidents are products of the author's imagination or are used fictitiously and are not to be construed as real. Any resemblance to actual events, locales, organizations, or persons, living or dead, is entirely coincidental.

AVON BOOKS
An Imprint of HarperCollins*Publishers*
10 East 53rd Street
New York, New York 10022-5299

First Avon Books paperback printing: November 2003

Avon Trademark Reg. U.S. Pat. Off. and in Other Countries, Marca Registrada, Hecho en U.S.A.
HarperCollins® is a registered trademark of HarperCollins Publishers Inc.

Printed in the U.S.A.

10 9 8 7 6 5 4 3 2 1

To CG, PB & SL,
my three favorite muses

Chapter 1

The Huntsman, Gentleman's Club
London, 1848

"**O**ne whining, overripe Hapsburg prince delivered safely to the cellar door at Buckingham Palace," Ross said, loosening his neck cloth as he slid a leather packet across the map table.

"At great risk to our personal fortunes," Drew added with a wry smile as he dropped into a wing chair. "Gad, Jared, the man's a bloody card sharp."

"You did leave him with a quid or two, Drew," Jared, earl of Hawkesly, asked, certain that the surly prince wouldn't soon forget his card game with Drew.

"Two quid *and* his hat," Drew said, propping his polished boots on the edge of the brass hearth fender.

"Good work, man." Jared gave Drew's shoulder an

affable cuff, pleased to be home and in familiar company, and to have the matter of the prince finished so neatly.

Neatly enough to finally have time to take care of some long-neglected personal business.

Brushing off the glint of a perfumed memory, a moment's guilt, Jared handed a report to each of them. "Fortunately we're finished with rebellions and insolent monarchs for the moment. A routine gun-running investigation."

"Ah, that American merchant ship," Ross said, flipping through the pages. "The *Pickering*. Impounded in Portsmouth."

"Customs found two thousand rifles," Jared said, pulling a map tube out of his saddlebag, "and countless crates of ammunition, all of it hidden beneath a shipment of Indian cornmeal."

"Guns and grain," Drew said, shaking his head, sobered considerably. "I'll wager they're bound for Limerick or Cork."

"My thoughts exactly." Word of the potato crop failure had reached Jared months ago in the China Sea, a blight that seemed to have only intensified. "Doubtless it's the Young Irelanders."

Ross tossed the report to the middle of the table. "Damn fools, if they mean to rise again. With martial law and another seventeen thousand of Her Majesty's troops on their way to Dublin."

"In any case," Jared said, adding Lord Grey's note to the report, "the Home Office has given me charge of coastal inquiries during the trouble in Ireland. We're to investigate the captain of the *Pickering*, his politics, the shipping company, the receiver, the warehouses. A simple, domestic inquiry—"

"Domestic?" Drew asked, a jaunty brow cocked at Jared. "An interesting choice of words, don't you think, Ross?"

"Absolutely," Ross said, his smile scheming and wry as he stood. Hazardous to the unsuspecting. "Because, as I recall, Jared leaves this morning on a domestic mission of his own."

So that was it, the blighters.

"Possibly the most dangerous mission of his life." Drew's dark eyes glinted like knife points, an expression as familiar as the easy drone of voices coming from the club room beyond.

"A lot you two blackguards know of marriage." Jared went to the map case beneath the bow window and yanked open a drawer. "Think what you will; I know what I'm doing."

Ross laughed, pouring himself a cup of coffee from the samovar. "But we also know what you *haven't* done, Jared."

"Couldn't possibly have done," Drew said.

"To the devil with both of you." Grateful that he was no longer prone to blushing like a callow lad, Jared lifted out the stash of maps and dropped them onto the top of the case.

"How long has it been since Hawkesly got married, Ross?" Drew asked. "Two years?"

"Longer than that, by my counting."

"Eighteen months, you bloody pair of magpies."

Doing a lousy job of ignoring their usual blathering, Jared found the map of the western England coastline and set it aside.

"Still, it's a loooong time to leave your bride *unattended*."

His bride.

The thought always stopped him in motion, left only the briefest image, burned into his memory, impossible to shake.

The blue-eyed mist of her, the silky promise of fire and smoke and long summer evenings. Or had she only been a mirage, heat shimmering off the harbor, the deep cerulean Egyptian sky?

"An eternity, Jared," Ross said, joining him at the map case, coffee cup in hand. "Especially for a bride that you didn't know . . . that you married in haste on the deck of your ship in Alexandria, and then left at the altar a minute later."

It had been at least *five* minutes later, Jared thought but thankfully didn't say aloud, because it would have been a ridiculous point to press. They all knew the reason that he'd had to leave Miss Trafford in Alexandria.

A convenient wedding at an inconvenient moment. As damnably inconvenient as this one.

"You'll have to begin the gun-running investigation without me. I'll be spending the next few weeks at Hawkesly Hall."

"Is that wise, Jared? Going home? What if, instead, Ross and I send word to your lovely bride that you died at sea in the service of your queen? That we tossed your rotting body reverently, but irretrievably, overboard—"

"Thanks anyway, Drew, but I'm fully capable of

making my own peace with Miss Trafford without—"

Drew sputtered. "Miss *Trafford*? Good Lord, Jared, you're in worse trouble than I'd imagined!"

Bloody hell, Drew never missed a slip of the tongue. And yet this was more than a slip—he'd been thinking of the woman as "Miss Trafford" all this time.

Kathryn Trafford, heiress and only child of the late Victor Trafford of Trafford Shipping. He knew little more of her than that.

Light eyes, bright as the sky, as blue as the sea. Sungold hair and ribbons and a bonnet that had fought the wind with all its might.

A deep memory of her mouth, softly red and full and firmly bowed. And frowning up at him, furiously working with resentment. Tugged at by her perfectly straight, white teeth.

Frown all you want, my dear wife, it was a business venture that wed us. Nothing more.

"A simple mistake, Drew, made out of habit."

Even Ross looked scandalized. "Do yourself a favor, Jared, and don't let your bride hear you call her Miss Trafford."

"She does know you're coming?"

"She knows, Drew." He'd written her recently . . . a few months back. Maybe six. But he'd informed her then that he'd be arriving home by the end of the year. And here he was. Early.

As to his delay in following her back to England after their wedding, he'd had no choice at the time. She would just have to be grateful that he had finally routed out some time to devote to their marriage.

And to their children.

Yes, it was time that he beget an heir to the Hawkesly fortune. With a few to spare. Miss Traff . . . *Kathryn* would surely be receptive to finally consummating their marriage.

He certainly was.

More than receptive. Eager, in fact.

"Ah! There you are, my Lord Hawkesly!" Arthur Pembridge had suddenly appeared at the door of the map room with his usual impeccable timing, impeccably dressed, impeccably composed. "Your trunk has arrived from your cabin on the *Garnet Moon*. Shall I have it delivered to the railway station?"

"And then sent ahead to Hawkesly Hall, Pembridge," Jared said. "Except my saddlebag here. I'll see to it myself."

"Ah, carrying a gift for your bride, then, sir?"

A gift?

Pembridge arched a well-groomed eyebrow, then cast him a half smile. "Doubtless too delicate an object to be transported by any means but your own hand?"

Damn! A gift. Leave it to Pembridge to think of that. Their man of affairs, who had saved him from countless missteps.

"Precisely, Pembridge." Jared patted his saddlebag as though he had a fragile treasure hidden there. "A gift."

Pembridge nodded an impeccable, glad-to-save-your-skin-sir smile and then left.

Drew was staring at Jared, aghast. "You forgot to get your bride a wedding gift, didn't you?"

"Bugger off." A gift was easy enough to acquire, though he knew virtually nothing about her. Her letters to him had been few and terse—sterile information, always seasons old and dripping with unspoken censure.

But she was a woman, after all, and women liked pretty things. Soft things.

"Oh, he's in trouble now, Ross."

He had crates of Chinese porcelain in the hold of the *Garnet Moon*. And silk. And perfume from Paris.

Ross straddled a chair. "How about some Belgian lace? All brides like lace."

A clock! There was a handsome floor clock stored at his hunting lodge, right there on the estate, inlaid with gold and mother-of-pearl. Very expensive—a gift from a grateful Swiss count. Which made the clock a gift suitable for any bride.

He'd stop at the lodge, have the clock loaded onto one of the panel wagons, if he could find someone to help him, and then have it in tow when he arrived home.

Easy enough. Ruffled feathers smoothed, her female temper cooled, pride easily purchased.

Excellent!

"Well, I'm on my way, gentlemen." Jared rolled the map into its case, tucked it into his saddlebag, then hooked the strap over his shoulder. "Do keep me informed of your investigation."

Drew caught Jared by the elbow. "Just one thing before you head off to this belated wedding night."

"What is it?"

Drew crossed his arms over his chest. "A wager."

"No." He'd long since stopped placing wagers against Drew. The man had the devil's luck, and a mind that stored and sorted every fact he'd ever learned. Jared brushed past him and out of the map room into the club room, with Drew on his heels, Ross close behind, laughing.

"Just a simple wager."

Jared laughed as he strode along the mezzanine with its gleaming mahogany balustrade and brass fittings, always pleased at the richness spreading out before him—the grand staircase, the thick carpets and luxurious furnishings, liveried servants and well-kept secrets.

The sinuous marble designs on the floor of the lobby below had been the crowning touch: a broad, inlaid crest, a lion rampant, a ship in full sail, and three swords, blades crossed.

The Huntsman—the grandest club in all of London. Prized for its grandeur, its exorbitant fees, its powerful, luminous, exclusive membership, the everlasting rumors about its mysterious owner.

St. Thomas, he was called. A duke, they whispered, doubtless a young European prince with too much money and power for his own good.

Let them think what they will.

Jared stopped one step down the staircase and turned to face his two friends, men he had loved and admired and trusted with his life for so long that it was second nature to him.

"No need for a wager, Drew. I'm fully confident that you and Ross will succeed in Portsmouth—"

"Of course we will." Drew laughed and draped his arm over Ross's shoulder. "My wager is far more personal and quite simple: that you'll be at least a week getting your wife into your bed. Seven days. I'll even mark it into the betting book."

Jared laughed again, because the huge man could be every bit as amusing as he was deadly serious, with barely a breath between. "You are completely mad."

"Not me, friend. You, if you really think you're going to just walk through her door for the first time in your married life and happily waltz your little bride into bed without paying a painful penalty for your neglect."

"First of all, my personal life has never been the subject of one of your frivolous wagers."

"Bloody hell, you've never *had* a personal life."

"Secondly, my marriage is bloody well none of your business."

Drew frowned and leaned against the banister. "Then you truly won't take the wager?"

Ross crossed his arms against his broad chest, a dare on his face. "At least grant us the warning."

"*Et tu*, Ross?" The solemn one of the pair.

Ross shook his head. "Let's just say that were I in your boots, Jared, I would tread lightly. Or better yet, I'd go barefooted and on my hands and knees."

An uncomfortable silence stretched out between them, the remains of Ross's quiet warning filling the gilded vaults above the lobby, drifting downward into the polish and brass, and settling hard on Jared's shoulders.

"Good then, Ross," he said, shaking off the unexpected hitch in his confidence. "When you decide to marry, do let me know and I'll be sure to take lessons from you."

Drew snorted, Ross only grunted and said, "Don't say we didn't warn you."

"Now if you'll both excuse me, I don't want to miss my train."

By the time Jared had left the Huntsman, he was once again feeling in complete control. And scoffing at Drew's absurd wager and Ross's warning, certain of his own success in the matter of his much delayed wedding night.

"As a matter of fact, I'll take your wager, Drew," Jared said under his breath as he climbed into a carriage outside the door of the Huntsman, "and I'll raise you a tenner."

Miss Trafford would become Lady Hawkesly in truth sometime tomorrow night because . . .

Bloody hell, because she was his wife!

Jared made Liverpool by evening. He spent a restless night at the Foxbury Railway Inn, then two more hours on a train and another hour in a post carriage, until he was finally trotting through the late September afternoon on a horse hired in Mereglass—his village— and rounding a familiar bend in the lane that led through the woods toward his hunting lodge.

The queen had granted him the lodge, along with the newly created earldom of Hawkesly and its magnificent hall, the town and the harbor, the mountains and the fields.

A heady accomplishment for a boy who'd escaped from a workhouse with the law on his heels and two young friends in tow. But fate had made him the queen's champion at twenty, her trusted emissary at twenty-one, and in the decade since, her clandestine intermediary in times of dire need. He gladly risked his life for her, for his country, and was well rewarded for it.

An occupational hazard which kept him away for long periods of time and the estate nearly deserted.

At least the lodge should be deserted. Yet as he cleared a hillock and its thick grove of yew, he was certain he'd seen a light where the lodge should be.

More than one light. And motion.

"Bloody hell!" Jared loped his horse along the winding lane, every switchback revealing more activity. Men and horses and then the sound of voices, until he reached the edge of the shadowy forest.

The instinctive habits of survival kept him from riding into the melee without knowing the facts.

The forecourt of the lodge was teeming with men, a half dozen just coming up the path from the river, bristling with fish and fishing paraphernalia.

His fish, of course! His lodge!

Bloody hell, and there was another group lounging at a long table under a tree, drinking *his* ale, from *his* tankards.

"Can I take yer horse, sir?" A boy was coming toward him, doffing his cap, an eager little hop in his gangly step.

"My horse?"

"Shall I stable 'im for ya?"

His stables, too? His hay and his horses? Damnation, his private hunting lodge looked like a bloody country inn!

"You do that, boy." Jared threw the groom the reins, grabbed his saddlebag, and started toward the courtyard, prepared to do battle with whoever the hell had taken over his lodge.

Which seemed to be doing a hopping business. Jared tried to brush past a trio of poachers, but the stoutest of them stepped in his way.

"I say, sir! Are you a course man or game?"

Bloody nonsense.

The lean one gave Jared a close look as he scratched at his thickly bearded chin. "No, Fitchett, he's got the look of the course about him."

"Nah, he's game, Gilmott." The younger man pointed at Jared with the tip of his fishing rod, not knowing how close he was to being tossed to the ground. "A grayling, I'd wager. At home on the Tay as well as the Tweed."

"Well then, what is it, man?" the first one asked, with a broad laugh, venturing a jabbing knuckle against Jared's upper arm, then wisely retracting the offense. "Breame here thinks he can tell a man's sport just by looking at him."

Seething with anger, Jared merely touched the brim of his hat and left them with a nodded, "Gentlemen."

Jared pressed his way through the blustering crowd, past the tippling squires and their tall tales—a seventeen-pound barbel, a dozen woodcock, bagging a hill hare with his bare hands. . . .

Bloody hell, someone had turned his lodge into a sportsman's retreat. And he was bloody well going to throttle whoever had done it.

Jared stalked through the front doorway and the entry passage, then into the brightness of the great room with its clerestory windows and it massive hearth ablaze with wood—from *his* forest, of course.

Last he'd seen the lodge, everything had been draped in dustsheets, from the furniture to the paintings and sconces and even the mounted game on the walls.

Now the place looked like a bloody hotel for country gentlemen, and smelled of roasted boar and woodsmoke, of brandy and leather . . .

And something else . . .

A haunting sweetness. Subtle. Familiar, somehow, blending with the other scents.

He stood in the center of the room, amidst the trespassers who were lounging in his plush chairs, their muddied heels grinding into the inlaid tops of his tables, into the thick carpets.

Drinking his whisky, by God!

Stolen from his cellar!

And served up by a tall, gray-haired barman, who was struggling with a keg behind a brand-new counter tucked inside one of the archways beneath the east balcony.

The man would damn well serve Jared the truth, else he'd find himself on his way to Newgate in the next breath.

"You there," Jared said across the top of the counter, startling the man into straightening.

"That fashed for a pint, are ya, sir?" His brogue was far thicker than the groom's. "So what can I do for ya."

You can get the hell out of my lodge, he wanted to say.

Instead, Jared leaned toward the man, wanting to take him by the collar and throttle the truth out of him. "You can tell me who's in charge here."

"Here?" The man frowned, scratched at the back of his neck. "Well, I am, I suppose. Curtis McHugh's the name, sir," he said, sticking out his hand for Jared to shake, retracting it when Jared didn't reciprocate. "In charge of the bar and the spirit cellar here at Badger's Run. And proud of the honor, I am."

"Badger's Run?" Like hell it was Badger's anything. This was plainly his hunting lodge on the Hawkesly estate. There was no mistaking where he was. "I'll ask you one more time, who is in charge here?"

"Here at Badger's Run, you mean?" McHugh smiled, sighed, nodded almost fondly. "Well, then, you should have said."

"I'm saying now, McHugh, as plainly as I know. Tell me who runs this place."

"Ah, now that would be . . ."

An odd expression drifted over McHugh's features, softened them, pinked his cheeks like a schoolboy's. He canted his head, then nodded over Jared's shoulder.

"That would be herself, sir. Comin' down the stairs." He sighed again, his smile gone wistful. "Our Lady Kathryn."

Miss Trafford?

Kathryn.

God, he hadn't thought for a moment that . . . never, ever imagined that she . . . that his wife was the . . .

A white-hot thrill ran through him, a remembered scent of flowers, anticipation. So powerful that it turned him on his heel toward the stairway that landed just below the balcony.

Holy hell. His wife.

Moving down the stairs like a cloud, the picture of

breathless grace, her hair cascading down her back like a curtain of silvery blond silk.

And she was coming toward him.

Or he was moving toward her in a room that suddenly seemed to be slanting and swirling.

Hell and damnation, he'd planned to meet her at Hawkesly Hall, to present himself with a proper greeting and the clock, fully in control of everything.

"Good evening, sir, may I help you?"

God, yes, wife, he tried to say.

But he only stood there blinking at her beauty, stunned to his soul, his mouth working like a fish into an utterly silent,

I'm home.

Chapter 2

"**M**ay I help you, sir?" she asked again, her silky words bewitching his tongue.

Maybe it was the soft lilt of her voice that scrambled his thoughts and mislaid his intentions. Or perhaps it was the familiar scent of her nearness that paralyzed him, that kept him from dragging her into his arms and claiming his marital rights on the spot.

But she was looking up at him patiently, as though he were simple, a frown of concern creasing her pale brows, winging them above her blue, blue eyes.

"Are you all right, sir? Perhaps you ought to sit down and rest." Now the enchanting woman had him by the elbow, her hot little fingers slipping into private folds, his own warm places, the woody scent of her propelling him wherever it was she was leading him.

"Sit."

He felt the backs of his calves against something low and cushy, watched as she spread her palm against his chest and then gave a little push. It wasn't until his backside hit a cushion that he realized he was sitting.

"Good God, woman!" Jared stood, fully in control again, except for his breathing, and a tight gripping in his belly, a callow erection that had him fully roused and wanting.

Wanting his wife and that moist, rosy mouth that pouted in thought as she peered up at him.

"Sir, you don't look at all well." Her eyes were enormous, fringed in sable. So blue. The clear blue of the Mediterranean, the Aegean, the Sandwiches.

Then he realized with a sudden, unbalancing twinge that she was calling him *sir*.

Not Hawkesly.

Or Jared.

Or husband.

But sir.

Sir!

As though he were an utter stranger to her, a lunatic besides. A threat that kept McHugh hovering over them.

"Did he speak to you at all, McHugh?" She lifted the hair at Jared's forehead with her fingertips, stunning him with her gentle touch, stealing the words that he'd been about to speak.

Don't mock me, woman, I'm your husband. But the words didn't make it off his tongue.

"Sure he spoke well enough, my lady. Spoke like regular toff, he did."

"I *am* a regular toff," Jared said, with a blustering sputter.

Bloody hell, he'd meant to say a regular *husband.* *Her* regular husband, but his mouth still wasn't working right and he was feeling like a regular fool.

A grin played at his wife's mouth, the slightest dimples winking from her cheeks, teasing him, he was sure. "Are you expected at Badger's Run, sir?"

"Expected?" He'd bellowed the question, felt it burn its way down his throat and into his gut.

Was this another game of hers? Like the lodge itself? Punishment because he'd been gone too long. This dodge and parry instead of a proper, grateful greeting. Surely she was expecting him—her husband—home.

Sometime.

After all, he'd written to her months ago that he would be arriving sometime this year.

"I'm sorry, sir. It's just that if you haven't booked your lodging ahead of time, then I'm afraid you won't be able to stay with us."

"Won't—" He choked on the rest of his words. On the very idea that his bride was turning him away from their bed on their wedding night.

Booked his lodging?

His *lodging?*

"We're full up for the entire weekend."

He was watching her lips instead of listening fully, consumed by the way they glistened as she spoke her riddles. "Full up?"

"The fishing tournament, you see."

"Tournament?"

"The second annual, I'm glad to say." She crooked an index finger his way, and then strode off toward the small office, just off the main room. "Very popular.

Now, if you'll simply tell me your name, I'll check my books for your reservation."

His name? A coldness settled across his shoulders. The specter of a topsy world, where day was night and strangers invaded his home.

Where his wife was pretending not to know him.

Or truly didn't.

Confused and slowed by this puzzle, Jared followed her into the little room. "Do you mean, madam, that you don't know who I am?"

She stopped behind a tidy desk and studied him earnestly for a short moment and then shook her head. "I'm sorry, I can't say that I do."

"You're certain?"

He felt her studying him, the hitch in her brow— a memory of some part of him that she must have dismissed—and then her cutting question,

"Why, sir? Should I?"

Of course she shouldn't. Five minutes in his company as she was rushed about in the hot, glaring sun on the deck of a ship in the faraway port of Alexandria, her foolish father dead only a day.

And a marriage thrust upon her from out of nowhere.

Why the devil should she remember him? Or care in the least? A reasonable possibility. And yet what would make her turn his hunting lodge into a bloody sportsman's retreat?

Something wasn't right here. Not right at all.

"Then if you'll give me your name, sir . . ."

For no other reason than a lifetime of perilous intrigue and a deep need to think through this very murky problem before taking another step, Jared looked his ravishing wife straight in the eye and gave her the name of his factor in Montreal.

"My name is Huddleswell, madam. Colonel Leland P. Huddleswell."

She blinked at him, then turned away to the large book spread out across her desk blotter. She ran her finger along the page, then looked up at him and said, just as plainly, but with a sigh, "As I feared, Colonel Huddleswell, your name is not on our books anywhere. So, if you plan to fish the tournament, you'll have to find a bed elsewhere."

Elsewhere but beside her? He nearly laughed at her wayward notion, but held his reaction close. If his beautiful, provoking bride thinks that he would willingly spend another night under a different roof than hers, she would soon learn otherwise.

But all in his own time.

Meanwhile, he would investigate her plans and uncover her strategies, her motives. Though revenge was the most obvious. To repay his high-handedness with her father's shipping business.

"Your pardon, Lady Hawkesly, but I don't think you understand me." Jared took a few slow steps toward her across the small office, stopping a foot from her, the rose of her lips reminding him that he'd forgotten to kiss her after their wedding ceremony. Not even a peck. "You'll find a suitable bed for me this weekend at Badger's Run, else I'll see you closed down for good."

"And how do you plan to do that, Colonel?" Her perfectly shaped breasts rose and fell sharply in her sudden anger, the points of movement and shadow against the linen of her shirtwaist sapping his concentration. The flick of her brow as riling to his will as her fragrance.

"I have my ways, madam. And more means than you could ever imagine. Now you'll give me a room, or you'll soon know the reason why."

Kate could easily imagine a great deal of mischief from this beastly tempered colonel who'd come marching into her lodge as if he owned her.

She'd never seen such a handsome man, certainly never at this close range. Close enough to savor his minty breath breaking across her forehead and the warm eddies riffling her lashes, her hairline. Muscles flexing beneath the skin of his smooth bronze jaw, the slight sheen of beard.

Ohhh, and all that bay- and leather-scented, steamy heat pouring off his finely tailored coat, seeping through her bodice, lifting the hair at her nape.

Distractingly handsome and imperious and rude and far, far too close at the moment.

So, for the second time in the same evening, Kate pressed the heel of her hand against his chest and gave a shove.

This time the man didn't budge an inch, beyond the taut bundle of muscles rippling beneath the wool and linen.

So, he thought he could frighten her, did he? Well, just let him try!

"Listen here, Colonel Huddleswell," she said, grabbing up a fistful of waistcoat and elegant, gold-crested buttons, and pulling him even closer, "I've survived the steaming jungles of Burma, three hurricanes, tigers, bears, pythons, a month icebound on an Arctic whaler, and a two-hundred-mile march through the Persian desert while being held prisoner of an angry warlord. So if you're thinking to frighten me, you have a long, long way to go."

The huge man had straightened from her with every item on her list, his mouth drawing into a fury, his dark eyes narrowing to dangerous slits.

"Say that again."

Taking the advantage of his sudden distance, Kate slipped away from him to the opposite side of the desk. "I'm only trying to explain to you, Colonel, that you can't frighten me with your bullying. And even if you could, I wouldn't be able to give you a room at Badger's Run."

The colonel had followed her around the desk. "What were you doing in Persia?"

"That's really none of your business—"

"You were taken prisoner?" The intensity of his question startled her.

"Years ago, if you must know. I was eleven and my father's ship had been captured in port and, well, it's really only a cautionary tale. Which changes nothing, Colonel." Befuddled by the man's scent, by the possessive fire in his eyes, Kate sidled away from him and again jabbed her finger into the registration book. "Here. You can see for yourself that I have absolutely no vacancies. Every room is filled for the next three days."

His smile turned sly and ominous as he came toward her, as though he were testing her and the air around her. "Then I'll take yours."

"That's quite enough, sir!" It wasn't his audacious suggestion that made her heart stumble over itself, it was the sullen darkness of his voice, the undermining rumble. She pointed to the fiddleback in the corner. "You'll sit there and behave yourself, Colonel, else I'll call McHugh in here."

Of course, he didn't sit, he only steadied his pace toward her as she backed away, around to the front of the desk. "You're a very beautiful woman."

The impertinent lout! She blushed instantly, like a silly debutante confronting her first rogue. "Thank you, Colonel, but I'm married."

That stopped the colonel midstride. He raised a bemused brow, then smiled ever so slightly, as though he were somehow pleased and trying to hide it.

"You don't look married." He leaned back against the desk, folding his arms across his broad chest, as though he had learned whatever he'd been after.

"Well, I am quite married. Quite."

The colonel pretended to look around her, as though he knew her sorry secret. "Where is he then? Your husband?"

"I . . ." She hated more than anything to admit that she was never quite sure where her husband was, hated even more that she wouldn't recognize him even if she saw him. "My husband is at sea, Colonel."

"He must be, to leave you here to manage all alone. That doesn't seem wise."

"I'm perfectly capable, sir." Capable of clouting the man on the head if need be. "But I can assure you that if he were here, he would tell you the same thing. We are full up and were not expecting you."

His face went stern and he tugged on the front points of his elegant dove-gray silk waistcoat. "But I wrote to you, madam."

"You did? When?" She certainly didn't recall the name Huddleswell. Or any kind of colonel at all.

"Months ago. I'm a man of careful planning."

"Why didn't you tell me that earlier?" Thoroughly flummoxed, Kate went to her filing drawer and opened it wide, hoping that she wouldn't find a lost correspondence.

"You gave me no chance." She could feel him watching her as she leafed through the drawer, a slow, searing heat from her nape all the way down her spine, jangling her nerves.

Must be all that talk about her husband—wherever the blighter was.

"No use dancing about the bush, Colonel Huddleswell." She turned to him, preferring to meet trouble with her chin forward. "I'm sorry, but I found no correspondence here with your name on it."

He shook his head dramatically. "I wrote to you in good faith, months in advance. You should have been expecting me."

Kate took a deep breath. "Then there's obviously been a mix-up between here and your home."

"There sure as hell has been."

"But to show my own good faith, I'll be happy to arrange a room for you in Mereglass—"

"I'll be staying here, madam, at Badger's Run."

"But the Cloak and Gander has rooms that—"

"Here." His surly frown loosened suddenly. "Because this is where you are holding your fishing tournament. And I want to be close to the fishing."

Kate couldn't help but laugh, though the man was being a right royal pain. "That's hard to imagine, sir. You're not the type."

He lifted a dark, defiant eyebrow. "Oh, and what type am I?"

"A regular toff. You said so yourself. Doubtless from a grand part of London. A paid-up member of at least three gentlemen's clubs—"

"Yes, madam, and with enough influence among powerful people to make sure that the Badger's Run closes tomorrow, on rumor alone."

Powerful people like her husband, if he were ever to hear of such a rumor. Hawkesly would never understand what she was doing here. But money was tighter than ever and she had so many expenses these days. And there was next month's shooting parties already scheduled, the money already spent on—

"Your decision, Lady Hawkesly?"

The blackguard looked ready and was doubtless able to do most anything in order to have his way. Not a man to cross. And, truth be told, she did have a spare room . . . of sorts.

Kate sighed, weary of the fight and seeing no other option. "Very well, Colonel Huddleswell, you can stay."

Now the blighter seemed surprised. "In your room?"

"Any more talk like that, Colonel, and I'll dust your backside with buckshot."

That too seemed to soothe him, brought on that

smug smile again. "So you do have a room, then? You were holding out on me."

"You'll understand the reason I didn't offer this particular room when you see it."

"It'll do."

"It'll have to, Colonel. In the meantime, you must excuse me. I've got an early dinner to serve to two dozen hungry fishermen, who retire before ten and rise at four in the morning."

Kate left the office for the dining room, angry at the colonel for defeating her so easily, angry at herself for allowing it when she had so many other more important problems to resolve.

The dining hall was paneled to the tops of the doorways in carved oak, plastered to the old coffered beam ceiling and encircled by heavily framed portraits of utter strangers alternating with the mounted heads of the fiercest kind of wild animal imaginable.

The diners were drinking and laughing and happily spending their money on the contents of her husband's wine cellar. Each man had a fish tale to tell her, adding minutes to her trek to the dais.

Remembering that the colonel would need to be seated among the other fishermen, she glanced up to find him leaning against the dining-room arch, arms crossed, his eyes moving over the crowd.

Good thing that his angry glare couldn't light fires, else the entire room would be ablaze. And at this point a meal seemed the least of his interests.

Well, let him starve.

Kate quieted the group merely by raising her hand.

"I want to welcome all of you to the second annual Fisherman's Regatta at Badger's Run."

A roar of approval went up and Kate couldn't help looking up across all the heads to find the colonel, not surprised that he was frowning.

"You'll have three days to score your best catch in each category. In whatever order you choose. The best overall fisherman, by weight, wins."

"Auch, if only you were the prize, Lady Hawkesly, instead of a case of your finest."

Kate smiled down at the man, always amused at the way his moustache bobbed. "You're a dear, Squire Fitchett, but it's no good trying to influence my opinion. The tournament will be judged again this year by our wonderful gamekeeper, Whelan Foggerty."

Foggerty nodded gravely to the applauding crowd, his deep pleasure crinkling only the corners of his eyes, before he stepped back against the sideboard.

"Submit your catches out in the courtyard, under the tent, and then take them to the kitchen to be dressed out by Mrs. Driscoll and her skilled kitchen staff and readied for our own tables." The rest would be smoked and preserved to feed all the hungry mouths up at the hall.

Kate raised a glass to her guests. "My very best wishes to all of you, and to your unlucky quarry."

The lot of them rose as one and the toast ended with a three-part hip-hip-huzzah.

Kate took a deep breath as the food began to flow from the kitchen like a river, then worked her way through the tables toward the door, trying to forget that Huddleswell was waiting for her there.

Colonel Leland P. Huddleswell.

Harumph and twaddle! He didn't look anything like a Huddleswell, let alone a Leland, or a P.

Not with that rakish black hair so carelessly its own style: wind-tossed and shot with gold, nearly reaching to his collar.

And yet he did carry himself and his arrogance as though used to having complete command of any situation.

Even this one.

She'd best show him to his room before he caused an even larger disturbance, and let the dust settle where it may. The night was only just beginning, and with the new child now living at the hall, and the shipment to finish organizing, it was only going to get longer.

Kate paused in front of her surly guest only long enough to say, "If you'll follow me, Colonel Huddleswell, I'll show you to your lodgings, though I doubt you'll be satisfied with anything I can give you at this late hour."

Or at any hour, for that matter.

Chapter 3

Jared let the sweet, woodsy breeze of her wash over him as she brushed past him, her breasts high and taunting, the weight of them shifting as though unencumbered by a proper restraint, her hair flowing down her back.

Calling himself every kind of a fool for not ending this charade immediately, he followed her into the lobby, past the frowning McHugh, who was carrying a case of Hawkesly's best Jamaican rum toward the kitchen.

"This way, Colonel." His wife had stopped on the landing above, amiable and patient. She had a smile that welcomed and challenged and made his skin ache. No wonder her erstwhile guests seemed to dote on her.

Feeling roundly jealous of every man in the place, Jared started after her, his path still unclear, his mind a teeming muddle.

He'd barely gained the first step when a thunder of footfalls rounded the newel and a small child went rocketing past him and up the stairs, using his knee as a pivot pole.

"Wait for meeeee!" And flew right up into his wife's arms as though she belonged there.

What the hell?

"Sarah, sweet, I'm so glad you found me!" The child received a snuggling embrace. "Whatever would I have done without your good-night hug?"

"You'd miss me terrible."

"I would, indeed!"

"Who is this?" Jared asked sharply, riding out a boiling, unfamiliar jealousy.

A child he'd not been told about before the marriage? Another man in her life? A dead husband? After all, he'd known damned little about the scheming woman that he'd married in such haste.

"There's the little groundling." A lean-shouldered, elderly woman bustled past Jared and up the stairs, her arms outstretched. "Time you be abed, Sarah, before the wee folks carry ya off."

"Not the wee folks, Mrs. Rooney!" And then a tremendous squealing and giggling came out of the little wriggling body as his wife tickled and juggled the girl and her wild limbs until Mrs. Rooney was carrying the bundle in her own arms safely back to wherever the devil it had come from.

"And who was that?" he asked again, sure that he hadn't been heard the first time.

"Mrs. Rooney," she said, her hand on her hip. "My ghillie's mum."

"I mean the child, dammit!" he said, aware that he'd made her flinch. "Who is she?" And what the devil was a ghillie?

A scowl flicked one of her brows. "You mean Sarah. She's Mr. Foggerty's little girl. Mrs. Rooney rounds her up for bedtime. Now come, Colonel, I'm sure you'll want to settle in."

She lifted the hem of her skirts and continued up the stairs, trailing her mysteries and her compelling scent.

He followed her for two more flights, suddenly wondering where she'd gotten the large staff required to polish the oak and brass.

And what about Hawkesly Hall itself? Had she closed it up completely? Had she turned it into a school for thieves, or debutantes?

"Your room is up here, Colonel." She opened a narrow service door hidden within the paneling and then climbed the narrowing stairs.

Jared followed, suddenly suspicious, not remembering this particular staircase. Or the stuffy heat—or the cool of the exterior stone wall. And certainly not the quarter turn of the stairs before she opened the door above and stepped into the corridor.

Feeling suddenly like a lamb to the slaughter, Jared stepped hesitantly past her, imagining that his devious, suspicious-acting bride was about to knock him in the head. He'd wake up in the morning with a throbbing headache in the hold of a ship bound for Nanking.

They were in the attic, low-ceilinged and dim, the uneven-planked passage lit by the last shreds of the orange sky sliding over the sill of a window at the far end of the corridor. He'd been so distracted watching his wife's hips swaying and shifting in front of him that he hadn't been counting the turns of the stairs.

"I warned you, Colonel. It's not what you're used to." She lifted a brow as she brushed past him and then continued down the corridor, her head just inches from the rafter beam.

And those perfectly formed hips swaying just slightly, dancing, beckoning his hands.

Cool your heels, old man, you've a shady plot to uncover.

And a marriage to begin.

He stooped his shoulders and started after her, losing her for a moment around a quick corner and then another, until she was climbing another, incredibly narrow, but shorter set of stairs and opening still another door.

"Your room, Colonel." She met him with a smug, poorly hidden smile. "Here in the old fourteenth-century bell tower."

Jared held back on the narrow landing, trying to focus on the woman's plotting, but enjoying the view of her ankles instead, intrigued by her sturdy boots, the dust and the polish and the scrapes.

Imagining those ankles bare and sliding through his hands, her calves and—

"Don't you want to see it, Colonel?"

He grabbed a breath. Grateful for the dimness of the stairwell, Jared swallowed and nodded as he started up the stairs. "I do indeed, madam."

"Watch your head." She was already in the room, covering the ridge of the sharply angled door frame with her hand and tugging on his sleeve to keep his head bent. "Here it is, Colonel, as unpleasant as I promised."

Jared found himself face to face, then nose-to-nose, with her as he slipped slowly through the doorway. Could have been hip to hip, if he'd pressed his advantage.

Which probably wouldn't have been a very good idea, given the moment and his head full of her scent and the roiling suspicions tumbling around inside.

"Badger's Run promised me a great deal, madam." He turned away from her too quickly and immediately crashed his knees into the foot of the small bed. He would have pitched forward, but the woman grabbed hold of his elbow and he turned back to her, closer than ever, his shoulders stooped.

"The room is quite small," she said after a long moment that seemed to confound her. "But it's clean, and has a number of amenities. A window that actually opens."

Jared had already memorized the room. "Yes, madam, and a miniature bed, a child's chair, a table the size of a dinner plate—and no place to stand up straight."

"I'm sorry. But you're very, very tall." She was gazing up at him, her nostrils flaring slightly, breathing too sharply for a solidly married woman.

She was smaller than he remembered from that long-ago, faraway afternoon: lean-limbed, her chin reaching only to the middle of his chest. Her hair was wilder, too, and lacked that huge-brimmed bonnet that had hidden her face from the sun and him and all the other distractions swirling around them on the deck of the *Cinnabar*.

Hiding her secrets even then.

"So how much do you charge for all this luxury?" he said, catching his hand on a rafter.

"Ten guineas for the weekend."

"Ten?" His neck aching from the angle, Jared sat down on the rail at the foot of the bed. "Holy hell, madam, ten guineas will buy me a year's membership in any one of London's finest clubs."

"Then perhaps you should go back to London, Colonel Huddleswell, if you're not happy with the price of your room at Badger's Run. Though I doubt you'll find much sport in fishing the Thames off London Bridge, and nothing I would care to eat."

"Your other guests—are they paying as much as you're charging me?"

"Eleven guineas." She took the two steps to the low, little window and closed the curtains. "After all, I couldn't very well charge you the entire fee. Not with your having to stay here in this room."

"How very considerate of you. What do I get for my money, besides this room?"

"The tournament, of course. It's the reason you're here, after all."

"That's all? No meals?"

"A reasonable extra charge."

"And drinks? What about that expensive cellar you were emptying?"

"McHugh will be happy to keep a ticket for you."

Gad, at least ten pounds a head lodging, and all

those meals and pints. The woman must be pulling in money hand by fist. And doing what with it? Buying herself gew-gaws? Jewelry? Gifts for her lover?

That thought hit him like a cold slap.

"If you'll tell me where your luggage is, Colonel, I'll have McHugh bring it up for you."

Hell. Pembridge had sent his cases ahead to Hawkesly Hall. He hadn't anything in his satchel but papers, and he couldn't very well send up to the hall for his luggage. Might not even be anyone there to receive it.

Well, he was already knee-deep in this messy story—why not jump in all the way?

"What do you mean, my luggage?" He narrowed his eyes at her, hopefully setting her off guard. "Aren't my cases here already?"

She straightened from him and frowned, her mind clearly racing backward through her busy day. "Already? What do you mean?"

Good! He had her on the run this time, pressed a bit harder with his wild story.

"I mean a portmanteau, two trunks, a half dozen cases. I sent my luggage ahead last night so that it would be waiting for me here. As well as my fishing . . . um"—blast, what was the stuff called?—"my gear . . . things. Poles and, um, whatnot."

Instead of cowering, his wife merely stood her ground and shook her head. "Well, I assure you, Colonel Huddleswell, that nothing of yours arrived ahead of you. I would have been informed by the staff and then the lot would have been safely stored."

"Unless it was stolen—"

Her cheeks flamed. "I do *not* employ thieves. How dare you suggest such a thing."

Possibly because you have seized my hunting lodge for your own purposes, without my permission.

"Because, madam, my bags are missing as well as my prize-winning fishing equipment, leaving me without even a change of clothes."

She touched her fingertip to the very center of her lips, surveying him. Then she sighed and shook her head. "Your visit seems to have been plagued with trouble from the start, Colonel Huddleswell. Perhaps it's an omen of things to come."

He'd been thinking the same thing, on this damnably delayed wedding night, in these very close and fragrant quarters. But blast the woman for saying it!

"What do you plan to do about it?"

"I'm going to suggest once more that you spend tonight in comfort at the Cloak and Gander in the village."

"I'm staying here." He crossed his arms and glared at the woman. "Now tell me how you plan to replace the contents of my luggage?"

She raised her shoulders and set her mouth. "You win, Colonel. I'll send McHugh up here with some clothes and a suitable toilet kit. And if you come downstairs for a few minutes early in the morning, I can fit you out with the appropriate tournament equipment. I'll need to know if you're a game man, or a course?"

Bloody hell, that question again. At least now he knew that it had something to do with fishing.

"Both," he said, refusing to be limited in any way,

and now wondering what the devil he'd said to make her lift both eyebrows.

"Well, I must say that I'll want to see you in action, Colonel. By the way, the fish start biting around half past four in the morning. Good night."

Then she turned and left him.

Just like that. On their bloody wedding night!

"Wait!" he bellowed, not at all certain what he was going to say or do when she turned back to him on the landing.

Only that he couldn't let her go.

Not that easily.

Not tonight.

"Yes, what can I do for you, Colonel?" He heard the implied *this time* in the lilt of her impatience. The fire in her eyes delighted him, the strength of her gaze, its skill at putting him in his place.

"Do I pay you now for a meal, or do you trust me enough to pay at the end of the three days?"

She huffed this time at his paltry game. "You can settle up when you leave. You'll have missed most of dinner, but Mrs. Driscoll will see that you're fed."

He damn well didn't want to be fed by Mrs. Driscoll. He wanted to share a meal with his bride. But she had hurried down the stairs as though trying to outrun him, as though he would allow her the distance.

He would have caught up with her but for the great, shining mahogany and brass object that loomed like a ghost on the last turn of the landing.

The floor clock! His well-intended wedding present to his wife.

Blasted woman, she'd already unwrapped it and displayed it in his lodge! He shoved aside the fact that the gift had been an afterthought, Pembridge's reminder.

Now he'd have to think of something else to give her. Something she wasn't already using.

Hell and damnation! Now the woman had disappeared entirely. He looked over the balcony railing and watched the sated guests pouring out of the dining room and filling up the great room, breaking out the card games.

And *his* brandy!

But no sign of his wife.

Perhaps she'd gone to speak with the cook. He hurried down the stairs into the mobbing crowed and cringed when he heard a familiar voice.

"There you are, Huddleswell!" It was Fitchett; somehow he'd routed out Jared's name. And now the rest of his party was closing in on him.

Breame took him by the elbow as though they were fellow conspirators. "Will you be fishing for trout in the morning, sir? Or will you be after the grayling prize?"

Damn and blast!

Chapter 4

⌒⌒⌒

What a prickly pest you are, Colonel Huddleswell!

And too handsome by far.

Kate hurried down the staircase, quickly dispatching the twinge of guilt at slipping away from the man when his back was turned; but the last thing she needed at the moment was a bull-tempered, contrary guest who promised nothing but a weekend of time-frittering trouble.

And she had so little time to spare.

"M'lady, there ya are!" Janie met her just outside the kitchen door with a large, painted tin, her face aglow with a grin. "Mrs. Driscoll said to give ya these marzipan biscuits ta take up ta the hall."

"Perfect timing, Janie. I'm off there right now." Kate was so glad to see the hollows in the girl's cheeks softening more every day, her green eyes growing brighter. "I hope you took a few for yourself."

"Tasted 'em for Mrs. Driscoll, m'lady. She said it was one of my new duties." Janie giggled. "So I took one for m'self and one out ta Corey in the stables."

"Now there's a young man with an appetite." Another miracle. Kate took the biscuit tin, then remembered her promise to Colonel Huddleswell. "By the way, Janie, one of our guests missed dinner; I told him that if he came to the kitchen, he might be able to get something out of Mrs. Driscoll."

"Oh, the pur man if he tries such a thing, my lady! But I'll give a watch out for him. Will ya be comin' back sometime tonight?"

"That depends on what I find up at the hall."

Janie's eyes puddled quickly. "How is the little girl faring?"

Kate smiled. "Much better, I'm glad to say." But Kate wanted to see for herself.

And to check on all the others.

And Elden had sent word in the afternoon that he was ready to move the next shipment to the Hawkesly warehouse on the Mereglass wharf.

With a wave to Janie, Kate grabbed her tweed cloak off the peg as she went out through the delivery door. She hitched her pony to the tilbury and was clattering down the lane toward Hawkesly Hall a few minutes later, the fear that she would arrive too late wedged firmly between her shoulder blades.

Though she really shouldn't worry. She'd left little Margaret in excellent care this morning, and much improved from the night before. Two days of proper nourishment and careful tending seemed to be working, though the lass was still weak and ghostly and as thin as a stick.

And sometimes they just came too late to be helped.

Elden was just closing his office door when Kate slowed and rolled past him toward the barn.

"Did you get my message, my lady?" he called, following with his lantern in his gangling gait.

"I did, Elden! Thank you!" she shouted back as she halted the pony just inside the stable yard. Elden reached her as she dropped from the tilbury.

"We've got a lot more to ship out this time than we had the last, my lady." The corners of his eyes crinkled as he grinned, his large ears flexing from beneath his cap.

"Father Sebastian will be delighted. Let's get it out of here as soon as we can." Before her husband could arrive to stop her.

Before the year was out, he'd said. Christmastide seemed too much to hope for.

Kate handed off the reins to the stable lad with the hope that she would head back to the lodge later, then followed Elden and his bobbing lantern down the corridor of horse stalls and through the double doors into the barn.

"The cribs are full, my lady," Elden said, holding his lantern above the nearest crib and thumping his fist on a lumpy sack of fresh cabbage grown in the gardens of Hawkesly Hall. "We've got carrots and turnips packed away in those empty wine and ale casks. So, come morning, I can start moving all this to the warehouse in Mereglass."

"Just in time for Captain Waring to arrive here from Liverpool with the *Katie Claire*." With a hold nearly full of grain. At least she hoped everything was going as well as it usually did. Because every moment's delay meant lives lost. "Thanks for all you've done, Elden."

"Mine was the simple part, my lady. You're the one who went and stole us a ship."

"I did no such thing." She smiled at the man.

"Took it right out from under your husband's own flag." Elden laughed and held open the barn door.

"The *Katie Claire* is mine." At least it used to belong to her—to her father's shipping company before Hawkesly stole it all away under the guise of marriage. "Besides, Hawkesly never uses the ship. Keeps it docked in Liverpool, like an old maiden aunt."

Or an unsuitable bride.

Damn the man!

"We'll all be thrown in jail if we're caught."

"In the brig, to be exact, Elden." Kate continued out of the barn and through the stables, anxious to see how Margaret was doing. "Especially if anyone ever looks too deeply into the activities of the Ladies' Charitable League."

But how else could she fill all those hungry bellies? The English Parliament had chosen to ignore the cries of starving children and she had chosen to avenge them.

"No word from Lord Hawkesly?" Elden followed her toward the porch at the side entrance of the hall, lighting the way with his lantern.

"None." Doubtless there would be hell to pay when he returned.

Not that her husband's opinions mattered at this point. By all measures of wedding rituals, she and his lordship weren't truly married. So the course of the future—*their* future together—was entirely dependent upon the man's character.

He was either a worthy man or an unworthy one. Only time and his choices would tell.

"I'll cross that bridge when he comes home. If he ever does."

"He will eventually, my lady—"

"And I'll be ready for him." Ready to spit in his eye.

Or confess, or ignore him—

Or run for her life.

"Pardon me for saying it, my lady, but I pity the man," Elden said, laughing lightly as he lifted his cap and scratched at the back of his ear. "Won't know what hit 'im."

"Yes, well, my husband should have nothing to complain about. It's been nearly two years and I have increased the output from his fields—"

"And you're giving away the profits."

"Not the profits—the harvest. Which I'd have done anyway, so I'm saving the blighter his own cash. Hawkesly Hall is my house as much as it is his—at least while I'm mistress here." However long that would be after the man returns.

"And Badger's Run? His lordship might have already heard of the place himself. You've made it quite the retreat in sporting circles. And with that I'll say good-night to you, my lady." Ever the rascally Irish gallant, Elden held open the door for her then tipped his cap as she passed by him through the side entrance.

"Good night, Elden Carmichael." *God be with you, dear, sweet man.*

She could always count on Elden to keep her thinking beyond the moment. Like the fact that Badger's Run had gained a reputation that might bring on unwanted guests.

One in particular whom she wished had never heard of Badger's Run.

Demanding and rude.

Probing and wary.

A compelling scent.

A nameless danger.

With any luck the colonel had forgotten about her and was carousing with the other guests. He'd better be, for all the trouble she went through to satisfy his complaining.

"I'm sorry, Colonel, but I can't say where the lady is just now."

Jared was full up with the load of muck they'd been shoveling at him in his own home. He leaned on the counter at the bar. "You *can't*, McHugh? Or you won't?"

McHugh snorted and fisted a towel into a pint glass. "She's a busy woman, is our Lady Hawkesly. What with Badger's Run, and the hunting park and this tournament and all the other . . . well . . . you can imagine, sir. A woman all alone in the world." McHugh gave a vague nod toward the foyer.

He could imagine far too much of a woman alone and independent; especially this woman, with her unorthodox persuasions. "No, McHugh, I cannot imagine the lady's whereabouts. Not after nine o'clock at night."

Not with two dozen "sportsmen" sniffing round the corridors of his hunting lodge, leering at her like a pack of jackals.

McHugh shelved the pint glass with others. "Our lady does her best work after nine."

"Meaning what?"

McHugh glared at him. "Take yer mind outta the bog, sir! I mean that the lady's much too busy before then with supper and the staff and meeting the demands of her guests to get any real work done."

Bloody guests and their bloody demands. "I don't much care about the others, McHugh, I want to speak with her ladyship. Now."

McHugh leaned his elbows on the counter. "Look here. I don't know what your interest in Lady Hawkesly is, or what you think you're planning, but you'd best be warned that she's a married woman."

"So I understand." To his marrow, he understood.

McHugh leveled a corkscrew at him, a plainspoken, unequivocal threat. "Then you'd best understand that the lady's off limits to you, sir. And to every other man jack hereabouts. Or they'll know the reason why."

Hell, now he was being taken for a skirt-sniffing scoundrel. "I've no plans to overstep the bounds of propriety, McHugh." At least not in public.

"You'd best heed what you say. Lord Hawkesly isn't the sort to share."

He bloody well wasn't! Especially not his bride.

"So this Hawkesly fellow—what's he like?"

"Dunno, Colonel." McHugh dried another pint glass. "Never met the man."

Yes, and that was another troublesome matter; he hadn't recognized a single member of the staff, and yet there seemed to be dozens of them, each and every one of them with a treacle-thick Irish brogue.

"And yet Hawkesly pays you your salary?"

"Well, no, sir, her ladyship does."

With his lordship's money!

"And what a dear lady she is to work for. The finest this side of heaven." McHugh had grown wispy-eyed again as he dried another pint glass. "Has the courage of a bear, stubborn like a badger, smarter than any dozen of them lords." He stopped and squinted suddenly at Jared. "Here I am, goin' on an' on."

"Please do, McHugh." The man was a font of information about his wife, more clues in his little investigation.

"I shouldn't really. The lady won't stand for any gossip, can't abide a liar for a minute, and admires nothing more than a genuine sportsman."

Especially one with a full purse. "Does she?"

"Believes it a sure sign of patience and honesty and nobility of spirit."

He'd been wise not to give himself away when he first arrived. The woman was one mystery after another.

He'd just have to acquaint himself with the fine art of fishing. A good cover story had saved many a mission from detection and disaster. And if he was to play the expert fisherman come morning, he was going to need a bit of private practice tonight.

"My thanks, McHugh." Jared placed his empty glass on the counter. "Oh, and since my baggage never arrived at Badger's Run, I'd better round up some suitable fishing gear for the morning. Any ideas?"

"Well, then, you'd be looking for Magnus. He's our ghillie."

That again. Good God, what the hell was a ghillie? Sounded like some sort of fish ailment. "Where would I find Magnus this time of night?"

"Fast asleep, to be sure, in a cabin just down the path from the game house. But he won't be likin' you wakin' him, tomorrow comin' as early as it does for him."

He'd not be likin' losin' his job either. "Where's this game house?"

McHugh drew in a long breath. "Out the east gallery there, past the kitchen building, over the bridge along the road to Hawkesly Hall. Keep to the lane on the left. You'll see the game house on the side of the hill."

He knew the building—an enormous old haybarn.

"Good evening then, McHugh." Figuring that he needed his cloak for this walk in the woods, Jared started toward the stairs and his pillbox-sized room, but then realized that he hadn't any idea at all about what kind of fishing gear he would need from this Magnus fellow.

Doubtless the man would then take his suspicions right to her ladyship. But where the devil would he find enough information to cover his story?

The library. Of course. With any luck, the woman hadn't leased out the room for a paper mill.

But the library was just as he'd remembered it,

though the high-back chairs were now occupied by a
half dozen card players at two tables. The books and
bookshelves reached halfway up the walls and above
that, more trophy-mounted boar heads and grizzly
bear and many-pointed bucks.

Hoping to find a book on the fine art of fishing, Jared
worked his way around the perimeter of the shelves,
avoiding the gaming table and finally finding what he
was looking for just to the right of the fireplace.

But hell and damnation, there wasn't just one book
on fishing, but a few hundred.

From *The Flyfisher's Way* to *Chalk Streams and
Their Flora* to a ragged copy of something called *The
Compleat Angler*, and a stack of well-thumbed *Hearth
& Heath* magazines.

He took a chance and yanked a very small book off
the shelf, *Hook, Line and Spinner*.

All he wanted to know as he thumbed quickly
through the book was what the hell kind of rigging to
use. No, it seemed the word for all the gear was
"tackle." And the bloody pole was a called a rod. And
it came in sections. And the best were made of
bamboo . . .

Bloody hell, what a waste of time! He ought to be
seducing his wife, but here he was studying up on flyfishing!

Drew's challenge hit him hard in the belly. *You'll be
at least a week getting your wife into your bed.*

"Do come join us, Huddleswell! Give your luck a
bit of exercise with the cards before the tournament
tomorrow."

Jared had been so occupied with his search, he

hadn't noticed Fitchett at one of the card tables, and now the man was waving eagerly at him from across the library.

"No cards for me tonight, Fitchett," Jared said, purposefully scanning the shelves for helpful titles, for one or two that made a least a little sense. "An early morning, you know. I'm off to bed with a few good books."

He hoped to bloody hell. He grabbed five off the shelves randomly, in rapid succession and would just have to hope for the best.

"Ah! One of my absolute favorites, Huddleswell!" Breame appeared at Jared's side and tapped the cover of the top book in the stack. *The Blue-Winged Olive and How to Tie It.* Know it by heart, myself. Rereading it to inspire yourself, I expect?"

"Indeed, Breame." *To inspire me.*

Jared left the library for the privacy of his own room, where he could sit alone and investigate the particulars of flyfishing.

On his wedding night.

Don't say we didn't warn you, Hawkesly.

Damnation!

Chapter 5

"**Y**ou want me to pack up his lordship's what, my lady?"

Kate outstretched the linen shirt, shoulder to broad shoulder. Enough to clad that brawny chest she remembered from her wedding day. "His drawers, Tansy. His underclothes."

"Then his lordship's come home, has he?"

"No." Thank God for that! "To be loaned to one of the guests at the lodge."

Yes, plenty of shirt here for the colonel. In fact, a perfect fit. Trousers, waistcoat, and jacket, right down to fancy gilded buttons.

"You've a guest who forgot to bring his own drawers?"

"Not exactly, Tansy. Misplaced baggage." Or some such story that she didn't believe. "I hate to ask this of you so late, but would you please send the lot down to the lodge sometime tonight?"

"Gladly, my lady." Tansy was already folding the shirts, humming.

Kate left the closet where she had stored away Hawkesly's wardrobe, and ducked again into the infirmary to take another look at Margaret, and found Rosemary in a chair beside the huge bed. Both were fast asleep.

Never able to keep away from the new ones, she peered into Margaret's sleeping face, searching for those dreadful signs of a failing heart. But her hollow little cheeks were beginning to pink and her breathing was steady and deep. And she had actually smiled earlier.

"Sleep well, angel." Kate held back a kiss on the forehead, not wanting to wake her, and made it out into the corridor without disturbing Rosemary, either.

Kate and her pony knew the long lanes between the hall and Badger's Run as well in the deepest midnight as she knew it at midday. She also knew that a light burning this late in the main room of the game house could only mean that Magnus was working far beyond his regular hours, when he had no reason to be.

His gratitude time, he called it. Repaying a debt to her that she refused to recognize, that he insisted upon.

"Ya saved my life, m'lady," he would always say, "and my dear ma's."

She hadn't really, had only offered him a job that she desperately needed doing. But Magnus would always frown at her denials, so now she let him mutter his gratitude and put in his extra hours.

But not tonight—at least she'd try to convince him to retire. It was nearly eleven and she feared for his health, though every day he was looking more and more as though he were merely lean, rather than a victim of the famine in Ireland.

She hitched the pony and the tilbury near the patch of daisies at the fence rail in front of the game house, crossed the planked porch, then unlatched the door and entered the vestibule to odd sounds coming from the large room beyond, with its carefully stored tackle and traps and lures.

"Magnus, what are you doing here so late?"

But it wasn't Magnus.

Colonel Huddleswell stood in the middle of the barn, stripped down to his crisp white shirt, his breeches and his boots.

His neckcloth was gone entirely and his shirt unbuttoned to the center of his chest.

He was standing like a dashing fencing master, poised in mid–*en garde*. Only instead of an epee, the colonel was wielding a clunky old greenheart fly rod, a loop of line caught up in his left hand.

A breathtakingly fine-looking man, his black hair slightly askew against his high forehead. His stance perfect; arrested motion. Long, powerfully corded thigh muscles, clad in black buckskin.

Absolutely stunning.

When she finally stopped her unseemly tour of the man's form and found his eyes, her heart gave a clunk and then started thudding against her ears.

"Can I help you, Colonel?"

He relaxed his stance and his grip on the fly rod

some, his brow dipping from something like slight surprise to his usual brooding impatience. "No, Lady Hawkesly. You can't help me at all."

"You shouldn't be in here."

He flicked that brow again. "And you shouldn't have lost my luggage."

"I—" She didn't lose anything of his, but she was long past arguing the point. "And what exactly are you doing? Casting indoors, in the middle of the night?"

"I'm . . . testing."

"For what? Termites?"

"For quality. And fit." He rested the butt end of the rod against the floor, loose elbowed, his dark scowl a stark challenge.

"Why now?"

"Since I'll be using a fly rod which is entirely new to me—not my own custom-made to my exacting specifications Henderson's greenheart, I thought it wise to take my time in choosing the very best among your"—he flicked a dismissive hand toward the wall of her very finest rods—"rental items."

Irked at the man's insult, Kate went to the rack of fly rods and lifted out the best of them.

"If you're looking for the best we have, Colonel, then you might like to try this one. It's a split bamboo, with agate guide rings, a ridged-cork grip."

He scowled at her, suddenly reminding her of someone that she knew—though she couldn't quite put a name to him. "The one I have will do."

Such an odd choice. An ancient fly rod, when he'd just touted the grandness of his own.

"Still, you might want to use a better reel than that old brass thing."

"What I want is the time to acquaint myself with this particular fly rod."

She didn't know what to make of his strange attitude, or the fire in his glare as she gazed up at him.

"Are you purposely trying to handicap yourself for tomorrow's tournament?"

He grunted and deepened his scowling. "My intentions are none of your business."

Jared wanted nothing more than for the woman to leave him alone because time was short and she was distracting. Because he was battling a red-hot urge to lean down and taste her mouth, to indulge in the dampness glistening on her lips.

So inviting. Warm. And damn, if it wasn't beginning to plague the devil out of him that he had completely forgotten to kiss her the day they were married.

And that he couldn't really make up for it right now.

What a hell of a way to spend his wedding night. He couldn't let her stay here any longer. He damned well couldn't let her see him try to cast the lure. Not with this relic of a fly rod, which had looked like the drawings in the book, but was apparently, simply laughably old.

And damned dangerous. He'd already hooked the seat of his trousers with the nasty furred and feathery weapon that was on the end of the line. He'd only just released the hook when the woman walked in on him.

Now she was drawing up the end of the line, expertly pinching the small feathered object between her fingers and giving it a careful inspection.

"Ah, a hackle red spinner."

Damnation, he understood dozens of exotic dialects, but the woman seemed ever to be speaking nonsense.

And studying him too closely.

Still he couldn't let her know who he was. Not until he discovered what the devil she was up to with her guests and her secrets and this so-called spinner thing.

"Exactly," he said, wondering if there was such a thing as a book of fishing flies. And forever hearing Drew's wager echoing inside his head.

"You're not planning to use this tomorrow, are you?" His bride looked amused and scandalized enough for him to know the correct answer.

"Of course not."

She laughed and let go of the fly. "Good! After all, what would a trout or a salmon make of an April-hatching fly in the middle of September?"

"Indeed." He felt entirely stupid, his pride laid flat. "The thing was already on the end of the line when I picked up the rod. I merely—"

"Well, that explains it." She *tsk*ed and shook her head. "Doubtless one of the boys left it on after using the rod last spring."

One of the boys?

"You didn't by any chance bring along your own fly box, did you?"

He gave her a purposeful frown, pleased with the flexibility of his lost luggage cover story and the fact that he had read up on fly boxes and knew exactly what she was talking about this time.

"No, madam. It was packed along with my other gear. Now if you'll excuse me . . ." He needed her to leave him to his practicing. The night was waning and this flyfishing was turning out to be more difficult to master than he'd expected.

"Then I suppose you'll be needing to borrow one of our fly boxes." Before he could answer, she left him for a tall cabinet against the opposite wall, and he followed her like a pup. "We have an excellent selection of William Blacker's salmon patterns, developed specifically for Badger's Run's three chalk streams."

"Have you?" Damn she smelled good—like moonlight and talc and warm sheets.

She opened the wire-meshed cabinet door, pulled down a flat wooden box, and lifted the lid to a wild display of bundled feathers and fur and bright dangly things. "We're very up to date here at Badger's Run."

"I should hope so."

"You'll find everything you need here for landing a trout: sedges for evening, and spinners and—" She touched the ends of other boxes on the shelves. "Duns and smuts and quills." She turned back to him, obviously pleased with herself. "Everything you need."

Thoroughly beguiled by the gentle lilt of her voice, the length of her fingers and all that marvelous hair, Jared rested the rod against the edge of the cabinet, and then leaned in to his wife. "Where did you learn all this?"

"All what?"

"Flyfishing and game birds and deer parks. These are men's pursuits."

She fit the lid back on the box. "And I've had to make my way in a man's world, haven't I?"

"Why is that, Lady Hawkesly?" he asked, feeling accused and tried and found guilty all in one breath.

"My dear father passed away nearly two years ago, I have no brothers or uncles, and as for my husband . . ." She shrugged and turned from him to shut the door. "Well, as I said, I've had to learn to live in a man's world."

"But why open a sportsman's lodge? Surely Hawkesly has no pressing need for money."

"Why would you assume something like that?"

Because you're married to me, and I'm as rich as Croesus.

"A supposition," he said instead, shrugging, not quite ready to hear her explanations.

"I can assure you that marriage to an earl doesn't mean unlimited wealth."

Bloody hell, it certainly did with *this* earl! It meant that she had plenty to eat without fishing for it. Or shooting it or trapping it. A limitless wardrobe, a magnificent, one-hundred-room roof over her pretty little head. "Then what does it mean, my lady?"

"Marriage to an earl?"

"Yes."

She shrugged and then leaned back against the counter as she slowly exhaled the weight of the world. "I'm sure I wouldn't know."

Bloody hell! "What does that mean?"

And what the devil was she doing with all this money she was making?

"It means that . . . well! It's just plain none of your business." She fixed him with a glare, then brushed past him. "Now if you'll excuse me, I'll be on my way."

Blasted woman. "I need a landing net."

She stopped with a harrump, then pointed to a wall of nets. "Take your pick, sir. Take anything you need with my best wishes. Good night."

Jared watched the woman leave, flinched at the crack as the door slammed behind her, at the softly lingering scent of her.

"Good night, wife," he whispered, wanting more of his bride than just her scowling impatience. He wanted to understand her and her suspicious enterprise. Something was making her work like a demon and he was damn well going to uncover the reason.

He spent the next hour wrestling with a nastily barbed fly on the end of an utterly uncontrollable horsehair line. He hooked his trousers twice more and then his shoulder, until he finally lodged the hook in the back of his hand.

"Damn and blast!" Cursing the woman and her bloody lodge and every trout in the bloody kingdom, Jared gathered up what looked to be a reasonable tangle of rod and reel and fly boxes and a landing net—whatever its purpose—and hiked back to the lodge.

His lodge.

To *his* bed. His empty bed.

And he'd only just piled the ungainly stuff into the tiny chair in the corner of his misshapen room when he heard a light knock on the door.

And his wife's soft, sultry voice from just beyond the panel, calling his name.

"Colonel Huddleswell."

No—the *other* man's name. Damnation! He yanked open the door. "Yes?"

She was standing like a supplicant—hair askew and still damp from the moonlit air, her arms loaded down with a pile of folded clothes.

"The clothes I promised you." She brushed past him and lay the pile out on his bed. "Two days' worth. I'll see that you get more."

"Where did you get these?"

"Up at the hall."

"When?"

"Earlier." She looked up and cocked her head at him. "I hope they'll fit you. I'm pretty sure they will."

"You were there tonight? At the hall?" Without telling him? Though she had no reason to tell him anything about her activities.

"Yes. Fortunately, you and my husband are nearly the same size."

"Are we?" Imagine that.

She studied him, then held up a pair of trousers, and studied him again. "Very nearly, Colonel."

"Yes, how fortunate for all of us." For him, his bride, and that neglectful husband of hers.

"Yes, well. I've brought you a goodly supply of everything you should need. Shirts, collars, waistcoat, trousers. Outerwear and . . . under." She flicked a glance over him, an assessing heat that licked like fire. "Um . . . and socks and, well, everything a gentleman might need for a weekend's proper sporting."

Ah, wife, if we were sporting properly, we'd have no need for clothes at all.

A riotous thought that roused him and plucked at his resolve.

"I suppose I should say thank you," he said. For offering him his own clothes from his own wardrobe in his own hall. And yet his heart seemed to be softening toward her, making excuses, rationalizing.

"Say whatever suits you, Colonel Huddleswell. But you're welcome." She righted the tottering pile of shirts, smoothed the suede lapel on his favorite tweed jacket, and then worked her way around the bed, toward the door. "Breakfast is served at four—"

"In the morning?" He kept forgetting the early hours of these flyfishermen. Weary to his bones, Jared drew his fingers through his hair.

"A full country breakfast, in the dining room." She stopped and stared at him for a long moment. "Dear God, what have you done to yourself?"

She moved the three steps toward him and caught his wrist before he could react, began inspecting the dried blood on the back of his hand.

Though he was hardly paying much attention; not with her palm so warmly supporting his, her fingers laced with his, their tips playing idly against the underside of his wrist, the brush of her breath against his skin.

Enough to drive a man over the brink.

"It's a . . . nothing at all, madam." He tried to pull his hand away, but she held fast and only peered closer at the dark red splotch.

"I know a fishhook injury when I see one." She looked up at him in horror. "How did this happen?"

Hell. Was hooking oneself a flyfisher's sin? A sign of incompetence?

"I . . . um—" God, her fingers were soft. And warm. Stunning.

"Were you actually casting overhead when I found you in the game house?"

Not knowing what truth to tell the woman, Jared shook his head and then answered, "Well . . . yes."

She huffed. "In the near dark, with an armed fly, and hardly any clearance in any direction?"

"I told you I had little choice, with new tackle to contend with and the tournament tomorrow."

"You could have blinded yourself!"

She was worried about him. Excellent. A smile begin to blossom in his chest, and then a sharp, suspicious twinge.

She wasn't worried about her husband, but Colonel Bloody Huddleswell.

"I didn't blind myself," he said, hearing the snap in his voice.

"Stay put. I'll be right back." She slipped away in a cloud of her heady fragrance.

Now what? Feeling more trapped than he'd ever been, caught inside his hastily prepared disguise, Jared listened for her footsteps, so nearly silent as she padded down the stairs and along the corridor just below.

Had his carelessness— no, his utter clumsiness with the fishhook and that blasted rod given him away? Had she guessed his identity? No, not his identity, but the fact that he'd lied about being the greatest flyfisher of all time.

And wouldn't she wonder why a grown man—a highly decorated colonel—would lie about a thing like his flyfishing skills?

"All right, give me your hand, Colonel." He'd only just turned to straighten the tangle of tackle in the corner when the woman returned with a small pot of something.

"What's that you've got?"

She patted the corner of the bed and said patiently, "Sit here, please. That's a nasty cut, and it could get a whole lot nastier."

"And you have a cure?"

She displayed the wide-mouthed jar and its tattered label. "Mrs. Rooney's ointment."

Feeling a bit more at ease, less on the spot, Jared sat. "Ah, Magnus's mother."

"Yes. I keep lots of it near at hand. Her ointment has kept many a sportsman from succumbing to his follies."

"You've seen a lot of these injuries?" So she wasn't accusing him of false credentials after all.

"More than I care to count. Not just fishhooks, either. Head wounds and scrapes and twisted ankles, not to mention the occasional set of bruised knuckles." She wiped at the wound with a warm, damp piece of flannel, her touch firm but gentle.

Practiced. Making him wonder all the more about the woman he'd married.

"So Badger's Run is a dangerous place to visit?"

"I'm saying that in general men seem to have no sense about them when it comes to wounds."

Men. Multiples of them. A bolt of jealousy shot through him and he shifted closer to her, taking possession of her by resting his knee against her leg.

"It doesn't hurt at all," he said, challenging all those others who'd come to her before him with their whining.

She smiled and shook her head. "That's the problem with most men. Fatal, false courage, when a bit of attention could save a limb or a life."

"A bullet wound might be serious, madam. Or a knife wound, the slash of a sword. Believe me, this fishhook is merely an irritation."

"I suppose you've been shot?"

"A few times."

"Where?"

"Canton, the Punjab, Montreal, a few other places. Oh, and once in London."

"Great heavens!" Her sympathy seemed genuine, and still she held firmly to his hand. "You've been shot that many times?"

"And shot *at* many more times." How much dare he tell her? "It's the nature of my profession."

"Which is . . . what? Besides a colonel in the army." She was peering too closely at him. "You've made it sound like you're a gambler or a highwayman."

Captain, earl, spy. Her eyes sparkled with interest, perhaps even admiration.

"Foreign service, actually. You see, I came by my rank honestly."

"And your wounds." She went back to her ministrations. "So you've been to China and India?"

"Often." He let her dab a gob of Mrs. Rooney's greasy ointment on his cut, relishing the care she took and the cool of her fingers.

"Have you ever been to Egypt, to Alexandria, specifically?" She suddenly seemed to purposely avoid looking up at him, letting her hair hide most of her face.

His throat went dry. He didn't know what to say, beyond a feeble-sounding, "A fine city."

"We were married there."

We? Jared's heart stopped cold.

"Lord Hawkesly and I."

Dangerous waters. He didn't like this kind of spying. The brittle knife edge, where time raced ahead of him and the risk mounted.

Where quickly and correctly calculating the stakes often meant the difference between life and death.

"Are you married, Colonel?"

He inhaled, needing clean air to clear his head, but only drawing in her compelling, distracting scent. He was finally able to answer,

"Yes," he managed. "I am."

To you, he nearly said. But he still sensed danger so he held back.

Kate knew exactly where this feeling of heat and stumbling shyness and these thrilling sensations in her fingertips were coming from.

They were coming from him: Colonel Leland P. Huddleswell. From his broad, warm palm and the depth of his gaze.

And from a haunting familiarity that had plagued her from the moment they met.

And here she was feeling the urge to confess to a total stranger what she'd hardly broached to herself in all these years.

This just wouldn't do. She was very married. And when Hawkesly finally did come home, it was vastly important that she be able to look him honestly in the eye.

Especially the eye she planned to spit into.

"There!" she said, with too much enthusiasm, putting the man's hand on his own knee before standing. "That should feel better soon."

"It does already."

He stood, towered above her, knocking his head on the slant of the ceiling. "Thank you, Lady Hawkesly. Please give my best to Mrs. Rooney."

"Yes, good night, Colonel." Feeling her face begin to flame, Kate took her leave with as much dignity as she could muster, writing off her girlish reaction to the colonel as completely natural. He was an immensely dashing, startlingly handsome man.

And those dark eyes! Oh, how they probed and alighted where they shouldn't!

She hadn't had time for many girlish fancies in her life. And this one was definitely without any kind of future.

Now if she could only remember what her husband looked like.

If she'd only gotten a good look at him.

Beyond his great, broad height.

And his midnight-dark beard.

His long hair whipped in the breeze off the bay.

His features hidden in the glare of the Alexandria sun.

And a wedding that took but a minute, before he was off down the gangway without a backward glance.

The blackguard.

A good crack in the shins with her best boot would be a fine greeting after all this time.

Should he ever decide to come home.

Chapter 6

"It's a fine, flapping winner of the first order, Lady Hawkesly!"

"A beauty, Mr. Gilmott." Kate stepped back from the large, wriggling trout dangling from the end of Gilmott's line. "But to be fair, the next few hours will tell."

"Ha! Old Fitchett's going to wish he hadn't been so puffed up about winning! Imagine, him the flyfisherman and me the lowly duck hunter." Gilmott chortled and waddled off across the forecourt to record his contender with Foggerty in the tent pavilion.

Kate stood just outside lodge door, surprised how smoothly the tournament had run this morning. The first round was winding down. Men were returning to the pavilion with their catches to compare techniques and tell their stories, resting only long enough to down a quick ale and grab a box lunch before they headed off for the afternoon's fishing.

A perfect day. Warm and softly breezy. The occasional cloud to break the solid blue.

Still, Colonel Huddleswell would probably find something to needle her about. Some tree out of place, or his toast gone cold. She could only be grateful that he had yet to seek her out this morning. Something of a miracle.

"A message's come to you from the hall, my lady." Corey swabbed his shock of blond hair from his forehead and handed Kate the message.

"You look worn to the bone, Corey," Kate said, brushing a spray of straw from his sleeve. "Have you eaten?"

"Just now, up at the hall."

Then Corey had been filled to the brim with hotchpotch and oat bread, like the mob of others. "Poor lad."

"It's back to work, my lady. Them horses get hungry too." Corey hurried off toward the stable.

Kate was about to stuff the message into the pocket of her breeches to read later, but a niggling sense of unease made her open it instead. She read Miss Rosemary's blockish hand with a nagging dread.

I give ya a good morning, Lady Hawkesly, and word from Elden that he left for the wharf at Mereglass with the first of the wagons. The new lass is sitting up. Were you expecting a trunk?

A trunk?

And a message come here from London for his lordship.

From London? Dear God, then Hawkesly must be on his way home! Oh, but please, not yet.

This was only September! There was still so much to do. The tournament and the *Katie Claire*, the children and Father Sebastian's soup kitchens! She wasn't ready.

But perhaps she was jumping to the wrong conclusion. After all, this was merely a message *to* her husband *from* some unknown party in London. Which wasn't absolute proof that his arrival was imminent.

It might just be a stray invitation to a ball from one of his social cronies. Or a note from a long-lost friend.

Blast the man and his arrogance! Believing that he could marry her, disappear for nearly two years, and then just show up to start their marriage when it suited him.

Well, it doesn't suit me at all, Hawkesly, not right now.

Trying to decide on when she could wedge in an extra visit to Hawkesly Hall in the midst of her impossibly busy day, Kate tucked the note into her pocket, then hurried off to the recording pavilion and the crowd watching Magnus chalk in the weight of Gilmott's trout.

"Eighteen pounds, three ounces, sir," Foggerty announced in his unflappable drone.

"I knew it!" Gilmott preened as Foggerty held the trout aloft as though it had just won a boxing match. "The biggest of the morning!"

It was indeed a large rainbow for this late in the season. "What stream did you take it from, Mr. Gilmott?"

"Yes, where, Gilmott?" Fitchett shouted from the edge of the crowd, laughing as the other fishermen joined in the questioning.

"Yes, where, old boy? Tell us!"

"Not likely!" Gilmott snorted, then hurried off toward the lodge, obviously pleased with himself and his newfound celebrity, surrounded by his equally happy chums.

The tournament was a remarkable success—so far. Easy profits piling into such a large and empty bucket.

Please, God, keep Hawkesly away from home at least until Monday.

By then she'd have the strength to face his certain wrath and be in control of her own.

"Been a good catch all around, my lady." Foggerty dropped Gilmott's trout into a bucket with other fish.

"If the catch is good this year, Foggerty, it's because you and Magnus have turned our streams into the finest fishing waters in the country."

"Just doin' my job, my lady."

"Thank God for that, Foggerty." Knowing that the man disliked the slightest hint of flattery, Kate studied the recording board as he ambled away, and found the colonel's name, but nothing listed beside it. "No word yet from Colonel Huddleswell?"

"Yet, my lady?" Magnus strolled up and snorted. "No insult intended, but I'm thinking that the colonel will need more than a bit of luck if he's going to land a keeper."

"Don't tell me the man is still prattling on about our

losing his favorite split rod and flybox? It would be a perfect excuse to explain the one that got away."

"If you want him to leave Badger's Run a happy fisherman, you'd best to send 'im off to the Glenwater Bend, about a half mile upstream from where Mr. Gilmott got that rainbow. Fish aplenty there. An' 'at's the only way he's gonna bag anything. All the big ones seem to be comin' out of the Glenwater this summer."

"If I find the colonel, I'll send him that way." The Glenwater Bend was a just bit off the road on the way to the hall. Two birds with one stone. She could examine the message to Hawkesly—without opening it, of course—and then there was that odd trunk that Rosemary mentioned.

Plagued by the sense of impending doom, and the distressing feeling that she would find her husband waiting for her on the steps of Hawkesly Hall, Kate hurried past the smokehouse, the air around it already sharply aromatic with the first stock of fish for the coming winter. After checking in on Mrs. Driscoll and her crew of fish cleaners, Kate saddled up her little mare and trotted off toward Hawkesly Hall, by way of Glenwater Bend.

She tied up the mare on the hill above and picked her way down the riverbank through the fading ferns and bracken.

If the rainbow trout were here in abundance as Magnus believed, she'd let him know when she returned from the hall.

"Splash me, Grady! Splash me!"

Kate smiled at the sound of the swooooshing of water, then Healy's happy shriek and Grady's hooting laughter that followed. The imps shouldn't be playing in the chalk stream with the tournament going on.

For that matter, they shouldn't be this far from Hawkesly Hall.

"Splash Dori now, Grady! An' Mera, too!"

"Me, now, me, meeeee, Grady!" Dori called out in her squealy singsong.

Gracious! The whole gang of them must have wandered down from the house. She stepped around the brambles and over the fallen hornbeam, ready to shoo them away. But she paused above the rocky pool and its sun-dappled gilding, wrestling with a grin and that pesky lump in her throat at the sight of the children playing.

Just playing. Doing what all children were put on this good green earth to do. Fearless, untroubled hearts, full bellies, a place to snuggle up and be warm.

"Hey, look up there!" Justin was pointing at her, his eyes bright, his dimples deep and winking even from across the stream. "Lady Kate's here!"

"Oh, watch me, Lady Kate! Watch me!" Little Lucas stuck his arms out like a pair of wings, stiffened, and then abruptly fell over backward into the water with a shallow splash.

"Excellent, Lucas!" Kate called out as the boy rocketed up with a squeal and an explosion of water.

"Guess what, Lady Kate!" Healy wobbled toward her atop the stepping stones.

"What, Healy?" The other children swarmed past the tottering boy.

"Grady can swim clear across the stream! All in one big breath."

"Just like a pike!" Mera shouted, her fist dug into the thick, black fur at Mr. McNair's massive scruff. The dog lumbered gently alongside the little girl, patient, devoted, that huge, goofy smile lighting his large hound eyes.

If only Mr. McNair were Prime Minister! He wouldn't let the children starve.

Kate really ought to be chiding them about playing so far from the hall, but how could she resist kneeling to meet their hugs and their laughter? The little ones holding on tightly; Lucas and his cap, Dori squishing kisses onto Kate's cheek, Healy climbing into her arms, Mera with one hand in Kate's and the other wrapped around Mr. McNair's neck.

"So you're a pike now, Grady?" Kate asked.

"He's incorrigible, Lady Kate."

"Incorrigible?" Dear Glenna must have learned another new word today. Another to add to the plates of fear that she used to armor herself. "Ebullient, I'd call him."

"Ebullient?" Glenna frowned more deeply as she stood apart, her curiosity never failing to distract her. "What does that mean?"

"You'll find it—"

"In the dictionary, I know." She folded her arms across her chest and glared at Grady. "I was just saying that I told them not to leave the hall grounds."

"Spoilsport!"

"Yeah!"

Kate stood upright, her arms still full of Lucas. "Glenna is only looking out for your best interest, children. And frankly, I agree with her."

"With Glenna?" Grady swabbed his cheek with his forearm. "Why?"

Glenna sniffed. "Told you so."

"Children, please." Kate used their proximity to gather them with her arms and herd them up the bank, far away from the rainbow pool. "We're hosting a fishing tournament at Badger's Run; it's our job to make sure the contestants have the very best time. Else they might not come back next year."

"What's a turmanent, Lady Kate?" Dori grinned up at Kate, thrusting the end of her tongue through the great gap between her front teeth.

"It's a fish race!" Justin shouted, his cunning alive in his eyes. "Right, Lady Kate?"

"Not exactly a race, but a contest. Whoever catches the biggest fish after three days wins the prize."

"We can win! Come on! Let's go, Justin! I saw a big one in there!" Grady threw himself backward and stumbled down the bankside into a gorse bush, Mr. McNair grabbing the tail of the boy's shirt before he rolled to a stop. "Oh, yuck, Mr. McNair! Get off!"

"The tournament is for our guests, Grady. You must promise to keep away from the streams and the fishermen until I say you can play there."

"Ah, but, we really could—" The dog sat down on Grady's leg, pinning him to the ground.

"I mean it, Grady. And you too, Justin. And the rest of you. You're to stay clear of the streams and the lodge and the contestants. For the next three days."

"Then get this blinkin' hound off me!"

Grady shoved at the dog, but Mr. McNair merely

lapped his tongue across Grady's face and the children burst out laughing; even Glenna smiled.

"Call him off, sweetheart," Kate said to Mera.

"Come, Mr. McNair!" Mera stretched out her little hand and the dog lifted himself off Grady, then loped to her side. "He likes the new girl, Lady Kate."

"Mr. McNair likes Margaret?"

Mera grinned broadly. "I do too. I let him stay with her last night. Miss Rosemary didn't see."

Rosemary doubtless did see. The woman missed very little and loved the faithful old dog every bit as much as Kate did.

"A man came to the house today, Lady Kate." Glenna posted herself beside Kate. "On a fast horse."

"Yes, I know, Glenna. Thank you." The message for Hawkesly, all the way from London. Just the thought of what it all might mean gave her stomach a twist.

Certain doom for all her hopes and plans, because the man himself wouldn't be far behind the message.

And what would he think of all the children?

A slice of cold fear sped down her spine; the image of them on their own again, unprotected.

Not that she'd ever abandon a one. But she could do so much more for them here.

"Can we go get apples from the orchard, Lady Kate?" Healy was still in her arms, nose to nose with her, his bright red hair smelling of leaves, his shoes drizzling.

"What an excellent idea, Healy."

"Good, good, goooood!" The boy grunted as he hugged her neck fiercely.

"Why don't each of you pick ten apples apiece and then take them back to the three Miss Darbys for supper?"

"Apple pudding and jam! Oh, boy!" Dori pulled at Healy and the boy slid out of Kate's arms and into Dori's.

"Will you be eating with us tonight?" Lucas asked, the breeze tousling his light brown hair.

"Probably not tonight, Lucas."

"Pleeeeease!"

"I'll be two more nights at Badger's Run. It's not so far away from the hall. And I'll stop by at bedtime, and each morning. You'll hardly know that I'm gone."

"Yes, we will!" The little charmers.

She started herding them again. "Now off you go to the orchard—then right back to the hall."

"Follow me!"

"Shhhh . . . quietly, Grady," Kate said to the boy. "The fishermen need—"

But Grady had scrambled back up the embankment and was already speeding down the twisting pathway into the woods, the other children taking after him, Mr. McNair loping along beside Mera.

"I'd best go follow them, Lady Kate," Glenna said with a huff far older than her twelve years, "else they'll end up at Badger's Run begging sugar off Mrs. Driscoll and pennies off the guests."

"Your hair looks very nice today, Glenna." The girl's neat little cap was tied beneath her chin, a thick plait hanging down her back.

"Really?" Glenna touched the deep red curls that ringed her forehead. "How do you mean, good?"

"It's getting to be a very pretty shade of auburn."

"Is it?" It really was, shining and thick in the noonday sun. A year of proper food and sleep and warm clothes had done that.

"You know, Glenna, I'm sure that I have a pale pink linen cap with a winding border of embroidered lilacs along its brim and all the way down its ribbons. It's just your size, and it's yours if you'd like it."

She gasped in utter disbelief. "For me?"

"You're nearly thirteen, Glenna Connett, a young lady. About time for something special just for you."

"Gosh. Thank you."

Kate continued up the embankment. "We'll see about finding it tonight. Now you'd best run along and keep the children out of trouble."

"Yes, Lady Kate." Glenna dipped a proper little curtsey, not even bothering to hide the brilliance of her smile as she sped off after the others.

Old before her time, sister to Healy and Grady, Doreen and Corey. Courageous and terrified, fiercely protective of her siblings.

Dear, sweet Glenna, who had watched her own father and then her mother and three little sisters die of starvation before her very eyes.

If Father Sebastian hadn't found them in time . . . But he had and he'd brought them here to her.

And there were so many others where they came from.

She'd learned quickly that to try to save them all was to risk everyone.

Child by child, heart by heart.

*   *   *

" 'Holding the fly rod firmly in one hand, and the line itself lightly with the index finger of the other, raise the rod nearly vertically, to the, uh!' "—Jared adjusted the line in his left hand and then peered closer at his scribbled notes he'd balanced on the rock beside him— " 'to the half-eleven position . . . ' "

He took the prescribed stance exactly, for the hundredth time that morning, pointed the fly rod at right angles to the stream, and raised it vertically to what he damn well hoped was exactly half-eleven.

And as he did so, the long, airy line, and then the olive dun fly, went sailing gracefully behind him, over his head. He then flicked his wrist to send the fly forward and out and, damnation, if the fly didn't plop right into the middle of the stream.

"Well, I'll be damned! Ha!"

That wasn't so difficult! Fly fishing! Hardly worth the worry of an entire night. It had only taken a bit of study, some practical application, and, once again he'd perfected a skill that had confounded others before him.

He watched the fly travel lightly atop the eddies, pleased with himself, with the day, and the dappled sunlight on the crystalline river.

His bride would have no reason not to believe that he was a flyfisher of great—

Suddenly the line stiffened. "What the devil?"

The long pole arched sharply and nearly shot forward out of his grip.

A fish? The water churned like a volcano, bubbled midstream.

Bloody hell, he'd caught a fish! A bloody Mako shark, by the thrashing power of it!

He yanked hard on the grip and the fish rocketed out of the water, whipped and wriggled as though offering up a direct challenge to him, then it dove again, already taking a hard, silver flashing course downstream.

Heading straight for a sharp bend of boulders and a thick stand of reeds.

Where he would surely lose the bloody thing.

"Oh, hell!" Jared stepped gingerly along the bank, following his catch as it shot over rocks and mossy lumps, yanking on the madly arching pole, amazed that it didn't snap.

Blast it all! He had to at least bring in one decent sized fish; his reputation and his cover story depended on it. These flyfishers were damn serious about their sport.

His bride seemed just as serious.

And oddly knowledgeable about fishing.

He could see the fish just a few inches beneath the clear water, speckled and rainbow-sleek and enormous.

He played it for a while, moving closer to it. But just when he was sure that it was tiring, the damned thing took off again, belying its size and dragging him off the bank and into the stream, right up to his calves.

"You've hooked a big one, sir!" A boy appeared out of the reeds ahead of him, standing astride a boulder overhanging the sharply bending waters.

"Away from here, boy!" Jared suddenly felt the complete fool, wrestling with a fish that was dragging him deeper into the middle of the stream.

"I c'n net him for ya, sir!" The boy looked ready to go in after it, headfirst.

Hell, he didn't need that kind of help. "Leave it be, boy. I'll bring him in myself."

"Who you talkin' to, Grady?" A much younger girl scrambled through the reeds and the water toward the field of boulders, flashing Jared a toothless smile.

"Go away, Dori!"

"Uh-oh, Grady! I think you found one of those fish men we're not s'pose to bother!"

"Shhhh, Dori!" the boy bellowed. "You're not supposed to shout."

"What kinda fish is it?" came another voice from somewhere behind him.

Jared grunted and stumbled forward even faster over the moss-slick stones that lined the stream bed, trying to at least keep the fish in place. "I'll thank you to leave here, boy."

"Hey, what's the matter, Lucas?"

His audience was multiplying by the second, with children popping out from behind willow bogs and fallen trunks, a full half dozen of them, and then the biggest damned dog he'd ever seen.

"There 'e is! Get 'im now, sir!" the first boy shouted frantically, as Jared sloshed past the projecting boulder where the boy was perched. "Reel 'im in!"

Reel him? Hell, the knob on the handle! He'd forgotten it was there.

Not that reeling helped him much at all. He kept stumbling forward with the force of the current and the fish's monumental struggle. He reeled in a foot or two of line at a time, trying to stay upright while the children followed him downstream along the bank.

"You're gonna win if you bring him in, sir! You're gonna win!"

"Catch him!"

"Woof!" The huge dog was loping alongside the stream now, keeping perfectly level with him.

"Help the fish man, Grady!"

"Don't you dare, boy!" Jared shouted as he slipped on a stone and went down on his backside for an instant, stumbling upright in the current with the next step.

Now the demon fish made a hard course for a shallow pool on the far side of the stream, away from the clamoring children and bounded by willow and thick with reeds, obviously trying to shake him.

"Not while I still have a breath in me, old man!" Jared followed the fish, reeling in more and more line, unwilling to surrender a single inch as the beast tried to hide itself in the vegetation.

"You've almost got him!"

Damn right I do!

Wet to his chin and now prepared to die for this particular prize, Jared threw himself into the reeds and onto the wrangling fish, holding fast to the fly rod and his pride.

He struggled with the fish, reeling and reeling, hearing the children cheering him from the other bank.

"The fish man did it!"

"He caught him!"

"I hope he wins!"

"Woof!"

Jared made a sweeping grab for the line where it had hooked the fish—a fat rainbow trout, he was certain—and then stood up, turning toward the opposite bank to display the beauty to his audience.

But as he turned, he realized that the voices were gone, and the children.

Vanished like some fairy clan.

Everyone, that is, but his wife, who was standing in the sunlight on the opposite side of the stream, her hands shaping her hips, and a very odd look in her eye.

He'd never felt so exposed in his life. So wet. So unsure of himself.

How much had she seen?

And what would she think of his "technique"?

"Well, then," she said, raising her hand to her brow, shielding her eyes from the sun, "you've got a lovely, large rainbow trout there, Colonel Huddleswell."

Trout, indeed. He was hard as hell for her, had a lovely, large erection, right here in the middle of an icy stream.

Which she must not be able to see, because that was a heady grin lighting her lovely face.

Enigmatic and amused.

And beautiful.

And, bloody hell, she was wearing a pair of trousers!

Chapter 7

"**W**here the devil are your skirts, madam?"
Hell, the woman was nothing but shapely
legs and captured sunlight and clouds of untamed hair.

Standing right there in the open, where any man
could see her!

"Where are my what?" Her lilting, laughing challenge hopped across the stream and slammed into his
chest.

"Your skirts! You've forgotten them!" His gut
molten hot with a wild need to shield her from prying
eyes and groping hands, Jared started across the
stream, working hard against the current and the slippery stones, his catch flopping and tugging on the line
behind him.

"Don't be ridiculous." She stepped easily along the
root-tangled bank, coming even with him. "I haven't

forgotten anything. It's my custom to wear trousers on tournament day."

"Your custom?" Struck momentarily speechless, Jared stopped midstream and pointed at her legs with the tip of his fly rod, waggled it at her. "Replacing your . . . your skirts with britches is your custom?"

She laughed again, lightly, plucking at the excess tweed of her britches tucked into her boot tops. "Great heavens, don't tell me you're a prig? I'm shocked! And you a man of the wide world."

"I'm hardly a prig." He was . . . proper. Protective. At least when it came to his wife. And she was almost naked.

She gave another laugh, good-natured and coercive, teasing his ears, tempting his heart. "But you don't approve of my working garb?"

He bloody well didn't approve! Not of his wife romping around the countryside in little more than a linen shirtwaist and a pair of woollen underdrawers. No wonder the denizens of Badger's Run flocked round her, slavering.

Nothing left to their imagination.

Or his.

"Damnation, that's not a proper costume for a lady." He slogged up onto the bankside, leaving the sorry fish to thrash around at the edge of the water, still attached to the line.

"It's quite proper if you're a woman, as I am, who manages a sportsman's lodge, which I do." And as though to prove this outrageous statement, she waded past him, deeper into the pool, and pulled a thickly branching root out of the stream. "As you can see for yourself, skirts would get in the way of my work."

"Work that you don't need to do. I can't believe that your husband would approve of . . . this?"

God, she was beautiful. Standing to her ankles in the stream, the sunlight sparkling gold and red behind her, making a halo of her hair. Her cheeks glowing pink, her nose unfashionably honeyed with a constellation of freckles.

And that blue, unfettered, unflinching gaze piercing him through.

"I truly don't have time to care whether my husband objects or not. He's hardly earned the right to have a say in what I do, let alone in what I wear."

There was a stinging blow. "Nevertheless, he's your husband. According to the laws of God and man, the right became his the moment you became his wife."

"That remains to be seen. Now, where's the rest of your morning's catch? It needs to be recorded." Her smile was as cynical as the single brow she arched at him. She pointed toward the huge trout whipping around in the pool, the force of it yanking at the line wrapped around his fist. "Or is that it?"

Damned distracting woman. "Released as I caught them. Anything under twenty pounds is hardly worthy of recording."

"Twenty pounds?" A disbelieving laugh. "You're certainly sure of your luck."

"I've no use for luck. Fishing is all about skill." A great big lie, but he watched her face for some indication of how much she'd seen of his bumbling flight down the stream.

Had she been part of his audience through the whole

bloody incident? Judging his ungainly skills as he careened through the water, deciding that he was a liar as well as a toff?

"That may be true, Colonel. But Rooney and Foggerty have done a fine job making our fisheries the best in the county. A strong breeding of fish, clean, challenging waters, quiet reserves—"

"Quiet? Then who the devil were those children?"

"Ah . . ." She cast him a rueful smile and stepped out of the stream, tossing the root into the brambles. "My apologies if they disturbed your sport. They're full of spunk, but they're good children."

"Yes, but where did they come from?" He'd never seen them before. "We're miles from the village."

Kate wondered once again why such a thing as the children should matter to the colonel, beyond the children frightening the fish. But why did he take everything about Badger's Run so personally? The tournament, the wine cellar, the other guests, the staff, her britches . . .

And why was it that just looking at the man, staring at him, really, made her feel as though she were standing on the edge of a hazardous precipice?

Waiting for something.

Or someone.

"The children come from . . . well, all over." It was the truth and she didn't want him to think they'd be around tomorrow to ruin his fishing again.

"Are they poachers? Children of poachers?"

"Hardly. But even if they were, they are nothing to concern yourself with. Unless of course, you were my husband come home to taunt me. Which you're not."

Great heavens, why the devil did she say that?

Because Hawkesly's clothes fit him perfectly.

More than perfectly. Even soaking wet, with his dark hair crisp and curling against his forehead. The fine, broad linen shirt beneath the dripping tweed of his unbuttoned waistcoat, molded like a second skin across the breadth of his chest.

His cravat hanging loosely at his collar.

His trousers fit just as perfectly, flat across his stomach, clinging to his thighs, his triangular hips, the buckskin shifting as he heeled the fly rod into the ground and caught her chin with his cool, water-sweet knuckle, tipping her gaze up to his fierce one.

"If I were your husband, I'd do far more than taunt you."

Her heart took a sideways leap, dancing with the danger of him. There was something familiar here too, his overwhelming nearness, the sound of his breathing, the feeling of him. His height and the breadth of his shoulders, the way he blotted the sun from the sky.

"Then I suppose we're both fortunate, Colonel." Kate stumbled backward out of his reach, able to breathe again, and think. "All I can promise is that you won't see the children again. Come, you'd better get your fish to the recording table. Where's the rest of your gear?"

He narrowed his eyes at her for a long study, then grunted and nodded upstream. "That way."

Kate started off along the bank, satisfied at the man's grumbling as he wrestled the trout out of the stream, at the crunch and snap of his footfalls as he followed. She rescued his rucksack and fly box from a boulder, then held open the large creel.

He dumped his wrangling catch into the basket,

dropped the lid and shouldered the strap. But the buckle on the creel had caught his watch chain and yanked the watchcase partially out of his pocket.

"Careful, Colonel, your watch." Kate tugged it the rest of the way out of his pocket, then turned it. "I'm sorry, it's soaked."

And its embossed gold case seemed familiar somehow.

The crest on the front, perhaps. A shield bearing a ship and a lion and three crossed swords. Arrows through it and a ribbon on each side. It gave her a vague, looming feeling of something always nearby. Something that she'd purposely avoided for a long time, never looked very closely at.

Something she'd seen in London, on a building? No, closer than that. On board a ship? Or here, at the hall, perhaps?

Something overhead, overhanging, forever looking down upon her.

"Blast it all," he said, lifting the watch by the chain, "I've ruined my watch."

His watch? *His?*

A chill trickled down her spine.

Yes, that was the trouble. The watch couldn't belong to Colonel Huddleswell.

Just as he couldn't have arrived yesterday wearing gilded buttons on his coat with the exact same crest.

Because now she knew exactly where she'd seen that ship and the lion and those swords.

That crest couldn't possibly belong to the colonel.

Because it belonged to . . . dear God!

She glanced up at the man, her heart stopped, her pulse gone dry.

"It's a lovely watch, Colonel," she said as offhandedly as she could manage. "Where did you get it?"

He frowned and rubbed the back of it against his waistcoat. "I had it made for me in London."

Please, God, it can't be true!

"When?" She could barely ask the question, because she already knew the answer.

"Three or four years ago."

Hawkesly's crest! The same one carved above the doorway arches at the hall.

And into the face of the fireplace mantels.

And emblazoned on the buttons of the coat he had arrived in yesterday!

His crest.

Him!

The bastard!

Kate shoved at his chest, stepped back from his nearness, letting the watch dangle below his waist.

The message for Hawkesly. It had come to the hall, because the sender had assumed that her husband had already arrived at the hall. And the trunk was also his, sent ahead of his arrival. But he'd come here instead—to Badger's Run.

Because . . . why? To tease her? No.

Because . . . he was a malicious, contemptible, betraying, spying scoundrel.

Now the lout was blithely listening to the back of the watch, as though he hadn't a care in the world. "It's stopped cold."

And I know just how it feels, Lord Hawkesly.

Cold. Betrayed.

Her bloody wandering husband home for an entire

day and he hadn't even had the decency to introduce himself.

Blast it all, he'd spent this whole time lying to her, making sport, spying on her, pretending he was the world's expert flyfisherman, or whatever the devil he was doing.

But why?

"A bit risky, isn't it, Colonel Huddleswell," she said, steadying her breathing, "to take your watch with you into the stream?"

He looked up at her as he fisted the watch and shook it. "An unfortunate misstep, madam. Not planned."

So blasé, Lord Hawkesly, so completely in control. "But quite fortunate that my husband's clothes fit you so remarkably well."

He raised a brow and studied her, then said slowly, "I'll have to thank him someday."

The overbearing blackguard! Feeling her anger begin to crawl out of her chest like a flush which he might take for passion, Kate picked up his fly box and rucksack then stalked the rest of the way to the path, safely out of range of the temptation to shove him back into the stream.

She stopped at the top of the weedy bank and turned back to him. "You might get your chance to thank him very, very soon."

"How's that?" He narrowed his gaze at her, shouldering his creel and starting up the embankment, like a monster rising out of the sea in pursuit of her. "What do you mean, soon?"

Yes, what the devil was she doing, taunting him? Her

mouth went dry. "I have every reason to believe that my husband is on his way home, even as we speak."

"Oh?" He'd made the embankment without straining a muscle. "What makes you think that?"

She kept a good step away from him, wondering how he could possibly have become larger in the last few minutes. "Just a bit of detection work on my part. Evidence coupled with speculation."

"What sort of evidence?"

Your bloody self, in the flesh, you bloody blighter. Standing right here in front of me, looking smug and sure.

Baiting his wife.

Taking his advantage.

Learning her secrets.

The children! Kate's heart dropped into her knees, making her want to run. Dear God, he'd find the children at the hall.

A single day spent in Hawkesly's company and she knew for a fact that he would never understand what they meant to her, and surely never allow her to continue her work with them.

Well, she'd just have to slow Hawkesly down in his snooping and give herself a time to plan an explanation, or an escape.

"You were speaking of this evidence of Hawkesly's return."

Kate swallowed back the lump of fear and started down the path toward her horse, forming her plan as she strode along in front of him. "Ah, yes, well . . . It isn't much, really. Just a letter that has come for him."

"A letter?" She could hear the restraint in his voice, a dangerous darkness. "It came to Badger's Run?"

Kate couldn't help the little laugh that popped out of her chest, pleased that she had confused him, if only for the moment. "Now, why ever would a letter come for my husband to Badger's Run?"

Hawkesly drew in a breath as though to speak sharply, but then shook his head. "Of course, it would come to Hawkesly's estate."

"Hawkesly Hall, actually. Yes, the message came to Hawkesly Hall." She was about to step over a fallen beech, when she felt his huge hand on her shoulder, a tugging that sat her down hard on the thick trunk and brought his face to hers.

"When, madam?"

"Well, let me see . . ." Kate pondered this slowly, with a finger to her lips and a sigh. "I think it was sometime . . . ummmm . . . last night."

"Last night?" he said with a deeply satisfying bluster that straightened him. He shot a glance toward the hall, with a deadly accuracy.

"Or was it early this morning?" Kate said, tapping her cheek, suddenly recognizing her recklessness as part of a growing plan to throw him off balance. Because she had so few other weapons to wield against him. "Not that it matters. He's not home yet."

He leaned down to her, making her bend backward to keep away from the soft, distracting brush of his breath against her mouth. "It matters a great deal."

"Why?" Confess, you blackguard!

"Because . . ." Hawkesly leveled a finger at her, then lowered it. "Because it means that . . ."

"Yes, that my husband is on his way home."

"Perhaps." He took a sudden, uncaring stance, giving a shrug. "It could also be a simple greeting from a friend."

"If that's so, then it's the first he's received since I've lived there as his so-called bride." The word bounced across his mouth, then brushed back against hers. "So I can only assume—"

"Where did it come from?"

"From?"

"Was the message to your husband posted from London? Portsmouth? Where?"

So Hawkesly *was* expecting a message from someone. "Hmmmm . . . I'm not sure. But I believe it was a private message, not sent through the royal post. And I don't recall any markings on the outside to indicate its origins." Not that she had even set eyes on the thing yet. Kate slipped her legs over the log and stood up with the fallen beech between them. "But now that you mention it, I think I'll just run back to Hawkesly Hall and open the message myself. Just in case—"

"No!" He'd not only stepped over the log, but he'd caught her upper arm. "You won't!"

"I know it's not entirely honest—"

"It's thoroughly dishonest, madam!"

"But, after all, he is my husband. My helpmate. Maybe this will tell me how soon he'll be home."

"Why do you need to know right now?" His face had grown stormy and dark. "Are you planning a happy surprise to welcome him?"

With a brick to the forehead. "Hardly."

"You don't sound very pleased at the prospect."

"I'm feeling quite the opposite." A little truth wouldn't hurt him.

"Bloody hell, you haven't seen him in nearly two years!"

"Exactly the problem." Though the blighter could only have known how long her husband had been gone if he were the culprit. "Reuniting with my husband is a moment that I've been dreading for all that time."

"Dreading?" The man looked incensed, dropped his creel on the log.

"As I would dread a visit from the very devil."

"Why is that?" His frown deepened. "Have you done something that he'll not approve of?"

"You mean besides wearing these britches and turning his abandoned hunting lodge into a sportsman paradise and loaning his clothes to a perfect stranger and . . ."

"And . . . ?"

And so many other things she could never tell him, things that he'd discover for himself soon enough.

"And so you see, I need to know his plans before he arrives, because . . . well, I'm afraid."

"Afraid of what?"

Kate touched his damp sleeve at his elbow, dallied with the folds in the linen, playing the defenseless damsel as she whispered, "Of him."

He grunted. "You're afraid of your husband?"

Kate sighed deeply. "Dear Colonel Huddleswell, I'm terrified of him."

"You're terrified of a man you knew for all of ten minutes?" He'd slipped there in his facts as well. She'd never mentioned the brevity of their wedding day to anyone, ever. The shame of it had burned her cheeks for months afterward.

Kate shook her head and leaned seductively against his arm, slipping her hand through his, causing the man to sputter. "Ten minutes was more than enough to know the kind of man he is. I know his reputation. Hard-tempered and cruel."

Hawkesly's mouth worked as though trying to form an answer. His breathing deepened to a near growl as she leaned more completely against him, her breasts moving lightly against his chest. "Where did you hear that, madam?"

"It's true." And it felt so wonderful to be seducing him against his will, nearly as wonderful as the thrill of her nipples playing against the wool of his waistcoat. "Will you stay with me?"

"Stay?"

"Please, Colonel." She held tightly to his spellbound gaze, savoring the rodlike hardness at the front of his trousers, the heat of him. Like dancing in the moonlight, in the middle of the day. Too bad that it couldn't last.

"Madam, do you know what you're doing?" She'd obviously scandalized him.

His perfect, put-away-in-a-box bride.

"Promise that you'll stay beside me when my husband comes. To protect me."

His face had gone fuming red, his eyes on fire as he took hold of her forearms and stood her away. "I bloody well will not!"

"I know we've only just met, but I feel like I know you very well." She grabbed hold of his shirtfront and pulled him down to her, till they were sharing every breath. "Better than I know my own husband. Isn't that amazing?"

Then she kissed him, pressed her mouth against her husband's, just to startle him, to put him firmly in his place, expecting coolness, but finding a kind of heat she'd never felt before.

Searing and slick, tasting like the creek, the sun when she nibbled. Quick became languid, rhythmic. She kissed him until her knees sagged, until he was kissing her back.

Until he was breathing like a stallion and growling like a bear.

Until she knew she had to stop. She pulled well away from him, her raging bull, who looked anything but fully in control.

She clasped her hands together over her heart and said in her most seductive voice, "Remember, Colonel, I'm counting on you."

And then she bolted from him into the wooded pathway, found her mare and rode hard toward the hall. She planned to beat him there, to hold off the moment of reckoning for as long as she could.

Jared stood rooted to the ground, his brain sodden and slow, his groin on fire with unslaked lust for her, his juices roaring through his veins.

"She kissed me," he heard himself say, dazzled, slack-jawed and staring after her, gazing toward the shadowy opening in the forest.

He was thrilled, burning, anticipating bliss in abundance with his bride, and yet . . .

Something was wrong here.

Not that she had kissed him, but that—

"Bloody hell!" His innocent little bride had just kissed another man!

Chapter 8

❧

And that bloody kiss of hers wasn't just a peck of appreciation.

Or a simple *thank you for your kindness, Colonel Huddleswell.*

Or *blessings on your rainbow trout.*

No, that kind of kiss needed a private chamber and golden firelight and softly scented silk.

And the sanctity of a marriage bed. . . .

"Damnation!" Seething with a green-tinted jealousy that was becoming far too familiar, Jared climbed the rest of the way to the road, but the woman was gone.

Vanished again without a trace, though he could still feel the imprint of her breasts against his chest, the arching shape of her mouth!

Doubtless off to plant another rousing kiss on another unsuspecting guest.

The hell she would! Jared stalked the mile to the lodge at full steam, and dropped his creel and his catch on the recording table in front of Magnus. She must be here somewhere, his flighty, faithless wife flirting with everyone, trailing a school of sportsmen in her wake.

"Damn fine rainbow you landed, Huddleswell! Congratulations, old man!"

"Thank you, Gilmott. Now if you'll excuse—"

Breame joined them, followed by Fitchett. "What did you catch him on, Colonel?"

Hell, another bloody fishing inquisition. But he'd learned one thing about anglers—they prized secrecy. "Now that would be telling, gentlemen."

"A green bumble?" Gilmott clicked his tongue and raised his bristly brows.

"Wooly worm? Midge pupa?"

"A family secret, Fitchett," Jared said, scanning over the tops of their heads for any sign of his wife.

The taste of her mouth was still on his lips, the warmth of her breath, her palm against his chest, playing with the buttons on his waistcoat.

"Now, if you're needing a partner tomorrow morning, Huddleswell—"

"I won't be, Breame." Jared left the forecourt and strode through the lodge and up to his room for a change into dry clothes. He struggled with the steamy wool and the wet linen and the stubborn buttons until he was sweltering hot, every move trapping him more tightly inside his clothes.

Blast the woman for her treachery! He'd expected obedience and patience and above all, faithfulness in a wife. Instead he'd wed himself to just the opposite.

She kissed me! And it burned him still.

A half hour later he was descending the stairs, fully charged with confronting his wife.

Magnus would know where she was. He got halfway through the forecourt when he was stopped by a young man who was offering him an envelope. "This is for you, sir."

Jared took it and glanced down at the familiar seal. One so nearly like his own, in a hand he knew well. And on the front:

The Right Honorable Earl Hawkesly
Hawkesly Hall, Lancashire

In Ross's hand.

"Where did you get this?"

"Just now, up at the hall. Lady Hawkesly said for me to tell you that it belongs to you, sir."

"To me?"

For him, Hawkesly. Not Colonel Huddleswell. Which could only mean—

Damnation! So the brazen woman had known who he was all along! She'd been playing him, reeling him in slowly like one of her precious fish.

"Where's her ladyship now?"

"At the hall, sir. Leastwise, she was when I left 'bout a quarter hour ago."

"Thank you, boy."

Minutes later Jared was in the saddle, the tick of outrage magnifying in his brain, the inconceivable realization that he'd been duped. Betrayed by an utterly shameless slip of a woman who'd had too much idle time on her hands for too long.

A danger to herself and to him, to everyone and everything around her.

That was about to change.

He was soon galloping down the treed slope and over the stone bridge that emptied into the long drive up. Hawkesly Hall popped into view a portion at a time, its high, honey-gold limestone fence wall and the steep gable of the east wing beyond that.

The angular vista brought him up short, stopped him in his tracks.

Hawkesly Hall. The seat of his success, his titles and achievements.

And yet familiar to him only in its angles and color and size. Whenever he'd thought of the place that he called home, it was from this vantage point. Off-center and always from outside the stately standards of the massive stone gateposts and the intricate iron gate standing between him and the hall.

A rattling, lonely distance he'd never felt before now. Because Hawkesly Hall had never really been a home to him. He knew very little about it—hadn't stayed there more than three months total in the four years he'd owned it.

A stranger in his own home.

Perhaps it was time to give country house parties and balls. Here, where life was cool and serene.

Or would be once he'd regained control.

Jared gave his horse a quick heel and cantered decisively through his front gate, only to come to a gravel-strewing halt at the edge of the circular lawn.

Or what had been a lawn the last time he'd been here. Now it looked more like a broad meadow, tall grass and daisies. Complete with three goats grazing in the center alongside a half-dozen sheep!

"Grady, dooooon't!" The wailing screech came from behind him, advancing, becoming a long peel of laughter.

And then a golden-haired little girl ran past him, laughing, followed by a blond lad, lanky and familiar, and then that same huge, black hound, loping and barking.

"It's my apple, Grady!"

"But I'm the apple monster, Mera, and I'm after you! Grrrrr!"

The same children.

"Ha-ha-ha-ha! Eeeeeek!" The trio went running off around the corner of the house, the boy growling, lumbering after the little girl.

Had the woman no sense at all, inviting all the wild children from the countryside to run like rabbits all over his estate? Where the devil had they all come from? Where were their parents? More precisely, why did they seem so much at home here?

"Whatever game you've been playing, my dear Lady Hawkesly, it going to end right now. Whether you like it or not."

And he had no doubt that she would not.

He dropped from the horse as he reached the front steps and was just tying the reins to the hitch ring when the laurel hedge that skirted the foundation of the hall began thrashing violently.

"This way!" Which precipitated a stream of noisy children pouring out of the hedge.

The one in the lead saw Jared and stopped. "Look, Dori! It's the man from the river!"

"Hello, sir!"

They suddenly mobbed around him as though he were a dancing bear at an exhibition.

"Did your fish win, sir?"

Jared felt a tug on his coat sleeve. "It should win, sir! It was the biggest fish I ever seen."

"Are you going to eat it all yourself?"

The eldest girl took the boy's hand, frowning hard. "Healy Connett, you know very well that Lady Kate will make the man share."

Jared caught the girl's eye, his only hope to wedge in a word between all the shouting and shoving. "Where's Lady Hawkesly?"

He got a deeper frown from the girl. "She won't like you coming here, sir. Guests aren't allowed at the hall. They're supposed to stay at the lodge."

"She'll allow me, young lady." The girl cringed and bit at her lip and he was instantly sorry for his gruffness. "Please tell me where I can find her."

"I'm here, my lord."

"She's there!" The little girl who was missing her two front teeth grinned up at him and pointed to the top of the wide stairs and his heart took off like a rocket.

Kate was standing above him on the porch landing, framed between the two white columns like some painted goddess. She'd changed out of her britches into a soft yellow, spriggy dress and an apron, and was now surrounded by the swarm of children.

"He's come to see us, Lady Hawkesly, the man who caught that big old fish!"

"Yes, I recognize him, Justin."

"I warned him that you don't allow guests on this side of the wall."

"I think we'll have to make an exception in this case, Glenna."

"But he looks dangerous, Lady Hawkesly."

"It's all right, Glenna, I'll handle the matter from here on." The woman drew herself up in a square-shouldered challenge. "Please take all the little ones to the kitchen to help the Miss Darbys peel all those apples."

Who the bloody hell were the Miss Darbys?

"Boys, you'll go on with Jacob and gather firewood— lots of it. Winter will be here in no time. Go on, now, please."

His wife's gaze never left his as the mob of children broke into separate swarms and sped away with their leaders, leaving the entrance suddenly quiet but for the birds and the winnowing breeze and the thunking of his heart.

She stood still and staring, her feet planted firmly, her chin high, as though the porch and its tall, palladian arched roof had been a hard-fought hillfort that she planned to defend to the death.

"Welcome home, my lord." As frosty a welcome, as cynical, as they come.

"And a bloody fine welcome you've made it, wife." Filled to the brink with righteous anger, Jared started up the stairs, steadily closing the distance between them. "You should have confessed immediately that you knew who I was. You should have said."

"*I* should have said?" Her eyes flashed blue-green beneath an arching brow, the only movement she made in her defense. "How, Hawkesly? I hadn't the slightest suspicion who you were when you barged into Badger's Run, demanding a room."

"Like bloody hell, you didn't."

"If it hadn't been for the engraving on the front of your watch, you'd still be leading me down your merry path."

"What do you mean, my watch?" He stopped on the step just below the landing, suddenly, clearly, remembering the change that had come over her at the stream, the shove she gave him and the passion and then the kiss.

"The bloody Hawkesly crest, sir. It's everywhere in the hall; on the hearth and the doorway arches, on the stationery. The ship and the rampant lion and those swords. Not only emblazoned on every buckle and coat button in your wardrobe, but on the buttons that Colonel Huddleswell was wearing when he arrived. I just hadn't made the connection until today."

Indeed. His cover detected by one tiny detail that he'd completely overlooked. The crest. An error like that in the field could get a man killed.

Hell, the woman had distracted him to the point of danger right from the start.

"Hardly an excuse, wife."

"And what is your excuse for your unforgiveable behavior? You were purposely misleading me. Not letting on that you were my husband. Why? I can't imagine what your reasons were."

"My reasons were sound." At least they had seemed to be at the time. He took the last step up onto the landing, though keeping his distance while he tried to decipher her plot. "Not only were you doing a land-office business in my hunting lodge, but you acted as though I were a stranger! In my own home."

She looked at him through narrowed lashes and said slowly, "You *are* a stranger to me, Hawkesly. How in blazes was I to recognize you?"

"Because, as I recall, you were standing right next to me when we were married."

"And you looked like a bloody pirate at the time, with a pirate's beard and wild hair, a cutlass as long as your leg—"

"I looked like a pirate?" Damnation, he was beginning to sense a flaw in his logic, a hasty accusation. Perhaps she truly hadn't recognized him.

"And that was nearly two years ago, thousands of miles from home, and in a shameful hurry, with me still in mourning for my father, and only after you had dragged me from his ship onto the deck of yours."

Wildly exaggerated. "I didn't drag you anywhere."

"You married me without notice, without giving me a voice in the matter."

"Entirely your father's doing."

"My father would never have given me to you against my will."

"He left me no choice, woman. We were partners in his cargo and in his ships. He owed me."

"My father owed you a *wife*?"

"It was a business matter between the two of us."

"Ha!" She leveled a finger up at him, spoke between her teeth. "You wanted Trafford Shipping, plain and simply."

He wanted *her*. He might not have known it at the time, but he did now. He wanted the crimson heat of her anger and the rise and fall of her chest. The ice-blue fire of her eyes. "There was nothing simple about the transaction."

"I know the shipping business, Hawkesly. I lived it all my life. The company was mine when Father died. You and I could have easily struck some sort of bargain with his ships and the cargo. You had no right to force me to marry you just to secure your profits."

Jared had finally gotten near enough to his prickly wife to cup her soft chin and tilt her crystalline blue gaze to his; he intended to get past her into the house, try as she might to trip him up with her wrangling. "I didn't force you into marriage with me."

She gave an unladylike snort and raised her brows sharply as she took a long step backward. "As I recall, your marriage proposal was exactly, 'Stand here and keep quiet, woman, or you'll know the reason why.' "

Jared opened his mouth to rebut the woman's memory, but her claim rang true with his own memories of the day. He hadn't any choice at the time but to take control of her assets. Her father had died with a hold full of treasures stolen from the tomb of an ancient Egyptian king. The foolish man had been duped by thieves into shipping the politically dangerous contraband. The ship's manifest was in Jared's own name and the authorities were about to board. There were three ships at stake and a small fortune. Not to mention a long stay in a hellhole of a prison.

"I was in a hurry, madam."

She laughed from deep inside her chest, a rare and rich sound. "You were as arrogant then as you are now."

"Which signifies nothing." Best to firmly lay down the law. "You are my wife and that's the end of it."

A larger laugh, longer and deeper. "The end of this mockery of a marriage."

He didn't like the sound of that. "Meaning?"

"I'm weary of this." She dropped her shoulders and sighed hugely. "I've already confessed to Colonel Huddleswell how I've been dreading the return of my husband. I was right about everything. Now I suggest you go ask him."

Kate wanted to toss the man into the privet hedge, but she turned away from him and started toward the front door instead, fearing most of all that he would see the tears of outrage welling in her eyes. He'd surely measure them as a weakness instead of the overwhelming fury she felt, the humiliation, the sense of gross injustice that she'd been hiding even from herself.

How dare he—

"Come back here!" He caught her by the apron strings before she'd gotten two steps from him and pulled her back against his sizzling chest. "So you truly were dreading my return, wife?"

"With all my heart, Hawkesly."

"Not just playing a role for the colonel?"

Kate pulled out of his grip and whirled to face him. "You are the most arrogant man I've ever met. And don't call me 'wife.' You haven't earned the right. You've been no kind of a husband in all this time. And as far as I'm concerned, I have none now."

"I don't know where you've come by your wayward ideas, wife." He looked suddenly taller, his shoulders broader, his eyes grown utterly feral as he advanced on her. "But I'm giving you fair warning that everything around here is about to change."

"Lady Kaaaaaate!" Mera came running up the steps, with Grady and Lucas on her heels and a happily yapping Mr. McNair lumping along behind them all.

They piled up around Kate, a noisy jumble of excitement wedged between her and the frowning Hawkesly. "Look what we found!"

Grady threw open a sack and raised it up to her. "Mushrooms!"

Kate peered inside. "Morels! Why, Grady, that's wonderful."

"I got a sackful, too!" Lucas shoved his sack in front of Grady's.

The children knew that the morels were not only expensive and rare, but that they would fetch a pretty purse from her contacts in London.

"Did you bring your big fish, sir?" Mera asked Hawkesly, who stared down at the girl as though she were a gnome come from the woods. Mr. McNair took a firm place beside the man, leaned his bulk against his leg.

"The fish? I, uh . . . no. It's back at the lodge."

"Did you win?" Mera asked, slipping her little hand into Kate's.

Hawkesly paused, glaring, as if considering whether

or not to answer. "I won't know until later."

Kate said nothing during the exchange, the simplest test of a man's heart.

He wouldn't pass.

"I hope you do, sir. So does Mr. McNair!"

Hawkesly looked up at Kate, his eyes narrowed, his mouth unsmiling, his nostrils flaring.

Foul-tempered beast! All was lost. She'd never be able to trust him. She turned the children from him. "Run along into the kitchen with those morels, Grady. The Miss Darbys will know what to do with them."

"Yes, ma'am."

The children and the dog took off into the house with their usual speed and brawling, Hawkesly staring after them.

"Who are they?" he asked, his gaze still following the children as they tumbled into the house.

"The oldest boy is Grady Connett, the younger is Lucas Howell, and the girl's name is Mera."

He focused on her again, her mouth and then her eyes. "And who, by chance, is Mr. McNair?"

"The dog."

A muscle squared in his jaw and then he asked carefully, "Where do they live?"

Kate sighed right out loud. Caught. No use dodging the truth about the children any longer. He'd find out on his own as soon as he entered the house and saw the rest of the evidence. Besides, she had no intention of making excuses for the children.

But Kate was saved an immediate answer as the door opened and Rosemary popped her head out. "Apple pudding, Lady Hawkesly, or just plain applesauce?"

"Pudding, please."

"It'll mean the last of the cinnamon."

"I'll have some brought in the next time the—" Dear God, she nearly said the *Katie Claire*. "Next time I make a marketing trip to Preston."

"You're a kind woman, my lady." Rosemary's smile flattened suddenly and she wagged her wooden spoon at Hawkesly. "Is he stayin' for dinner, then?"

No. "We'll see."

"Fine then," Rosemary said with a sniff toward the man as she closed the door.

Hawkesly was fuming as he turned her sharply to face him, pointing over her shoulder, his nose nearly meeting hers. "And who was that?"

"Miss Rosemary Darby." Kate pulled away and rescued a wooden spindle that one of the children must have misplaced from their bowling game and decided that it was time to face the consequences, the full force of his anger, and take him into the hall.

"I asked who that woman is."

"She's a cook here at the hall."

"What happened to Mrs. Archer?"

She couldn't very well tell him that the very capable Mrs. Archer was the first to volunteer to work at Father Sebastian's soup kitchen.

"Mrs. Archer needed a holiday from all the work here, so I sent her to . . . Italy."

"Italy?"

Kate opened the door, hoping for at least some sense of order inside the house. But there was nothing that could soften this kind of blow; might as well have been a clack against the head with a cricket bat.

Hawkesly stepped into the foyer then stopped abruptly to stare at the telltale row of little coats and hats hanging on hooks along either wall of the foyer, the little boots standing below each and the benches.

A nice, neat line of children's belongings, looking very much at home in his castle.

"What are all these?" He grabbed a coat by the neck, inspected it at arm's length. "The place looks like a poor school."

As though on cue, the children came running toward them from the direction of the kitchen, Rosemary close behind, calling them back. Then Tansy and Myrtle joined their sister until the gang of them were clumped around Kate.

"I'm so sorry, my lady," Rosemary said, "but the children got a sudden notion that—"

"No, they're all right here, Rosemary. I actually have a very important announcement to make. And I want you all to hear it."

"You're going to read to us?"

"No, children. Please listen." She stopped them before they could begin shouting their usual list of fairy tale requests. "I would very much like you all to meet Lord Hawkesly."

There was a long silence as everyone took in her information.

"Hawkesly? You mean like you, my lady?" Glenna asked, puzzling it out before the other children had. "The one that's your husband?"

For the moment.

"Yes, Glenna. Lord Hawkesly has finally returned from sea."

"In a boat?"

"Does he like hedgehogs?"

"Where will he sleep, Lady Kate?"

But in all the stunned confusion that followed, the three Miss Darbys said it best in one single voice:

"Have mercy on us all."

Chapter 9

"**W**hat the devil? What's happened here?" Hawkesly stared down at the children, then up at the walls, surely taking an inventory, obviously ready to explode with anger.

But Kate certainly wasn't going to let it happen here in front of the children and the staff; they were wide-eyed enough already.

"Come with me, Lord Hawkesly." Kate swished past him, knowing that he'd follow her like a beast stalking its prey. "This way and I'll try to explain."

He caught up with her as she entered the library she'd turned into a schoolroom. "You'll do more than try, madam. I'll have the whole of your deceit this instant. To begin with, I had six suits of very expensive armor standing along those walls! What have you done with them?"

He hadn't even noticed the library itself. Wait till he saw the parlors! Kate stepped back to close the door but found the three Miss Darbys peering past her into the library, muttering to each other, their worried glares fixed on her husband.

"Will ya be all right in there, my lady?"

"I'll be fine, Myrtle." Kate pushed her shoulder against the door, but Myrtle pushed back.

"But he's so . . . big."

"I can handle him." It took Kate's fiercest scowl, but she finally got the door closed.

Even before Kate turned, she knew that Hawkesly was looking daggers at her, following her every move, speculating. Yet she wasn't prepared for the heart-stopping sight of him when she did meet his gaze, standing there against the shelves of books and the massive marble fireplace, staring at her with those dark, incising eyes.

So ruggedly elegant, with his arms crossed against his chest, his hair half wild, his shoulders as broad as the mantel, his temper barely tethered. A pirate once more.

But rather than explode, Hawkesly said quietly, intensely, "What the hell are you running here? A school for local ruffians?"

"Hardly."

"What then? An orphanage?"

Kate had been ready to explain just that, but he'd stolen her momentum along with her words. "Not an orphanage, a home for orphaned children."

Jared was sure that he hadn't heard her right—sometimes outrage became such a roar in his ears it drowned out the sense of things around him. "A what?"

"I'm sure you understand the meaning, my lord: children who have no parents, no home, nothing to eat, to wear—"

"Damn it, woman, I know what an orphanage is." He'd goddamned lived in one long enough, before the workhouse and the streets of London. "What you haven't told me is why the hell my wife is running one in my home."

"And *mine*. Funny, but I didn't notice that you were here to have an opinion one way or the other. I was the only one living in this huge house, and so I did what I thought was right."

"And what was that? Place an advertisement in the county newspaper offering Hawkesly Hall to the local Poor Relief Committee?"

"Don't be absurd."

"Absurd is that my library is now littered with these benches and little trestle tables. That instead of tapestries and expensive, historically significant Spanish armor, my hallway is now hung with tiny coats and hats. I can only assume that the upper floors look like a dormitory."

She raised a self-righteous brow. "Well, they have to sleep somewhere."

"Not in my house."

She tsked at him, then shook her head. "It's amazing that all the time you've been gone, I've been imagining that you would say that very thing, in that very way, when you found out what I'm doing. 'Not in my house,' " she said in a low voice, shaking her head. "Just like that. I'm only sorry that you've proved me right."

Then the woman turned and made it all the way to the door. "Where are you going? We're not finished here."

She turned back to him, lifting her hand off the door latch. "Oh, but we're quite finished, as I knew in my heart that we would be the moment you came home. We obviously have nothing more to say to each other on this or any other subject. So good afternoon."

"We've plenty more to say."

"No, we're as far apart now as we were when you were halfway around the world. Now that you've returned, it's time for me to leave. And don't worry, I'll be taking my . . . orphans with me." She turned to go.

"Stop right there." Jared felt his feet glued to the floor by the absurdity of this discussion. "You're not going anywhere."

"The sooner done, the better. I'll start packing them up immediately, but I would appreciate you allowing us to stay the night. It's hard enough to move nine children in the daylight, let alone—"

"Nine children? Living here? Where the devil did they all come from?"

She faced him full on, her hands clasped placidly in the folds of her apron. "Ireland."

"Ireland?" Bloody hell. The telltale brogues on every tongue.

She took a deep breath, one that seemed to infuse her with a reckless kind of courage. "The children are from Wicklow, mostly, south of Dublin. Oh, and we've one from the Scottish Highlands. Margaret. She just arrived."

"Good God!" She'd gotten her orphans from Ireland, of all places. A teeming mass of hunger, too many mouths, not enough to go around.

"I hadn't really planned on this when I arrived here. It all happened quite by accident."

"You accidently invited nine Irish orphans to live in my house?"

She arched that fawn-light brow at him, a powerful condemnation. "*Our* house. And there were only five at first."

His head aching with the woman's prevaricating, Jared took her by the upper arm, led her to a fiddleback chair. "Sit right here and tell me everything."

She sat, crossing her arms and jutting out her chin, looking very much like a belligerent captive. "There's nothing much to tell."

"I want every word." And then, damn it all, he wanted *her*. Tonight.

She rolled the words around inside her stubborn mouth, then finally sighed impatiently. "It was just a few weeks after I arrived here after our wedding. I thought I'd make a visit to Mereglass—down to the village, so that I could become familiar with the villagers and the shopkeepers." She stopped for a moment and studied him, as though mulling over the next part of her story.

"Go on," he said, prepared to sort through her falsehoods.

"When I arrived, there was a great commotion coming from the headlands, along the cliffs. Apparently a small boat had run aground and broken up on the rocks with ten refugees from the famine in Ireland on board. Only eight were still alive. Two men, five children, and a priest, all of them nearly dead of starvation, let alone their journey."

"So you brought them to Hawkesly Hall."

"How could I not? There wasn't enough room in the village for all of them. And they needed such a lot of care."

Bloody hell. "Like putting out a dish of cream for a kitten. You let them stay."

Her face went cold, a look of disgust that made him glance away, to the mezzanine above and its shelves and shelves of books. "When the men recovered, they wanted to work for me. So I let them."

"Who?" Though he already knew the answer to one man. "McHugh?"

"And Ian. He works the stables here at the hall. As to the children, they were orphans when they arrived. A family of children whose parents were dead of the famine and who were now without anyone to take care of them."

"And you believed that person should be you? A woman alone—"

"What a blathering thing to say. I might have been alone, but I was not without resources."

That was a certainty. She seemed to be capable of making gold out of straw, no matter the risk.

"You've explained five of the children. Where did the others come from? All of them shipwrecked and plucked out of the sea?"

"We've only had the one disaster. Mostly the children were . . . um . . ." She stopped and chewed for an instant on her lower lip and then flipped him an impatient frown. "Most have been brought here by Father Sebastian himself."

Jared didn't like the turn of this tale. "Father Sebastian? The priest that you rescued."

"He was nearly dead when we found him, but he lived to continue his original mission—"

"Which is?"

She looked him straight in the eye, challenging and defiant. "Which is aiding the wretched poor in Ireland who've been tossed aside by the fat, sightless criminals in Whitehall and Westminster."

Hell and damnation, a wife with a rebel's political leanings. His fault entirely. If he'd only come home sooner, he could have headed off her wrong-headed opinions.

He held back his temper. "And just what is your association with this renegade priest?"

"He's not a renegade." She stood, fisting her hands against her hips, fire blazing deep in her eyes. "He's a devoted man who is willing to sacrifice everything for the well-being of others. And I'm doing my level best to help any way I can."

"By sacrificing yourself to every wide-eyed child with a heart-cracking story?"

"How dare you!" Her cheeks went hot, her mouth hard. "There are thousands of starving, orphaned children in Father Sebastian's parish."

"None of whom is your responsibility," he said with as much equanimity as he could muster.

"Starving children are everybody's responsibility, no matter where they are. If you'd seen what I've seen—"

"You'll stay out of it." He damn well couldn't have his wife crossing the Home Office with her inciting opinions. Embarrassing the queen. He was a peer. An influential member of the House of Lords. An agent of the Crown. "The Irish troubles are not yours."

"They are not *troubles*. They are children. Innocent, helpless children. They come to me like lifeless bags of bones, dressed in rags, with hollow eyes and hopeless hearts. They need food and clothing and someone to care about them. It's the very least that I can give."

"Don't be a fool." False hopes and grand plans. He'd learned long ago never to involve himself too personally. "You can't take on an entire famine by yourself."

"Unfortunately, no, but I can take on a small portion of it, and I can win. I am winning, in my way. With a little creative enterprise—"

"Ah! Like Badger's Run." He understood now. She needed to raise money for her little cause.

"Yes, Badger's Run. I had to feed the children somehow. It was important to be self-sufficient and portable, just in case things went badly." Her laughter was dry as dust. "I suppose I needn't ask again about the children? Whether or not they can stay here tonight . . ."

One night would only mean a dozen more and he couldn't have that. "I want no part of your little famine-relief scheme. I thought I made that clear."

"You've made it terribly clear." She nodded, her disappointment a powerful indictment against his character. "I should have made better plans. Now if you're finished with me here, I've got to get the children ready."

He caught her arm as she reached the door, stopping

her because letting her out of his sight seemed a dangerous move. "Oh, I'm not anywhere near finished with you."

"I'm afraid that whatever it is, it'll have to wait." She jabbed a practiced and pointy knuckle between his ribs, startling him off balance, then escaped through the door.

"Come back here." He missed her by an inch, then threw himself into the corridor.

But she was already in the main hall, surrounded by swarms of children, each of them looking up at her in rapt adoration. "Dori, I need you to help put the spoons on the tables."

"Oh, goody! Come help me, Grady!"

"What the hell are you doing?" Jared asked from the edge of the mob. "We have unfinished business."

"You and I are completely finished. Now if you'll excuse me, I have many things to do while the children eat their dinners."

"To the devil with the children—"

"Somehow I knew you'd say that." She scooped up the little red-haired boy and started toward the kitchen. "Come, Lucas, you can help me pack up the pantry."

Jared stopped her, midstep. "Where the hell do you think you're going, madam?"

Two pair of eyes stared back at him. "I'll thank you not to curse in front of the children," she said, as though he were a child. "We'll be out of here soon enough. Then you can curse all you like, till the air is a lovely shade of blue." She pulled away.

"Damnation!" he said out of habit, but well under his breath.

She spun around and scowled at him, then continued on her way down the stairs, trailing children in her wake.

By the time he swam through the little mob she was inside the pantry and he was standing just outside, where he couldn't quite see her.

"Now don't crowd, children," she was saying to all the out-stretched hands. "There's plenty for everyone to do."

"Hand it all to me," the elder girl said. "I'll stack it all on the table!"

"Thank you, Glenna."

"I insist on speaking with you now, madam." Jared tried to shove forward, feeling as though he were bobbing on a troughy sea, making no headway as the children jostled him and each other.

"I'm sure it'll keep." A stream of bottled carrots started flowing out of the pantry, traveling on a current of thin arms and little fingers, landing in the care of the efficient little Glenna.

"What are we doing, Lady Kate?"

"Packing, Mera."

"Are we going on a holiday?"

"That's exactly right, Healy. The apples are coming next," his wife called from the pantry, and there followed still another stream of apple jars flowing past him.

Jared finally made his way through the children into the pantry, grabbing hold of the next jar, interrupting her efficient flow.

"What are you doing, wife?"

"I'm packing food for the children. We have a long

way to travel tonight and many mouths to feed in the morning."

"You?" Bloody hell, she was talking about leaving herself. "You're not leaving here."

She raised her brows. "Are they staying?"

"No."

"Then neither am I. We'll be out of here tonight, if you'll get out of the way."

"Tonight?" Talking to her was like standing in the midst of a typhoon. Nothing but wind and motion.

"You're obviously in no mood to let us sleep at the hall tonight."

"Don't be absurd. You're not going anywhere." Hell, he'd just gotten here.

"I have no choice. It's actually the best for both of us."

"How's that?"

"We're still not completely married, if you recall."

"Oh, yes we are." Or would be tonight.

"But not really. Not without accomplishing that wedding-night ritual. If you know what I mean."

He knew exactly what she meant. Understood it quite deeply, especially here in this close pantry with its clouds of cinnamon and pepper. "A detail only."

"A stroke of luck for both of us in the long run."

"Stroke of luck?" He wasn't feeling at all lucky at the moment.

"Are there any more apple jars, Lady Kate?"

"In just a minute, Jacob." She frowned up into Jared's face. "That way, you'll find our marriage-that-never-was uncomplicated and quite easily annulled.

Best of all, I'll require no maintenance from you. It'll be as though we were never married."

He caught her by the shoulders and made her look at him. "Are you mad?"

"I'm finally quite sane. Sad, but definitely sane." She bent around him and, smiling fondly, she handed an apple jar into Jacob's small, dirty hands. "There you are, dear. Now, Lord Hawkesly, if you'll excuse me, I have more jars to move and a wagon to fill. If we can borrow such a thing—"

"Stop—"

"It'll be full dark in three hours; I have to get the children fed, dressed, and to the parish church by then." She fixed a withering scowled on him. "Now move, please. You're in the way."

Jared had faced down lethal assassins, powerful politicians, pirates, prelates, and the queen herself, but he'd never been so hard-pressed between a rock the raging sea.

She spread her fingers against his chest and gave a slight shove. "Now, go, please."

He took hold of her wrist and held her hand against his chest. She must have felt his heart slamming around inside there—whacking against his ribs in frustration and blazing anger and a roaring lust.

"Truce," he said, finally, breathing like a buck in rut and needing to think this out, because the lunatic woman seemed bent on following through with her threats.

"Truce?" She shrugged, sniffed at him. "What could that possibly mean?"

Damnable woman! "It means . . ." Hell, he didn't know what it meant. "Peace. For the moment."

"But it doesn't mean that the children can stay."

He sighed out the breath he'd been holding. "We'll talk about it in the morning."

"A stay of execution?"

"In the morning, I said."

He couldn't believe that the woman was even thinking about turning him down. Dragging this clot of children through the dark countryside to God knew where, when he'd just offered her exactly what she'd asked for. But he could see the clockwork of her thoughts, the glistening intelligence behind her eyes.

"And now I have a personal question for you, sir."

Doubtless another impossible one—will you let me keep the orphanage? "What is it?"

Hot little spots of pink bloomed high on her cheeks. She took a long breath and then whispered with an aching tenderness, "Where have you been for the last eighteen months?"

A simple question, but its softness stopped his heart, tanged his mouth with the taste of dry metal. He tried his best to say the right thing.

"Busy," sounded good.

"Bastard." She spun on her heel and would have started toward the door but he caught her arm and held her close.

"My business keeps me occupied."

"Too occupied for your wife, I know. Even now. You haven't the decency to offer me a simple explanation. That's all right. I understand."

"I'm in shipping."

"Ballocks, my lord," she whispered. "My father was in shipping and when we weren't traveling with him my mother always knew where he was and that he was thinking about her. He was a good husband and a good father."

But a lousy merchant and a damn fool who couldn't even take care of his daughter.

"In case you haven't noticed, I'm home now."

"How disappointed you must be to find it full of orphans and refugees and a wife like me." She went on before he could respond. "I'll take your stay for tonight, my lord. But we'll be gone from Hawkesly Hall by tomorrow evening. You can count on it."

Chapter 10

❦❦❧

"All right, children, go wash up. It's time for supper." Kate clapped her hands, knowing that her face must be flaming red as she brushed past Hawkesly and into the kitchen workroom.

Between the fragrant closeness of the pantry and Hawkesly's overwhelming presence, and the blackguard's insulting dismissal of her simple question, she could hardly breathe.

He was too *busy* to come home to her.

Good then, Hawkesly, you'll not miss me when I'm gone.

She shooed the lagging children toward the wash-up room, sweltering from her simmering anger and the blatant heat of her husband's stare.

Feeling exposed and oddly off-center, she ventured a glance at him and managed to say blithely, "You're welcome to stay here and eat with us tonight."

He frowned. "You're eating here?"

"I nearly always do. I promised them." She carried a flour sack full of bread out of the kitchen and up the stairs into the dining room, not knowing what to make of Hawkesly trailing her so closely. "But you needn't stay for our pot of chicken stew. Badger's Run is serving not only trout and salmon but our best venison."

He stopped at the dining room archway and Kate felt every moment of his watching her as she put a small loaf of bread to share between every two bowls.

"I'll stay," he said, clearly a challenge to her, though he looked thoroughly disgusted by the prospect and angered by the practical changes she'd had to make in the dining room. A shorter table, equally sized benches, completely stripped of breakables and delicate brocades.

Vagabond children, an invisible wife, and a plain-faced stew. Not exactly the sort of fare that her husband would be used to in his social circles.

A pity that he hadn't departed in a huff; the last thing she needed was to have the man following her around, noticing things. Bumping into Elden, because Elden would be hard to explain. Not so much because he was hauling off the Hawkesly harvest to the warehouse at Mereglass for shipment elsewhere, but that she'd commandeered the *Katie Claire* for the purpose, without Hawkesly's permission.

"Suit yourself, my lord—"

"*Jared*, blast it all! My name is Jared."

Jared. She'd almost forgotten it, had never spoken it

aloud. And yet try as she might, she couldn't get her tongue around it. It seemed far too intimate.

And intimacy of any kind was the last boundary she wanted to cross with him. An annulment was the answer to both of their separate problems.

"I'm sorry about your name . . . Jared, but we were never formally introduced. Not even that day we were married."

"But we were indeed married. Bloody formal enough for anyone."

Kate was saved from answering by a thundering rush of footsteps clumping up the stairs from the kitchen level and rolling toward them down the corridor.

"I must warn you that supper with the children can be deafening."

With her next breath, the children came pouring past him through the doorway to stand at their places at the long table with its sawn-off legs.

Kate took her own place. "Jacob, if you'll lead us in tonight's grace."

"Dear, kind Lord. Thanks for the apples. And our new blankets. And for making Margaret better. Your friend, Jacob Kilfinnan."

Supper began with its usual chaos, the three older children running off to the kitchen to help bring up the serving bowls, the others sitting down in the rumble of scraping benches.

Hawkesly was still watching from the doorway. She was about to motion him in her direction, to squeeze him in beside her, but she heard a familiar voice.

"You c'n sit beside me, sir!"

Hawkesly's puzzled gaze moved twice up and down

the table until it finally landed on Lucas, sitting just below him.

"There's room right here, sir," Lucas said, through his indomitable smile, patting the small space on the bench beside him.

Hawkesly met her gaze, his eyes dark with irritated impatience, his chest rising and falling with frustration. Maybe he'd turn and leave right then and there. Instead he squared his jaw, took two strides to Lucas's side, and then lowered himself onto the bench.

And lowered and lowered, until his long, powerful legs bent sharply to accommodate the short table and the even shorter bench. The poor man was nearly folded in half.

And Lucas was beaming with pride.

The soup came like a much-heralded parade and the children ate every drop of it, then every crumb of bread and bite of apple pudding.

Hawkesly had taken but a spoonful, and a corner of the bread that Lucas forced upon him. He said little as the children chattered all around him, telling wild tales of sea serpents, and trying to best each other for his benefit. But his eyes followed each one carefully, his face a mask of disinterest.

Or something else, unreadably buried. Perhaps worth trying to uncover had she the time, or the inclination.

Supper ended as it always did, with the three Miss Darbys marching into the hall:

"Bowls to the right, children," Myrtle announced in her singsong chortle.

"And spoons to the left." Rosemary always, purposely, pointed to the right, and the children always called out her error and pointed to the left, laughing.

"Helpers follow me to the kitchen!" Tansy trilled, holding up her wooden spoon like a general's baton.

They all looked toward Kate as she stood. "And all the rest of you have a few hours left to play inside before bedtime."

And baths and a half-dozen stories. The routine had become dear to her, security for the children.

"Hooraayyyyyyy!" The room cleared a noisy moment later, leaving her eyes burning and her throat tight with tears that she couldn't allow herself to shed. Not in front of her husband.

Things would be fine. She had started over once before, she could do it again.

"They eat like a pack of wolves," Hawkesly said, studying the room as though suddenly assessing the full magnitude of his losses.

"We scavenge where we can." Kate stooped to straighten the bench. "But I assure you, the children are grateful for anything at all. It pleases me that they finally have enough."

He only grunted and stared at her.

"You didn't eat much tonight. The three Miss Darbys would be injured to the quick to know that you didn't like their stew."

"I wasn't hungry." He set his mouth in a line. "Now if you'll excuse me, I need to see to something in my chamber."

His chamber? Oh, no! Kate's heart took an unbalancing spin as he left the dining room and started down the hall toward the massive main stairs in the foyer.

"No! Wait! *Jared*!"

He turned sharply, his eyes brightening, stirring a little storm in her chest. "Yes, Kathryn?"

"You can't . . . ummm . . ." Kate made her way toward him, feeling a bit like a fox approaching a hound, prepared to leap out of his reach. "What I mean is that—"

"I can't what? Can't go to my own chamber?" He narrowed his eyes.

"Well, um, it's just that it's been more than two years since you've lived here."

He raised a challenging brow. "But I do still live here. Don't I?"

"Of course. You're the master of Hawkesly Hall. And you're home now."

"And I have a bedchamber, don't I? A large, comfortable suite of rooms, if I recall."

Kate wanted to close her eyes and spend a wish that his room was just as he'd left it. Just *poof* and everything would change. But life didn't work that way. "Yes, the master's chamber is very comfortable. Attractively furnished."

"Good. Then it hasn't changed a whit, has it? Again, if you'll excuse me." He started down the hallway again, bound for the entry and the grand staircase.

"Let me do it for you . . . husband." The word got his attention as she hoped it would.

He stopped in his tracks and then turned so quickly that Kate came within an inch of colliding with his broad chest. He was looking down that long, slightly skewed nose at her. "Will you then, wife?"

Will I what? nearly came flying out of her mouth,

but she remembered just in time: She was going upstairs to get something for him, to keep him safely out of the upper level until she and the children were long gone.

"Certainly . . . husband. I'll be right down." Kate managed to walk around and then past him and all the way to the foot of the grand staircase before he stopped her with the darkness of his question.

"What is it you're getting for me, exactly?"

"Ah . . . um . . ." Kate caught her hand around the thick, claw-footed newel and just stood there, looking at the man, dumbstruck to her knees. "I've forgotten."

"Actually, I never said what I wanted from my bedchamber."

"You didn't?"

"No." He strode toward her across the wide entry. "So I'll just go myself. I won't burden you."

"But—" She tried to catch his elbow as he passed her on the stairs, but his muscles were as thick and as unpliable as the branch of an oak.

"Do come along, if you'd like."

She would dearly love to stay behind and hide somewhere, but there were innocents to protect from his temper once he reached his chamber and she was the only one who could do it.

"Yes, I think I will come." Knowing how guilty she must look, Kate took two steps at a time and passed Hawkesly just as they reached the upper floor railing.

"What the hell . . ." He stopped again to scan the two-storied stairwell, frowning at the wallpaper and the empty walls. "Where are my Joseph Wrights? And my Turners?"

Sold at auction in New York to pay for Indian corn probably wasn't exactly what the man needed to hear after agreeing to their little truce and letting the children stay the night.

"Your what?"

"My paintings."

"Oh, taken down and stored away from the children." A bald-faced lie, but with any luck he wouldn't discover the truth until long after she and the children were out of his long and doubtless vengeful reach.

"And the porcelain case clock?" He nodded toward the corner where the clock once stood.

"Especially the porcelain case clock. Grady and the older boys learned cricket last spring from a party of young men from King's College who were staying at Badger's Run. And well, you know how boys are."

Feeling that she was chattering her way toward blurting out the truth before he was ready to hear it, Kate smiled with a confidence she didn't feel and started toward the master's chamber.

And the trouble he would find there.

But the trouble was standing in front of the chamber door in her nightdress, holding tightly to the latch as though she'd fall over.

"Margaret!" Terrified for the girl, Kate scooped her into her arms and carried her through the doorway into the anteroom. "What are you doing out of bed?"

"I'm feeling lots better." Though the little waif was still just a bag of sticks.

"Tomorrow you'll be better still, as long as you get your rest."

"And eat lots of apple pudding." Margaret grinned

broadly, then slipped her thin arms around Kate's neck.

"Always the very best medicine." Kate kissed her temple, wanting to believe that there was a little more flesh there tonight than the night before.

"Who's that man over there?"

Kate had almost forgotten Hawkesly—as much as one could forget a thundercloud, or the threat of a typhoon. Ready to brave anything for the sake of the little girl in her arms, she turned slightly and found the huge man standing just inside the doorway.

"That's Lord Hawkesly, Margaret. He's . . . well, this house belongs to him."

"So goes the rumor," he said in a voice far more distant than the space between them.

"Lord Hawkesly, this is Margaret O'Banyan. She just arrived three days ago."

" 'Lo, sir." Margaret had turned her head toward Hawkesly, though she stayed snuggled under Kate's neck.

Hawkesly said nothing.

"If you'll wait here, my lord, I'll see that Margaret gets back into her bed, and then you and I can . . . discuss the matter." Kate carried the feather-weighted girl into the next room.

But Hawkesly hadn't waited in the anteroom: now he was standing in the doorway to the sickroom, his cold, dark expression speaking volumes. Condemnation and the end of any chance at a further reprieve. They might even have to leave tonight.

"The big dog came to see me today." Margaret's eyes were already drooping as Kate lowered her into the bed and pulled up the covers.

"Mr. McNair is a fine friend and protector, isn't he?"

"He give me a kiss on my hand."

Jared tried desperately to look away from his wife's gentle touch, from the child and those hollow, beseeching eyes.

He'd seen enough of hunger, had felt it deeply enough to know that he didn't want it in his house. Ravaged limbs, unseeing eyes, the stubborn dead who ought to know when to lie down.

And yet here his wife had been secretly crowding his home with the leavings of a famine. Caring too much for her own good, when there was nothing of substance that she could do.

Now pressing her lips to the girl's forehead and whispering softly, "Miss Rosemary will be in with your milk in just a little while. Sleep well, sweet."

" 'Night, my lady."

"I'll leave the door open."

She blew a kiss at the girl as she backed away from the bed, watching all the way, nearly bumping into him. But she turned at the last moment and caught his arm.

"This way, so we don't wake Margaret again. She needs her sleep."

He stopped her in the middle of the room, right where his marble-topped writing table had once stood. "Damn it, woman," he whispered, "you've turned my bedchamber into a sickroom."

"Because it happened to be the best choice of all the rooms in the house. Quiet, isolated from the other children, with a separate room for a nurse."

"It's the master's suite. Sacrosanct. A man's retreat. Mine."

"Then I apologize," she whispered, bewitching him with the scent of lilac as she wrapped her warm fingers around his wrist and led him out into the main corridor. "I had misunderstood your intentions completely."

"That a man's home is his castle?"

"No," she said, glancing back over her shoulder with those wide, bright eyes, as she trailed him along the hallway toward some unknown destination. "I had assumed that if you and I had come home together after our wedding, we would have shared a chamber and a bed."

He stopped midstride, startled by her frankness. "You're damn right, we would have. Will. Share a bed."

"Ah, then wouldn't that have made the master suite mine as well as yours?"

The woman was a Gordian knot of logic. "So where did you store my clothes? In the attic? Out in the barn? What about the trunk I sent ahead? Or have you given everything of mine to the children to play with in the garden?"

"Your trunk is downstairs, unmolested. Everything from your chamber is right in here. Safe and sound." With that she unlocked the large linen closet on the opposite wall and opened the door wide to a neat array of shelves and baskets and the pungent aroma of camphor.

"Much obliged." He felt thoroughly shelved.

"I've one request, though," she said, the brashness gone from her voice and her eyes.

He laughed at her sudden humility. "Only one?"

"Please don't move back into your room until tomorrow afternoon. I don't want to have to move Margaret tonight. As you saw for yourself, she needs all the rest she can get."

Jared slammed his palm against the door frame and leaned into her face. "Bloody hell, woman, I'm not going to evict a sick child from her cot."

She pressed her lips together, in disbelief or in gratitude, he wasn't sure. "Thank you for the reprieve. I promise that we'll be packed and gone from here by tomorrow noon at the latest. A good evening to you." She lifted his hand and put the key to the closet in his palm with such tender care that she was halfway to the back stairs before Jared knew she was leaving.

"Just a damn minute."

"Ah, there you be, Lady Hawkesly." One of the Miss Darbys poked her head around the corner, smiling fondly. "Elden's looking for you."

"Oh! Excellent, Rosemary. I'll see him right now." Kate shot him a worried glance, then disappeared down the stairs like a wisp of smoke, leaving him with Miss Darby bustling toward him, a tray clattering with a small pitcher, a cup and a saucer.

"Evenin' to ya, Lord Hawkesly," the woman whispered, shyly padding toward him. "Just going to look in on little Margaret. C'n I get you anything?"

She waited, unmoving, until he asked, "Who is Elden?"

"Ah, Elden Carmichael. A dear man. My lady's estate manager. Anything else?"

"No. Thank you." Except what the devil had happened to old Hopwood, his own estate manager?

"Good then, just give a call and your wish is ours." The wiry woman hurried down the corridor and into the sickroom.

The very chamber that he still planned to share with his bride as soon as he could close down her orphanage. Surely the parish church could find room for them, or the relief commission in Preston. The sooner they were dispatched from his property and from his wife's care the better. A clean break was best. Because he damn well wasn't going to let her just up and leave in the morning. He'd lock her in the cellar first.

He had come home to a madhouse, run by a madwoman who happened to be his wife.

His beautiful, wild-eyed wife, who had packed him away as though he'd died, his personal effects stored away in a room no larger than a closet.

He rifled through eight baskets before he found his razor and shaving kit. If he was going to spend another night at that damned Badger's Run, he was going to have a fine Wilkinson blade and razor to shave with come morning.

And then what?

Where were peace and contemplation?

And what about the marital bliss he'd expected to find here in the bosom of his home?

Let the woman tend to her noisy little projects, he had work to do. A new assignment from the Home Office that put him in charge of investigating suspicious activity around the English ports. He was expecting a crate of papers from Lord Grey that would keep him busy during the day.

Now that he'd come home from the high seas, he had a land-bound lifestyle to sustain, in an elegant house with liveried servants and a wife, and he certainly couldn't accomplish it all with his wife in open rebellion and the place overrun with orphans.

He grabbed a few of his handkerchiefs out of a basket, shut the closet door and as he stuffed the kerchiefs into his coat pocket he ran into Ross's message.

In all the confusion, he'd never read the bloody thing! He yanked out the envelope and scanned Ross's neat hand, wondering how the man had learned anything new about the gun runners so quickly.

14 September 1848

Hawkesly, old man:

Nothing yet about the Pickering. *But scuttle from Whitehall is that Trevelyan is up in arms about a theft of grain from his warehouse in Southampton. Discovered by Hunter Claybourne in the course of his business at the Claybourne Exchange.*

If anyone could expose a misplaced sack of grain, it would be Claybourne.

Drew and I should be in Portsmouth by the time you receive this. Will contact you as soon as we learn anything more. In the meanwhile, sit back, old man, and enjoy the ride. Unless, of course,

*you've not yet managed to catch your little filly,
let alone saddle her.*

> Your encouraging friend,
> R

"Thanks, Ross, and may God rot your socks."

Granted that a breach of more than eighteen months was a bit too long between the "I do" and the wedding night. But he hadn't been able to help it at the time. And he planned to explain it all to her in private sometime *tonight*.

If he could find the woman after he penned a reply to Ross.

He sorted through the closet and finally found the basket that held the contents of his desk: paper and envelope, pen, ink, his seal and a stick of wax. By the time he found a writing surface, he was downstairs in the dining room straddling one of the tiny benches. His oil lamp brought one of the children to him like a little moth.

"Hello! I know how to write my name! D-o-r-i!" The little girl who was missing all four of her front teeth managed to shove herself against his arm, dropping a glob of ink in the center of the page.

"I'm glad of that . . . Dori. But I'd be just as glad of a moment to write in silence."

It wasn't to be. The room filled with children who rummaged paper and pencils from somewhere and were now crowding around his lamplight, taking turns drawing and writing.

"Let's play school!"

"I'll be Lady Hawkesly!" shouted Glenna, poking a pencil into the air. "Now, children, you must hold your pencils just this way."

Starving orphans? Hell, they didn't know what starving meant. These were robust young limbs, shiny, clean hair, white teeth.

Suddenly two of the Darby women appeared like shepherds and shooed them all up the stairs, offering their apologies and displaying an impossible amount of patience.

He tried to finish his message to Ross in the over-whelming quiet, but he found it far more oppressive than the children's simple chaos. Because he could so easily conjure the image of his misdirected wife galli-vanting around the countryside with her orphans in tow.

Because he knew that she would do just that, if he al-lowed her.

Because, of all the things he'd learn about his wife, he was sure she wasn't the sort of woman who made idle threats.

His only choice was to extend the "truce" a few days while he made a few inquiries.

More important than that, he needed to launch this marriage before the woman found an excuse to scuttle it.

To finish what he'd stupidly left incomplete.

To make her his before the sun rose tomorrow.

Chapter 11

⟋⟍

"**W**e should have plenty of grain for the soup kitchen this month, Elden," Kate said, dragging the oil lamp closer to the ledger on Elden's desk, carefully tallying the column of numbers one more time. "If Hopwood's accounting is correct—and heaven knows the man is minutely accurate—then we still have a hundred twenty tons of barley in the warehouse at Southampton . . ."

"And something near to two hundred tons of wheat and . . ." Elden had perched himself on the edge of the desk and now squinted down at the ledger. "What's that last column?"

"A hundred tons of Indian cornmeal." Kate leaned back in the chair and breathed a long sigh, the prospect of getting caught at her intrigue keeping her from feeling any sort of relief. "We're holding steady at the warehouses in Bristol and Liverpool, and Hopwood is going to make another acquisition in Plymouth."

Great heavens, the enormous risks they were all willing to take.

"M'lady, if the government ran the Relief Commission as well as you run the Ladies' Charitable League, there'd be no famine at all." Elden popped the last of a meat pie into his mouth then went to the office door.

"If I thought I could change things, Elden, I'd storm Whitehall and stage a coup."

"God help us all." Elden laughed and jammed on his cap. "Just one more trip to the wharf, one more wagon, and the barn will be empty. Ready for the *Katie Claire*."

"Do take care, Elden. It's dark out there on the road." He gave her a wink then disappeared into the shadows on his way toward the barn.

So many people giving so much of themselves.

And far too many who gave nothing at all. Men like Jared Westbrooke, earl of Hawkesly.

She slipped back into Elden's little office, gave the account book one last tally, then tucked it behind a barrel of garden implements.

Another secret she could never share with her husband.

She had kept an eye out for him during her meeting with Elden, expecting him to burst through the door at any moment. But he'd never come looking for her, though she been gone from the house for more than a half hour.

Tansy and Myrtle were scrubbing up in the kitchen when Kate finally returned to the house, humming together in their slightly imperfect harmony.

"His lordship's gone, my lady, if you're looking for him," Myrtle said, her eyes glinting at Kate.

The woman never missed a thing. "How long?"

"Not ten minutes ago. Said he had a message that needed to be sent."

"Then he's probably gone back to Badger's Run. And I should too. I need to stop by the tackle barn and pick up the prize for this evening's award." And Lord knows what kind of trouble Hawkesly might bring down on them all. Like tossing all the paying guests out on their backsides.

Tansy giggled. "A right lovely man to be following after, my lady. If you know what I mean."

"Handsome doesn't make up for bad timing, Tansy." Kate grabbed one of her cloaks off the peg at the back door. "I don't know why Hawkesly chose to make his grand entrance at this particular moment."

Myrtle smiled fondly as she patted Kate's cheek. "And aren't all husbands just like that, my dear? No sense of when to come and when to go."

The perfect description of Hawkesly.

"Don't listen to her, my lady," Tansy said, "Myrtle's never been married."

"Haven't been to the moon either, sister dear, but I know for a fact that it's made of cheese."

"Then you know as much as I do on the subject of marriage, Myrtle." Kate laughed and gave both women a hug. "Still, I'll keep your advice in mind."

Kate saddled her little mare and rode off toward the tackle shed, certain that she'd catch up with Hawkesly along the way.

Unless the blackguard decided to send his message from the village, which would put him right on the main road, sure to encounter Elden and his wagon.

But as she reached the tackle shed and let herself inside, she realized that the man must have ridden like the wind because she should have caught up with him by now. Even in the darkness, along an unfamiliar track . . .

No, not unfamiliar. Hawkesly must be quite familiar with the shortcut to the lodge.

And the road to the village.

And the wharf.

To the Hawkesly warehouse.

"Good evening, wife."

Kate whirled toward the voice in the doorway, already knowing its source, the sound of it in her ears, the way it rattled her heart and angered her.

Hawkesly! Like the near mythical creature he seemed to be, her husband was standing in the doorway, taking up its height with his shoulders.

There seemed to be something almost feral about him, as though he'd been stalking her through the woods. As though he'd been riding ahead of her on the trail, had heard her and decided to slip into the shadows, and trail her once she passed his cover.

Which could only mean trouble.

"Good evening," she said as lightly as she could manage, fumbling to light the oil lamp on the workbench. "Is there something I can get for you? More olive blue flies? A larger creel?"

She heard his leagues-long footfalls against the plank

floor as he entered the room and the stark finality of his shutting the door.

"What I want is to understand why a wagon just left my barn under cover of darkness, loaded down with I don't know what."

So he'd seen Elden after all. No matter. This little secret paled in comparison to the others she would keep from him forever.

"Cabbage. And carrots. And other crops. Heading for market. We've worked hard all summer. Now that the harvest has come, it's time to sell."

"To market where?"

"Preston this week. Our green goods have done very well there."

Hawkesly didn't look satisfied in the least with her explanation; he looked . . . hungry, voraciously determined as he continued his inexorable stalking toward her, tall and darkly encompassing.

"Elden," he said, slowly mulling the name, one eyebrow cocked devilishly. "I don't recall having an Elden on my payroll."

"You do now." Kate stood her ground, ignoring the weakening in her knees and the clattering in her heart as the man approached in his beastly way. "His name is Elden Carmichael. I hired him well over a year ago."

"As what? A cabbage broker?" He peered down at her, making her back up a step and then two.

"Elden is my estate manager." She bumped her backside into the workbench, making the bamboo poles clatter.

"You're wrong there." He reached behind her, gliding his hand between her elbow and her waist until he was leaning his palm against the bench top, smelling spicy, oddly sweet, of Tansy's cinnamon apples. "Martin Hopwood is the estate manager at Hawkesly Hall."

"*Was* the estate manager."

"Was?" His frown deepened. "What happened? Is Hopwood dead?"

"Of course not." But she could hardly explain that he's become her grain procurer for the Ladies' Charitable League. "Martin Hopwood is nearly seventy years old. He's not as strong as he used to be."

"Hopwood is as hardy as an ox."

"Which shows just how long you've been away." Kate slipped out from under his prison and carried the lamp toward the office. Hawkesly followed like a thunderstorm. "Master Hopwood was growing frail, his eyes dim, his bones achey like the autumn wood, as he used to say. I couldn't bear to see him suffer any longer so I pensioned him off to live with his daughter and her family in Devonshire."

"Without my leave?"

"You weren't here. But you'll be glad to know that I hear from the dear old man quite often and he's very happy in his new situation." Says he loves the life of an intrepid scallywag.

Hawkesly glared at her in silence, then took the oil lamp from her hand and stalked to the center of the room, hooking the handle to a rafter peg. He looked even more devilish with the lamp still swinging, making the shadows dance and deepen across the planes of his face as he stalked toward her. "So if Hopwood wasn't here, then all those letters I sent to him about the estate accounts—"

"Answered by me, Hawkesly." Kate turned away from him and went to the shelves of baskets. "I not only wrote those reports to you, but also everything that went to your banker and your broker in London."

"You?" He laughed deeply, as though he thought her efforts a great jest.

"The work needed doing and there was no one here to do it but me. I'm not the sort of woman who sits back and waits for someone else to take care of my problems."

"Not until now. From this moment on, *I* will take care of your problems for you."

She nearly laughed: the impossible man *was* her problem. A stone in her shoe.

A hole in her heart.

The sad truth was that deep inside she'd been hoping for something so much better from him.

"Taking on all my problems for yourself is a generous offer, Hawkesly, but an annulment will take care of everything."

When the man only stared at her in a stony fury, Kate assumed he was finished with her, so she picked up the box of metals and ribbons then turned back to him with a shrug.

Jared would have followed his wife, but she'd staggered him. Bloody hell, she'd just dismissed him, tossed him out of her life!

He found his voice as he reached the woman and her mare. "There'll be no annulment."

She stuffed the flat wooden box into the small saddle

pack. "Better annulled than to live married and apart for the rest of our lives. We tried that already and, personally, I found it unsatisfactory."

Certain that the woman was about to mount her horse and gallop away into the night, Jared clamped his hand over hers and turned her.

"Dammit, Kate. I came home to begin our marriage, to at last take up where I left off. And I bloody well plan to do just that. You're not going anywhere."

She looked at him gravely. "If I stay, Hawkesly, the children stay."

"Don't be absurd."

"Then I'm sorry, but you're just too late." She sighed and turned and reached for the saddle horn, but he caught her again by the waist, with both hands this time and turned her easily, unable, unwilling, to let go of the slim, curving shape of her. Hips and rib cage and waist.

"What do you mean too late?"

"Just that if we had started our marriage immediately, like a normal newly wedded couple, I would have doubtless discovered our incompatibilities a little at a time. The fact perhaps that you snore or womanize—"

"I do neither!"

"Or have poor hygiene habits—"

"I happen to have impeccable hygiene habits, as you will find out!"

"Or, worse, that you lack compassion for those less fortunate than you; for homeless, starving children as an example. If I'd learned this in the steady course of our marriage, then I would have known this trait of yours and accepted it and I would never have taken on the children." She caught her lower lip with her teeth for an instant. "At least I don't think I would have, because I wouldn't have had the opportunity."

You're damn well right you wouldn't.

"But since you left me instead to make my own way, I've taken a path that you could never find, let alone follow, one that I cannot possibly abandon." She shaped an impatient hand against her hip and canted her head at him. "Now do you understand how unwise it would be to begin a marriage, when we already know how badly it will end?"

It occurred to Jared just then, with the light of the moon setting off pale fires in her eyes, making silky, silver strands of her hair, that his wife might just be lunatic enough to believe her own logic and to follow it all the way to its tragic and inevitable end.

He was equally certain that she not only intended to do just that, but that she was entirely capable of it.

So it seemed that his marriage rested at the moment on the tousled heads of nine ragamuffin children.

Hell and damnation. Formidable little foes.

"Stop right there, wife."

She had one foot in the stirrup, her hand on the horn. She tipped her head back as though weary to the marrow and searching for strength in the treetops, spilling her hair down her back. "Please, I've got much to do tonight. The tournament awards, arranging for food to be packed for the children, sending word to Father Sebastian—"

"Not to mention a wedding night with your husband."

"What?" She froze.

Time to be delicate with her. "I don't need to remind you that we haven't consummated our marriage."

"Dear God." She whirled around to face him, her eyes huge, her fingers to her mouth as though they would contain the sound of her little gasp of horror. "You actually mean to force yourself on me, to bed me in spite of all my objections."

"I've never forced a woman in my life." He took hold of her chin and made her look him directly in the eyes. "Where the devil have you gotten these outrageous notions about me?"

She shook her chin free, raised it to him, suddenly a bit overdramatic in her breathing. This fearless woman and her bold threats. "Do your worst. But you might as well know right now that bedding me will not keep me here beside you."

He could play that game too. Couldn't resist wrapping his fingers in the silky ends of her hair, or pulling her against his chest and whispering close to her ear, "Ah, my dear, you've never been bedded by *me*."

He felt her indrawn breath against his cheek, and the wide-eyed lifting of her gaze against his heart. "No, I haven't. But then whose fault is *that*?"

Her unmistakable, straightforward challenge whispered against his mouth zipped through him like a bolt of lightning, lodged in his groin like a roiling storm.

Drew and Ross might have been right after all. That he should tread lightly here, to carefully negotiate his way into this unfamiliar, labyrinth of a marriage.

Humility in the face of truth.

Honesty, because he owed her that.

"It's my fault entirely, Kate."

"Then, please . . ." She took a long, shuddering breath, and grabbed hold of his lapel as though to steady herself. "Please don't compound your mistake by insisting on consummating our marriage when there's—"

"No hope?"

"Exactly." The word found its way through the linen of his shirt, burning through his skin to the center of his chest. "No hope at all."

Responsibility. He'd long understood the word, but had never felt the meaning of it so completely. It was nudging at him to do something.

To be something, someone to Kate.

He could at least try.

"What would hope look like to you, madam?" He watched her face as she glanced up at him with a frown that pinched her brows.

"What do you mean?"

What *did* he mean? "Would your image of hope for our marriage include an apology from me?"

She sighed and shook her head vigorously, as though to shake out the very thought of such a thing between them. "There's no need for that."

He'd known all along who his rivals were, yet he didn't know quite what to do about them. How to work around the obstacle they presented. "Then this is truly all about your orphans?"

She threw out another sigh. "I'm utterly serious about leaving with the children, no matter what you do to me."

"And if I offer to find them a suitable home?"

She cocked her head, hands on her fine hips. "What do you mean?"

Nine children to place for her. "I'll arrange somewhere for them to live."

She eyed him, as skeptical as ever. "You mean to make Hawkesly Hall into a permanent orphanage?"

"No—"

"There!" She huffed and had her foot in the stirrup an instant later.

"Give me a chance." Jared caught her by the waist again, and turned her sharply, glaring down into her face in the hopes that she would listen to him for once. "I'll find something for them. I promise."

She narrowed her eyes to diamond glints. "If not Hawkesly Hall, then where?"

"God, woman, how would I know? I just now thought of the idea."

She considered him for a very long time. "Do you mean this, Hawkesly?" She grabbed hold of his sleeves at his elbows and pulled him closer. "You're not just trying to patch things over for the moment so that you can trap me into staying, because—"

"Tempting, but I wouldn't dare."

She studied him for a very long time, tracking her eyes across his mouth and then his lashes. "And in the meantime, while you're looking, where do the children stay?"

Much as he hated to imagine his house filled with chaos, he said, "At Hawkesly Hall."

"But you will find them a real home, like you promised."

"Yes."

"Safe and clean and dry and heated, and above all, nearby."

"Christ, woman, I'll do my best."

His outburst made her step backward and study his face even longer; one last, long perusal before she finally shrugged and nodded reluctantly, her judgment of his motives still obviously reserved for later.

"And in return, my lord, I shall do *my* best."

Jared wondered what kind of trouble her best might get them into in the years to come, wondered most of all at the astonishing sensation of comfort and peace that had settled across his shoulders.

An important battle won. But only the first of many.

"Does your best include calling me something more personal than 'my lord'?"

She caught her lower lip between her teeth, then gave a nervous laugh. "Yes, of course—"

"Jared."

"Jared," she said, as though his name would need hours of rehearsal.

"A good try."

Her smile went sideways and demure and focused directly on his mouth, as though she was hungry for him, or curious. And if it weren't for the pale, blue wash of the moonlight, her cheeks would be a blushing, bridal pink.

"And I'm Kate."

"Yes, I know." Great God, he was rocking slightly sideways on his heels, feeling a little giddy and shy, like a stumbling, inexperienced bridegroom.

Hell, he might even be on the verge of grinning like a bloody fool.

"You drive a hard bargain, Kate."

Christ, here they were, married. The woman standing so boldly in front of him was his wife. His bride. He felt the tether between them just now as he hadn't that sweltering day so long ago, or any day since.

And tonight he would complete the bargain. She would be safely and entirely his. In the fullest sense.

A day later than his unspoken wager with Drew, but timely enough, considering.

And well worth the wait.

"Welcome home, Jared. And thank you."

His blood surged at the silkiness of her voice, the promising embrace of it, after he'd so thoroughly bunged up the situation. The callow feeling vanished, replaced by a ripe, rip-roaring craving for her.

For all of her.

"Remind me often, Kate, what a fool I was for not returning sooner."

She was standing just inches from him, moonlight glistening on her lips, beckoning him closer, her scent of heather and loam embracing him and tugging at him.

"Perhaps it's time that you find out for yourself what you were missing when you were so busy that you couldn't come home to me. All that I hinted about to Colonel Huddleswell earlier today."

"That was hardly a hint you gave the old colonel, Kate. You nearly killed him." Jared slipped his fingers through her hair, stunned by the easy way she tilted back her head, the sound of her sigh sending his pulse pounding through his veins, pooling heat in his groin.

"Oh, goodness," she whispered through a bowed smile. "I'd wondered . . ."

"Wondered what?" Jared caught her around the waist with his other arm and lifted her closer.

"Ohhh . . . about this sort of thing." She moved her hips against him, his groin, the constant erection there, purposefully, as though she understood what it meant and was set on driving him out of his mind. "About being, well . . . wifely with you."

"Wifely, indeed." Christ, the woman was sultry and soft, and oh, so pliable. With her mouth upturned and damp and mere inches from his, her breath against his.

"Because this is good, Jared. Very good." She drew in a deep breath along his neck, and if he wasn't dreaming all this, that was the tip of her tongue, tasting the underside of his jaw, sliding down his throat.

"God, woman." His patience spent, his pulse wild, he enfolded her, marveling at the perfect fit of them, the thrumming heat, and when he closed his mouth over hers, he tasted honey and heather.

"Ohhh, my!" She moaned against his mouth, made little, kitteny sounds in her throat as she raked her fingers through his hair and then dragged him closer. "You taste of cinnamon, Jared. Not like the colonel. Not anything like I imagined for all those months you didn't come to me."

She climbed even deeper into his embrace, as though she couldn't get enough of him, nibbled and tugged. An excellent trait in a bride, passion so easily aroused. One he planned to encourage.

"What did you imagine instead, Kate?" Roused to the edge of decency, and only barely aware of the fact that they were out here in public view, Jared backed up against the thick trunk of an elm and pulled her against him, fitting her neatly between his legs.

"I imagined salt and sunlight, and yet nothing like this. Nothing beyond the simple kiss of a bridegroom on the deck of the *Cinnabar*...." She kissed him madly, his cheeks and his brow. "Not all this, Jared. Not the feel of you against me, your hard places and your soft. Your hands—they're so wonderfully large—and your delicious mouth and your tongue—certainly never your tongue or your teeth!"

"Christ, woman, you'll stop that right now."

"What? Why?" She looked up at him, her hands cupping his jaw.

He could barely catch his breath, let alone control the urge to grind hard against her, to lay with her on the loamy floor of the fragrant woods. "If you want our wedding night to be later tonight in our chamber and not right here outside the tackle shed where anyone could find us, then you'd best stop right now."

To his great regret, Kate stopped her kissing and pushed an arm's length away. "Tonight? You mean to consummate our marriage tonight?"

He caught her waist, missing her heated curves, trying to pull her against him. "As soon as you can decently remove yourself from your guests."

"No, that won't do, Jared."

He was breathing like a rutting stag, the noise of it drowning out any other sound. "What won't do?"

She shook her head at him. "Consummating our marriage tonight."

He stopped breathing. "Why the devil not?" And then a thought came to him. "Don't tell me that you're . . . having your . . . woman's time right now? Because—"

"My . . . ? Oh. No, that's not the reason. It's just that. . . ." She shrugged lightly, caught her finger in his watchpocket. "It . . . well, it just doesn't seem right to me."

"Not right?" He straightened. "What do you mean? You just kissed the bloody hell out of me."

"Kissing is one thing. Consummating is entirely another."

"Good lord, woman! You've just spent the last half day chiding me for neglecting you all these months, for not beginning our marriage—"

"I'm dreadfully sorry if you got the wrong idea," she said, clearly upset, clearly a lunatic. "But I can't just leap into bed with a man I don't know."

He caught her by both arms. "I'm your husband, dammit. Of course you know me."

She sniffed. "Who makes your shoes?"

"Galeno and Chavez. In Madrid."

"I didn't know that. What was the last book you read?"

"*Hook, Line and Spinner*. Why?"

"Your favorite soup?"

"Curry. Blazes, woman, you're mad!"

"I might very well be completely out of my head, but since you don't know me at all, you can't be sure one way or the other."

"Enough!"

"Which I'm not, by the way."

"Not what?"

"Mad." She exhaled as though she'd been carrying a huge burden for a very long way. "Don't you see, Jared, I don't know a thing about you. I'm just . . . well, if we had been properly betrothed . . ."

"We weren't. And that's that."

"But if we had been properly betrothed, we'd have had time to get to know each other before we married. Small talk and lemonade and balls and whist until three in the morning. That's what normal couples do."

"I'm aware of that, but times weren't normal." And there wasn't anything the least bit normal about the woman he married.

"But now that times are somewhat normal, I would like very much to have you court me, as though we had been recently betrothed."

Jared blinked away the staring dryness in his eyes, flinching at the painful scrape against his eyelids. "Court you?"

"That's right. It's a simple enough request, easy to fulfill. You can call on me properly at Badger's Run or Hawkesly Hall, and we can take long walks in the woods or by the chalk streams."

"What the hell do you think we've been doing for the past twenty-four hours?"

"We can also sit in the library and have tea and discuss books that we've read."

"Madam, our libraries have both been overrun by untold multitudes of unwelcome pests."

"We can share a quiet meal together—"

"Where?"

"The where doesn't matter in the least, just that we do it properly. It's not like I'm asking you to change the tides, or wrestle an alligator. Only that you and I take a bit of time to learn a little about each other before we share our marriage bed. So that we're not utter strangers when we do come together as husband and wife. I don't think I'm asking too much. Not after all this time."

After all this time? Wasn't that the point!

Jared stood in stunned amazement, realizing that somehow she'd managed to perch herself astride her horse, the reins in hand as though she were going to ride out of his life and go blithely back to her own.

He opened his mouth, but couldn't think of a thing to say that wasn't a howling curse or a plaintive bellow, so he said nothing.

"So will I see you at the lodge, Jared?"

His jaw aching, nearly locked, he somehow managed a strangled, "I'd be . . . delighted."

Her smile shamed the moonlight. "Good," she said in her simple triumph that ought to grate but only made him feel like the lust-starved, slavering beast that he was. "Till then, husband."

And in the meantime, he would burn.

In more ways than he could possibly count.

Chapter 12

❝**H**e's my *husband*!" Kate held fast to the saddle horn for fear of melting right off the horse. For the memory of Jared's strong bronze neck, the broad heat that had poured off his chest and down the front of her blouse, setting off little, tingling fires.

"He's home and he's mine!" Her cheeks were still blazing hot and her heart was still rattling out of control as she tried to fit the word to the man.

"Husband!"

And he wanted her in his bed.

Tonight!

Oh, my, what a glorious delight that would have been. A night of sultry, sizzling pleasure with her husband. His kiss, his touch. All that thick-muscled heaviness of his body pressing against hers.

A torrid, erotic dance, hinting at her favorite Aba-

santi celebrations. Swaying, singing bodies and firelight, drumbeats and heartbeats, writhing limbs and
glistening skin.

Only this time she wouldn't just be watching,
wouldn't be left alone at the fire with her imagination.

At least she hoped her wedding night would happen
soon. If all went well, and Jared kept his promise to her
about the children.

And if he never found out about the warehouses and
the activities of the Ladies' Charitable League.

Feeling just like a dazzle-eyed schoolgirl, Kate whistled the rest of the way to Badger's Run, whistled and
giggled to herself and grinned like a fool. She entered
the stable yard at a trot, her face hot and her smile too
huge not to draw suspicion from those who knew her
well.

"Evenin' to ya, Lady Hawkesly." Corey met her in his
eager, lanky gait and held the reins under Sunny's bit.

"Good evening." She felt dazed and a bit giddy as
she dropped from the saddle onto watery knees and
hurried off toward her office via the kitchen carrying
the box of prize metals and ribbons.

She burst through the kitchen doorway, startling
Mrs. Driscoll, who stared at her. "What the merry devil's gotten into you, Lady Hawkesly?"

Was it that plain? Her blush deepened. "Nothing,
Mrs. Driscoll, just running behind time, as usual."

Because my husband has just come home and kissed
the daylights out of me. And he promised he would
care for the children! And I'm going to do my best to
believe him.

"Well, my lady, supper's on schedule, if that'll ease your spirit. Here, lovie, have a taste."

The rail-thin woman poked a succulent piece of perfectly seared trout into Kate's mouth.

"Dear lord, that's delicious." It was no wonder Badger's Run was gaining a reputation for fine dining. "My thanks as always, Mrs. D."

Kate hurried off to check on the dining-room linens, then made her way through the lounge, already crowded with boasting fishermen, to speak with McHugh about the reserves in her husband's wine cellar.

Jared's cellar . . .

Lord Hawkesly.

Oh, dear. What was she going to tell the household staff about the sudden arrival of her husband?

Far more daunting, what would the guests say? They were under the mistaken assumption that Jared was Colonel Huddleswell, a cranky, opinionated flyfisherman who'd had great luck with a trout.

She couldn't very well explain that he was actually Lord Hawkesly in disguise—not only their host, but the lord of the manor and her husband? It would seem as though Badger's Run were playing some bizarre trick on their unsuspecting guests. And it would hardly be fair to award Jared the daily overall weight prize for fishing in his own stream.

He wouldn't be at all pleased with her plan, but he was going to have to remain Colonel Huddleswell until all the guests were gone.

She'd best get her story straight with him as soon as possible and come up with some believable explanation as to why she had to disqualify Colonel Huddleswell and his enormous rainbow trout from the competition.

"McHugh, if you happen to see my hus . . . um, I mean Colonel Huddleswell, please have him come find me. I'll be in my office for a while."

"Done, my lady. I heard the colonel caught himself quite a rainbow this afternoon."

"Didn't he just, McHugh."

Kate found Foggerty's list of the contestants' names and their catch weights waiting for her on her desk blotter, and busied herself putting together the ribbons and metals for the day's winners. But her concentration kept wandering off toward Jared and all those kisses, along her throat and beneath her ears. His hands, his mouth.

Her thoughts were sneaking upstairs and through the door to his bedchamber when she felt him standing in the doorway, watching her. Her fingers fumbled and the fish medallion clattered to the desktop.

She chanced a look at him, savoring the sight of him, from his tall boots, up the length of his fine wool trousers, his waistcoat and jacket, to his neckcloth and then his unreadable expression.

Amusement, caged anger, certainly impatience with her, though he was leaning easily against the jamb as if he hadn't a care in the world.

"Ah, there you are, Colonel Huddleswell."

He arched a brow and a slight smile. "So it's to be that game again, wife."

Afraid the man would simply abandon their ruse, Kate hurried to him, tugged him into the room by the crook of his elbow. "Please, it has to be. At least until the tournament is over and the guests are gone."

"Absolutely not. I refuse to play the avid sportsman for another two days."

"Then how do I explain you to everyone?"

He caught her chin with his crooked knuckle and said with complete sincerity, "You'll tell them I'm your husband. Simple enough even for the obnoxious Squire Fitchett."

"Then how do I explain you disguising yourself as Colonel Huddleswell? Won't they wonder why you'd do such a thing?"

He narrowed his eyes. "I don't much care. Against my better nature, I've agreed to postpone bedding my bride in order to pay her court—"

"Which she very much appreciates." Though her cheeks were pinking again with the thoughts of him. "However, if you don't wish to continue to play your part as Colonel Huddleswell here at Badger's Run, then you'll just have to stay with the children at the hall."

"The hell I will."

"I don't know how much you care about your reputation, but you can bet that word of your odd disguise and your even odder deception—in your own hunting lodge—will eventually make its way back to your friends and colleagues in London and cause quite a stir."

"Let them . . . oh, hell." He glared at her, scrubbing silently at his jaw with his closed fist, giving the whole matter deep consideration.

"Well, am I to call you Colonel Huddleswell for a few more days?"

He inhaled as though he planned to bellow a curse, but the air came out in a long growl. "Once again you have me by the nape. And I don't like it one damned bit."

Not wanting to seem too pleased with herself, or with him for being so cooperative about the situation, Kate shook her head. "I'm afraid we've no other course."

"Make no mistake, there are always 'other courses' in every situation. It's the weight of the cost that decides the matter."

"But this is only temporary and not the worst thing in the world." For some reason that had something to do with the need to touch him and all that seething maleness cooped up here in her office, she brushed a thread off his sleeve. "After all, you certainly can't complain about having to spend a few idle days fishing."

He captured her hand and imprisoned it flat against his chest. "Madam, if I never see another fish, it'll be too soon."

"Come, Jared, pouting doesn't become you. You needn't give up fishing altogether just to spite me."

"Spite has nothing to do with it. It's the plain fact that I've never fished before today and that I—"

"Never fished? Don't be ridiculous. You—"

"Shhh . . ." He lifted her by the hips, and slid her onto the edge of her desk, then peered closely. "I thought you were interested in learning everything about me before you let me into our marriage bed."

"I am." Though she wouldn't mind learning what those big, hot hands of his would feel like against her skin.

"Then you'll start out by believing that I know nothing at all about fishing, save that which I learned last night by reading and this afternoon by chasing that bloody trout down the stream."

But he'd looked every inch the expert in his flyfishing stance. "What about the tackle you claimed that we . . ."

"Lost in transit?"

"You made a huge enough fracas about it."

"A complete fabrication. Just like Colonel Huddleswell. Why would I—your husband—have brought my fishing equipment with me when I didn't know a thing about Badger's Run or any tournament?"

He was making sense, still— "But you managed to hook that huge rainbow trout—with all that ancient tackle."

"I hooked it, but I didn't land it, exactly." He pushed up from the desk.

"Then how did you bring it in?"

"Well, I . . . um," he said, shrugging, "I fell on the bloody thing."

No wonder he'd been wet to the bone when she'd found him in the stream. "You fell on the fish?"

"Right on top of it, I'm afraid, in the middle of a reed bog. You mean you didn't see me take that fall?"

"You fell?" Kate couldn't contain the giggle, though she covered her mouth with her hand. "I was busy shooing away the children."

"Go ahead, laugh. I suspect I looked the perfect fool. Especially to those children."

"Jared, really! They think you're wonderful." He grunted at that. "And I'm not laughing at you."

"At whom then, the trout? Don't blame him, he was just doing his best to survive."

Kate laughed even harder, letting herself down from her desk. "You've truly never fished before?"

"As God is my witness." He raised his hand, glancing at the red mark just below his thumb. "And I've got all the injuries to prove it."

She took hold of his hand, loving the size and the strength of him. "Your injury looks better."

His voice grew soft. "Perhaps you can tend my wounded thigh later tonight? And my shoulder." He sat down easily on the edge of her desk, thrusting his legs out in front of him, the rippling power of his thigh muscles making her palms tingle.

"I'd be glad to." If she could resist the temptation to tend more than his wounds. "But why pretend that you were Colonel Huddleswell, the legendary flyfisherman?"

"For the same reason that you pretended to be Lady Hawkesly, the proprietor of Badger's Run, when all the while you were my wife."

"I wasn't pretending; I was just trying to survive. But you were actually spying on me."

"I confess, I was." He flicked that piratical brow at her, making her smile. "I was damned suspicious. I still am. My wife, the proprietor of a sportsman lodge. Hell, woman, I had to uncover your motives."

But he hadn't yet, at least not all of the delicate complexities of her venture. With any luck, he never would.

"Instead, I uncovered yours: plainly to deceive me."

It had only been a toss-away comment, meant to remind him that his deception hadn't worked, but a darkly exciting gleam came into Jared's eyes.

"To study you and then expose you, but in the end to bed you."

"You shouldn't keep saying that." It made her cheeks flame and struck the breath from her.

"It's the truth. I want you."

There she went again, her limbs and her will melting away as he shaped his huge hand to her cheek and slipped his fingers into her hair.

Perhaps she ought to establish a few rules between them before he took matters too far.

Rule number one—

"Oh . . . Jared." He kissed her, his mouth a soft, hungry heat against hers.

"I want you here in your little office." He kissed her more fiercely than before, nibbling, possessive, his breathing unstable as he pulled her closer. "And in our bed—"

"Our . . . you . . ."—shouldn't! But he moved his hands up her sides, his fingers softly kneading, his mouth probing hers.

"And I wanted you out there in the woods, beside the stream, and in it."

"Jared, I don't think this is a . . ." Kate couldn't think at all through the silky pleasure swimming along her skin, could barely hear the tapping sound on the door and then the panel opening.

"Lady Hawkesly, Mrs. Driscoll wanted you to. . . . holy bleeding hell!"

Kate met McHugh's startled gaze with one of her

own, feeling as though she'd been caught with her hand in the sugar sack. "McHugh, I . . . ah . . . Hello!"

But McHugh had already lifted a murderous glare at Jared, his brogue a harsh, drilling burr. "Sir, you're no kind of a gentleman. And if you're not gone from this place within an hour, I'll be coming after you myself, with my shotgun loaded and barking."

"Wait!" Kate caught McHugh's sleeve as he turned to leave and yanked him into the office. "McHugh, it's all right. He did nothing that I didn't encourage."

McHugh's glare darkened. "No, lass. I warned him once before. The bloody blackguard knows exactly what he's done. As well as his fate if he doesn't—"

"She's my wife, McHugh."

Kate took in a breath as Jared came to stand just behind her, a dark, embracing heat that could have been his arms for the strength of it.

"Your what?"

Jared stepped around Kate like a cloud obscuring the sun, as though he were trying to protect her. "Lady Hawkesly is my wife."

"You're a damnable liar, Huddleswell." McHugh pointed past Jared. "The lady is married to Lord Hawkesly. So you'll keep your bloody hands off her."

Jared's arm went toward McHugh, and Kate grabbed for it, fearing that her husband was going to deliver a blow to the very faithful McHugh.

But Jared's hand stopped abruptly in front of McHugh's chest, his fingers extended. "And I must thank you for keeping watch over her in my absence."

A handshake, not a blow.

Still McHugh frowned his implacable suspicion at

Jared's hand and then at his face. "Ha! So now you're saying that you're Lord Hawkesly?"

"Because I *am*."

"He is my husband, McHugh. Jared Westbrooke, earl of Hawkesly."

"Ha! That's what the blighter's told you, my lady?"

Jared withdrew his hand. "My apologies for not owning up when I first arrived. But there were other considerations at the time."

McHugh whipped around to Kate, scowling fiercely, and jabbed his thumb over his shoulder at Jared. "This true, m'lady? He's Lord Hawkesly?"

"He is absolutely." But McHugh was reacting just as the other staff members would when they learned the truth about the colonel. "But his identity is somewhat of a secret at the moment, so you mustn't reveal anything to anyone else until I say it's clear."

"Auchhhh!" McHugh dropped his shoulders and shook his head in disgust. "You didn't even think to tell me his lordship had returned."

She felt Jared's sizzling gaze on her, a warning or a question, she couldn't determine. Not that she would ever reveal the shameful truth to anyone—that she hadn't even recognized her own husband.

"Suffice it to say that the matter couldn't be helped."

"Ha!" McHugh glanced up at Jared and grunted. "A fine way to treat the folks who love ya so, my lady. Not even letting us know that your neglectful husband has come home."

"McHugh, please—"

"Don't be worrying yourself, my lady. I'll get over it." McHugh snorted, still assessing her husband with a furious eye. "But he'll take some getting used to, this one. Evening to you both."

"Wait, please," Kate said, stopping the man at the door.

He sighed as he turned back. "I'll not say a thing to nobody, my lady."

"I know that, McHugh. But you came in here to tell me something and you haven't."

"Ah, yes. Ya distracted me, my lady, with your . . ." He waggled a scandalized finger at Jared and then at her. "Well, you know very well what the pair of you was doin' when I come in here."

"You had a message for me?"

"Only that Mrs. Driscoll wanted you to know that supper was being served. Just trying to do her job." McHugh grunted again, then left, but not before elbowing the door wide open.

"McHugh needs a good flogging. Insolent old codger." Her husband crossed his arms over his broad chest; every bit the importuned king.

"A man who lost his entire family to the famine." Kate grabbed a prize ribbon and a medallion off her desk. "You'll treat him with respect; he's been a rock to me."

"Seems you've gathered yourself a whole quarry full of them. Enough to get on quite well without me."

"Quite well. But now that you've come home you'll have to learn to behave around here." She poked the ribbon through the hasp of the medallion.

"*I'll* have to behave?"

"And that's just one of the rules I've decided to invoke while you acclimate yourself to life in the country."

Jared decided against even the slightest hint at the bellow of laughter that threatened. An ordinary wife wouldn't dare such an affront.

But then again, he was beginning to believe that he hadn't married an ordinary woman.

Which pleased him to the depth of his bedraggled, undeserving soul.

Chapter 13

"Rules?" Jared marveled at the extraordinary way her mind twisted and turned, at the way her slender fingers worked the ribbon so expertly without her paying attention to the task. "Such as what?"

"You're on dry land now, Jared. The code of the high seas doesn't apply."

"I promise not to flog anyone."

"And no *threats* of flogging either." She threaded a pin clasp into the dangling ribbon. "Civilization relies on common rules and laws. And so must you and I if we're going to . . ."

"To what, Kate?" Not that he had any intention of abiding by her regime, but he'd learned long ago never to stop an opponent from delivering valuable information.

"To . . . to keep our promises to each other."

"I promised to protect you with my life and I will."

"I don't need your protection. I need cooperation."

Nevertheless, she was going to bask in his protection anyway. Daily. Hourly.

"Oh, you mean that other promise, my dear. So does this mean that you'll allow me to bed you someday, as long as I follow your rules?"

"You know very well that's not what I meant." She dropped another beribboned medal on the desktop and picked up another set.

"But that's what you said."

"Is that the sum of your thoughts? Taking me to bed?"

"Yes." The simplest of answers, entirely honest because she scrambled his mind with her fragrance.

"That's very shortsighted of you, as far as our marriage is concerned."

"I'm sorry, but to be specific, just now it's your hair that's distracting me."

"My hair?" She touched the back of her head, threading her fingers through the wild gilded ends, shifting her shoulder, baring more of her neck, every inch the siren, though he doubted she understood the effect.

"Your long, lovely hair. I imagine it spilling out across your naked shoulders and our linen sheets, curling on my pillow, wound up in my fists."

She opened her mouth in a perfect O. "Why are you going on like this?"

So she was capable of surprise.

"I thought you wanted to learn all about me."

"I do. But this is not the kind of information I intended us to learn about each other. At least not right now."

"But it's the subject at hand. It's what I'm thinking. Constantly." He stayed rooted to the carpet, keeping her well out of his reach, for fear of taking her right to the floor. Tossing that damnable courting promise right out the window. "Though right now I'm beginning to think about that shirtwaist you're wearing."

"What about my shirtwaist?" She pressed her hand across the soft rise of her bosom, so perfectly defining her shapes and slopes and peaks, tightening the pressure in his groin.

"First of all, I noticed that you don't wear much of an undergarment. Nothing to keep you still . . . if you know what I mean." Even now her breasts were buoyant, dancing, his imagination out of control as she took a dangerous step closer to him.

She gave a delicately shy little laugh. "Why ever would you notice a thing like that?"

"Which naturally makes me curious about how you would taste beyond those buttons." Despite his better judgment, he caught a button, tugged lightly on it.

"Lord Hawkesly!" The woman blushed instantly, like the sun hitting the underside of a sunset cloud. "You'll stop that kind of talk right now."

"I'm just being honest. You asked me if all I thought about was taking you to bed, and I answered as clearly as I could."

"I didn't mean for you to give me a minute-by-minute explanation."

"Too bad, because I still have the most delicious image in my head from this afternoon, the perfect shape of your legs."

"You can stop trying to shock me, Jared; it won't work. As I told that blighter Colonel Huddleswell only yesterday, I've been to places that you can't possibly imagine. I've seen things." Her eyes took on a sparkle, her voice thickened to honey. "Amazing, unforgettable things. So I understand completely."

"I don't think you do. In fact, you'd bloody well better not understand." He didn't like the fierceness of the blush he'd cultivated in her, a deep crimson that might not be entirely of his making.

"Oh, but I do."

"All right then, what have you seen?" Doubtless nothing more than a young woman's fertile imagination at work.

She closed her eyes and sighed, took a deep breath of something exotic. A memory? "Never mind."

"I want to mind. I want to know."

"At the proper time."

"Which is when?"

"When I know you better. In the meantime, I think you'd best redirect your thoughts."

"Impossible. I've no control over them."

She paused and quirked her head, too interested. "Really?"

"Completely out of control. Ever since the moment you came down that stairway yesterday, and I realized that you were my wife. I couldn't take my eyes off your mouth."

"You couldn't?"

"My only thought then was to kiss you." He brushed her mouth with his.

"And now?" she breathed against his cheek.

"To kiss you, of course."

"Oh, my." She sighed, seemed to catch herself, then stuck out her arm like a battering ram against his chest. "But you have to stop this, Jared."

"I can't."

"Then just don't tell me about it."

"So you're actually allowing me these thoughts about you. Your mouth, your hands, your lack of undergarments. You just don't want me tell you about them."

"Exactly." She sniffed at him, then snatched up another ribbon. "So that's Rule Two; keep your thoughts to yourself."

Feeling smug, Jared tempted fate and leaned against the desk, just inches from her furious industry.

"And what if I happen to slip and wonder aloud about the taste of your collarbone or your . . . earlobe." He liked this teasing, the way she stood up to it, challenged him and tried to ignore him. He lifted the cascade of hair off her shoulders, wringing a stunning gasp out of her.

"Behave yourself." She batted at his fingers and missed, then let out something that sounded very much like a giggle.

"Now that seems to be the trouble, Kate. I'm behaving like a normal husband who desires his wife."

"You shouldn't. Not yet." Despite her denial and her half-hearted attempt to brush away his fingers, she let him play along the downy soft ridges of her ear. "We're not completely married yet."

"Oh, yes we are. But I've agreed to court you, to confess my heart. And so you're learning this about me, my attraction to you. I just thought you should know."

"All right then, I'll grant you this . . . oh, lovely, yes . . . this heady, wonderful feeling that you stir in me. Which makes me believe that we'll fit together well in our marriage bed."

"More than well." God, his hands ached to hold her. All this brazen honesty between them was going to kill him if he let it go on, the raw nakedness of it clinging to his skin, cramping his groin. The shapely column of her neck as she tilted her head to his touch.

"So in the meantime, husband, we need to accept this attraction as a basic truth between us, and a pleasure to come. But I do need to know more about you than merely the taste of your mouth."

"Jesus, woman." He sucked in a sharp breath as a bolt of lightning shot through him, sending him off the desk and to the chest of file drawers.

Her blush had matured and her breathing slowed as she blew out her cheeks. "I suppose we can manage with but two rules between us, Jared."

"And they are . . . ?"

"Respect for what I've done here . . ."

For turning his life upside down.

For selling off his crops.

And his wine cellar.

For filling his houses with hordes of children and blustery old flyfishermen.

And his head with some kind of preposterous, illogical hope for . . .

He wasn't sure what he was hoping for, or how to go about capturing it. Or that hope wasn't a dangerous commodity to carry around unguarded.

But the blasted woman had managed in little more than a day to force him to look at things differently.

"Go on, Kate. The other rule between us."

"Distance."

"Distance?" He didn't like the lifeless sound of that. Not at all. He couldn't get enough of the scent of her, couldn't give it up. "What sort of distance?"

She judged the span between them. "Well, I suppose two feet will do. One foot when necessary."

He nearly laughed with relief, but thought better of it. "And if I agree to keep to your rules, how will I know that I've done enough courting?"

He could see her hiding her smile behind her efficiency. But it was there and pleased him to his soul.

"You'll know, Jared. You'll know."

With that spicy invitation, his bride picked up the ribbons with their attached medallions clanking together in her palm and left the office.

And blast it all, if he hadn't just agreed to spending another night away from her, in separate beds.

Bloody hell, in separate rooms.

Not a wedding night in sight.

What was it that bloody smart-ass Drew had said? Something about the madness of believing that he could just waltz Kate into his bed without paying dearly for his neglect.

He was paying for it, all right, with fevered imaginings of her tight-fitting trousers, bones that ached from wanting her, not to mention a scraped knee, bruises, and a constellation of fishhook wounds.

But he had always prided himself on the unshakeable strength of his honor, had honed it on kings and princes, pirates and popes.

So how had it happened that a beautiful young woman whom he'd wed out of necessity had the power to turn his resolve into pudding?

Not that it mattered in the least. He was doomed to burn for her.

Because he didn't have the slightest idea how to go about courting her.

He found her in the dining room a few minutes later, flushing slightly at the cheering applause from the sea of sportsmen as she took her place in front of them.

"A good day's catch, gentlemen," she said in her musical voice. "Records in nearly every category. Congratulations!"

As before, the crowd cheered and huzzahed themselves and toasted each other with Jared's own wine. Though it all made more sense to him tonight.

She made more sense to him. His entrepreneurial wife and her wild schemes.

Her confident declaration that she didn't need him or his protection.

When it came to announcing the daily prize for rainbow trout, and he saw that she was puzzling out the fairness of awarding him the medal, Jared stepped into the room and waved at her.

"In truth, Lady Hawkesly, I must disqualify myself from the rainbow category."

The crowd turned toward him and grumbled.

Kate's eyes grew wide, twinkled at the corners. "Surely not, Colonel Huddleswell? Yours was the largest fish of the day!"

"Indeed, it was. But I didn't actually catch the damn thing legally."

"What?" Her question ricocheted around the tables. "Do say?"

"I'll be damned." And other exclamations of disappointment and approval.

"Actually," he said, "I didn't reel him in as the rules require. One of those technicalities that I couldn't help at the time and didn't realize until just now."

Jared watched her hide another smile. "If you're certain, Colonel."

"Absolutely, my dear Lady Hawkesly. Rules, as you know, are rules."

She frowned at him, sparks lighting the corners of her eyes. "Civilization relies on them, Colonel. And so do tournaments. So I declare Mr. Gilmott the daily winner in the rainbow trout division."

And so the evening went, Kate dashing from one incident to the next and Jared keeping a close eye on her.

Strictly in a courting effort to learn more about her. A mission he was beginning to enjoy.

Especially when she would catch his glance from across the room, or include him in her machinations whispered against his ear.

"How are you at the game of hazard, Colonel?"

Ross had always referred to him as a bloodthirsty shark. "Tolerable, Lady Hawkesly."

"Excellent. Then would you mind joining the table

in the corner? Been a bit too much drinking there. If you could go settle them down, I'd be so very grateful."

Gratitude would do for now. "I might ask how *you* are at the game of hazard. Strictly out of curiosity, of course."

"We'll play a hand sometime and you'll find out for yourself." She left him with a wink.

He watched her from the distance of the rowdy hazard table as she moved around the lounge, and heard her congratulating the daily winners and commiserating with the losers, listening to their raucous tales of the monsters that got away.

Dazzling them as easily as she dazzled him.

Fortunately, with the fish inclined to begin biting just before dawn, the evening ended suddenly and hours earlier than it would ever have in London.

Jared helped McHugh muscle the drunken Breame and Fitchett into their rooms, losing track of his wife for the first time all night.

A single wick had been left burning in a lamp on the bar. "Any sign of my wife, McHugh?"

"M'lady said to tell you she was off to her chamber." McHugh cleared his throat. "Whatever that means to ya . . . m'lord."

"It means that you're too insolent by half, McHugh." Though Jared couldn't help but like the man.

"Just watchin' out for my lady's interests, my lord. Habit, I suppose. Nothing changed from last night, far as I'm concerned."

"I wouldn't expect it to. Lady Hawkesly thinks the world of you."

McHugh's chest rose. "Does she now?"

"And her word is good enough for me. Good night to you." Jared left the man rubbing his knuckles across his jaw and started up the stairs toward his garret room.

So his bride had slipped off to bed without even a "good night, husband."

That wouldn't do. She'd offered him a foot's distance from her and he was bloody well going to take it.

Weary to her bones and yet simmering with excitement, Kate shed her clothes, slipped into her nightgown, and then dove under the counterpane.

Married!

She was actually married to that amazing man she'd left prowling around downstairs. He'd been such a presence throughout the evening, it seemed as though she'd spent the entire night on his arm.

Yet she'd spoken only a few dozen words to him.

And coward that she was, she'd waited until he had gallantly offered to help McHugh with the more unruly guests before scurrying to her room like a rat and locking the door safely behind her.

It might have been wiser to go back to the hall and sleep in her regular bedchamber, instead of up here in the maid's corridor. It was just easier, quicker, to head off any problem guests if she stayed at Badger's Run during the tournaments.

Problem guests like Colonel Huddleswell.

At last the stairs had gone quiet, the long case clock on the landing just now striking twelve.

Married!

"Good night, wife."

"Jared!" Kate would have screamed but she'd sensed him there at the foot of her bed in the instant before he'd spoken. "What the devil are you doing here?"

He was an enormously tall silhouette between her and the window, and then a deep pressure against the mattress as he sat down beside her.

"My room is a good seventy feet from here and up two flights of stairs." She could just see his eyes, glints of moonlight.

"What are you blathering about? I know where your room is. How did you get in here? I very carefully locked the door."

"Then you've just learned something new about me, my dear; no lock can hold me."

"You're a lock pick!"

"When I need to be, and tonight"—she thought she heard his boot drop to the floor—"I needed to be."

"To get into my room."

"As I said, because my room is at least seventy feet from you. Possibly a hundred."

That was definitely a boot! "And Mrs. Driscoll's room is just across the hall. What are you doing here?"

"I'm sleeping beside my bride." She felt the full weight of him against the mattress, and then his head hit the pillow beside her.

"You're doing nothing of the sort." Kate shoved at his shoulder and scooted to the end of the bed. "You promised."

"So did you, my dear. You promised me a foot and I'm taking it." He tugged at the blanket.

"Are you mad? What foot?"

"According to your rule, I need to stay a foot away from you, so I'm taking you at your word."

"You know that's not what I meant."

"The truth is all in the details, Kate. Now lie down. It's past time to sleep. Those bloody fish start biting before dawn, you know."

She couldn't have this, couldn't have Jared's huge, magnificent body throwing off his heat all night. She'd never get a moment's sleep for fear that he would try to gather her into his embrace.

For fear that he wouldn't.

"Please go back to your own bed."

"This *is* my bed."

"It's *mine*."

"Proving my point. Now stop chattering and go to sleep. I've promised not to touch you and I won't." The bed seemed to settle with his huge sigh.

He was fully clothed, the devil, his arms tucked under his head, his breathing leveling out so quickly she was sure he'd suddenly dropped off to sleep.

"Jared?"

"Shhhh." He patted the bed beside him. "To sleep now, wife."

Wife. And this huge man lying so casually in her bed was her lawful husband.

And lawfully he had every right to do anything he pleased with her, or to her, short of murder.

But the lout was just lying there, as subtle as a thunderstorm, as encompassing, courting her in his own overwhelming way.

Protecting her, even from himself.

Her husband.

She suddenly realized with a flooding warmth that there couldn't possibly be a safer place in the world for her to sleep tonight than right here beside him.

"Do you snore, husband?"

"I'm sure you'll tell me in the morning."

Kate caught herself smiling as she settled in beside him, as she felt him measure off exactly one foot.

A far greater distance than she'd imagined it to be. Lonely and cold.

She slept deeply beside him all through the night, waking to the gray light of dawn and an empty room.

And the curious, half-empty feeling that he'd been only a phantom.

Chapter 14

~~~ ⟳⟲ ~~~

Jared gladly kept his distance from the fishing tournament for the next two days, perfectly satisfied to have Colonel Huddleswell's luck take a bad turn, but bloody impatient to begin his marriage to his astounding wife.

Though he tried to resist, he had found himself following Kate like a lovesick pup, this woman in perpetual motion.

With a quicksilver mind, endless patience and a fiery, focused temper when she sensed injustice.

Silky, soft hands that could gentle a weeping child or stir him to passion with as much skill as when she baited fishhooks or chopped cordwood. And those compelling, sky-blue eyes that missed nothing and embraced everything, everyone.

Including him, in the most provocative ways and when he least expected it.

By the time Badger's Run finally emptied of its hordes of irritating guests, Jared had somehow managed to survive three long, sleepless nights lying but one duly agreed upon foot from his wife.

Never touched her.

Never kissed her.

Burned.

But in that quiet, peaceable time between the darkness and just before dawn he'd not only learned everything about the cultivation and maintenance of a profitable chalkstream, but that his wife was remarkable.

Had courage enough for an entire regiment. Could make him laugh at himself. Would fight like a tigress for the things she loved.

And that wresting back control of his estate from her after these long months away wasn't going to be simple.

This was the calm before the storm.

Fortunately, he had already set the impeccably efficient Pembridge on the trail of suitable situations for his wife's orphans, and had heard excellent news from his man of affairs this morning.

Identified a plethora of parish farms and relief homes in Manchester and Birmingham for your unfortunate children, my lord. Each one eager to do business with you.

"They're not *my* children, dammit."

My every hope for your happiness, sir, and that your lovely bride is enjoying your generous wedding gift.

The impudent old rascal. Though he didn't know what the devil he'd do without Pembridge, who had save him from many a gaff, saved Drew and Ross as many times.

Yes, it was all going amazingly well. And now, at long last, the library at Badger's Run belonged to him again.

No, this wasn't Badger's Run, this was his private hunting lodge, reclaimed through his wife's efforts and welcoming as it had never been before. Though the housekeeping staff had been dashing madly around with clean linens and feather dusters, mops and brooms, Jared lounged in a library chair at the large writing table, rereading Drew's recent message.

Hawkesly, Lord High Inquirer of All Matters Coastal:

The clown.

Holding the captain of the Pickering *for questioning. Guns and ammunition impounded in Portsmouth. Indian cornmeal impounded in Customs warehouse in Liverpool. Investigation into Trevelyan's missing grain has led to the same in Lord Grey's own warehouse in Liverpool. Interesting, eh?*

Not half as interesting as the prime minister's message that had arrived the night before.

Must make passage safe and pleasing for V to visit Ireland as soon as possible. HM is anxious to meet her loyal Irish subjects.

"All seven of them?" Jared said to the absent prime minister, giving the message a toss and grabbing a clean piece of paper from the stack. "Blast it all, I've got larger fish to fry at the moment."

"I thought you'd given up fishing, Colonel."

Jared looked up from the blank page to find Kate standing at the library door, a brimming tea tray in her hands, her hair piled loosely atop her head, and that stunning smile teasing at her lips.

He stood as she entered, his heart giving an unruly kick to his pulse. "I thought I was alone."

She paused beside the table. "Then I'll leave your tea and won't bother you further."

He caught her hand as she reached for the teapot. "Please, Kate, bother me."

Her eyes followed his as he lifted her hand to his mouth and left a kiss on her palm.

"Oh, Jared." Her sigh riffled against his forehead.

There now, *that* was courting.

Damned rousing.

"Amazing as it may seem, I had just been sitting here thinking how desperately I needed you to come bother me, to distract me with this sweet scent of yours—and, well, here you are." Jared bent toward her ear. "Making all my wishes come true."

"That wasn't my inten—oh, Jared, you, it's . . . !"

He touched his lips to that scented place below her ear, tasted her softness, reveled in the lightness of the breath she took, in the plain fact that she grabbed hold of his sleeve and hung on.

"Actually, Jared . . . oh, my!" She giggled softly when he caught her earlobe between his teeth and tugged lightly. "But I've . . . I've invited . . ." Now she was tilting her head, exposing her throat fully to his mouth.

"You've invited . . . who?" *Privacy.* Lordy, he wanted long, private moments with his bride. "Because I want you alone, Kate. And to be finished with all this courting business."

"Yes . . ." She sighed with a little mewling. "But I've invited—"

An indelicate throat cleared in the doorway. "Your pardon, my lady."

Kate's eyes widened at him. "Janie!"

Janie?

Kate jumped backward out of his arms then hurried to the door, straightening her skirts with an unsubtle yank. "I'm so glad you're here. And the others too. Come in."

Others?

"Sure, just as you asked, my lady." The trembling maid sidled into the library, her disapproving gaze locking onto Jared's face.

The others entered from behind her, at least a dozen staff members, lining up in front of the shelves of books as though they assumed they were about to be shot and had accepted their fates.

"Thank you all for coming." Kate had recovered entirely, her hair tidy again, save for a strand at the back of her neck that he so recently had wrapped round his finger. "And thank you for another successful tournament. Our guests left Badger's Run very happy, with plans to return."

The hell they would.

She applauded the staff and they shuffled and

blushed and nodded their adoration at her. "You're most welcome, Lady Hawkesly."

She raised her shoulders and took in a deep breath. "And now I have a very important announcement to make."

She glanced back at him, shyly, a conspiracy between them, and then he suspected what she was about to say.

"You'll notice that Colonel Huddleswell is the only guest that hasn't left Badger's Run."

The staff's virulent silence was answer enough, a wall of hostility directed at him, the rumors of his indiscretion already passed between them.

"The truth is that this man was never a guest here, and his name is not Colonel Huddleswell."

Now the staff gasped and muttered, glancing between each other as though planning to rush him in defense of their lady's honor.

Kate silenced them with a gesture. "This man is actually Lord Hawkesly—your employer and my . . . husband."

A leaden silence thudded into the room, hung in the air like a sulfurous cloud, lasting for what seemed like minutes of horror and shock and indignation.

Kate nodded Jared forward to stand beside her. "Ladies and gentlemen, may I present Lord Hawkesly."

No one spoke, only stared until Jared was about to break the silence when his wife continued.

"And to answer your question as to why we didn't announce that he had arrived home: We couldn't just then."

"Why ever not, my lady?" Janie asked, staring at him, her words cracking as she spoke.

"Because Lord Hawkesly is . . . um . . ." She looked up at him as though demanding that he go along with whatever explanation she offered. "He's a spy."

Bloody hell! How did she know? And why the devil would she announce such a thing to a room full of strangers?

Everyone gasped. Janie's eyes widened. "A spy, sir? What kind?"

Kate turned to Jared, looking relieved, innocently pleased with herself and her blithe explanation, when she'd just hit a bull's-eye.

"Which is the reason I couldn't let on to you who he was. What kind of spy did you say you are, Jared?" She blinked up at him, leaving his mouth dry as dust and his thoughts scrambled.

"I'm . . . not."

"Not?" She shot a near lethal frown at him.

"Not really a sp—" but he couldn't bring himself to say that in front of the staff. Couldn't contradict Kate's explanation for his not identifying himself from the start.

Bloody hell.

"Yes, Jared?"

"I suppose I am at liberty to say that, although I am retired as of . . . today, I shall always be willing to give my life in service to our queen and to our country and to all it stands for."

The lot of them sighed at him, cocked their heads as if suddenly seeing him through an entirely different lens. Smiles erupted, nods of approval. Waves of applause.

Pride in their lord.

"I thought as much, my lord."

"How exciting!"

"Welcome home, sir."

Kate raised her hand again. "He was here during the tournament to keep an eye on one of our guests. Please, no speculation as to who it was. The matter has ended safely."

Jared grabbed her hand and pulled her against his side. "May I speak with you alone, wife?"

"Of course." She turned back to the staff. "Thank you all for your patience and loyalty."

The staff left the library a changed mob, no longer seeking his blood, but beaming back at him as they closed the door.

Kate was beaming at him too. "I'm sure they believed us, Jared."

"That I'm a spy?" He sat back on the edge of the table and studied the woman. "What the devil were you thinking?"

"What other kind of person would mask their identity and have their wife go along with it?"

Jared opened his mouth to explain her foolishness, but a sharp knock sounded at the door.

" 'Scuse me, my lord, my lady." It sounded like the boy from the stables.

His wife threw open the door and pulled the boy into the library. "Come in, Corey."

"Yes, m'lady. A message come for . . . um, for his lordship." Corey was peering at Jared as though seeing him for the first time. "For you, my lord."

Jared met the boy at the door and took the message. Another from Drew. Making him wonder if it wouldn't be more efficient if he just packed up his wife and took her back to London. "I'm obliged, lad."

"Yessir. There's a fellow waiting for an answer from you. Mrs. Driscoll's givin' him supper."

"All right. Give me thirty minutes." It must be urgent if Drew needed an immediate reply. The boy sped away as Jared opened the envelope.

"You need a full-time messenger."

"Indeed."

Kate loved the rumble of his voice and the dark curl of his hair, admired the planes of his face as he concentrated on the paper in his hand.

"Damned strange, Drew," he said as he dropped the message among the other papers on the table. He pulled out the chair and sat, looking determined.

Feeling suddenly quite married to the man, Kate poured him a cup of tea and set it on the table. "I don't really know what your business is, Jared. Besides shipping, that is."

He cast her a wry, sideways glance, then slipped a blank piece of paper in front of him. "My commercial interests are varied."

Stubborn, arrogant man. "And they are . . . ?"

"The usual." He wrote a few words and then took up the message again and studied it.

Deciding it was time that she learned as much as she could about his business, Kate poured herself a cup of tea and pulled up a chair near his table.

"By 'the usual,' husband, you mean the opium trade, and the transport of stolen antiquities, slavery, rum, gun running . . ."

He looked up with another of his crooked, to-swoon-for smiles, utterly devilish, as though she'd struck the perfect note with him. "You might say that."

"You're a slaver?" She sat straight up, horrified. "I don't believe it. You can't be! It's illegal. It's reprehensible! If you are, then this is the end of us."

He looked her square in the eye, wearing the inscrutable expression that she was beginning to distrust and adore in the same breath, then took a handful of her blouse and pulled her the last inch toward him, his mouth nearly touching hers, the graze of his fingers hot between her breasts.

"Do you really think that badly of me?"

"I still have no idea what to think of you. I don't know you, remember?" Except that he smelled of paper and woodsmoke and shaving soap. And his hair had a charming mussiness about it. "*Are* you in the opium trade?"

"No." His whole expression changed, serious and straightforward as he lightly touched his mouth to hers. "Nor do I transport stolen antiquities"—another kiss—"or smuggle slaves, or rum, or guns. . . ."

Good. Good. Very good! Honorable and delicious. Then she pulled away and studied him. "So, husband, are you a Tory or a Whig?"

He grinned and leaned back against the chair, clearly amused. "Neither."

"A party of your own devising?"

He laughed. "If only that were possible." Inscrutable again, he grabbed the pen and started writing.

Feeling wildly brave and more and more a part of his life, Kate picked up the nearest message and read as far as the first line. "Who's 'V'?"

"Our mad queen."

She hadn't expected that answer. "You mean 'V' is Victoria?"

"One in the same. And as usual, she carefully asks my opinion, but in the end she'll ignore my advice."

"You advise the queen?"

"No, my dear, Albert advises her. The rest of us merely flap our wings."

Albert, the prince? And who exactly were "the rest of us"? Just who was this man she'd married? "But you do sometimes advise the queen?"

"I do my best."

An advisor to the queen? What exactly was a shipping magnate doing advising the queen? He'd looked like a Barbary pirate when she married him, but what was he really?

He'd written a dozen lines already, but she watched him scribe the words,

Stop her, Drew.

"Stop who, Jared? The queen?" She leaned on her elbow beside him, admiring this other side of her husband.

"If he can."

Just like that. "Isn't that dangerous? Dashing off orders to the queen of England?"

"Sometimes it takes a very long stick to reach the woman and her pride." His powerful, bronze hand skimmed over the page as he wrote, each stroke emphatic and elegantly male.

"What is it the queen wants to do that makes you

think her mad?" But then Kate remembered a single word that struck at her heart.

Ireland. It was there in at the end of the note. The queen wanted to visit her loyal subjects.

"She wants to make a royal pilgrimage to Ireland next month." He underlined the word *foolhardy* twice.

Kate straightened, shocked by the possibility, her contentment swamped by a cool, deeply abiding anger. "Then the woman really must be mad."

He paused in his writing and turned slowly in his chair to study her fully, looking suddenly defensive of his queen. "What would make you say that?"

"Because her loyal subjects are starving to death over there. They have to blame someone. What better target for their anger and despair than an English monarch who dares set her plump, pampered foot on Irish soil in the midst of a famine? That isn't just foolhardy, Jared, it's arrogant."

"For a monarch to show concern for her subjects?"

"What an inconsequential word that is. She's 'concerned.'"

"Believe me, she is."

"Ballocks!" She sat on the edge of his writing table. "People are starving by the thousands because Parliament has decided not to feed them, because the poor obviously deserve the potato famine."

He narrowed his dark gaze at her, dragging his tongue across the inside of his cheek. "It's not quite as simple as that."

Kate set her jaw. "I don't know what could be made more simple to the queen than making sure the children of her kingdom are fed. Her own seem to be. Surely she has power enough to command the actions of her ministers. Give them a royal order to purchase all the Indian corn that can be found in the world. Then give it away at the relief depots instead of selling it to people who have no money left."

He stared at her still, coldly unwavering. "Politics."

She turned away from her husband, deeply disappointed in him, fearing what else this might mean for the future. "Well, if the queen truly accepts that scant justification, if she doesn't have courage enough or care enough to stand up and fight Lord Russell and that bastard Trevelyan—"

"It's not a matter of caring—"

She whirled on him. "That's all that matters to a starving family. Caring enough to do something. So if you can't convince your queen against this royal visit, then tell her that she'd better watch her back when she arrives in Dublin, because . . ."

Jared stood, bracing his boot on the chair seat and leaning close. "Because what, wife?"

"Because it's dangerous. You know that yourself, else you wouldn't be advising her against her visit. Am I right?"

He snorted as though she'd caught him, and turned back to composing his message. "More right than you know. The only thing more dangerous than a fool with a rifle is a mob of foolish rebels who think they can best the Royal Guards."

"At least they attempt something."

"Firing the docks and running guns won't gain them anything but prison, or worse."

"I can't imagine anything worse than watching help-lessly as your children die one by one."

He muttered something at her, doubtless one of his dismissive curses, then scribbled off a few more words that Kate didn't quite catch before he folded the paper and shoved it into an envelope.

She trailed him to the door. "I hope you're not saying that a man ought to just abandon his wife and children to starvation instead of fighting for their right to eat a decent meal."

"What I'm saying is that a man would be a fool to trust a handout from his landlord or the Relief Commission or Trevelyan or anyone else, for that matter." He yanked open the door and handed the letter to Corey, who'd been leaning faithfully against the opposite wall of the hallway. "A shilling for you, lad, and one for the messenger. Tell him to hurry."

"Yes, m'lord!" Corey grabbed the two coins then shot away down the hall. Kate shut the door behind him, feeling as though she needed to protect the young man from Jared and his type.

"And what of the thousands of children like Corey whose parents died and left them to fend for them-selves? Should they trust a handout from their landlord or Poor Relief? Or do they scrabble around on the land, eating grass?"

Jared stared at her through darkly lashed eyes, their color turned silky black and smokey. "The wise ones take what they can, while they can, and then do for themselves as nobody else will."

What a cold and distant thing to say. "A child shouldn't have to live that way."

He lifted his cup of tea to his lips. "No, but that's the brutal truth. Take what you can, from whatever hand is open, and hope to hell you can duck in time before the blow lands."

She'd never heard him talk this way. "Surely you don't believe that, Jared."

"It's a hard lesson, but it serves well. You've only to look at your own mob of orphans to see it at work. They've all taken what they could from your lessons. They'll doubtless do well wherever they land."

Her stomach dropped. "What do you mean, wherever they land?" Yet she already knew his answer; that he was planning something bleak and solitary.

"This is as good a time as any to tell you, Kate." He poured himself another cup of tea. "I believe I've found places for them all." He sat in his chair, lordly and commanding, as though the discussion was over.

"Places?" Kate could hardly breathe, felt a weight settling hard on her chest. "They have a place. Here. Perhaps not in the hall, but somewhere nearby. A home of their own."

"I promised to find suitable housing for each of the children, and I have done just that." He gathered up a stack of letters.

"Where? What kind of housing?" Doubtless some horrid stone box in the middle of the city? Some kind of warehouse for children.

"Parish farms, relief homes—"

"You did this without asking me?"

"The problem was mine to solve. And I've solved it."

"If you think you're going to send my children into

slavery, you'll just have to think on that one again. I won't allow it."

"Kate, they're not your children. They're strays—"

"But they've been put into my care—"

"And a parish farm is a far better place than a brutal Manchester workhouse."

"But these children came from farms. Mucky little bogs of mud and peat, and shriveled, rotting potato plants. They've served their time in hell. I won't send them back there."

"This is England. Our farmers plant more than potato crops."

"But the children don't know that! They've found refuge from the terror here, apples and mushrooms and cabbage. And I won't let them live in fear of want ever again. I love them too much to ever allow that to happen."

"Enough." He capped the bottle of ink. "I've made my decision. It's the best for all, and that's that."

She swallowed the lump in her throat, her regrets for what might have been. "I knew you didn't understand the situation. That you would never understand. It's just not in you."

"Bloody hell, woman, what would you have me do? Adopt them all?"

The idea brought her up short. She'd never considered it before. Of course it was impossible at this point.

"And saddle them with you for a father? Not on your life Lord Hawkesly." Her heart aching, Kate shook her head at him, sorry that he had simply refused to change, because he had goodness in him somewhere. She was sure of it. The children had seen it plainly, right through all his blustering anger. "I'm just glad that you showed your real colors at last. Before I let myself . . ."

"Let yourself what?"

"Before I let myself be married to you completely. Be assured, my lord. The children and I will be gone by the end of the week. Good night."

Kate left him to his small-minded, impoverished notions, regretting that she and the children were back where they had started five days ago.

Her heart aching, but a host of plans already swirling in her head.

Chapter 15

For the umpteenth time since meeting his presumptuous bride, she'd left him standing speechless and immobile.

"Come back here, Kate!" Stark silence, of course, though the door still rattled where she'd slammed it. Not that threats seemed to mean a damn thing to the woman.

Or promises, or good intentions.

Hell, what orphaned child wouldn't be grateful to live on a farm, with plenty to eat and a dry roof over their heads and a warm coat and a change of clothes. He'd have been thankful to have had half as much when he was a boy.

"Kate!" He shouted her name again as he reached the main corridor. And again in the middle of the lounge.

"Yer wife's gone off to the hall for the evening, my lord," McHugh said from behind the bar.

"Damnation!"

"Said something about the children."

"Double damn."

Janie appeared from out of nowhere. "Are you wantin' something, my lord? More tea?"

"I was looking for my wife."

"Ahhhh . . . have you lost her again, sir? Or shouldn't I be asking that? Some sort of spy dealings?"

"Yes, Janie. It's a professional situation. I'll be working in the library, if I'm by chance needed by the lord of the admiralty." Not that he expected to hear from the admiralty at the moment, but hoping to end this whole spy matter once and for all.

"The admiralty?" The woman dropped another curtsey. "Oh, my, yes, sir!"

"Good. And would you please have my belongings moved from that little garret room in the rafters to the suite on the second floor."

"Done, sir."

He stalked back toward the library. He'd be damned if he was going to follow Kate to Hawkesly Hall tonight. There was nothing that she could say or do to change his mind at this point. He'd made his decision about her orphans, she'd just have to bloody well learn to live with it.

With *all* of his decisions! Because however much she protested and wrangled with him, he wasn't going to let her leave him. Or their marriage. She was his wife and had no choice in the matter.

Hell, that's what he got for not keeping a tight rein on her from the beginning. For not sending her home from Alexandria with a minder, an entire entourage of keepers. But how the devil was he to know she'd take on the world singlehanded?

Now it looked like he'd be still another night without claiming his bride, this time without even exercising his one-foot rule.

So he worked on a half dozen reports and compiled a half dozen more and dined in silence. Hours later he slipped into an icy bed in the best of Badger's Run bedchambers instead of that bloody little garret prison cell.

But his sleep was fitful and stuffed with nightmarish memories of an empty belly and long wintry nights without a blanket.

Of the workhouse and Squire Craddock's unerring aim with a board.

Of doing his best to protect ten-year-old Drew and the younger, foolhardy Ross.

Of failing little Thomas so completely, finding him curled in the corner, dying, his small, twig-thin body broken and bloodied by Craddock's unquenchable anger.

And now came the new faces into his dreams: his fiery-haired wife and the boy Grady, the dog and Mera, Dori and her missing teeth. The new one, Margaret, her eyes still as death.

He fought with his demons until well after dawn, and he was just dropping off to a softer sleep when he woke instantly to the sound of Kate's voice from a distance.

He felt the pillow beside him, but it was cold. She was gone. No, she hadn't been there all night.

The large window in his new room overlooked the forecourt of the lodge and the excitement below.

"My Douglasses!" Kate was shouting with an excessive amount of glee for so early in the morning, and about some man named—

"Douglas?" Another shot of jealousy zipped through him. "Who the devil is Douglas?"

A wagonload of barrels was just being hauled into the forecourt by that Elden fellow, met there by Corey and Kate.

But barrels of what?

Jared dressed quickly and was stalking toward his wife a few minutes later. "What is all this, Kate?"

She turned in his direction, blinked at him with those clear blue eyes, the morning sun glinting red on the ends of her hair. She hadn't a smile for him this morning, but that compelling intensity was there.

"Douglas fir seeds, Hawkesly." She patted the side of the wagon fondly. "From the tree that grows so prolifically on the west coast of North America."

Seeds? "I know what a Douglas fir is. I ballast my ships with timber on every return from the Fraser Valley and make a damned good profit by it. What the devil are you doing with barrels of seeds?"

"Last spring I learned from one of our Scottish guests at Badger's Run that the Douglas is hardy and quick growing and sprouts very readily from seed." She came toward him with the fierce confidence he'd come to adore, her hips moving like honey—smoothly and succulently, like no other woman's he'd ever noticed.

Honey that he wanted to dip into, to taste and caress. And if he wanted to partake of her any time soon, he would have to keep up his courting dance.

"You're not answering my question, wife. Why?"

She stuck her fists against her hips. "I need the seeds because I plan to reforest the Hawkesly estate."

"You're going to do what?" He knew better than to trust one of the woman's lunatic explanations.

"Let's show him, Elden." Elden was already at the tailgate, using a pry bar on one of the barrels.

His heart sank with the weight of her foolishness. Replanting a forest?

She pointed to a label pasted to one of the lids. "Directly from Edinburgh."

The woman was mad. "Purchased from one of the guests who stayed at Badger's Run?" So far she seemed to be a remarkably astute business woman. But she was, after all, merely a woman. Prone to fancies and charlatans and orphans and fast-talking sportsmen with barrels of seeds to sell to the unsuspecting.

"Mr. Lyons was very knowledgeable about cultivating healthy forests, and shared with me the many benefits of reforesting where the trees have been cut down and nothing replanted. Come, I'll show you." She went to the edge of the courtyard and pointed to a steep, starkly cleared hillside. "Do you see the devastation?"

"That was cleared centuries ago, Kate. And look at that slope. It's impossible to replant."

She looked up at him as though she were going to offer another of her wild-eyed theories, then blew out a sigh and shrugged. "Nevertheless, it needs doing as soon as possible. The hillside is slowly washing away. Magnus says that it's the major cause of damage to the chalk streams."

Convinced that it was best to point out the many errors in her plan as early as possible, Jared walked back to the wagon where Elden had pried open the lid of one of the barrels.

Expecting to find anything but seeds, Jared was surprised that the barrel was indeed full of them. Definitely Douglas fir. He reached in and lifted out a handful of the little brown pips, recognizing the fragrance of a thick western Canadian forest. A pungent, autumn smell.

He glanced at his wife, who was looking up at him in simple triumph.

And you're going to plant them how? he wanted to ask. And when? Millions of seeds, across an enormous hillside made of rock and ridges.

But she seemed quite proud of her efforts and certain that all things were possible.

Besides, a project of this magnitude, not to mention its potential for frustration and failure would keep her out of other trouble for months on end. Simple for him to monitor.

And it would keep the children off her mind once they'd all been sent away to their new homes.

"I hope you slept well, Jared." Her brows were winged, her eyes honest and searching for something in his own.

"I slept alone." And damned if he hadn't missed her like his own heartbeat.

"I'm truly sorry for that. And for the reason." She gave an impatient little huff. "Now if you'll excuse me, I have to help Elden get the seeds to the meadow barn before it rains."

She flounced off to the wagon and pulled herself up

into the bench seat beside Elden. The stoically silent man had the decency to tip Jared the brim of his cap as they passed him.

Feeling utterly spurned, Jared battled the urge to demand that Kate stay behind. But he had already learned the hard way that the woman was made of stubbornness and resolve.

And despite their difference of opinion about the orphans, he still intended to court her until she succumbed.

Besides, she couldn't avoid him forever.

Kate resisted the desire to turn back and look at Jared still standing in the courtyard. She had missed him dearly last night, him and the honorable distance he kept from her through the last three nights. Missed the soft, steady sound of his breathing.

A perfect man in every way but the one that counted. He simply lacked a heart, or refused to use the one he had.

"My lady, I couldn't tell you this with his lordship nearby, but the *Katie Claire* will be docking in Mereglass tomorrow afternoon."

"That's wonderful, Elden." A half day to load the harvest goods from the warehouse. Another day to get to Dublin. A day for the food to start arriving at Father Sebastian's soup kitchens. Yet it always seemed such a long time, an eternity to the children whose lives depended on their next day's meal.

"Wonderful, my lady, unless his lordship discovers her in port and goes aboard."

"We can't let that happen." Kate jounced sideways

into Elden's shoulder as the wheel hit a chuck hole. "I'll just have to nail Jared into his room."

"Or perhaps just keep him busy, my lady. . . ."

It wasn't until Kate was opening the barn door and Elden was driving the wagon forward that the perfect idea occurred to her.

"I've got it, Elden!"

"Just don't tie him up, my lady."

"You get the *Katie Claire* loaded and I promise to keep Jared safely occupied." Somehow. Kate dropped the tail gate, climbed into the bed and found the single crate. "But in the meantime, if I understand correctly, the seeds need to be measured out and packed into small, silk bags. Here, I'll show you what I mean."

Even with following the instructions which had come inside the crate with the little bags, it took them nearly an hour to make the perfect seedbag.

"With a few helpers, my lady, I'll have these finished by tomorrow afternoon." Then Elden fixed a look at her. "Though I admit that I agree with your husband on one fact."

"And that is?"

He nodded toward the barrels. "You're more than a bit mad."

"Oh, ye of little faith." She left Elden and hurried along the lane toward Hawkesly Hall. If she and the children were going to be gone within the week, then she had a lot of work to do. And letters to write. Contacts to make.

"Woof!" Mr. McNair! Just around the bend in the road, and Mera would surely be nearby.

"Do you see 'em, Jacob?" Lucas, too.

Doubtless she'd find the whole pack of them up to some mischief. They were still a bit too far afield from the hall, but at least they couldn't be harassing some poor fisherman like they had Colonel Huddleswell.

Dori saw Kate and came running toward her, flinging herself into Kate's arms. "Lady Kate! He's helping us! Come see!"

"Dori, what is it?" Then Kate saw the rest of the children, in the woods just off the road, their attention fixed on the upper branches of an enormous, overhanging hawthorn.

"Children, what's going on here?"

Glenna grabbed Kate's hand and pulled her toward the tree. "Justin bet Grady that there was a baby eagle in the nest up there and then didn't the two little fools climb up and get themselves stuck."

"His lordship's trying to help 'em down."

His lordship? Jared?

Then she saw his big bay just off the road, the reins wrapped through the branches of a willow.

Traveling with a gang of ruffians, husband?

Once she stepped beneath the canopy she saw the man himself, halfway up the tree, one foot anchored on a thick limb, the other braced against the trunk, his arm outstretched toward Justin's foot.

"I can't come down yet, sir," Justin said, all the boasting gone from his voice.

"Then hold right where you are. I'll try to get closer."

"Lady Kate's here, sir!"

"Is she now?"

Kate found herself staring up through the thick webbing of limbs into the unreadable eyes of her husband.

"Good afternoon, wife. Enjoying the woods?"

Dear God, the man was powerfully muscled from this angle. From any angle, really. So difficult to believe that he was as hard-headed as a stone.

"What can I do, Jared?"

"Catch us."

The children screamed and rushed around the base of the tree.

"He's joking, children. You're not going to fall, are you, Lord Hawkesly?"

"Of course not." He looked solid as a rock up there, capable of most any act of courage.

Well, she couldn't just stand there and watch. "I'm coming up."

"No, you're not!" Jared's bellow shook the branches and the leaves and made the children cry out again.

But Kate had always loved tall places—trees or mainmasts or flagpoles; she could shinny up most anything in the blink of an eye.

Moments later she was gripping a branch and bracing her feet on the limb where Jared had just been, and he was now nearly level with Justin, a good thirty feet off the ground.

"Do you ever behave, wife?"

"Come, Justin," she said, ignoring her husband and the grim and dangerous set of his white teeth, "show Grady how to climb down."

"I don't need no help!" Grady had thankfully crammed himself between the trunk and a sturdy limb about ten feet above Justin's head, and didn't look like he was going anywhere, anytime soon.

"You won't fall, lad, I've got you," she heard Jared

say to Justin. "The trick I use when I'm a hundred feet up, hanging onto the yardarm is to try not to look straight down."

"Then what do I do next, sir?"

"I'll steady you down to that lunatic woman on the limb below . . ."

"I am not a lunatic, sir!"

And neither was her husband in this particular case; he'd made Justin laugh and eased his fear in a most amazing way.

"Watch out, then! I'm comin' down, Lady Kate!" Justin's lanky legs churned above her, his face pale with concentration and damp with sweat as Jared guided him lower and lower, until Kate had a grip around the boy's waist.

"Got him, Jared. Good work, Justin."

"Delivered safely, wife." Jared let go of Justin's wrist and the boy flung his arms around Kate's neck, nearly knocking her off balance.

"Told you I could."

"I had no doubt, Justin." Kate carried him down another limb, closer to the ground, before he scrambled proudly the rest of the way, to the cheers of the other children.

One down, another to go.

"Hey, this is easy!"

Kate looked up to find Grady sitting on Jared's broad shoulders, and Jared working his way down through the limbs, nearly blinded by Grady's handholds.

By some miracle they all made it safely to the ground a few tense minutes later.

"Justin Cleary, I've warned you about making wagers. And the rest of you children about taking them. You especially, Grady."

Grady pointed up into the tree. "Justin said there was eagles—"

"And if Justin had said the nest was filled with golden seashells?"

"In an eagle's nest?" Grady narrowed his eyes at Justin. "I'd tell 'im he's stupid."

Justin butted his chest against Grady's. "You're just sore because—"

Jared caught them both by the collars and easily separated them.

"A rule of thumb, gentlemen." Jared scowled at both boys, catching their wide-eyed attention. "If ever someone wagers you a tenner that he can make a farthing disappear from his own hand and then find it behind Lady Hawkesly's ear, believe that he can do just that."

He winked at Kate across the heads of the boys and sent her heart spinning wildly.

"A farthing from behind Lady Kate's ear?" Grady laughed, swatted his belly.

Justin joined in, nudging his friend. "Who'd ever make a wager like that?"

"I would," Jared said, letting go of the boys and revealing a penny farthing between his fingers. "Because I know how it's done."

"How?"

"Watch carefully, now." He nicked the edge of the penny with a knife blade, then held up the coin again. "Proof that this is the very same penny as the one I'll find behind the lady's ear."

The children gathered around him as though he were a piper, to peer at the coppery coin, then followed him as he walked toward her, his smile cocky and sure, as though he actually believed he could perform such a mountebank miracle.

"You shouldn't tease them, Jared."

He said nothing, but displayed the coin in front of her while the children flocked around them to get a closer look at her husband's foolishness.

"You see the coin in my hand, my lady?"

She saw more than that behind his eyes, surprisingly more. "Of course."

"I see it too, sir!" Dori wrapped her fingers in Kate's skirt.

"Me, too!" came the ever-present chorus of rowdy little voices.

"Woof!" And Mr. McNair.

"Watch carefully, ladies and gentlemen, while I make this farthing disappear from my hand and then reappear behind Lady Hawkesly's left ear."

In the blink of an eye and with a great deal of show, Jared grabbed the coin from between his fingers with his opposite hand and closed it inside his fist. When he opened that same fist in the next instant the coin had disappeared.

"It's gone!"

"Where'd it go?"

The children frantically searched the sky and the ground and behind their own ears, until Jared finally announced:

"Is the penny here behind the good lady's ear, I wonder?" With another great show, he slipped his hand slowly through Kate's hair and paused a breathless moment at her ear. "Why, I think it is!"

She felt the lightest touch of warm metal against her nape, and then his hand appeared again in the midst of his audience with the same penny shining from between his fingers, knife-nick and all.

"He did it!"

Marvel of marvels, he had.

And won the children's devotion in the bargain. They cheered and jumped like jacks, and her husband hid his pleasure in a flexing muscle in his jaw.

It hurt her that he felt he needed to.

"Lesson learned, boys?" she asked Justin and Grady, who were gazing up at Jared in worshipful adoration.

"How'd you do that, sir? Will you show us how?"

She shook her head at Jared. "Next you'll be teaching them pickpocketing."

His eyes darkened, and an utterly wicked slant lifted the corner of his smile. "There are worse occupations, madam."

Spoken as though he knew of them firsthand.

"Off you go, children, his lordship is going to keep that secret to himself. For your own good, I might add."

The air filled with disappointed groans, scattering among the leaves that were beginning to tumble from the huge tree.

"Now, back to the hall with all of you before it starts to rain. I don't want any of you sick. And the Miss Darbys are doubtless looking for you to help with lunch."

"But, Lady Kate—"

"I said now, Grady!" Kate frowned at him, cutting off another bid for freedom.

"Beat ya there, Justin!" Grady took off, dust flying, the rest of the children following close behind.

"Thanks for looking out for them, Jared." She watched for his reaction and found none at all.

"I haven't changed my mind."

"Neither have I." Except that he'd seemed so comfortable with the chaos, so genuinely concerned about Justin and Grady. Perhaps he had a heart after all. She just needed to find it in time. "But whether you like it or not, you just made nine new little friends. Treasure them while you can. Good afternoon, Jared."

"Dammit, wife!"

But she'd already started down the lane toward the hall, hoping he would stop her, or follow.

It took him only moments to ride up beside her, to lean down, scoop her up off her feet, and into his lap.

"What do you think you're doing?" He'd clamped his arm around her waist so she couldn't move, beyond leaning away and staring at his square jaw with its dark unshaved edges.

"Where were you going?" he asked against her ear.

"To the hall to help arrange for taking the children away from here."

"Chatter all you want about leaving me, Kate." He heeled the horse forward down the lane. "You're wasting your breath. I cannot, will not let you go. No matter what you threaten. I'm responsible for your well-being."

"I can take care of myself." She folded her arms across her chest and focused her attention on the laurel hedge that marked the boundary of the hall itself. "I'll sign papers to that effect. You won't even miss me. Except that the hunting season starts in three weeks and you'll have two dozen hunters show up at Badger's Run for their tournament."

He stopped the horse and turned her chin. "Hunting season?"

"Deer and boar. Badger's Run is as famous for its hunting as it is for its fishing. And hunting season beats the fishing season hands down. We'll be full to the brim for a month."

"No, we won't."

"There's nothing to worry about. The tournament practically runs itself. Magnus and Mr. Foggerty take the hunters out in organized shooting parties. With plenty of ghillies and brush beaters. They know what they're doing."

"Absolutely not. I came here to the country because I want my life back. *Our* life. Which means privacy."

If the lout wasn't careful he was about to have all the privacy one lonely man could stand. "I'm sorry, but there's nothing to be done; you can't call off the shoot. You have reservations paid in advance—"

"I can damn well do whatever I want to do."

"And what good has that brought you so far, Jared?"

A muscle worked beneath his jaw. A hard place that she wanted desperately to soothe with her palm.

But he grunted and gave a heel to the horse, then rode the rest of the way to the hall in silence. He halted at the base of the wide entry stairs and let her down to her feet.

"You'll have dinner with me tonight, wife."

She chose not to answer that particular demand, asking instead, "Did you receive your wooden box from London? Elden delivered it to Badger's Run with the Douglas seeds."

"I saw it."

Though the box had given her a fright. It had been sent by Lord Grey.

"Do you advise Lord Grey as well as the queen?"

"On a daily basis." His smile had a wry slant to it. "I am a spy, after all."

Then the blackguard cantered off through the gates.

A spy, indeed.

At least his box of papers would help keep the man busy while Captain Waring brought the *Katie Claire* into Mereglass tomorrow.

But not half as busy as a seductive wife on a mission to distract him any way she could.

Chapter 16

Jared couldn't tell if he was bleary-eyed from a day's worth of reading or just bored. Lord Grey's conglomeration of evidence and unimportant pieces of stray information were dry as dust, and just as old, compiled over the last two years by the customs office in Portsmouth.

And now this honeymoon had turned completely on its backside. A battle of wits one moment, a breezy kind of joy the next, all of it tinged with Kate's threat to take the children and leave him.

He had isolated himself even more from the comings and goings of the staff. The suite of rooms at Badger's Run rivaled anything at Hawkesly Hall, with a huge bay window in the anteroom, spilling late afternoon sunlight across his work table, and a fireplace and a goosedown bed in the bedchamber, though the suite lacked the echoing sound of children's laughter and the Darbys' mouthwatering baked goods.

And Kate. She was gone from him too much of the time.

It seemed he would be having dinner alone tonight, as he had last night, despite his demand that Kate eat with him, and he didn't like the idea one damn bit.

"Your pardon, my lord—"

As though he'd conjured her out of thin air, Kate was standing in the doorway, a bottle of wine in one hand and two glasses in the other.

"Kate?" He got to his feet, as suspicious that she would appear just now as he was enchanted with the picture she made. Janie and another maid were peering into the room from behind her, both loaded down with heavy trays.

"If you're not too busy, I thought you and I would share supper here tonight."

"I'll make room in my schedule. Come in."

Without another word, Kate flashed him one of her seductive smiles and in moments a private banquet was set on the small round table nearest the hearth, complete with linens and silver, candles and wine, and another table was heaped with platters and tureens.

Kate's smile was slightly off center as she closed and locked the door, her eyes glittering, a brow arched with one of her tantalizing secrets.

The question was: Why?

"To what do I owe the honor?"

She shrugged. "I just haven't seen you much in the last day or two. Have you been *busy* with your work?"

He laughed, wary of that little trap and prepared to

offer up a bit of his pride. "Could I have been more boorish, Kate, or any more foolish? Too busy to come home to you?"

"We all have our foibles, Jared. I've completely forgotten it."

Like hell she had. What the devil was she up to now? Letting him off the hook so easily and with such a fiery glint in her gaze? "Are you planning to seduce me tonight?"

Her eyes widened. "I . . . I don't think so."

He knew her better than that. She had something up her sleeve. But if it involved a bit of seduction, then he'd go along with her as far as she wanted to go.

"Let me know if you do and I promise to be entirely cooperative."

She laughed. "I'll keep your offer in mind. But you must be famished, Jared."

"Likely to perish." Starving for her as he hadn't for any other woman he'd ever met. Hadn't had one since his compelling marriage to his elusive bride.

God knows, he'd not set out to be celibate in the separation, but his opportunities had been few and his sense of loyalty to the woman he'd married had been stronger than his desire for another.

So here he was, rattling with need for her. For this particular woman who was standing beside the table, their marriage still unconsummated, though he'd been here a week as of today.

"Shall we eat, then, before Mrs. Driscoll's feast gets cold?"

And he wondered again at this sudden attention, what he was supposed to do about it, what he would be allowed to do. "What exactly are your plans for me?"

She lifted a brow. "Plans?"

"You've obviously prearranged this private dinner."

"I did."

"Dinner and wine and then what?"

"Scintillating, revealing conversation between us. Uninterrupted, at our own pace."

Jared let go the laugh that bubbled in his chest. "So you are courting me now?"

"Of course not." Then she frowned and reconsidered, setting her index finger against her upper lip. "Well, I don't know." Her eyes widened.

"Indeed." Pleased with himself, with her, with this proper game of hers, whatever her motives, Jared decided to go along with her play and went to her side. "You're very good at it."

"Am I?"

"A natural." He pulled out her high-backed chair and gestured for her to take her place, then poured two glasses of claret.

"It's the best from your cellar. I hope you don't mind."

"I would have minded if it weren't the best." He handed Kate the glass, lingering as her fingers met his around the gentle bowl, before raising his own glass to her. "To courting, my dear."

"To . . . courting. And to the freedom to change one's mind." She lifted her glass in his direction, her gaze an unflinching challenge to his stance on her orphans.

He almost called her on her blatant intent, but then she put the rim of her glass to her lips and delicately sipped, leaving him staring, lovelorn, his heart racing like a rabbit's.

"To anything you wish, my dear." Anything at all. He sat back in the upholstered chair as she stood and went to the sideboard, admiring the view as she then ladled a hearty-looking vegetable broth into his bowl.

She was so unmindful of her place, so widely skilled and unafraid of failing.

Unpampered and determined. Where did that kind of independence come from in such a young woman?

"Persia!" he recalled suddenly, sitting up straight with the memory of a week's old disagreement with her.

"Persia?" She blinked at him.

"A sudden recollection that you told me you'd been held prisoner by a warlord. . . ."

"Oh, that," she said as she easily ladled herself a bowl of soup. "I was just trying to make a point with you. That you couldn't intimidate me."

He relaxed a little. "So you were just spinning a tale about the Persian warlord?"

"No. It really happened. But it was nothing. Only a bit of posturing between my father and the local shah."

"Good lord, you actually were taken hostage?"

"Technically."

"For how long?"

"Nearly a month." She sat down and dipped her spoon into the chunky liquid.

"And?"

She paused, the spoon poised at her mouth, her brows drawn in confusion. "And what?"

"Believe me, I know the ways of these warlords." He leaned forward across the small table. "Always on the lookout for stunning young brides, the younger the better, to add to their harems."

"Stunning?" She laughed and smiled brightly at him, her eyes glittering with amusement in the lamplight. "I was neither stunning, nor in any danger of being wed unwillingly to Uncle Ashraf."

"Any woman who is as beautiful as you are now had to have been a stunning young lady. Tempting to any man looking for a bride."

"Not Uncle Ashraf, not ever. And I'm hardly a stunning beauty."

"Like bloody hell, you're not." He took her hand and leaned on his elbow across the table. "Gad, woman, you'll be the talk of London society."

She laughed as though that were the funniest thing she'd ever heard. As if she couldn't imagine just how magnificent she was. "Jared, please. Your soup. It's getting cold."

He jammed a spoonful of soup into his mouth, swallowed a chunk of carrot whole, then returned to his wife's wild story. "Why do you call this Ashraf 'uncle'?"

"He was as close to me as one; I can't remember not knowing him and his family."

"Are you mad? He kidnapped you and held you for ransom."

"Not really." She fanned a skeptical hand at him, grinning. "Only because he and Father were at odds over the price of a shipment of dates and myrrh."

"So Trafford didn't mind that his daughter had been abducted. You were part of a business deal?" The man had had absolutely no scruples.

"Am I going to have to wield your spoon for you? Please eat."

Jared grabbed another swig of soup. "I'm not letting this matter of your abduction drop. And *then* I want to know about your being stranded on an ice-bound whaler."

How the hell did a man keep a woman like his foolish wife out of trouble when she seemed to thrive on it?

"You're making too much of everything. My father would never have let me go if I had been in danger. I was best friends with Uncle Ashraf's three middle daughters. He loved me like an uncle, treated me like a daughter. And my uncle knew that Father would never leave port without me, so kept me at his court so that they had to meet and negotiate a settlement. They did, and then I left with my father. Reluctantly."

"Reluctantly?"

"Because I got to see my three friends and my uncle but once a year at best and I knew I'd miss them terribly. In fact, I wangled an extra week with them. And I turned twelve while I was there." She grinned impishly at some grand, myrrh-scented memory.

"And this ice-bound whaler you spoke of . . . how old were you then?"

"Fifteen."

"Why the devil were you out at sea on a whaler? Did your father know this?"

"Of course. I was a passenger on my way to Boston, as Captain Ostein's favor to my father."

"Boston by way of the Arctic? What the bloody hell happened?" Not that he really wanted to know the details; they would only add to his restless nights.

"It was purely by accident. We lost a mainmast in a hurricane off Nova Scotia. It was late in the season and we were set adrift and forced above the Circle and trapped for six weeks in a hard freeze."

"Good God, woman! You could have perished in dozens of ways, freezing to death being the kindest."

"But I didn't. And so now I know how to hunt seal with a spear and render an entire whale, from bladder to blubber."

His pulse racing with helpless anger and fear of the future with a wife like Kate, Jared stood and paced to the fire. "Where was your mother in all this?"

She sighed and leaned back against the tall-back chair. "My mother died when I was eight. The love of my father's life. I miss her so."

"And so you were raised by a foolish father who should have left you home with an aunt where you would have been raised properly, safely."

She stood abruptly, scowling at him as she picked up her empty soup bowl and his half-eaten one. "I'll not have you insulting my father. He was the very best. A fine man and a finer father."

"Who encouraged you to run wild across the Seven Seas, completely unchecked."

"For which I am more grateful than you could ever imagine. I have no regrets about traveling with my father." She paused and studied him, a smile lurking at the corners of her mouth. "Though now that I think about it, if it weren't for him selling you part of his shipping business, I wouldn't have been forced to marry you."

Jared suddenly couldn't imagine that. Missing out

on a life with her. "And I would have regretted that, my dear. To the end of my days."

A dimple appeared on her cheek. "That's a long time."

God, she was beautiful! "It's just that I'm not used to a woman so . . ."

"Well traveled?" He watched this complicated woman uncover a steaming bowl of carrots, following every move as she set it on the table beside her plate.

"Indeed. Most of the women of my acquaintance stray no farther than their dressmakers."

"Then I doubt these ladies have witnessed the fertility dance of the Abasanti tribe?"

His blood stopped its shooshing, midbeat. "None that I know of."

She shook her head as she reached for the silver serving spoon. "A pity, that."

"A pity?" He knew exactly which dance she meant. Red, musk-scented flames rising in a moonlit night, naked skin veiled in silk and glistening with oil and sweat. Undulating lines of dancers curling around the leaping fire and each other, the dance increasing and increasing in sound and frenzy until bodies were writhing in pairs on the ground.

"A pity, Jared, because it's a most . . ." She glanced down at the flames leaping in the nearby hearth and he could have sworn that she rolled her shoulders and dropped her hip—only the slightest movements, but provocative, erupting out of memories, not imagination.

"It's a most what, Kate?"

She looked up at him as though surprised to see him

and then thoroughly pleased. "The dance. It's a wonderment."

"Are you saying that you've witnessed this ... dance yourself?"

She bit her lower lip and nodded. "I've actually danced it."

Bloody hell! His wife, dancing like a pagan spirit. "When?"

"Two years ago." The memory must be fresh. "Just before you and I were married."

"You danced naked and oiled?"

"And well veiled. Not exactly acceptable in a London ballroom, I know, but it's the custom of the Abasanti. So I would have felt out of place if I hadn't worn the costume."

"Or not worn it! Dancing naked until ... good God, woman!"

"Dancing until I thought it best to step out of the line and let the others find their joy."

Joy! Now there's a euphemism. "You didn't finish the dance?"

"Heavens, no. I'm not Abasanti. It wouldn't be proper." Untouched, if he could believe her. And she was not capable of that kind of dishonesty.

"Christ, Kate. I've seen these primitive affairs myself, and—"

"Then you know how the Abasanti end their fertility ceremony?"

"I sure as hell do."

She smiled and then sat back in her chair and sighed deeply, sadly. "It's too bad, really, because I had been hoping that you and I would try the dance ourselves one night."

"What?" The word stopped halfway out.

"It would have been fun, Jared. You and me and a bonfire in the woods. If we had stayed married."

"What?" He could only watch as she lifted a trio of long, buttery carrots onto his plate.

"Not outdoors then, a hearth would have done, or a candle. And a music box. I already have the scented oil."

"Do you know what you're proposing, Kate?" His blood leaped at this unfettered streak in his bride.

She spooned a few carrots onto her own plate. "To dance with you in the moonlight." She laughed brightly.

"God, Kate, have you a proper bone anywhere in your body?"

"I don't know what you mean. Proper?" She sat down in her chair, her jouncing making the carrot roll off the serving spoon. It hit the edge of her plate and landed on the blade of her bread knife.

"How do I begin counting your improprieties, Kate? They are legion." Deciding that the urge to bury himself in her softness was dangerously near to winning, Jared spun away from her.

"How do you mean? I know very well how to conduct myself in society. At a ball or the opera. I play the pianoforte and I sing."

"How did you find the time to learn? You were raised at sea, traveled the desert with barbarians, which is doubtless where you learned to wear trousers." Though God alone knew how she had contrived to turn an elegant manor house into an orphanage.

Feeling safely distant again, he turned back just in time to see her stick a tine of her fork into the wayward carrot then lift the tip of it to her mouth.

"I'm sorry, Jared. But I don't consider any of my behavior improper."

But, God, she was. Oh, so very improper. Exotic and wonderful.

And his. If he played the right cards, in the right order.

He stared, gaped, as she drew the tip of that fat, butter-glistening carrot between her lips.

His bones ached, his penis raged with lust for her, a weather vane, a thick iron rod to her mystic, magnetic north; it wanted her.

He wanted her.

He watched the carrot disappear inch by inch into her mouth, in tiny succulent nibbles, while her gaze wandered his face, innocent of guile, but flushed with passion.

His throat had dried with his feral breathing, but he managed the best warning he could, considering the rawness of his nerves. "Here's my situation, Kate. If you don't stop with your talk of dancing naked, and your manipulation of that lucky vegetable as though it were part of me, then I can offer you two choices."

He saw her swallow, admired the long column of her throat as she sat upright. "And they are?"

"That one of us leave the room immediately—"

She frowned fiercely at that choice, which pleased him. "Or?"

"That I take my marital rights here and now."

She blinked at him, touched her lips with her fingers. "I'm quite sure you wouldn't."

"Don't tempt me."

"You wouldn't without my permission, no matter how tempted. Or how much you bluster about it. I've learned that much about you. And that speaks volumes about a man's character. And I'm counting on your character, Jared. Counting on it in so many ways." She grinned at him from across the table and his blood surged again, his erection harder than ever, determined to have its way.

As eager as he was to delve deeply into this woman who hunted whale and rode with warlords—

And wished for him to dance naked with her in the moonlight.

Kate wondered if she hadn't taken this whole ruse a little too far. Because the only thing going through her mind at the moment was:

You'd look so very fine dancing naked in the moonlight, husband.

Sleek.

Glistening.

Corded and bronze.

Standing there in his fine wool jacket and his crisp white linen shirt, a tiger ready to spring.

Wondrously fine!

Not that she could risk saying that just now without accepting the explosive consequences. She wanted to be his wife in every possible way. But the children had to come first, no matter what.

And the *Katie Claire* was docked in Mereglass with

her pilfered cargo. Another hour and the ship would be safely out of the harbor, heading toward Dublin.

And in the meantime Kate might find herself breeched and boarded and her plans foundering.

"Your carrots are getting cold, Jared." Her nerves jangling, flushed to the tips of her ears, Kate leaped from her chair to the sideboard to serve the peas.

"Damn the carrots." He began stalking slowly toward her, an utterly untameable look in his dark eyes. "You never cease to amaze me."

He was wearing that intoxicating smile again, the one he wore just as he was about to kiss her, his finely sculpted lips parted and hungry looking.

"About what?"

"You were wearing a prim bonnet when we married." He threaded his warm fingers through the hair at her temple. "But you are the most brazen woman I've ever met."

"And you looked like a scallywag at the time, hardly a merchant or a stone-headed, prudish advisor to the queen."

"Or a spy." He arched a dark brow then took a long breath. "You were right, by the way."

It took Kate a moment before she realized what he meant. "You're a spy for the queen?"

"And for the Home Office and the admiralty and at the prime minister's discretion."

The Home Office? Her husband spied for Lord Grey? "You must be joking."

"Not a bit. Which took me aback the other day when you announced my secret to the entire staff."

Kate backed away for a better look at him, the devil in her midst. "Why didn't you stop me?"

"I tried."

"Not hard enough." On top of everything else, her plans and schemes, she might have put his life in real danger. "You let me babble on. You should have throttled me."

"I should have kissed you." He reached out to her, cradled the back of her head between his large hands. "God knows I haven't done that nearly enough."

His dark eyes were shining, his teeth glinting white through his wicked smile, his cheeks warm and his mouth a dazzling heat against hers.

She was deeply hungry for this, for him, her husband and spy, for his breath to mingle with hers as he delved deeply with his tongue and danced with hers.

"That is a fine claret, Jared." She felt him smile against her cheek, then against her mouth. "Rosy." A kiss. "And rich." Another kiss.

"And you're buttery sweet, wife." This one low at the base of her throat where her pulse raced and his fingers played at the buttons at the front of her shirtwaist. Unfastening the top one and then the next few fell before she could lodge a feeble protest.

"Where are you going, Jared?"

"Inside," he said, dipping his head, following his fingers with his mouth until he was hovering between her breasts, kissing her there.

Inside! Dear heavens, she was in way over her head with this foolish plan to keep him occupied.

"I really shouldn't let you. . . ." But there she went,

slipping her fingers through his hair at his nape and pulling him closer to this heady danger.

"Oh, yes we should. I should have come back to you months ago." The brazen man laced his fingers beneath her backside like a sling, then dropped with her into the chair she'd just been sitting in, landing her in his lap.

"I didn't really mean to go this far." So very, very far, that she had now slipped her legs around his waist and was straddling him in a thoroughly indelicate pose.

And feeling like a princess riding her knight, nuzzling at his neck and squirming her bottom against his thighs.

"I mean us to go much farther than this, Kate." He was taking such blatant advantage of her position on his lap, slowly unfastening another button on her shirt and another. . . .

And she wasn't trying very hard to stop him, this delicious man who could scuttle her plans. "We can't, Jared."

"Beautiful, Kate." He drew his thumb across her nipple and she found herself gasping from the pleasure, laughing in little breathless bursts.

Her heart was a muddle of wanting him, his hot, heavy body, of wishing the impossible and knowing this wasn't wise.

This wondrous intimacy with him. When it had no future.

And still she let him draw aside her shirt at her shoulder, let his mouth pull and tug and travel a giddy path along her collarbone, while his warm fingers teased and taunted.

"Please, Jared!" Now she was begging for more, enchanted by a deep yearning for him that had smoldered inside her since that day on the deck of the *Cinnabar*.

Their wedding day. So brief and confusing, and now this uncontrolled wanting, when she knew that she shouldn't.

That she couldn't possibly.

"This isn't working, Jared."

He murmured against her throat, still teasing at her breast with his fingers, making her gasp and tug at his shoulders. "It's working fine, wife. Don't know how it could be working any finer."

"Please—"

"Unless we were in that big bed in the next room, and even then I don't think it would matter. You couldn't taste better than—"

"No! Stop!" This wasn't right. She couldn't go on playing him the fool. Not even for the sake of the *Katie Claire*. There must be other ways to distract him. She scrambled off his lap, the cool air hitting her nearly bare chest like a fist. She started buttoning up her shirt. "I can't, Jared! There are still too many differences between us."

He remained in the chair, a caged bear, breathing like a stag and glaring at her. "Not this, certainly. We plainly want each other."

"But I want a family I can love and respect in all things." Not knowing what else to do with her hands,

Kate finished serving the peas with a sharp clank of the spoon.

His brow dipped in a look of dismay. "You don't respect me, Kate?"

"Not in the way I would dearly love to."

And the potatoes.

"I don't know what to say to that."

She couldn't bring herself to look at him, because she couldn't muster much respect for herself at the moment.

"There's not much to say, except that your supper is ready." And she had to stay here with him. To keep an eye on his activities.

To offer up herself completely should he suddenly insist on going to the village.

But he didn't insist, only glared and snorted and shook his head at her. They ate a cooling supper together, played a game of cribbage. She read an entire issue of the *Hearth and Heath* gazette cover to cover while he went to work on his snowbank of papers from Lord Grey.

Sometime during the long evening, the mood between them became more comfortable, the fire warmer, the brandy richer, sweeter. He never touched her again, but she could feel him as though they were skin to skin. She must have fallen asleep in the chaise, because she woke up near dawn lying on his bed.

She was still in her clothes, draped by a silken counterpane, Jared snoozing on the pillow beside her, boyishly innocent and dashingly masculine at the same time.

A dangerous combination with so much at stake.

Regretting that so many things had turned out so very badly, Kate slipped out of bed and made her way toward Hawkesly Hall, leaving a good part of her heart at Badger's Run.

Chapter 17

"Gone again!" Jared glared at the empty place in the bed beside him, the dent in Kate's pillow.

Stubborn, befuddling woman.

She'd sprung his courting trap then escaped to God knew where. But not for long. He planned to spend his day with her, whether she liked it or not. To tag along in her adventures, with the rowdy orphans or without.

He could take it.

Pembridge had yet to get back to him on the particulars of their placement, but that sort of thing took time. He'd instructed the man to check on the living conditions himself. That too would take time. But would smooth the way for Kate to accept what was best for her orphans.

He dressed for the cool morning and was just heading down the stairs when the treads beneath his boots gave a sharp shake.

And then a great booming sound rocked the walls.

Then the ceiling and the prisms hanging from the sconces on the landing started to dance.

Cannon fire!

"Bloody hell!"

Booooommm!

And another! A twenty-four-pound mortar if he'd ever heard one.

Coming from the north, near the sea cliff.

Holy hell! Suddenly terrified for Kate, he took the stairs three at a time and sped toward the stables.

"Are we under attack, my lord?" Corey's eyes were saucers, even as he handled the saddle with the unshakable ease of a seasoned soldier.

"I'm going to find out, Corey." Who would be shelling his estate? And from where? The sea? And *why*?

He hoped to hell that Kate was well out of range. And the children! Please keep the wily little scamps at the hall and out of harm's way.

Jared mounted the bay moments later, and galloped north toward the barren cliffs, where the barrage seemed to have come from.

He followed the main road for nearly a mile under a dark, blustering sky before he was almost knocked from the saddle by the roar of another shot.

He must be nearly on the weapon, could even see the smoke rising from above the scrub and the scree at the base of the treeless cliffside. He turned off the main road into a narrow, recently traveled lane, ignoring the foolish chance that he was taking.

He knew better than to gallop headlong into danger, but this attack was different, some kind of madness.

Smugglers? Gun runners?

Completely stumped, Jared dropped silently from the saddle and secured the bay's reins to a tree. Then he crept along the line of brambles until he heard voices.

One a gruff male voice and then a lighter baritone and then . . . Kate?

Captured? Kidnapped? A stone dropped into the pit of his stomach. Fearing the very worst, seeing only the slightest movement through the thickness of the underbrush, Jared threw himself into the clearing, ready for anything.

Anything but Kate, and a six-inch-carriage cannon, Elden, a fizzing torch, Magnus Rooney and an awe-struck audience of children scattered a hundred feet behind her in the trees. She was wearing those bloody trousers, an oversized coat, and a flop-brimmed hat.

What the devil was she doing?

"Stand away, children!" she shouted.

The lunatic was about to fire off another volley!

"Cover yer ears, ya little dodgers!" Magnus shouted.

"Firing now!" Kate then touched the torch to the fuse, turned away and covered her own ears. Five seconds of sizzling silence later the cannon went off.

Kabooom!

The children squealed. And Jared followed the object's trajectory, a high and wide arc that ought to look like a cannonball in flight, but wasn't at all.

It seemed to be a large ball of wad, and as he watched, it broke open suddenly, then exploded into a dark brown cloud above the rocks and brush, about as far up the sharply banked hillside as it could go. Whatever the cloud was made of started falling to earth and made Kate leap for joy.

"It's going to work fine!"

Another round of cheers echoed across the hillside.

Jared was on the woman in the next second, grabbing the torch from her hand and turning her to face him with the other. "What the devil do you think you're doing, Kate?"

She frowned in a thin line. "I'll ask the same of you."

"Then sorry, madam! Don't mind me! I'm just out here looking to see who was firing on Hawkesly Hall with a six-inch cannon!"

"Hawkesly Hall is quite safe. I know what I'm doing."

"Then please tell *me*, so that I'll know too."

She yanked her wrist out of his hand. "I'm planting Douglas fir seeds."

"I want the truth, Kate." A vein in his forehead began to throb. "Are you planning to pitch a battle against Parliament?"

"Now, that's a fine idea. But I'm busy at the moment planting seeds."

"No, Kate, you were firing off a cannon."

"Like they've been doing on plantations in Scotland for nearly a hundred years."

"Planting?" By God, the woman looked utterly truthful, with the sudden wind lifting her hair and scattering the leaves that littered the rocky ground.

Unconvinced, because she'd played him the fool too many times before, because it was all so absurd, he went to the wagon near the stand of willows and pulled out one of the wads.

And found a six inch diameter silk pouch packed tightly with fir seeds. He turned back to her scowling, stunned and amazed at the woman's devices.

"And this is how you plan to plant this hillside? By bombing it with balls of seed?"

"That's exactly how Nature does it, if you think about it. Branches fling the seeds from the cones into the wind from hundreds of feet in the air. So it makes perfect sense to use a cannon to do the same thing if you haven't any trees yet." She pointed behind him into the sky. "Especially when a big storm is going to be blowing in off the sea, bringing lots of rain to soak the seeds and help them to germinate. The conditions couldn't be better."

She was explaining all this as though it made sense in her eccentric world. "But with a cannon?"

"Brilliant, isn't it?"

As though to prove that she held the power of nature in her hands, the wind whipped up again, stirring the leaves and sending a cloud bank scudding across the sun.

"Are you mad? You could have been killed!"

She stepped back and laughed with an indulgent amusement. "Don't be ridiculous."

"Dammit, Kate, there's nothing ridiculous about blowing yourself up or those children!"

A crack of far-off thunder drew her eyes away toward the peak, then she turned to Magnus and Elden.

"Hurry, Magnus! Let's move the cannon on to the next site before the storm makes land."

"Stop right there, Kate!" Jared grabbed her hand when she would have reached for the cannon hitch. "That cannon's not going anywhere."

"Please, let's not argue. The seed needs to be scattered before the storm comes. It's my best chance for the forest to take root this fall."

"I'm not going to let you use a cannon—more's the point, woman, where the devil did you get it?"

She flicked a brow. "In the village, behind the smithy. It's apparently off an old ship. I didn't think you'd mind. I cleaned it up and made it fit to—"

"*You* did? You repaired a cannon?"

"Cleaned and oiled the barrel and the wheels. And cleared the fuse channel. You saw for yourself, it fires just fine, though it does pull a bit to the right."

"What the hell gave you the notion that you know anything at all about cannons?"

She drew back again, amused again. "I'll admit that I've never been tested in the thick of battle, but I served for years on my father's ships. I can clean, load, and fire any one of a dozen different cannons, with my eyes closed. So if you'll pardon me . . ."

"You're not going anywhere!" He hadn't bargained for this kind of wife, one who believed that all children should be cherished, who fired off cannons and . . . and danced naked in the moonlight.

But he did want her, wanted everything about her. The brightness of her eyes and this unorthodox tree-planting scheme.

But, blast it all, how much courting was a man expected to do?

"Please let me finish the job. It's the last thing I'll ever ask of you."

He doubted that, but as he studied her more carefully, the cannon and the wads of seed and the steep hillside, the plan began to lose some of its folly.

"You learned of this technique where?"

"From the Highland company that sold me seeds."

"Bloody, crazy Scots."

"They were very specific and I followed every step of their instructions."

He couldn't believe he was even considering this. "And the seed isn't harmed in the blast?"

"Not if it's packed specially to keep the heat away from the seed itself."

Still he couldn't quite believe that shooting fir seeds worked, so he nodded up the hillside. "Show me then."

"Very well." She begrudged him a tight smile with those luscious lips, then said, "Go on ahead of us, Magnus. Set up and then wait for me. Children, you stay there in the woods until I call you."

The little wide-eyed mob had been so quietly behaved, or so utterly terrorized, that he'd nearly forgotten they were there.

She started up the hillside, battling the wind that rose up the mountain, that lifted the brim of her hat and the loose strands of her hair.

He followed her, admiring the unorthodox view, her coattails flapping, the shape of her thighs, her backside shifting beneath her tweed trousers as she clambered up the incline.

She stopped abruptly about a hundred feet up and picked up a seed, holding it out to him as he approached. "See, Jared, unharmed and ready for the rain."

He inspected the seed for damage, its color and shape and its wing. He looked down into her eager face. "The fact that there's no damage doesn't lessen the reality that this is a lunatic idea."

"Give this hillside three years of sun and rain, and these little brown seeds will be trees as tall as your knees. Good enough to harvest ten years after that. I think that's pretty miraculous."

He felt an odd stinging at the backs of his eyes. "You've got too much in that pretty head of yours, Kate."

"Are you going to let me continue?" She waited for him to speak.

"Under my supervision."

Her little sigh made him feel barely tolerated. "All right, then, but we'd best hurry. Mrs Driscoll's elbow has been giving her pains."

"Which means?"

"The storm will be here by late afternoon. And it's looking to be a big one."

"Come quick, Lady Kate!" Grady was standing below them, waving his hands. "The seed wagon's stuck."

"Don't move it, Grady!"

So much for supervising, he thought as the woman started loping down the hillside, as agile as a mountain goat, beating him to the bottom.

She was already under the tailgate, consulting with Magnus. "Looks like the axle has split in the center, so the wheels bind up when it tries to move."

"I'll go fetch another wagon," Magnus said.

Kate sighed as she rolled out from under the wagon and looked up the threatening sky. "Which puts us well into the early afternoon."

"Possibly not," Jared said, waving Grady over. "You, there!"

"Yessir!"

Forever amazed at the boy's good-natured eagerness, Jared lifted a bulging wad of silk out of a keg in the wagon bed. "Think you can carry a few of these to the next spot?"

The boy smiled and stuck out his arms. "Give 'em over, sir."

Jared had loaded four of the wads into Grady's arms, when he heard the other boys running toward them from the woods.

"I c'n take more 'n that, sir!" Grady said, eyeing the friends who swarmed around them.

"Me too!"

"And me!"

"If you all take care," Jared said, looking up to find his wife shaking her head at him.

"Follow Magnus, then, lads," she said to the boys as Jared loaded up their arms with the bags of seed.

"There, you see, Kate," he said as soon as the children were well out of hearing, "they seem to enjoy working, as any boy does."

Kate's condemning frown returned, harder this time. "Hawkesly Hall is not a parish farm, Jared. Or any kind of an orphanage. It's their home." Her eyes lost their fire. "At least it was. Now let's get on with the planting, while we still can."

The hare-brained woman then picked up an entire keg of gunpowder and staggered off after the others, her knees bowing under the weight, her shoulders sagging.

"I'll take that," Jared said, catching up to her and lifting the keg onto his shoulder.

"I can do it!"

"Not as well as I can. Now go back and get the torch and the flint."

He left her standing on the rock-strewn path, wondering how she was going to react when he refused to allow her to go running off with her orphans.

"You're a monster, Lord Hawkesly!"

Then an acorn bounced off the back of his head.

No, she wasn't going to take the news at all well.

Could she possibly chew through rope, he wondered? God knows she would try.

Damnation! What the hell was he going to do with her?

Jared continued to monitor the storm through the afternoon. It brewed slowly, rainless, but increasingly windy until the clouds piled up darkly against the mountain and the first isolated drops began to fall at exactly four o'clock, just as Mrs. Driscoll's elbow had predicted.

"Just this last shot, Jared, and we'll be finished!" Kate shouted over the wind and the splatting rain as she bent to light the fuse. But she paused there again too long, too close to the cannon.

"Stand back, Kate!" Jared reached out for her, then hauled her backward against him as the cannon fired.

It went off at the same time as a satisfying crack of thunder, the pair of sounds echoing across the cliff face and tumbling down the swale.

"Isn't it marvelous!" She pointed up at the explosion of seed as the wild wind took hold of it and tossed it against the steely-gray clouds.

"Indeed." A provocative, powerful sight, even in the half light, with his untried bride shaping her back against his chest, her round, perfect bottom tucked up against his groin and the front of his thighs.

They'd sent Magnus and Elden back to the hall with the children to outrun the storm, and now Jared was alone with this unorthodox woman, thinking randy thoughts about her and the dark woods behind them.

"At least you'll think of me, Jared, whenever you look toward the hills and its sea of green."

"Think of you? What makes you believe that I would ever stop?" He turned her in his arms as a huge glob of rain landed on his shoulder.

"The forest that will grow here someday—you'll remember me by it when I'm long gone and out of your hair."

"You're not—" The rest of Jared's reply blew back against his mouth with a blast of wind and rain as the sky dashed against them.

"Come," he shouted, grabbing her around the shoulders and leading her toward the shelter of the trees and the place he had left his horse.

"The cannon." She stopped and tried to wriggle away. "And the powder."

A blinding blast of lightning bored into the side of the peak above them, the crack of thunder too close and nearly deafening them.

"Leave it. I'll buy you another." As many as she wanted. He gave a yank on her hand and she followed him deeper into the forest.

They slipped and slid through the brambles of the sloping woods as the sky lit up behind them and the thunder rolled down the hill.

Jared had lost a mast or two at sea in sudden, unpredictable storms just like this one, but he'd never been quite so concerned about taking cover, about safety.

Her safety, whether she cared or not. Though she sprinted through the underbrush and between the oak and alder like a gazelle across the Kalahari.

And he could have sworn that he'd seen the glint of her smile more than once, and her delighted laughter among the peals of thunder.

"There's the horse, Jared!" The huge bay seemed unconcerned about the storm, and stood steadfastly as he mounted, then dragged Kate up behind the saddle.

"Hold on, wife!" Reveling in the heated feeling of Kate slipping her arms around his waist, pressing her chest against his back, Jared gave the horse a heel and started along the road just as the sky opened up with a drenching downpour.

"Lord, I love a good storm!" she shouted into the wildly swirling air, pulling herself more tightly against him.

"And a good dance in the moonlight, I hear?"

"You heard right, Hawkesly." Her laughter rippled along his ribs and lodged in his groin. "Now to the hall, please. I need a bath."

Now, there's an enchanting idea!

The image of Kate standing naked and glistening in a bath rode just ahead of Jared, dragging him hard against the wind. He galloped up to the entrance of Hawkesly Hall with his beautiful wife drenched to the skin and clinging to him.

"You needn't carry me," she said against his ear as he lifted her down from the saddle.

"My pleasure, I assure you." He raced up the stone staircase, his head filled with plans of courting and seduction, soap and warm water, and Kate.

But his fantasy vanished the moment he carried her over the threshold and right into a sea of children.

"Is Lady Kate hurt, Lord Jared?"

"What happened to your legs, Lady Kate?"

"Why are you all wet?"

Kate looked up at him with a wan smile. "You've been most gallant, my lord."

"A lot of good it's done me." Jared reluctantly set her on her feet, clearly recalling his vow that morning to follow her through her day and wondering how he'd survive it.

He cleaned up down the hall from the master's suite which he and Kate ought to be sharing, stole a listen at the door to her bedchamber as she splashed around in the tub while regaling Rosemary with tales of shooting off the cannon.

He ate supper with his knees crammed against the

underside of the shortest table in the kingdom, and finally dozed off in the library to the third reading of the *Brave Little Tailor*.

"Are you sleeping here tonight, Jared?"

He woke with a start, lying on his back on the carpet, nose to nose with his wife. Close enough to kiss her and so he did. Pulling her mouth gently to his, just in case she got away. Or was a dream. Or a phantom.

"Am I what?" he asked, nibbling on her softness.

"It's after eleven and I'm off to bed. Are you going back to Badger's Run, or will you be sleeping here?"

"With you?"

"No room. I've got Dori and Mera and Mr. McNair with me tonight."

"I should have guessed." He sat up, his head stuffy with sleep. "Off with you, then. I'll go back to the lodge in a few minutes."

She straightened and studied him with her impatient goodness. "You're not a half-bad man. A few lessons would do you a world of good." She bent and kissed his forehead, then left him to the dimness of the library.

Lessons be damned. His body as exhausted as his soul, he lay back for just a moment, and then dropped off like a rock.

He awakened to the sound of little voices whispering above him. And then a huge tongue washed over his face.

"Mr. McNair!"

"Good morning, Lord Jared!" came the full chorus.

He swabbed his face dry with his sleeve and then found a half dozen pairs of eyes staring cheerily at him.

"Lady Kate was going to meet you at Badger's Run," Grady said. "Boy is she going to be surprised."

Not half as surprised as he was: At the ache in his bones, or the larger one in his heart as a bolt of laughter rumbled out of his chest.

Chapter 18

❝**I** think I've packed enough clothes for the children, Elden.❞ Kate inventoried the contents of the trunk one last time, then fastened it tightly before helping Elden slide it into the back of the wagon.

"Two wagon loads of clothes and shoes and blankets and food for nine little ones seems plenty to me."

"Until they each grow another two inches." Thunder rumbled off the sea and up the little valley, signaling the second storm since three days ago, when they had planted the hillside.

More rain meant damp trunks, even with canvas covers for the wagons. So she'd wait a day or two more until the weather cleared and then leave Hawkesly Hall for a place of safety with the children.

She'd hidden the wagons and their cargo from Jared in the meadow barn because the man wouldn't understand. He hadn't come right out and said it, but she knew that he would never willingly let her leave him or their marriage. Despite his worldly travels, he lived by traditions. And a wife belonged at home, cleaving to her husband, no matter how wrong-headed he was, or how badly they fit together.

Or how grand she felt to be in his powerful arms.

"We need to be getting back to the hall, Elden, before his lordship comes looking for us and finds our contraband."

"Better that he finds a few trunks of clothes, my lady, than a half dozen warehouses filled with grain stolen from your dearest enemies."

"Lord Grey will never miss a grain of it. At least his children won't starve for the lack of it. The bloody bastard." She helped Elden drape the canvas over the trunks. She was just locking the door when a voice rose over the growing wind.

"Lady Kaaaaa-thryn!"

"That's Ian. Here we are!" she shouted, hurrying out into the lane where he could see them in the coming darkness.

He came running toward them from around the bend, his eyes widening when he saw her. "My lady!"

"Great heavens, Ian, what is it? One of the children?" Her stomach was already knotted with fear.

"Not that. A boat's having trouble out in the bay. They think it's the *Fairheart*."

"Father Sebastian's little longboat?" Nothing more than a launch with a sail. Hardly a boat at all, especially in a storm like this. "Dear God, Ian! I hope he doesn't have children with him this time."

"What shall we do?"

"Ride to the lodge, Ian. Tell Lord Hawkesly and Magnus that I'll meet them in Mereglass. Elden, go to the hall and let them know what's happened. I'll take my mare."

Minutes later she was galloping down the road toward the village, wishing that the light weren't fading so quickly and praying for the wind to settle and the waves to carry the little boat safely into Abbey Cove and not onto the rocky headland.

She rode hard against the wind, made the crowded quay a half hour later. Dozen of villagers watched the longboat inching its way toward disaster, a tiny, dark shape in the steely-gray half light.

"Did you see it, Connell? Is it the *Fairheart*?"

"Certain of it, my lady," Connell said, tossing a rope to his son on the lower dock. "Gibson's boys were up on the old abbey ruins collecting gull eggs and saw the boat enter the mouth of the bay just as the storm come in."

"Fought against the wind and that damn tidal current for such a long time without goin' anywhere," Avery shouted from below, clamping his arm across his cap, "then the boat just give up its mast and its sail."

"Now it's adrift, my lady. Sure to run up onto the rocks out there on the point. An' the tide's rising fast."

Please, not again.

The storm had paused in its rampage, opening a large hole in the west of the sky, letting the bright, placid moon limn the violent sea and the cliffs and the darkly forbidding promontory opposite the village.

Kate could barely see the boat for the depth of the waves and crashing surf so near it. She could feel it being drawn up against the ragged rocks.

"Did the Gibson boys see anyone on board?"

"Four or five, maybe. Too small to be sailors or fishermen."

"Then Father Sebastian has children with him."

"Me and Avery thought we'd get as close as we can. Pluck some out of the water."

"Dear God, look!" As Kate had spoken the words, the little boat seemed to lose any kind of will. The next wave lifted it a dozen feet into the air, spun it, and then swallowed it inside a foaming curtain.

Everyone on the quay ran toward the edge, watching in horror as the waves sunk away from the ragged ledge in a frothing rage and left the little boat wedged among the rocks.

"I'm going out there to the point. Connell, you and Avery, do whatever you can to rescue anyone. But please don't risk yourselves."

"Now, where's the fun in that, my lady! You just be careful yourself!"

Kate gathered two other men and as many ropes and lanterns as they could round up then rode along the rocky rise toward the cliffside and the point beyond it.

The cliffs jutted out into the sea like a gnarled, thick-knuckled finger, curving like a claw, narrowing as it stepped down to a flattened shelf where it finally reached the water.

As she galloped along the path at the base of the

High Watch crags, she kept her eye on the boat, holding her breath with every crashing wave as the vessel pitched and rolled in its precarious perch.

More terrifying, she couldn't see a soul inside.

Kate led the rescue party across the flat, grassy plane of the upper ledge and then drew up the horses as near to the edge as they dared, fighting the slashing wind that was trying to push them backward.

"Do you see anything, Wallace?" Kate shouted, looking desperately for any sign of life, inside the longboat or bobbing on the surface.

"Nothing, my lady."

A wave swelled and loosened the boat slightly, then shoved it harder into the rocks, tipping the stern toward them before the surf crashed again.

But the sight had left Kate's heart soaring. "They were still there, Wallace. Did you see them? Three, at least. Clinging together in the bow."

Wallace swabbed his eyes with his coat sleeve. "'At's what I saw too, my lady."

"Thank God! Can you tie the lantern to something, Ben? Let them know we're coming." Give them some hope to hold on tightly to.

Wallace crawled closer to the edge and hung over it slightly. "Looks like we're gonna have to climb down this cliff face to that flat area there," he said.

"About twenty, twenty-five feet," Kate said from beside him. "But it's the only way to get anywhere near the boat."

"Right, then, Lady Hawkesly. I'll get—"

"No, I'm going down there, Wallace."

Wallace grabbed her by the elbow. "Oh, no you're

not, if you don't mind me sayin', my lady. His lordship would have m'hide if anything should happen to you. I'll go."

"I won't let you, Wallace. I'm the lighter of us three." She wrapped a rope around her waist. "You and Ben will have to stay up here and act as anchors."

Ben had managed to wedge the lantern into a crag just below them and must have heard the last of Kate's orders. "You're right, Wallace, Hawkesly will kill us."

Kate handed Ben the end of her rope. "Tie yourself to the other end of mine, Ben. In case it gets rough out there."

"In case it's rough? It ain't hardly gonna get any rougher!"

"Use the other ropes if you need to add more length. Wallace, you do the reining for me; I'll give a yank when I need more rope."

"I'm beggin' you to let me do it, my lady."

"Just hold tightly and guide me, Wallace. As soon as you have another man to spare, secure him with a rope and send him down! I'll need help with the children."

Kate knew the cliff well enough to start over the side without pausing longer than the realization that the landscape was vastly different now in the stormy dark than it had been when she brought the children here in the daylight to play in the tidepools.

Only this time she was climbing straight down the hard way, rather than having the luxury of waiting for low tide and the strip of sandy shore that exposed itself along the base of the cliff on a sunny afternoon in July.

"Down, Mr. Wallace!" She straddled the wide rocky columns of basalt, leaping from side to side as Wallace and Ben let out the rope a few feet at a time.

"Yeeouuch!" Though she only whispered it, as the wind shoved at her suddenly and her boot wedged for a moment between two rocks before she bounced away.

"I'm down!" she shouted as she felt solid rock beneath her feet. She turned from the cliffside, bracing herself against the wind.

There it was! Should be as easy as that to rescue the passengers. A hundred feet in front of her: the underside of the bow projecting just above the edge at a dangerous angle. Thankfully still in one piece, though no sign of people from this vantage point.

"Father Sebastian!" Kate shouted for him, but the wind stole her words.

She put her head down and shouldered forward into the blinding gale. But the few yards she gained had only shoved her sharply sideways as she battled the stinging salt spray and the driving wind.

The sea seemed to rise with a sudden surge and a towering wave hit the promontory broadside, washing over the rocks and knocking her flat, skidding her across the rugged surface toward the edge.

And plunging her right over the side, her motion slowed, and her thoughts so oddly clear:

Jared isn't going to be at all happy with me.

"Where's my wife, Mercer?" Jared pulled the fisherman closer, certain he'd heard wrong in all the noise and chaos on the quay.

The man pointed into the dark bay. "There, my lord, you see that light out on the point? They musta put up a lantern on the cliff."

"They?"

Magnus had told him only that there was a foundering vessel out there somewhere, and Ian had said to tell him that she was on her way to the village.

Doubtless to supervise the rescue.

With her hands tied behind her back.

"She's out there, my lord!" Mrs. Foster from the inn tugged on his sleeve. "Out on the point where the boat's grounded itself."

"On the point?" Hell, all he could see was a black, glistening cliff and the frothy white breakers pounding at the rocks. "She's out there?"

"With Wallace and Ben, I hear. Must be them just below the light, sir."

Lunatic woman! "I need my horse. And as many hands as we can muster."

He was on the road short minutes later, followed by a half dozen able-bodied men. Most of the villagers were already perched along the rim of the bayside cliff, helpless, despondent, eager for someone to act.

"Here's another lantern, Lord Hawkesly."

"Hurry, help them, if you can!"

"And your lady."

Kate! She was an impossible woman to protect. The wind gave a tear at his coattail, driving the cold and wet into his bones like a dread.

He grabbed the lantern and kept riding, his gut churning, replaying his last moments with her.

That blissful assurance that they fit perfectly together, that he would easily be able to change her mind about things.

As he approached the high-shouldered, jutting head-

land he could just barely make out two dark figures sil-
houetted against the edge of the cliff, standing a few
yards apart, both far too large to be Kate.

"Where is she?" He flung himself off the horse and
ran the rest of the way.

"Mighty glad to see you, your lordship!"

"Don't tell me you let her go over the side."

Jared steeled himself against the buffeting winds, his
gaze following the sharp play of the rope from Wallace's hands into the darkness, where it dipped and
bent around a huge, slick-backed rock below and then
across the moonlit surface.

"She's a bullheaded thing, your wife is, sir. Almost
lost her once over the side, but we've got a good hold of
her now."

"Bloody hell!" With nothing but a rope keeping her
from being tossed into the raging ocean.

"See her there, my lord?"

He panicked for a moment, his heart stopped as he
searched the crags, never to beat again if he lost her.

And then there she was in the sheeting rain, struggling her way across the shiny surface of the rocky shelf
toward the longboat that teetered on the edge.

"Keep it steady, men. I'm going down there." Jared
wrenched on his gloves and grabbed hold of Wallace's
rope, following it hand over fist down the face of the
cliff, leaping the last half dozen feet.

"Kate!" Hell, she couldn't possibly have heard him
in the howling wind. "Hold on, you little fool!"

His little fool.

His heart.

He followed the rope and rounded the massive rock only to run right into the full, blinding, battering force of the wind and a sudden surge of the sea that shoved him back against the rock.

He looked up from under his sleeve and saw Kate straight ahead of him, but too close to the edge. His heart leaped and he called out her name again.

An instant later she was gone, swept away by an enormous wave.

"My God, Kate!" Jared yanked hard on the rope as he followed it to the craggy edge, catching sight of her once as a wave lifted her above the rocks and then dropped her back into the sea.

The rope went blessedly taut; she was still tied to it. "Hold on!"

Jared braced his feet against the rocky edge and held fast to the rope, taking up yards and yards of slack as the sea rose again.

"Kate!" One more yank and she came toward him on a shoulder-high wave, shooting forward, both arms outstretched, riding the crest like a miracle served up from the deep.

"Jared!" Her eyes were wide with surprise when she hit him square in the chest and hung on. "I'm so glad you're here!"

Glad! Bloody understatement. He twisted as he went crashing to the hard ground, taking her full weight across his stomach.

He grabbed hold of her with his arms, so happy to see her that he could sing out loud, angry enough to spend the next week shouting at her. "You'll be glad, woman, that I don't turn you over my knee and paddle you for this foolishness."

But she was squirming to get up, even as the next wave skidded them a few feet.

"Later, if you must. The boat's getting loose!" The woman was already on her feet, tugging at the rope where he was lying on it.

"You're going back up where it's safe!" He stood and pointed to the promontory, saw more lanterns bobbing along the edge and that there were two other men roping their way down the cliff.

"Come, Jared!" His foolish wife was tearing at the rope around her waist, straining to get away from him.

"I'm not going to let you . . ."

"Father Sebastian!" She was staring at the boat, her eyes fixed on something.

"Are you mad?" Even as Jared shouted over the wind a wave dumped a stumbling curtain of water between them, knocking her off balance.

"He's right there, Jared!" She righted herself and pulled at the rope and his hand. "Don't you see!"

A thin, dark-clad figure was struggling to rise from the bow of the bedraggled little launch, a large bundle tucked under his arm.

"He's got one of the children!" Kate fought forward against the wind and the rope and Jared could do nothing but follow her, hoping to reach the man before his wife could leap into the foam.

"Katie, my darlin'!" the water-logged old man bellowed. "I knew you'd come."

"And you're a miracle worker, Father."

"Where the devil do you think you're going, Kate?" Jared tried to keep the boat in place as she clung to the starboard gunwale, leaning forward to look into the dark hull.

The damn thing was a disaster waiting to happen, on the brink of breaking up, the priest looking so exhausted that he couldn't stand, let alone help himself.

"How many, Father?"

"Two. And a babe." The priest had a child in his arms, maybe a boy, Lucas's size.

"Where are they?" Jared asked, not seeing anything else in the boat.

"She's under the seat, holding on like I told her to do. And the babe's basket is tied to the bench."

"You're coming out of there first, Father," Jared said, hoisting himself up onto the gunwale and taking hold of the man's bone-thin elbow. "Let's get him to the cliffside."

"Give me the child, Father," Kate said, taking the bundle and wrapping him in her arms as though they were the warmest of cloaks.

"He's Michael," the priest said, as though baptizing the boy on a quiet Sunday morning.

The bow pitched and rolled and Jared finally reached in and lifted the chatty old man from the boat.

"Take them both, Jared. I need the rope and they need your strength and your weight to make it across the flats to the other rescuers."

Damn woman was right. "You stay here, Kate. Don't move a muscle."

Kate knew she couldn't keep her promise, but agreed

anyway, anything to get Jared going. Anything to bring him back in time.

He'd been a kind of miracle himself.

Her handsome Neptune, guiding her safely out of the sea, there on the shore to catch her when she fell.

She held dutifully onto the bow and let him get far enough away that he couldn't see her well through the dark and the spray, then stepped up on a rock and hoisted herself over the gunwale into the boat.

"Hello, there? Come out. You'll be on dry land in just a moment."

"I'm too c-c-cold."

She barely heard the little voice, but it was a bright beacon to her in the shadows. A little moonlit face peered out from under the middle bench and she grabbed her up, wondering how she had survived the trip with so little meat on her bones.

"Damn it, woman, I told you not to move." Jared was half a leg over the gunwale.

"Here, Jared." Kate clawed her way up the thick, shuddering ribs of the inner hull to the bow with the little girl tucked under her arm. "Take her."

"Come out of there."

"Please, Jared." She raised up the child and he finally took her, his eyes hot in anger. "There's one more. The baby. I saw the basket tied beside the oarlock. Quick, before we lose the boat to the next wave."

"Stay put, Kate. Please." He disappeared into the spray with the girl in his arms.

And then Kate heard the terrifying scrape of the hull against the rocks.

A grating, sliding backward sound. As though the

ocean was suddenly draining out of the bay, sucking them downward.

"Hold on, little baby." She balanced herself and slid toward the bench, trying not to drive the boat backward any faster. She had to loosen the basket.

Or the baby.

He was a bundle of soaking wet blankets, a band of sheeting keeping the blankets inside the basket. She wrenched at the basket, but it clung to the bench. She finally yanked off the band and lifted the bundle from the basket.

"Come now, little love." She clutched the baby against her chest, riding out the force of a dousing wave against her back, wishing the child would move or cry, fearing the wet chill that seeped from the blankets.

"You'll be warm and dry soon. I promise." But just in case, she jerked the rope that was around her waist up far enough to secure the bundled child to her chest.

Before she could start for the bow, the sea disappeared suddenly. The boat lost its purchase on the rocks and slid backward for what seemed like hours.

The rope around her chest went slack and then just as suddenly taut as the stern finally smacked against the ledge below, throwing her to the floor with the baby.

"Kaaaaaate!" Jared's dark face appeared fifteen feet above her, the other end of the rope in his hands, wrapped around his waist. "For God's sake, hold on."

She heard the ocean surge from behind her, felt the boat begin to rise again. But this time the bow dipped and scraped along the rocks as it rose.

The wave shifted and the water swirled, wedging the

prow into a gap between two rocks. The surf gave another surge, sending the stern up and over Kate's head, and Kate into the churning water.

She closed her body around the baby, grabbed her knees and held her breath as the sea scraped her over the rocks.

Bring us up, Jared. Please, my love!

The last thing she remembered before the blackness blinded her with a slamming pain in the side of her head was the rope growing taut and a deep, bellowing voice.

"Kaaaaaate!"

Chapter 19

Kate had wild, terrifying dreams of swimming against the thundering wind, of bundles bobbing just out of reach.

And Jared calling to her.

Of his arms and his mouth.

Of being held back, restrained by harsh bands of rope, when there were children floating down the chalk streams.

Or were they fish? Bright-sided schools of rainbow trout, sunning themselves.

So very cold and then hot as a fire.

Pinpoints of light and deep darkness.

"Kate." The sound warmed her ears and her arms and lifted her.

And came again sometime later. Warmer now.

"Wake up, Kate."

That's the trouble, she wanted to tell him. *Jared, my husband, my eyelids don't work.*

"Sleep, Father. I'll watch her."

Somebody's father? Hers? Papa? Oh, she'd love to see him again. And talk to him about her wayward husband, what to do with him. Because she loved the stubborn man, for all his faults. Now, if she could only open her eyes before her father could float away from her, too.

If she could just move her arms.

She worked on this problem of making her limbs move again until she heard a steady, mechanical noise coming and going from somewhere nearby.

It came softly in the warmth and then went away again. Coming and going. Soothing, familiar.

Like snoring.

It *was* snoring.

Jared!

Kate opened her eyes to a blinding pain in her head and a whirling dizziness. And a bank of soft pillows.

She was in bed? Where? Then she remembered and her heart stopped cold.

There'd been a storm. And children in a boat. Dear God, where were they? And Jared?

She sat up slightly, peered into the near darkness and then understood. This was her own little bedchamber at Hawkesly Hall.

And there was Jared! Safely sprawled out asleep in a rocking chair right beside the bed, his legs propped on an ottoman, the entire, long length of his frame covered in a counterpane that bulged oddly above where his arms crossed below his belly.

But thank God, he was safe. Sleeping. She wanted to kiss him, to throw her arms around him and make sure he was real and alive, to get a better look at him.

She carefully raised the counterpane, surprised at how badly she ached and in so many places that even the shifting of her nightgown hurt. Undaunted, she slipped her legs over the side of the bed.

The movement cleared her head of its fog, sharpened the details of her memory, the terrifying storm and the helpless baby.

Dear lord, where was the poor cold thing? And the other children?

And Father Sebastian?

"You're a damn fool, Kate." Jared's deep voice crossed the short distance between them, and circled her heart with relief. He was looking at her from the chair, not moving at all, his eyes open and narrowed at her.

And whatever had landed the blow to the side of her head must have addled her brains, because under the bulging counterpane he looked as though he were . . . with child.

"I'm so glad you're safe, Jared." He made a low, disapproving sound in his throat. "What happened at the cliffs? Where is everyone?"

"Convenient that you can't remember."

Her stomach wrenched, remembering the child she'd tied to her chest. "Where's the baby?"

"You could have been killed, Kate."

"Tell me, please." His evasion terrified her; he was hiding something from her, some terrible truth. She scooted closer, her heart pounding and her head swirling. "What happened to the boat? To Father Sebastian? The baby! What are you hiding under there?"

She pointed to the counterpane and he moved his hand slowly up to the center of the lump, spreading his fingers wide. "The luckiest damned baby that ever was born of woman."

"The baby? Oh, Jared!" Kate slid her stiff fingers over his warm hand and felt the roundness. "You have the baby here? Dear God, then he's all right?"

"*She* is." He glared at her as though the storm had been her doing, and she happily glared right back.

"Can I see her?" Kate reached to pluck aside the corner of the blanket, but he caught her hand gently.

"Not till she's warmer." He put his lips to the back of her hand, placed a tender kiss there. "Doctor's orders. The little thing is still sapping the heat out of me by the bucketful."

Then she wasn't out of the woods yet. "Was she hurt badly? What about the other children?"

"Not a scratch anywhere. Thanks to you. Except that . . . Christ, Kate, there's nothing to them." He sighed and leaned his head back against the chair, his movements slow and careful. "Twigs for bones, not an ounce of fat."

Tears stung the corners of her eyes, clogging her throat, putting a quaver into her voice, a powerful, too familiar blend of sorrow and outrage.

"That's how they always come to me, Jared." He said nothing in reply. She stood up on the bed step, wobbling on her legs and surprised that the room could dip like the sea.

He held tightly to her wrist. "Where do you think you're going?"

"To see the other children."

"They're in good hands. It's three o'clock in the morning. Get yourself back into that bed immediately or I'll tie you to the headboard. I swear, I will."

He would probably try and was probably right; swooning on the stairs wouldn't help anyone. She sat back down on the edge of the bed, suddenly wanting to hold the little girl.

"Has she eaten?"

"Four ounces of Rosemary's milky gruel. Went right off to sleep afterward."

Jared Hawkesly looked nothing like the scoundrel she had married. Nothing like a man who could give away orphans willy-nilly.

Especially with his oddly bulging belly.

No wonder he'd been such an easy man to love. He had so much to give, if he'd only try.

She wanted to run her fingers through his inky dark, newly washed hair, to tuck the stray strand behind his ear. But he seemed so protective of his special cocoon, as though he believed he were the only one capable of saving the child. The warmest chest. The strongest arms.

He was probably right.

"You've made a lifelong friend there, Jared." He only grunted and rocked the chair a little. "And you've made a friend here, too. You were pretty darn remarkable, husband. You saved us."

"Saved your fool neck." He turned his head and

gave her that look again: glaring and distinctly arrogant, but clearly pleased. "I owe you a paddling."

Kate tried not to smile at the notion of that. "And I suppose I owe you a thank you."

His glower deepened its fire. "A long, heartfelt, on-your-knees apology."

Never. Some things just had to be done any way they could. "What about you? Were you hurt?"

"Thrashed." Now she could see the red abrasions across his cheek, glistening with Mrs. Rooney's ointment. He must have more injuries elsewhere. "Just like you."

"Like me?" Of course. She could feel Tansy's bandages on her elbows and knees without even searching them out, and the sore stiffness on her temple. "How do you know where I've been injured?"

"Believe me, wife. I know everything about you."

"How do you mean?"

He turned his eyes to the ceiling, a smile lifting the corners of his mouth. "There's not an inch of you that I didn't take careful stock of tonight."

"You saw me without my clothes?"

"Completely naked, my dear. More beautiful than I had imagined. Though sadly we were not in the moonlight. And you were in no condition to dance."

Her own private rogue of a husband. "If you're trying to shock me—"

"I'm beginning to think that I'm the only one in this family capable of being shocked."

"Well, good. Because I'm not." She was, in fact, thrilled. Her pulse taking a sudden leap, before crashing into the bump on her head. A small price to pay.

Unable to resist him any longer, she sifted her fingers through the dark hair on his forehead. "Are you comfortable there, Jared?"

"We're fine."

We. How she loved the sound of that. He'd better watch out—for a hard-edged old crank, he was becoming extraordinarily attached to his little charge.

"Because there's plenty of room for you and, oh, . . . did Father Sebastian tell you her name?"

His breathing had deepened—the snoring man of her stormy dreams. "The good father didn't know."

"Then we'll have to name her."

She was going to ask if he wanted to have the bed, but he was snoring again, lightly, giving off his generous heat to the little one snuggled beneath the counterpane.

Enchanted by the heartening change in her husband's disposition, Kate pushed reluctantly back into the pillows, but couldn't stop looking at him.

"I love you, Jared."

She hoped her whisper made it all the way into his heart where it might do a little good.

She slept like a rock, and woke to the sun rimming the heavy curtains covering the tall windows. Jared was still asleep in the chair, the baby higher on his chest, a shock of blond curls tucked under his chin. And a hank of her own hair captured in the crook of his index finger.

He must have been awake at some time during the night; there was a new bottle resting on the side table—doubtless Rosemary's careful tending.

Feeling much healed and restless and satisfied that Jared and the baby were doing well, Kate carefully disentangled his finger from her hair, slipped out from between the covers and padded silently down the hall to the girls' deserted dormitory, with a change of clothes.

Anxious to see how Father Sebastian and the two new arrivals were faring, she dressed quickly in a proper skirt and shirtwaist, tamed her hair into a relatively organized plaited knot near the top of her head, and hurried off to the sickroom.

"Katie, girl, you shouldn't be up!" Father Sebastian frowned at her as she poked her head through the sickroom doorway.

"And you're a wicked sight yourself, Father." Kate threw her arms around his neck. "But you're alive and I'm so grateful."

"Takes more than a frothy bit of ocean to drown an old boot like me. It was the children I feared for this time. And you, my dear. Taking chances like that. Look at you! A bruise on your temple, your hands scraped to pieces. Your husband was beside himself."

"And I keep telling you, Father, that crossing the Irish Sea in the *Fairheart* is a damn fool thing to do, even in good weather." She glared at him as she straightened the sagging shoulders of what must be a borrowed coat. "You'll take the mail packet home."

"You're a hard woman." He grinned and scratched the thatch of gray hair that fringed his temples. "So, how's the little babe?"

"Still asleep on Jared's stomach."

"A good place for them both. I found her just in time, lass."

"Jared says she doesn't have a name?"

"Put into my arms by a young stranger as we loaded the boat. The lad said she was all alone in the world."

"Well, she's not anymore, Father."

He nodded toward the door to the hallway. "He's a good man, your Jared."

"The best, I think." But will the obstinate man know it himself before time runs out for them? "Are the other children doing well?"

He smiled and tugged on the end of his too-long sleeve. "Michael and Rachel are doing well enough to be in the kitchen with that mother bear, Rosemary and her sisters."

"Thank God." Kate sagged into a chair, her bones aching. "Did the *Katie Claire* arrive in Dublin on time?"

"Did indeed, my thanks to you. Mrs. Archer put her soup kitchen crew right to work and had fed nearly a thousand by the next day."

"Good, then the *Katie Claire* must be on her way back to Portsmouth for another round of grain running." And to think that Jared was a spy. Good thing he would never be interested in anything as piddly as a little grain pilfered from Lord Grey and his fellow devils.

Because the man would never see the justice in her choice of pilferees.

"You rest yourself, Father. I'm going down to meet the new ones." She took off down the back stairs but stopped herself from bursting through the kitchen door and frightening them. Instead, she straightened her clothes and entered quietly.

"Lady Kate!" Glenna was at the worktable, set for

the two children, obviously supervising. "Good morning."

Dear God, Kate would have known who the new ones were by their dreadfully hollow cheeks, the darkness under their dull eyes. Little faces, little arms, slumping shoulders. Even the spoons they held so tightly seemed too heavy to lift.

They had been scrubbed, and warmed by the Miss Darbys, their hair checked for lice, and now were dressed in clean clothes and bundled in blankets so that they looked like woollen bumps in the big chairs.

She swallowed back the lump of sadness and smiled at them. "Welcome to Hawkesly Hall. You're Michael, aren't you?"

Kate stooped beside the boy and received a worried nod before a smile crept into the corners of his eyes.

"I am so glad to meet you." She turned to the girl on her right, dull, shaggy blond hair, pale cheeked. "And you're Rachel," holding the girl's hand, to comfort and to judge her strength.

Her little grin seemed to sap her energy.

The three Miss Darbys weren't far from the table, armed with oatmeal and applesauce and a pot of warm milk at the ready. They had become as knowledgeable about feeding the starving as Kate had.

Too much food and the wrong kind would bring agony, too little was just plain cruel.

"Aren't they looking just fine, my lady?" Myrtle said, leaning between the two children to add an inch more each to their empty milk cups.

Kate laughed, then gently patted the boy on the shoulder and then his arm, feeling for the thickness of his bones. "I'd say so, Myrtle. Especially considering that wild boat ride last night. You were all so brave."

"You were too, Lady Kate!" Glenna was beaming at her, her hair covered with her new embroidered cap. "And his lordship! Father Sebastian told us."

"Well, we had a high old time out there, didn't we, Rachel? But next time let's wait till summer comes. We can all go out to the beach together, in the sunshine, pull off our shoes, and put our toes into the sea. No more riding the waves against the rocks, eh, Michael?"

His eyes were huge and followed Kate's every move. "No, ma'am," he whispered.

"And as for today," Kate said, running her fingers through Rachel's thin hair. "I think a little rest is in order. I know that I'm tired out after last night."

"I told them how good you are at reading us stories, Lady Kate." Glenna nodded expectantly at Kate. "Could you?"

"If you'll help me."

"I will!"

"All right then," Kate said, slipping an apron over her neck and tying it at the back, "shall we all meet in the library in a half hour for the exciting tale of *The Ugly Duckling*? Time enough, ladies?"

The three Miss Darbys all nodded, as always anticipating her needs. There would be no schoolwork today, the other children would be outside helping Ian and Elden clean up after the storm. Not making noise in the hallways.

But just as she thought Ian's name, he came down the kitchen stairs and through the door. "Your pardon, my lady, but I just saw two gentlemen in the lane, 'bout a quarter mile from the gate. Coming from the village way on a couple of hired horses."

"Guests?" They weren't expecting anyone. "Thank you, Ian."

"Dressed like a couple of toffs, my lady. Like his lordship." Ian grinned as he accepted a nut-topped biscuit from Tansy, then hurried out the back kitchen door.

Toffs, are they? Kate wondered, as she hurried up the short flight of stairs into the main hallway. Couldn't be early arrivals for next month's hunt; Badger's Run was closed until then.

Friends of Jared's? A couple of stray members of the Privy Council? A visit from Trevelyan, his bloody self? Or Lord Grey, looking for his lost sacks of grain.

Feeling suddenly rumpled from roof to cellar, she peered out the front window at the drive up, hoping that the circle was free of livestock.

But there were the three goats, so very like the three Miss Darbys that she never let the thought linger in her mind for fear of it ambushing her at the wrong moment.

"Can't resist those daisies, can you, girls?" Kate hurried out the front door, down the wide, stone stairs, across the gravel and into the unmowed patch of waist-high grass and flowers. She should keep it cut, but the animals seemed to love it here best, and gave such excellent milk.

"Come along now," she said, grabbing Chloe's and Buttercup's bell collars, grateful when old Ginny followed them into the drive.

She'd gotten only a few yards when Grady came

running toward her from around the corner of the house, Justin and Jacob right on his heels, the little ones following.

"Hey! Can we help you, Lady Kate?"

"Please do, Grady. They need to be penned for a few hours." Kate handed off the goats to the older boys, then dropped to her knees and caught the little ones as they surrounded her.

"Does your head still hurt, Lady Kate?" Mera asked, tugging on Kate's apron. "Miss Rosemary said you were sleeping."

"Miss Tansy said you and his lordship fished us more friends right out of the ocean!" Healy insisted on planting a kiss on Kate's cheek.

"My head is much better, thank you. And we didn't exactly fish them out, Healy. But we do have new friends." And visitors coming any time now.

"C'n we go play with the new children, Lady Kate?"

"Maybe you can meet them all tonight, Dori. They're very tired after their travels. So you must all be as quiet as you can today."

"We will!" Jacob shouted as he strained to move Buttercup by her collar. "Come on!"

But the goats were heading back for the patch of daisies, dragging the three boys with them.

"Not this way, girls!" Kate jumped into the path of the goats, waving her arms, which brought on a flight of flapping arms and shouting from the children.

"Hey, who's that comin'?" Jacob had popped his head up from the knot of goats and children and was stabbing his finger toward the stone gates.

Kate looked up from her struggles with the goats just in time to see two tall riders come loping easily through the entrance.

Toffs, to be sure.

"Stay right here, children," she said to her little mob, though she did welcome Mr. McNair padding along behind her, poking his wet, reassuring nose into her palm.

The riders met her halfway around the circle, both dismounting with a flourish, both as handsome as her husband, as tall and broad-shouldered.

The one with the boyish, lopsided smile stepped forward with a charming nod. "Good morning, madam. This is Hawkesly Hall, isn't it?"

"Indeed, sir. And I am Lady Hawkesly. May I help you?"

The towering man drew back as though she had just stunned him. "You're Lady Hawkesly?"

He shared an unmistakable look of amazement with his friend, who then stepped forward with a fleet but appraising sweep of his gaze. "You're Jared's wife?"

"I am. I'm Kathryn."

"Well, dash me!" the man said, beaming at his friend, who grinned at her with a disarmingly sheepish slant.

"Do forgive us, Lady Hawkesly. I am Ross, Viscount Battencourt and this is Andrew, Viscount Shefford. We are—"

"Don't believe a word they say, wife!"

Kate whirled at the sound of Jared's voice rumbling across the courtyard, staggered at its power to start her heart thumping.

He was striding down the wide stairs, collarless, his hair a little mussed, clutching a blanketed bundle against his shoulder as though he'd been a father for years.

"Good God, Ross, I never thought I'd see it!"

Ross laughed and nudged Drew with a rowdy elbow. "Bloody hell, he's a quick one! What's the man been up to out here in the country?"

"Plenty, I warrant!"

Now the children were swarming toward Jared, grabbing hold of his coattails as he kept up his jaunt along the gravelly drive, the goats dragging the boys, and Mr. McNair leaving his post beside Kate at a lope.

"Keep away from the blackguards, Kate, they're dangerous." But Jared was smiling broadly at her and then at his visitors.

She hurried toward him too, her pied piper, and held out her arms for the baby as they met in the midst of the children. "How is she?"

"Wriggly," he whispered, smiling as he brushed her cheek with the back of his fingers, his eyes sparkling. "You look beautiful this morning."

"Why, thank you." A blush came rushing out of her bodice. "Now, may I hold her, Jared, or are keeping her for yourself?"

If he took the last as a challenge to his compassion, then she'd succeeded, though he looked so perfectly at home surrounded by the children and the goats. He lifted a dark brow and grunted as he carefully handed her the baby.

Such a spindly bundle of warmth and wriggling. No longer able to resist, Kate finally pulled aside the edge of the blanket and got her first look at the sweet little face.

"She's lovely." With a button of a nose and a cherub's mouth, a downy crown of silvery blond hair, and deep blue eyes that were looking intently back at her. And all the harrowing, heartbreaking signs of the famine that had stolen the child's family from her and brought her here.

"You're home now, little one," she whispered against the soft little curls as she looked up at Jared. "Home to stay."

Chapter 20

Home to stay.

Jared thought his heart might just leap out of his chest, launching itself toward Kate and the baby in her arms and the innocent little faces in the crowd around them. He knew that Drew and Ross were standing outside the knot of children, the pair of them lathered with questions, but he couldn't care in the least. Couldn't drag his gaze from his wife and the baby, the tenderness in her voice, in her eyes, the love pouring from her.

Couldn't speak for the huge lump in his own throat.

"Is that the new baby?" Dori said, jumping like a jack to be level with Kate. "Lemme see her, please."

"One quick look, children," Kate said, bending slightly to the throng, "and then you must all go help pen up the goats."

Jared was overwhelmed by a feeling of protectiveness as he watched each child bend into the baby's face and grin or giggle or plant a kiss on the top of her head and then go speeding off toward the garden.

A special greeting from each of them, the little one's misfit, ready-made family.

"Not you, Mr. McNair." He grabbed the hound's collar just as he went diving toward Kate and the baby with his great lolling tongue and that goofy smile on his muzzle.

"Come along, silly doggy!" Mera scratched Mr. McNair behind the ears, and the dog went galloping off after the dark-haired girl who was wearing Kate's rumpled hat.

Kate stood, her gaze passing between the baby and him with an equal amount of adoration. Then she turned all that staggering radiance on Drew and Ross.

"Welcome again to Hawkesly Hall, gentlemen."

"Yes, welcome, Andrew, Ross. Old friends of mine, Kate." Jared caught her around the small of her back, fitting his hand into the curve of her waist, over that soft, slight rise at her hip. "And this is Lady Hawkesly, my wife."

"We've met your lovely bride, Hawkesly," Ross said, giving a sudden study to the baby. "But whose ch—" He stopped and scratched his head.

"Husband, I promised the children a story. I think I'll leave you to your guests for the moment." Kate smiled up at him, mischief in her eye. "You gentlemen will be staying with us, of course."

"You're most kind, Lady Hawkesly," Drew said. His

eyes had grown wide and staring as though he too had just begun to add up the months and the years and the age of the child tucked up in Kate's arms.

She started away a step and then turned back to Jared, touching him lightly in the crook of his elbow. "Be thinking of a name for her, Jared," she said, obviously playing this to Ross and Drew's fertile imaginations. "Something soft and sweet-smelling."

"The sooner the better, wife." It must have been just the right amount of scandal for her and her audience: She raised her brows, and his friends went stone silent.

He watched her go. They *all* watched her. Jared, wanting to gloat openly about that fine, if unfondled, bottom and her slender waist, Ross and Drew because they both deserved to burn, to envy him his good fortune.

"Christ, man, I had wagered that you wouldn't make it into your bride's bower on the first try, and now you've gone ahead and populated the whole bloody countryside in record time!"

"Jared, whose child is that?"

Whose child indeed? "We don't know, Ross."

"You don't know?" Ross barked the question. "Jared, do you know what you're saying?"

"And what happened to the pair of you, Hawkesly?" Drew pointed to Jared's forehead. "You both look as though you've been in a fistfight; scrapes and bruises. And I know that you'd never lay a hand on a woman. Even given the untenable position she's put you into."

God, he was enjoying this; twisting the blackguards on the pointy end of a scandal. Making them sweat for him.

"What position would that be, Drew?" He started rambling slowly toward the house, knowing they would follow with their horses.

"Now see here, Jared, you know that I would never presume to disparage your wife's character, but—"

"Because I would tear out your heart and throw it to the hogs." Jared kept up his steady pace, hiding his smile, certain that his friends were only looking out for his interests. Even more certain that he would do the same for them.

Ross caught up with him, his brow deeply fretted. "What Drew is doing such a piss-poor job of saying is that. . . . well, dammit, Jared, you've been gone all this time—"

"And she's got all these children about the place . . ." Drew added from his other flank.

"Wait! Had Lady Hawkesly been married before you? Yes, that's it! She's a widow."

"No, Ross, I'm Kate's first, and only, husband. There's been no one else before me."

"Excuse me for being blunt, but that's an infant she was just carrying."

"Not quite two months, Ross. Or so." Jared picked up his pace toward the house.

"She doesn't know?"

"Or won't tell you?"

"What the hell kind of excuse is that, Jared?" Drew hurried alongside him. "Where did she say the babe came from? The stork?"

"The ocean, actually." Jared laughed at the absurdity.

"The ocean? And you believed her?"

"I was there."

"You couldn't have been, you were with us two months ago. Hey, wait just a damn minute." Drew caught his arm and stopped him at the bottom of the stairs, lightning shooting from his eyes. "What the devil are you talking about?"

Oh, what bumbling investigators they had become. Off on a tangent when the facts were right in front of them.

"The new baby. Aren't you?"

"My God, Ross, I thought you told him where babies came from."

"He told *me*!"

Drew dragged his fingers through his hair. "Jared, your wife didn't get that baby out of the ocean!"

"Yes, she did, Drew." Jared finally couldn't keep his laughter inside his chest. "Last night during that storm. Like I said, I was there when the little fool rescued the baby, a priest, and two other children from a boat that had run aground on the rocks."

"She what? She rescued them?"

"Just in time, as it turned out." He shook off the sharp memories of the night, the incalculable loss if she hadn't acted when she did and the way she did, if she'd been swallowed by the sea. "She's a hardheaded woman, and there was a moment or two when I thought I'd lost her."

"Can't you see the blighter's been leading us on a merry chase, Drew?" Ross laughed and tied his roan's bridle to the iron hitch ring set into the stone block. "That's where all those scrapes came from."

"Is this true, Jared?"

"Afraid so, Drew. No scandal here."

"Then what about all the rest of the children? Don't tell me she rescued all of them as well."

That was the undiluted truth of it. Kate, the champion of the innocent. "She did just that, Drew. Rescued all of them, one way or another."

Had rescued so many other people along the way.

Even Jared himself had begun to feel the distinct tug of her unyielding resolution.

"So all these children are yours?"

His? Jared swallowed, caught in his own trap. Unable to imagine the hall without them.

Without Kate. Without her respect.

"Come on, let's go into the house," he said like the coward he was. "We'll find someplace quiet and you can report your findings. I'll send someone for your horses."

He led them into the house and opened the door to the south parlor, expecting the worst, but finding the usual half dozen hobby horses standing in the middle of the floor, a nursery's worth of doll cradles, dolls sitting up in the chairs, toy soldiers lined up along the windowsills.

Neat, but well used.

"Make yourselves comfortable," he said, moving the herd of horses out of the way of the settee.

"You sure fell into a patch of clover, Jared," Ross said, dropping his saddlebag on the low table. "Your wife is an unimaginable beauty."

Drew snorted and stood frowning, with his arms crossed high on his chest, obviously disgusted with himself. "And don't I feel like a damned fool."

"Kate will find your mistake in judgment amusing, Drew."

"You're not going to tell her what Ross and I were accusing her of?"

Jared laughed. "Believe me, she already knew what you were thinking. So take care. The woman's mind works at twice the speed of mine."

"Ha, so she did toss you out of her bed when you tried to climb in the first night."

He'd been expecting this ambush, had composed a dozen believable replies, but preferred, "Bugger off, Drew. Now sit and tell me why you've come. Unless it's just to plague me on my honeymoon, then I'll thank you to leave."

"You were right, Drew. She tossed him out of her bed."

Jared ignored Ross's jibe. "So, has the queen decided to take her grand tour of the Irish counties?"

The pair of them gave him the once over, but Drew finally said, "Postponed until late next summer."

"Let's hope she doesn't change her mind." Because he'd been thinking hard about Kate's view of the mess in Ireland, the motives and the mistakes. The responsibility. Still a powder keg.

Jared sat down hard in a chair opposite Ross, the low table between them. "So what did you do about the *Pickering*?"

"She's been confiscated by the navy." Ross flipped open his saddle bag and drew out a folio. "The good Captain Sewell is clapped in the brig until his trial, or until he cooperates, the grain in Liverpool, the guns commandeered by the Portsmouth armory—"

"And the feckless rebels waiting for the ship in Dublin arrested as conspirators."

"So that's the sum of it?" Jared sat back, feeling unsettled at the ease of the outcome.

"The end of the affair of the *Pickering*," Ross said. "But the beginning of a larger mystery that's causing all kinds of outrage and indignation at Whitehall and Westminster."

"What is it? Another Effington scandal? Or has George Hudson finally been revealed as the crook he is?"

"Not that I wouldn't welcome Hudson's end, but that's not it." Drew had been sorting through a stack of paper, found what he was looking for, then handed Jared a thin, bound book. "Hardly worth our efforts, but Grey seems to believe the matter is a major threat to national security."

"A scandal, at least," Ross said.

Jared paged through the book. "An accounting journal?"

Drew leaned back against the settee, propping his boot across his knee. "We picked it up yesterday at one of Lord Grey's warehouses in Liverpool."

"Don't tell me we're to investigate the man's clerk for embezzling?"

"For theft on a grand scale, carried out over the last six months. Frankly if the mousy Mr. Parkhurst is the culprit, he's the finest actor I've ever seen. No, it's more involved than that."

Then Jared remembered their earlier messages. "Ah, yes, Russell and Trevelyan have suffered the exact same losses."

"Beginning exactly at the same time. Charles Wood

has put his best auditors from the Exchequer on the investigation."

"Hardly a threat to the nation," Jared said, trying to rub the tightness out of his forehead, but running his thumb into a flinching bruise instead. "Has any of the stolen grain been traced? Grain sacks are sometimes marked with the name of the shipper or the granary. And has the grain been milled or is it unmilled?"

Ross lifted a shoulder. "Hell, I don't know. I didn't think to ask. I suppose it was unmilled. Just arrived from Ireland."

"Ireland? I doubt that, Ross. Exporting food from a country that's starving to death?" Jared picked up Grey's account book again and flipped through the pages. "That doesn't make any sense."

"Unless you're an absentee English landlord, like Lord Grey," Drew said as he stood and walked to the window.

Here was a clue, right in the journal. Facing pages of import entries from Dublin and Wexford and Belfast. All of them made in the last year.

"Bloody hell," Jared said, flattening the book against the low tabletop and running his finger down a telling list, "here's a bit of evidence. Wheat and barley, pigs and cattle, eggs, oats . . ." And all of it from Ireland.

Ross was leaning over the book, staring at the figures. "Evidence?"

"When the newspapers get hold of this story, it's going to be flatly embarrassing to the three most important men in the government. And that is a very large signature. Because whoever has arranged this theft has chosen his victims with great political care."

Drew nodded. "Ah, a protest."

"A rather quiet way to protest, isn't it?"

"Which is just the point, Ross. A practical theft carried out by a person with politics on their mind and mouths to feed by the thousands."

"Who would do that?" Ross sat back against the chair and stretched out his legs.

Besides Kate? Jared nearly laughed at the speed of that wildly preposterous thought.

He shook his head of his wife's suddenly distracting smile, her scent of lemon and cinnamon, and leafed through the other pieces of paper now strewn all over the table.

"What is the Ladies' Charitable League?" he asked, scanning a list of warehouses that Ross and Drew had made note of while they were in Liverpool.

"Just another of those relief committees' warehouses," Drew said, sifting through the account book again. "Must be three on the Brunswick Dock alone—"

"A relief committee?" Ross stood and ran his fingers through his hair. "Isn't this suddenly getting a little close to the mark?"

Jared had already made the connection and felt a guilty twinge. "Grain imported from a starving Ireland goes mysteriously missing from fat English warehouses owned by the Lords Russell and Grey, and that bastard Trevelyan. Add a zealous Irish famine relief organization and we've got ourselves a clever criminal conspiracy."

"Ha!" Ross clapped Jared on the back. "And Drew thought that coming here would be a waste of time!"

"I was just tired of your face, Ross."

"Enough, boys. Looks like you're going back to Liverpool for a little spying on the Ladies' Charitable League and any other relief committee you come across."

Drew snorted. "At least this time we won't have to sit in a palm tree trying to look like a pair of coconuts."

"That was your idea—" Ross's argument was cut short by a knock on the door.

"Ah, here you all are." Kate was standing in the doorway, her smile brightly focused on Jared, the baby snuggled under her chin. "I hope I'm not interrupting."

Ross and Drew burst into greetings and compliments and babbling bows.

Jared rescued her. "We were . . . reminiscing."

"That's good. I just wanted to make sure that Drew and Ross were settled in, and to apologize again for our chaotic first meeting."

Drew grabbed her hand. "My lady, may I say that your husband is a lout and doesn't deserve a wife like you."

Her eyes widened and she laughed, shifting the baby higher on her shoulder. "And may I say ballocks to you, sir."

Drew arched a wry brow at her and then at Jared. "You were right, Hawkesly, a lightning-quick mind. Dangerous in a woman."

"Even more dangerous in a wife," Jared said, feeling as content as he ever had, thoroughly pleased with himself.

"Are you married, Drew?" Kate asked.

"God, no! Who'd have me?" Drew relaxed against the sideboard. "Or Ross, for that matter. Jared went first into the muddy fray. And I think I'll stop talking before I step into it completely."

Jared found himself cupping his hand over the baby's head, an amazing feeling that seemed to run all the way up his arm and into his chest. "She's sleeping?"

"Like a champ. And I think I'll join her after I've settled our two guests into their rooms. Now, if you'll follow me, gentlemen?" She smiled at the men again, and again their mouths went a bit slack as they followed her out of the parlor.

Jared stayed behind to study the documents still spread out on the table.

More than that—to sort out his thoughts.

His head from his heart.

A cold, stormy sea and a fragile life.

A distant peace or intimate chaos.

His life was utterly chaotic at the moment, except for Kate, and the contentment that seemed to encompass her like a cloud of lavender.

No. Kate was the cause of the chaos. And the cure.

"Hell's teeth." So much for clearing his head.

He grabbed the first report on the top of the table. A sheaf of reports from the commissariat officer at Bantry, sent to Trevelyan.

" 'August twentieth,' " Jared read. " 'The wheat crops are poor and the oat crop smutted. Maggot and Hessian fly destroying the rest. The rain is unrelenting, potato rows turn to rivers'—Hell, that's not even a month ago."

An old familiar fear began to gather in the center of his chest, as though a hole had been opened, exposing his heart, his failings. He moved to the window for a sharper light.

" 'August twenty-seventh. The clearance of tenants

in arrears and the tumbling of their homes by landlords continue apace. Multitudes now living in mud banks and ditches like animals. The failure of the potato crop in Bantry is expected to be utter.' "

The more he read, the more his stomach dipped and churned and filled with helpless fear.

Dark memories and bleak glimpses into a future that he hadn't wanted to see.

But it stretched out so clearly before him:

Kate, leading the children into the garden like a piper, through the woods and out across a stormy sea to who knew what fate.

"You win, Kate." And she hadn't even been here in the room to debate him.

"Now he's talking to himself, Drew." Ross strode through the parlor door, wearing a new shirt and his hair combed, Drew following after.

"Then a game of hazard is in order."

Jared stood, prepared to face the music. "Actually, my wife and I have other plans."

"Sounds like a liaison to me, Ross."

"It is." A dance in the moonlight, if the weather holds. "And I need your help."

"Ours?" Drew laughed. "I rather expected that you'd have worked it all out yourselves by now."

No time to be cagey. "We haven't. Not at all. If you want the naked truth, I haven't touched her in a married way."

"But you told us—"

"A lie, Ross. I have my pride. Or rather I had it until I met Kate. As much as I hate to admit it, you were right, Drew."

"Ha!"

"Kate insisted that I court her. And that I agree to . . . well, that doesn't matter anymore. What does matter is that tonight, at long bloody last, will be our wedding night."

Drew rubbed his palms together. "Tell us how we can help."

"You must bluff my unsuspecting bride into going to the hunting lodge. I'll take it from there."

Ross snapped his fingers together. "We'll just tell her that you've been overcome by an interest in fishing and that—"

"She'll never believe that one."

"How about a leaking roof?"

"A fire?"

"Hell, Drew, let's just kidnap her."

Trusting that his friends wouldn't betray him, and satisfied that the other preparations for the night's marital revels were solidly in the works, Jared crept into his wife's bedroom.

She was sleeping soundly on her side, in the middle of the bed, her hair spread out in gilded tendrils across the mounded pillows, her hand resting fondly, protectively in the folds of the baby's blanket.

Selfishly he wanted to wake her, but she needed her sleep after last night's enterprise.

Would need it even more for tonight's celebration.

The baby jerked suddenly in her sleep, stretching her thin arms out of the blanket, fists whirling for a moment, her little mouth working and her eyes peeping open for an instant.

Jared tiptoed to the baby's side to repair the blanket,

but even in her sleep, Kate reached out and tucked the corners back into place, patting the baby's chest.

What a lucky child, to have found Kate in the midst of this very messy world.

Unable to resist, he leaned down and kissed Kate on the temple, a warmth, a downy softness. She smiled crookedly and sighed, disarming him with her honesty, filling his lungs with her scent and his groin with pure lust.

Knowing that he'd better leave while he still could, Jared backed out of the room, and went off to take care of his own preparations for this long-awaited wedding night.

Chapter 21

"**J**ared's been injured? Dear God!" Kate felt her heart stop, leaving an icy trail in her veins. She hurried down from the landing on the grand staircase, grabbed hold of Drew's coat sleeve, trying not to panic, because nothing good ever came out of panic. "How badly, Drew? Where is he? Take me there! Please!"

Ross was glaring at Drew. "Dammit, Drew." Ross took her hand. "Don't listen to him, Lady Hawkesly. There's nothing wrong with your husband."

Relief flooded her limbs, made her knees sag. "Then why did Drew say there was?"

Drew lifted his eyebrows to her, stammered in a most charming way. "I was . . . well, I thought." He glared at Ross and said through his clenched teeth. "I thought that was what you told me to say."

"What exactly is going on here, gentlemen?" Kate's

heart had settled some. Jared was fine. But his lunatic friends were a different story altogether. She hadn't known them longer than a few hours, but if they were colleagues of Jared's then they were clever operatives.

And they must be planning something.

Ross seemed to have found his way again. "Well, it actually does have to do with Jared. He wants to see you."

"Supper is in just a few moments. He's surely on his—"

"He won't be there," Drew said quickly, throwing a frown at Ross.

"Jared isn't coming to dinner? Why?"

Ross frowned back at Drew. "Something came up."

"Or certainly *will* come up," she heard Drew say to Ross out of the corner of his mouth. "Ouch."

Ross had shinned the man in the boot. "You see, Lady Hawkesly—"

"Please, call me Kate. And tell me the truth. Where is my husband going to be during supper? And why does he need to see me beforehand?"

The pair got stumbly again, Ross finally speaking. "The truth is that Jared's at the lodge. There's something there he needs to take care of and he needs you to be there with him when he does."

"That's for sure," Drew said, unflinching as Ross's elbow stuck him in the ribs.

"Why the lodge?" Kate asked, completely dumbfounded. "Has he found trouble there? Storm damage?"

"A fire," Ross barked on top of Drew's, "A leaking roof."

"Excuse me, what?"

Drew heaved a heavy sigh then tucked his arm inside the crook of her elbow. "I told you we should have just kidnapped her."

They lifted her by an elbow each, then hauled her out the door and down the stairs. Always gently. And loaded her with great respect into the hall's small, closed carriage that had been waiting in the drive up.

If she didn't know better she'd have to believe that they were abducting her for nefarious purposes.

At her husband's behest.

It all made perfect sense. Rosemary had set out a two-piece gown for her, slightly more elegant than she was used to, given an evening with the children. It was soft, pale muslin, the bodice buttoned down the front, lightly stiffened points at waist, a chemise and two frothy petticoats. A lacy shawl.

But hardly a suspicious wardrobe, because tonight they had two guests at dinner, sophisticated men who were used to elegance.

Who were both completely mad.

As mad as her husband.

But such thoroughly charming abductors that she kissed them both on the cheek as they let her in through the front door of Badger's Run.

The door closed firmly behind her, leaving her standing alone in the midst of the foyer, beckoned deeper into the dark, silent lodge by a pathway of candles perched on tables and in sconces and leading up the stairs.

"Jared!" Heaven knew where he was. The lodge had been closed up a few days ago, except for the suite that Jared had been using.

Which must be where he wanted her to go as she followed the flickering candles up the stairs and to the end of the hall.

The door was open a few irresistible inches, so she gave it a push, granting Jared his mystery, her heart long ago run wild with anticipation.

But there were still more candles, leading her through the anteroom into the warm glow of the bedchamber, which was awash with candle flame.

"Nearly two years late, my love, but I plan to make our wedding night well worth the wait."

My love. Kate knew the silky dark voice, had come to adore its force and its foggy depths. To look for it around unexpected corners. Now it came rumbling toward her, dancing on the sea of candle flame, and the power of it set off her pulse against her ears.

"You did this for me, Jared?"

He appeared out of the shadows near the velvet-draped windows, his smile devilishly dark, his hair a deep blue midnight, roguishly tousled and now long enough to reach his stark white collar.

He moved toward her, a menace to her willpower. But she stood there, enchanted by his towering shoulders, butterflies flitting and looping inside her stomach, her palms itching to slide over his chest.

The room smelled of him, of leather and bay and beeswax.

"For you, my dear wife, I would do anything."

Anything? Oh, how she wanted to believe him, and this lovely night he'd made for them, wanted desperately to stay and be his wife for ever and ever, wanted him to love the children who'd been sent to them, as he would have those who might have been born to them. But it seemed he hadn't yet found room in his life, and hers was already overflowing.

As incredible as a wedding night with Jared would be, she just couldn't let it happen, no matter how seductive he was. She'd already begun to compose a letter to her father's ancient solicitor about finding a suitable house somewhere.

And yet here she was, being openly seduced by the most amazing man she'd ever met. Though she knew exactly what he was up to.

"But I can't let you do *this* thing, Jared," Kate backed away from him as he came forward.

"This *thing*?" His eyes glinted in the candlelight, burned with an unmistakable hunger, looking too satisfied for her own good.

"You're courting me again." With a whole pantomime's worth of scenery and light and color, a fire blazing in the hearth and pillows heaped on the floor, and, oh, my . . . !

"A bathtub!" Steaming and scented, tucked into the bow of the window, the candles bright against the drapes. She ached everywhere. "Heavens, it would feel so grand! But I don't think it's a very good idea."

"I've given up courting you, my love. Tonight I'm going to make you my bride." He was so tall, so very close, slipping his arm around her waist, nudging her nearer, and bending toward her until he found her mouth and covered it fully, but far too lightly.

And not nearly enough!

She wanted to fold herself into his arms, to lose herself there forever, but that could never be, so she shoved both hands against his chest.

"No, Jared! I can't. You know why I can't."

"If I've learned one thing about you, my dear Kate," he whispered against her temple, nibbling there, his smile loose and tilting and far too bewitching, his eyes never leaving hers, making her pulse surge and her heart soar when it should stand firmly on the earth, "it's that you can do anything you set your mind to."

She shoved him again, a piddly, halfhearted attempt that made her feel weepy and unsure of herself. "Don't you see, I can't set my mind to do this thing. Not a wedding night with you."

He drew back slightly, his eyes wide, brows arched in mock offense. "Am I that loathsome?"

"That's not the point."

His smile turned utterly wicked, pleased with himself. "So I *am* that loathsome. . . . I had no idea."

"Don't tease me. I've told you why we can't be married or stay married."

He loosened his arms abruptly, but held her by the waist with his huge hands, his thumbs nearly meeting low across her belly. "Tell me again."

"You can't change my mind. I won't split up the children and send them off to parish farms. That would be unimaginably cruel."

"You've made that quite clear." He was being remarkably calm in the face of this prickly issue between them, smiling crookedly, his eyes such a lush and smokey midnight that she had to look down at his shirt buttons to shake his influence.

"And because timing is critical, I've already begun composing a letter to Mr. Biddle, my father's lawyer, to help me look for a suitable house."

He frowned down at her, a sumptuous, bay-scented heat pouring off him, seeping through the linen of her shirtwaist, playing against her skin. "Just what would this suitable house look like?"

"It doesn't matter what the house looks like." But she slipped out of his arms, swallowing back the irksome tears that were suddenly clogging her throat. "It just has to be safe and large enough and in good repair. Even then, if it's not too badly gone, I can have repairs made. The roof and rising damp and so forth. And it must also have room for the children to play outdoors."

"Sounds like a lot of trouble to go through for a wretched old house."

"Nevertheless it must be done. And so that's the reason that I can't stay here with you tonight." She swallowed hard against the truth. "As much as I would like—"

"As much as you would like what, my dear?"

"To stay here with you, you big lout. To have a wedding night and a marriage with you, because . . ." She stopped because she'd been about to give away the secret of her heart and now he looked so smug, as though he already knew that she loved him.

Adored him.

"Go on, please, Kate. Because why?"

"Because . . . it would be simpler that way."

He laughed. "Simpler?"

"Simpler to stay here with you and all the children, instead of packing them up and hauling them off to some unknown, unfamiliar place where they'll never be quite as happy as they are today. Instead of wading through all the legal muck of dissolving our wedded union. Instead of exposing the intimate details of our marriage, explaining that it had never been a real one."

"It feels quite real to me."

Her heart sank. "Please don't fight me on the matter. It's not real, Jared. We never finished it."

"But we will tonight."

Now her heart started clanging around inside her chest. After all this, he was going to demand his due. "Only if you force yourself on me. And I know that you would never."

"I won't have to. I guarantee that quite soon, you will be forcing yourself on me."

"You're a lunatic, Jared. Just like your friends."

"I'm not jesting. I predict that in a very short time you'll be freely tearing at my clothes, just as I will be tearing at yours."

"Do you plan to lace my wine with an exotic aphrodisiac? Fruitbat guano and powdered tiger's testicles? I won't drink it!"

He laughed. "Only you would know of such a compound, let alone speak of it in mixed company. But I assure you that you will be under the influence of nothing more, nothing less, than your own will." He seemed so serious, so sure.

"And if I thought you were the sort who would swindle a woman into your bed, I wouldn't be here. But you're not that kind. You're a good and decent man. The best I've ever known."

"Me?"

"You're courageous and respectful and intelligent. I love your sense of humor and your patience with me and with the children."

He showed his splendid profile, tilting a proud chin, posing for her like a war hero. "I'm deeply flattered, madam."

He wasn't! He was toying with her in the worst possible way.

"But you're also deeply flawed, Jared. You lack one critical element in your character. One that I cannot overlook because it keeps you from understanding."

"Understanding what? Grady's terror when he's alone in the dark? Or Glenna's fear of everyone leaving her? You think I can't imagine what a handful of rotting garbage tastes like?"

She didn't know what to say to the sudden somberness of his mood, the anger buried just below the surface. "I wouldn't expect you to."

"Then you don't know much about me, wife."

"I meant that you've lived a different life than the children have—"

"What makes you so sure of that?" He was looking right at her, daring her to believe him.

"They've been orphaned, Jared."

"So was I."

Kate blinked at the image. A little orphaned lord. "I'm sorry. But these children have grown up in unspeakable poverty—"

"So did I."

"What do you mean?" He must be leading her somewhere with this drama.

"I simply mean you to know that I understand the

children better than you might think, because I was orphaned sometime soon after my birth and lived in a filthy workhouse until I was fourteen, when I escaped with my life and my two friends."

"You're not serious, Jared." Though he looked deadly serious, and a little proud.

"It's no secret. I'm a success story. So are Drew and Ross."

"All three of you?" An impossible story, with a stunning ring of truth.

"Slept in horse stalls, ate garbage out of dank, back alleyways, and were glad to have found it." A muscle ticked in his jaw, his gaze so piercing that she suddenly knew that he was telling the truth, not spinning a yarn.

A spark of anger flared in Kate's chest. "Why are you telling me this now?"

"I thought I'd impress you with my lineage." Smug again, and offhand.

"Dammit, Jared, you're a pompous ass."

He finally looked offended. "Me?"

"You've known all along the horror that the children had come from and still you can find it in your heart to send them back there."

He blew out a huge sigh, scrubbed his fingers through his hair. "I told you plainly, Kate, from the beginning. I had been seeking homes for them, good parish farms or boarding schools, not the slums of Calcutta. I had no intention of sending any of them anywhere without paying a surprise visit."

"Don't you see, Jared, that's not enough for a child."

"I know that."

"Hawkesly Hall isn't an orphanage to them. It's not

a holding pen until we can place them elsewhere. It's their home, their sanctuary."

"Yes, I understand."

"You don't understand. We are a family. If you truly understood, then you wouldn't let me take them—"

"I'm not going to let you take them anywhere."

"It won't work to lock us all in the cellar."

"Don't think I haven't considered it. But I couldn't stand the caterwauling. So, I have an idea. It occurred to me today."

"Ah, you mean to toss us all into the sea during the next storm?"

"I thought of that too, but you'd only be tossed back to me, wife. Like happened last night on the cliff."

The rat. Kate crossed her arms over her chest. "Then what is your grand idea?"

He studied every part of her face, as though trying to judge her reaction in advance. "What do you think of Badger's Run?"

"I'm very proud of it."

"I mean the lodge itself. The building. Comfortable, in excellent repair, plenty of bedrooms, a large dining room, a first-rate library. God knows there's plenty of room to play outdoors—"

"You mean to turn Badger's Run into an orphanage?"

"Exactly." Jared expected the woman to have run toward him by now and thrown herself into his arms. But her feet were planted hard against the carpet, her fists balled against her hips.

And those were brilliant blue lightning bolts shooting out of her eyes.

"How dare you!" She stomped her foot, whirled on a heel and started for the door.

He arrived before she did, barring the way, locking it behind him. "Christ, Kate! Isn't that what you wanted? The children nearby."

"Nearby, indeed. Now move, sir, before I use my knee against your wedding tackle."

"My what?"

"I'm warning you." She pointed at his crotch. "Move out of my way."

"My God, Kate. What do you want from me? How much closer do the children need to be?"

She crossed her arms again. "Tell me, Jared, how much sense does it make having the children eat and sleep and bathe and attend school at Badger's Run, when we live more than a mile away in the hall."

"Perfect sense?" He flinched as he said it, because he knew that wasn't the answer she was looking for, had known the right one for some time.

"What if Mera awakes from a nightmare at two in the morning? What if the baby misses you? Or one of them has a fever, or a loses a tooth? Or needs a story read to them."

"Then you can just . . ." He shook his head, because he didn't know what else to think.

"They'll think we deserted them." She touched his arm. "Can you imagine having supper without them, Jared? And all their chatter, their laughter. Or living in that big house that's so quiet we can't sleep."

"What are you getting at, Kate?" Though he understood perfectly.

"We've become a family. Can't you feel that? I love

the children—every one of them. I need them with me as much as they need me. As much as you need all of us, Jared."

The back of his eyes began to burn. He'd known the truth, her ultimate expectation for some time now. He'd just hadn't wanted to face it, the choice he had to make.

Kate and a houseful of castaway children or his independence.

As much as you need all of us.

He felt her watching his every move, reading him, seeing into his heart and holding her breath in the hopes that he would find the right answer.

"There are twelve of them, Kate."

Tears welled in her eyes, a smile lifting the corners of her mouth. "Isn't that a miracle, husband?"

It was. It must be, because as their gamin faces blinked past him he couldn't imagine choosing from among them. This one stays, this one goes. Parish farm, boarding school, Bethnel Green, a squalid ditch.

"It means adoption, Kate."

"A lot of paperwork."

"And lawyers' fees." He felt the glow of a huge smile building inside his chest. "But cheaper, I expect, than an annulment."

Tears were streaming down her cheeks, catching up in her dimples before continuing their trip over the edge of her chin and down her throat.

Filled to the brink with love for this amazing woman, Jared lifted her hand to his lips and dropped onto one knee. "Will you marry me, Kate?"

"Oh, Jared, with all my heart, yes." She slipped her fingers between his and kissed where they joined.

And stole his breath away. Soft, pliable lips, deeply sabled lashes, her blue eyes looking back at him, her heart laid open to him.

"Then, my dear wife," he said, rising off his knee, wrapping his arms fully around her to gather her as close as he could, until her breasts were dancing points against his chest, her belly a welcoming cradle for his arousal, "you and I have a marriage to begin."

"A scandalous good thing, husband, because we've already got a passel of children."

And he had a lifetime's worth of courting still to do.

Chapter 22

"**O**h, Jared! I'm looking forward to this English consummation ritual that I've heard so much about." She reached her arms around his neck, squirming languidly against him, measuring his hardness as she smiled up at him.

"Sweet, not half as much as I am." His pulse suddenly pounding and steaming like a runaway train, Jared scooped her completely off her feet and held her tightly against him, riding a searing wave of temptation, a profound yearning to carry her to the carpet, to lift her skirts, and enter her sweetness. To explore and thrust and possess her.

"Besides, husband . . . oh, my!" She lifted herself higher into his arms, wrapped her legs around his waist. "Besides, I'd hate to waste all these lovely candles and that steaming hot bath and your devious plans to seduce me."

"To join you, Kate. At long last." God, if he could keep up with her, his virginal dance-with-me-naked-in-the-moonlight bride.

"You mean to join *with* me, husband." She caught his earlobe with her teeth and breathed the heady words, "In every way."

"Yes, that, Kate." Oh, God! The lovely woman clinging so perfectly to his waist was racing ahead of him, squirming and sighing, measuring the iron-hot stiffness of his penis with the pulsing rhythm of her hips while he was trying desperately to keep a steady, governable pace.

"I've been waiting so long for this, Jared." She sighed his name against his temple, churning up clouds of lust in his groin. "For your kiss." She touched her mouth lightly to his, again and then again, until she became his pulse and his heartbeat. "Waiting for you."

"Your witless husband, who hadn't the sense to come home to you."

"But you did come home, Jared, and I hope you mean to stay." She kissed him more fully, pulling him against her, moaning against his mouth.

"And stay and stay until long past forever." Starving for her, he lifted aside the linen of her gown and kissed her shoulder, filling his lungs with her scent of lilac and lemon until he thought he would burst with the wanting.

The fiery need for her.

An even greater need to make this night hers.

But their wedding night would end right now if he allowed her to continue her assault on his senses, his sense of honor, his self-control.

"Come, wife," he said, carrying her toward the hearth, "you'll have to slow down, or I won't last the night."

"Too exhausted for making love?" She quirked a look at him, then took a long, delicious time sliding down the front of him, her eyes flickering with fire as she meet his hardness along the way. "I can't believe that, Jared. You seem wonderfully sturdy to me."

"Kate, please—" But she'd already slipped her hand between them, was running her palm down his belly until she stopped at the front of his trousers.

"Especially right here." Her eyes bright with excitement. "Very sturdy."

Jared gasped and jerked her hand away. "I'm not tired in the least, wife. I'm just too interested . . ." God, this was going to be a long, amazing night.

"How can you be too inter . . . oh, I see." Still she danced her hips against his, blinked at him, primly disheveled, her hair escaped from its lose bindings, now a cascade of gold clouding her shoulders. "You're too interested in leaving the dance and the fire and taking me off into the shadows to complete our . . . union?"

"I don't think you understand at all." Jared felt a feral growl rising out of his chest, an urge to clutch at her bottom and grind his erection into her belly. But he merely kissed her, madly, held her firmly against him to keep her from moving.

"Thank you, Jared." She wriggled and moaned against him, taking his kisses deeply, bestowing her own with a sensual ferocity.

"For kissing you?"

"For taking such care tonight. It's all so perfect."

He found her earlobe and nibbled, wanted to chew and suck his way across her shoulder and right down into her bodice.

"Truthfully, love, the bath was Drew's idea."

She pulled away an inch, smiling, her mouth moist and pouty. "Do you know they're complete lunatics, and thoroughly charming? And I can only assume that they delivered me to you knowing exactly what you were planning to do to me tonight."

"That we'd be dancing naked in the moonlight, Kate. I'm afraid so. As a matter of fact, I put them in complete command of Hawkesly Hall while we're gone."

"The children will eat them alive. And the three Miss Darbys will feed them till they pop."

"Probably, but they'll all have had fun and will sleep till noon."

"What about the baby?"

He'd even thought of that, though she hadn't been his daughter then. Not officially.

"I told them to think of a name for her."

"Jared!"

"Don't worry about any of them. I've never seen a child or a dog who didn't take a permanent liking to those two right off."

She took a deep breath then settled herself with a long sigh. "Then it must be the company you keep."

"What do you mean?"

"If I wasn't in love with you before, and I have been since the day you married me"—*Bloody hell, she loves me!*—"then I would have fallen for you last night when I saw you with the baby on your stomach." She smiled at him wistfully, started working on the tiny buttons on the front of her gown.

"What are you doing there?" He watched the first three buttons pop open one by one, was entranced by the curving shadows that slowly revealed themselves between her breasts.

"I've been coveting that bath since the moment I walked in here." She reached down and brushed her fingers through the water then touched her lips.

He watched the drop slide down her throat, separate over the soft rise of her breasts, then reconverge as it disappeared into that sweet valley.

His mouth went dry.

"Will you join me?" She touched the damp trail, her fingers toying in the lacy folds at the top edge of her camisole. Then two more buttons succumbed, the panels falling aside, her gown sagging off one shoulder.

"Wait, love," he said, wanting to make this luscious moment last into tomorrow, wanting to peel her of every flounce and ribbon all by himself. "Let me."

"Undo my buttons?"

"Undo everything, remove every sweet scrap." His heart was thrumming, pumping molten lead through his veins and into his gut.

"As you wish, Lord Hawkesly."

"You are my wish." His nerves standing on end, he focused his fumbling way along the remaining half-dozen buttons that ran down to the stiff little point at the front of her bodice.

Though she wasn't helping his concentration, not

with her delicate fingers playing softly in the hair at his temples. "You grew up in a workhouse?" He looked up into her eyes, at her out-of-place question and found them watery and concerned, searching his face. "I can't imagine your life there."

"A long time ago."

"What a fine man you've become." She slipped her fingers between his, then kissed the underside of his wrist, stopping his progress in stripping her, swelling his heart as thickly as his rock-ridged penis.

A wholly different kind of throbbing, but just as steamy and sensual. That she thought him fine in any way.

Then she kissed him again, long and sweetly, with her tongue and her teeth, her fingers guiding his hand through the labyrinth of all those frustrating little buttons.

At the last, the front sprang open like a pair of heavenly gates, a mouth-watering invitation just for him, revealing a thin chemise, plain of decoration save for the short lacing of ribbon that ran partway down the front.

"God, Kate, you're beautiful."

A pallid description of the woman who had changed his life, his dreams. Who thought him wonderful.

"You keep saying that, as though it were true and I was some flower you plan to pluck." She touched that tasty hollow at the base of her throat.

"Now there's an idea, wife. To pluck you." Because she belonged to him and he loved her smile, its brazen tilt, her fingers laced between his as though she couldn't bear to let go of him.

"Pluck away, then, sir."

Oh, how he wanted to. To pluck and plunge and taste.

He'd spent half his days in the last two weeks watching her breasts tease against her shirtwaist, wanting them, wanting her to grant him the moral right to kiss and nuzzle them. Now he wanted to see them—in all their glory, to touch them, and suckle and grope in a most carnal way.

Yet, there was still another layer of cotton hiding them, keeping him from them.

A camisole and the formidable waistband of her skirt. He'd undressed more than a few women in his life, but this one stumped him with her scent, with the cool heat pouring off her.

"Shall I lend a hand?" She reached behind her, wrangled for a moment with something, then tugged on the skirts. It hung up for an instant and then slipped over her hips and slid down her petticoats.

Still another garment. Two of them. Like peeling an onion.

"Let me." He reached behind her this time, placing kisses along her nape as he worked, and they were gone quickly, a mound of cotton and linen pooled around her ankles, leaving her standing there in drawers to just below her knees and her untucked camisole.

"Well, now, Kate, that's an excellent place to start. Nearly naked."

"But not nearly enough." She tugged on the ribbon that was lingering in the cleaving between her breasts, but he caught her hand and the ribbon, kissed her fingers.

"All the time in the world, love." She watched his every move from under her long, sooty lashes as he hooked his finger into the criss-crossing, and tugged the ribbon through one hole then the next until it had fallen to his touch and the ends were hanging loose, revealing her buttery smooth skin, bathed in lemony shadows.

"I won't ask why you're so skilled at undressing women, husband."

"An old skill. Haven't used it for years." God, he want to taste her, to nibble and bite and swallow her whole. He kissed her there in her sultry shadows, touched his lips to her silky skin, felt her breath gusting against his temple.

"Truly, Jared? That you . . . oh!" She drew in a long, humming little breath as he slipped his hand inside her camisole, cupped his palm around the base of her perfect breast. "That you haven't had a woman since . . . yes, that's very, very ni-nice! Oh!"

Highly encouraged, flattered, his penis thoroughly engorged by her moaning, he drew aside the linen and revealed the lusciously rose nipple.

"Haven't had a woman since we married, Kate." He bent his head, would have lightly touched his mouth to the delicious looking peak, but she caught his face with her hands and stared into his face.

"You've been celibate?" Her eyebrows winged deeply, curved at their ends, her eyes searching his face. "All this time?"

A splinter of guilt wedged in his rib, because he hadn't set out to be celibate. "I have."

"My handsome, pirate captain, celibate?" She kissed him again, one of her softly succulent assults on his mouth which zinged him in the groin and drew a groan from him. "I'm amazed, Jared. All those woman in all those ports."

"But I had you to come home to."

She eyed him, unbelieving. "Some other reason."

Indeed. "I must have just known that you would be worth the wait."

"You're full of blarney, Jared. But just so you know that I'm not the sort to share my husband with anyone."

He smiled from deep inside him. "Not a chance, love." He kissed her neck and then trailed his mouth downward. "I promise."

"Good, because I . . . oh!" She gasped as he pulled aside the drooping camisole, wriggled against his hips as she leaned back in his arms, exposing more of her curves and shadows, making soft little noises as he continued his journey.

"I've wanted to taste you right here." He caught her nipple just between his lips, his teeth, and Kate gasped.

"Oh, my, you shouldn't have waited so . . . so looong, husband!"

Wanton to her very soul. He nibbled and tugged and rolled the delicous little delicacy on his tongue and between his teeth, while his marvelous wife mewled and pressed her hips against his erection.

"I'm a damned fool, love." For not rushing home to her, for not cleaving when he had the chance.

But then she wouldn't have been there to save the

children; Justin and Dori and Margaret and all the others.

And now that seemed utterly unthinkable.

"You're just going to have to make up for your inattention." She caught his gaze, now a bright, fiery blue as she breathed hard and impatiently yanked her camisole off one shoulder and then the other until she was bare and beautiful above her tiny waist. And now she was standing in her drawers, her skin shining gold in the candlelight, sleek and silky.

Drawers that were plain linen and nearly shapeless to her knees, opaque, and yet marvelously split right up the center, begging exploration.

"God, Kate, you've got my full attention now." Two perfect half-orbs, ripe and rosy-tipped, smooth as cream and meadow-scented. "All of it, for all time."

He was focused on the woman, having trouble thinking, or making sense of her leaving him to circle the bathtub. She cupped her hands into the water, took a sniff of it.

"My favorite scent."

Then it was his too. And he would have told her that, but she stepped over the edge of the tub and into the water, drawers and all, then disappeared to her collarbone beneath the surface.

"Ahhhhhhh, my bones ache, Jared. Thank you for this." She leaned back against the edge, closing her eyes, her scraped kneecap making a steamy island in the water.

"The bath was Drew's idea, remember." He'd never felt quite so frustrated, standing at the edge of the water, fully clothed, nearly barking like Mr. McNair. Wanting in. Wanting to play.

"I must thank him, then." She opened an eye at him, grinning. "I wish there was room for two."

There's damn well going to be! He shucked his neckcloth and his shirt and was about to shuck the rest when her foot peeked out of the water and then her leg, all sleek and shiny and tasty.

"If you're offering, Kate." He took hold of her foot and her bare ankle and knelt beside the tub, ran his hands down her leg, massaging his way toward her thigh and her wet drawers.

"Ohhhhhhhhhhhh, myyyyyyyyyy!" She slumped farther and Jared kept up his assault, changing to the other leg and then her arms, glad of the metal barrier between him and his wife's moans of ecstacy.

Because he was near the brink of his patience and planned to stay there until he'd brought Kate to her pleasure.

"I don't think I can move." Her voice wavered and hummed, her eyes were closed and her arms flung to the side.

"I promise you will, love."

Jared stepped out of his shoes and into the bath on either side of Kate's knees, straddling her waist.

"Jared, your trousers!"

"I couldn't wait."

She laughed and sat upright, staring up at him, assessing him from below his knees in a most provocative way. If he sat, all the water would flood over the side. So he slipped his hands around her and brought her to her feet, her naked skin and his bare chest meeting like slick fire.

"Mmmmmm . . ." She sighed and moved against him, sliding her fingers up his back, kneading his aching muscles, gliding her thumbs along his waistband.

Thoroughly enchanted, Jared, held her close, memorized her textures and spoke a silent prayer of thanksgiving.

Kate was sure that her heart would burst from her chest, that her blood would boil right out of her skin.

He was Neptune and Isis, a pirate and a spy. And suddenly a father.

Extraordinary in every way, his broad chest gleaming golden in the forest of candlelight, his smile as husbandly as it was roguish. She felt wanted and adored.

So enchanted with him that she hadn't noticed him lifting her out of the tub, until she felt her thighs meet the upholstered cushion of the bench at the foot of his bed, couldn't imagine what he was planning until he knelt, and nudged her knees open on either side of his waist, then pulled her into his arms.

"I'm soaking wet, Jared." Which didn't seem to bother him in the least, seemed to mobilize his hands and his lips and his tongue.

"I'll take care of that." He was breathing madly, hot bursts of air trailing against her skin, nibbling his way down the center of her breastbone, between them, making her lean backward on her elbow, making her giggle.

"What are you up to?"

"Paying attention to you. Very close attention."

The wicked way he said that sent her imagination running wildly away from her. Out of bounds. Because she was lying with her legs spread on either side of him, the split of her drawers open and visible should he decide to look.

Thoughts that turned her cheeks crimson and filled up her belly with a yearning that seemed impossible.

"How close do you mean?" Because he seemed enchantingly close right now.

"Much closer than this."

"Much?" She couldn't resist touching the damp cords of his chest, or spreading her fingers along the muscles rippling there, and deep in his arms. So well defined, so steadfast. "And to think, I actually believed you were a pompous, prig of a man named Colonel Huddleswell."

"I've played far worse roles than the old colonel." He bent his head and caught up her nipple between his lips, sucking a gasp out of her until he was simply ravaging her will, making her squirm and pull at his hair.

"Worse than Colonel . . . ohhhh!" She growled and drew in a breath between her teeth and leaned back against his arm, not quite knowing where to cling next, his shoulders, his arms. Wanting him, all of him. Wanting him completely naked.

And dancing with her in the candlelight.

"These have to come off, Kate."

"My drawers?" She reached feebly for the ties in the front, but he covered her hand, her head spinning with pleasure.

"But slowly. I have my ways." He cocked a brow at

her, roguish and dark as he caressed the inside of her thighs just above her knees, a sensation with its own magic, that made her feel completely shameless, filled her with a desire to open herself to him.

"You'll find that I have my ways too." Not exactly a way, but a thriving curiosity about how that fine, hot penis of his would feel in her hand once she got his trousers off him.

"I already like your ways." He nuzzled her breast, still breathing like a stag, grabbing one steamy breath after another as his mouth blazed a long, thrilling path of kisses between her breasts and then slowly, amazingly, down the middle of her belly, stirring up exotic sensations that seem to be gathering like a storm.

She sprawled against the end of the bed just behind her, felled by another wave of shamelessness, languid and lounging in her wet drawers, wondering what he planned as he massaged and kissed and made her flesh goose and all her muscles cramp.

Thoroughly distracted by the sensations he was causing, the breathless glow that was swelling between her legs, she hadn't realized exactly where he was heading with his attentions until—

"Jared?" She sat up, looking into the smiling face of her husband, his hair wild and his eyes filled with delight.

"Yes?" The lout knew what she was asking. He'd been toying with the tie at the waist of her drawers, tugging and teasing. Now he'd slipped his finger into the slit between the legs at the waist, was lightly drawing his fingertip across her belly.

"Do you know what you're doing?"

"And exactly where I'm going."

"Where?"

His eyes flashed. "Making up for lost time." He dipped his finger lower, as though to prove his strategy. "And paying close attention."

A stunning whisk through her curls. "Oh, my!"

He couldn't be thinking of getting that close.

"There," he said, grinning, the ends of the drawstring were dangling in his fingers, dancing against her belly and her nerves.

There, indeed.

He was still kneeling between her thighs, still taking his time with his tender threats. Though now he was pulling aside the tops of her drawers, peeling them back, exposing her most private place as though he were opening a Christmas package.

He grinned up at her, a young man in a sweet shoppe. "Ah, Kate."

Before she could stop him he settled his hand between her legs.

"Jared!" She grabbed his arms, quaking like an autumn leaf, staring at him as he began playing his fingers through her curls.

"Close attention." And then her amazing husband leaned into her and kissed her on the mouth, while he played his fingers at the joining of her thighs!

"Jared, please . . ." She couldn't keep her hips still, fell backward, grinding herself against his intoxicating hand, his fingers dancing through her damp curls.

"Didn't I say that you'd be begging me for a kiss?"

"A kiss? I wasn't . . ." She opened her eyes and realized that she'd turned completely brazen. She'd wrapped her legs around his waist, was arching toward him.

And then he kissed her! There! Pressed his mouth where his hand had just been and sent her senses reeling, shooting off little stars behind her eyes.

"That was a kiss!"

"Here's another"—he straightened some, a lusty look in his eyes, a beast sating himself—"unless you object. Do you?"

"No!" She didn't really need to shout. But it made him grin, made him dive back into his objective, this time with the tip of his tongue and then a slick, humid kiss. "Ohhhhh, soooo wonderful! Jarrrrrred!"

She wanted more of this. More of him.

"Closer still, Kate." He caught her attention and then slipped his fingers slightly inside her, moved them, feeding her wildest hunger for him.

"Jared, I want—"

"Yes, I can tell, sweet. But not yet."

"Not yet what?" She hadn't the slightest idea what he meant, but he nuzzled her one more dazzling time between her legs, and then became her broad-shouldered, nearly naked flyfisherman, the loss of his closeness leaving her aching and unfulfilled, breathless.

He would have stood up if she hadn't sat up straight and caught hold of the tops of his trousers. "Where are you going, husband?"

Two could play at this. *Should* play at it.

"To cool off."

"Not yet, Hawkesly. My turn."

They were eye to eye and he raised one of his arrogant brows. "Yours?"

"Oh, yes. I've always wanted to feel one of these." She pressed her palm against the bulging front placket of his trousers, and found a most magnificent shape beneath the wool—long and thick, rigid like a hot iron rod.

"One of these?"

And she knew exactly what it was, had seen a few in their pagan glory.

But this one belonged to her.

"Oh, this is very nice."

Nice? Jared could hardly speak for the breathtaking caress of her hand as she blithely, meticulously measured the details of his erection.

Length and breadth.

Rigidity. Which it was. In full rock-hard tumescence.

Applying just enough pressure in just the right places to finally make him grab hold of her fingers.

Her eyes glinted just inches from his. "You're not faulty in the least, Jared. In fact, you're working just fine. Though you're much larger than I'd imagined."

"And just how would you know how a man's equipment should be working."

"Never mind. I'll behave now." Her fingers sped down the front placket of his trouser fly until she'd freed the last button.

"That's enough." Certain that the woman meant nothing but trouble, Jared moved well out of her reach across the room, and shucked himself of his trousers and the rest of his clothes, tossing them aside.

He turned back to her, expecting to find his bride where he'd left her on the bench at the foot of the bed, eagerly waiting for him. But she'd vanished.

"Kate?" Candles blazed everywhere, leaving nothing but the darkest shadows beyond the flames.

"It's time." She had moved silently to the other side of the room, pillows piled in a corner and a candle on the floor in front of her.

She was standing utterly naked, her skin like gilded silk, her hair a cloud of the finest spun gold, her eyes bright and beckoning to him with her enchantments.

"Time for what?" Time to take all that beauty to bed. But she seemed to have some other plan in mind.

She smiled seductively at him, lifted her lacy shawl off the arm of the chair, then started dancing with it, a slow, serpentine flow of languid arms and sinuous thighs.

"Well, it's not a blazing fire." She turned her back to him, swaying that gorgeously rounded bottom at him, all undulating curves and two dimples that he hadn't known were there. "And there's no music."

So entrancing he couldn't stay away.

"It's not the jungles of the Abasanti, Kate, but I'm sure they would be pleased."

He was pleased.

He was ramrod straight and aching.

She was a glory of shadows and shapes and bobbing breasts, of swirling hips and golden hair, and that luxurious length of lace that she draped here and drew across there, hiding away her most savory details just as he expected to see them, taunting him, drawing him toward her.

Until he was standing in the circle of her light, reaching out for her, catching one of her kisses when she turned in her dance, his eager, unabashed wife.

"You're very like an Abasanti tribesman tonight, Jared."

Christ's bones, she was beautiful!

She swayed in place, regarded him steadfastly, boldly flicking her gaze downward across his belly to rest on his penis, staring at his groin, rocking the room sideways.

"And you, woman, are utterly wanton."

"I can see you so well under an Abasanti moon, my warrior husband." She draped the lace shawl over her shoulders and strolled toward him, smiling, her hips still swaying. "Celebrating your astounding prowess, proudly wearing two stripes of ochre paint along your jaw."

His extraordinary wife applied the imaginary ochre paint to his jaw with her fingers, following each with a line of hot, lingering kisses that drove him ever closer to the edge, that wrapped him in the heady scent of lilac and lemon.

"Dashes of deep red across your chest." Her fingers were like slow, sweet fire, had a wild rhythm of their own.

"And, husband, a thick band of dazzling violet from the base of your throat down the length of your torso—"

She slid her fingers downward, over his heart and then lower to the middle of his belly and downward until he realized where she was heading.

"Kate!" He would have caught her hand, but she stopped short of his arousal so he held back, watching her every move, watching her breasts bob, well within reach. "These Abasanti warriors must have nerves of steel."

"Men of great courage." She kissed him, dallied there with her tongue, then drew her fingers lightly down the bridge of his nose to his mouth. "Blue means that the warrior has raised himself up from a dark abyss to a place of great honor."

"So much for that piddling knighthood ceremony I went through at Westminster Abbey when I received my earldom."

"You do look fine in your ceremonial paint."

He felt fine. And good. And almost worthy of her.

"Is there another color?" He spread his arms, opened his palms to her dance.

"Orange, my husband, from your shoulder to the tips of your fingers." Her touch was slow and magnificent, soothing and raw, wild and sinuous.

She trailed kisses across his chest, spent a time tugging and licking at his nipples, nibbling, brushing her hips against his until he had closed his eyes and was moving slightly to her melody.

"Now, if I were an Abasanti woman I would devise my own band of color to bestow on my warrior."

He liked being Kate's own personal warrior, attended to with such care. "What color would that be?"

She rubbed her cheek against his chest. "A blend of two actually, a sunshine yellow and the green of a pine forest. Carefully applied from the buttocks forward around the hip to the—

"Kate!" Too late. Her wonderful hands. "Gahhhhhh, that's so fine."

She had flattened her palms and drawn them across his stomach and then in a single move, she'd fluted him with her exquisite fingers. Circled him, found his pulse and matched it.

"You're so large, Jared. And thick and hot. I love the feel of you."

He grabbed her shoulders, his blood sodden with the bliss of her touch. "Take care, Kate."

"I promise the best of care." Her hands blinded him with their pleasure, never still, stealing his will and his breath. Then she slipped to her knees and was kissing him, flicked her tongue across the tip of him.

"Jesus God, wife." *Stop!* But the word never left his mouth.

He let her hum and sway and nibble and gather his scrotum into her hands, let her fondle and taste, but when she took him into her mouth he caught her chin and dropped to his knees in front of her.

She was wearing a look of injured confusion. "You're disappointed?"

Jared growled out a shudder of restraint. "No, love, I'm nearly spent."

"So you like that kind of kiss as much as I do?"

He groaned again with the memory of her squirming under his kiss, the feel of her mouth around him. "To the depth of my soul, I do. Next time?"

"Later tonight?"

"If I'm still alive." He laughed and moved to sit on one of pillows that were scattered around them in the glow of the candle.

"I wish we could have been together on that far away South Sea island." She advanced on him until she was sitting in his lap, her legs around his waist, her face inches from his. "Dancing to the flame. I'd have chosen you, Jared. Above all the others."

"And I'd have chosen you." She'd started up her bewitching rhythm, shifting her hips until the tip of him was bumping against all that steamy moisture.

He bent his knees and gave himself a perfect trajectory. A simple thrust and he'd be through her maidenhead. But that would make him a selfish brute and he didn't want Kate to think that of him.

"I love this feeling, Jared." She draped her lithe arms around his neck and rocked forward. "Fitting so tightly against you." And then again in a steady measure. "So like a kiss."

He couldn't take his eyes off hers for fear of losing all his restraint. They were reflected flame and the stormy blue of the sea.

Every motion took him more deeply inside her, inch by inch, brought him up against a barrier that didn't seem to faze her. "Are you all right, Kate?"

"Mmmm . . . oh, yesss!" She gripped his shoulders and threw her head back, moaning in ecstacy. "But I think I have to . . ."

She plunged her hips forward, driving his shaft all the way to the hilt. "Oh!"

Her eyes went wide as saucers. "You're huge, Jared."

And he was rattling with lust for her, wanting to plunge and thrust and grind their hips together.

But he gritted his teeth and stilled himself inside her, savoring her heat and the slickness and the depth until he could finally speak, finally ask her how a virgin could be so worldly and open when it came to sexual relations.

He dropped his forehead against hers. "Kate, have you had experience with this position before tonight?"

"Once."

His heart fell.

"But only for a moment."

"Where? How?"

"After I left the Abasanti dance to go back to my own bed." She wriggled her hips languidly against him, taking his breath away. "I stumbled across a couple sitting just like we are. Obviously a private time, so I left immediately. But I've never forgotten."

"I'm glad of that." And straining along with her in this tribal rite. Rocking with her, as she raked her fingers through his hair and cupped his face in her hands, gazing into his eyes.

"Thank you for coming home to me, Jared."

"And you for not hitting me with a kettle."

She was breathless and riding him, slick and hot and ready for his touch. He slid his palm between them, fondled his way toward the heat of her, where she was rising up to meet his touch and then a husky throated sigh.

"Ohhhh . . . ooooo, Jarrrrrrred!" She grabbed his shoulders and crooned her way through her climax. A wild, guttural roar that set him off toward his own splintering release.

Kate heard herself tell Jared how much she loved him, but her words sounded more like a growl. And she was riding him, bucking and swaying on these waves of astounding pleasure. Troughs and crests and cyclones of heat.

And a deep need to cling to him, though he was looking at her with wildfire in his eyes, gripping her arms and then plundering her mouth as he thrust and rocked against her and cried out her name.

"My Kate!" He clutched her bottom and ground her closer to him with the same need that she had to bind them together.

"My brave warrior." She kissed him and nibbled at his ear and he looked at her with the sated eyes of a bear with a belly full of black currants.

"You've exhausted him." He wrapped his arms around her waist and fell back with her into the pile of pillows they'd tossed all over the floor, and snuggled her against him.

"Do you suppose it will work for us, Jared?" She scrubbed his damp hair out of his face, kissed his cheek and the corner of his smile.

"Will what work?" His eyes looked better focused now, glittering under his dark lashes.

"The Abasanti fertility rite. Do you suppose a child will be born from our dance?"

He glanced down at her, quirking his dark brow at her, his smile as warm as she'd ever seen it.

"Good Lord, woman, you gave me twelve tonight already. How many more have you got?"

Kate snuggled against him. "Imagine, husband, if we'd have had a real moon."

Chapter 23

"It's too quiet, Jared," Kate said, stopping in the middle of the foyer at Hawkesly Hall, suspicious of the utter silence.

"I sense a trap." Jared's well-trained eyes tracked up the stairs as though he believed someone might leap down on them from the landing.

Someone like Grady or Mr. McNair or Drew. But the stillness continued.

"Since they ought to be at their lessons right now," Kate whispered, fully suspecting a prank, "let's try the library."

She led Jared down the corridor, then pushed the door open and peered inside. The room was occupied by nine little scholars sitting upright at the school table.

And two big ones, lounging in wing chairs.

The lot of them silent, in suspiciously motionless

poses, the two men reading newspapers, each child reading a book.

Mera's was upside down.

Kate caught Jared's smile and said, "Nobody in here that I know, Lord Hawkesly."

"Nor I, Lady Hawkesly. Shall we go find our children?"

Dori burst off the bench. "But it's *us*, Lady Kate!"

The room erupted into spasms of laughter, the boys rolling on the floor, holding their bellies, the girls dancing in circles toward Kate and Jared.

Drew stood, smiling at Jared and then at Kate. "Just educating the troops for you while you were . . . otherwise occupied."

She would have to thank them one day.

"We named the baby, Lady Kate!"

Oh, dear, she'd forgotten that the children were working on that assignment. "That's just wonderful, Healy."

Kate looked up at Jared, afraid for the poor little thing, hoping for the best, realizing that they could always hide the name in the middle of a longer one.

"What name did you give her?" Jared asked, sitting on the table, eye level with Healy.

"Belizabut."

Jared threw Kate a shocked glance; Kate tried to hold up her smile as she repeated the name, "Beliza—?"

Drew smiled wanly and said to them under his breath, "Elizabeth."

"Elizabeth." Kate said, releasing the breath she'd been holding, catching Jared's wink and his smile.

"Elizabeth is a fine name," Jared said.

"That's right! Belizabut!" Healy clapped his hands

together then climbed easily into Jared's arms.

Kate watched the pair of them and the backs of her eyes began to sting. Healy was her son! Hers and Jared's. And he would always be.

So were Glenna and Dori, Grady and Justin, Mera and all the others. A full dozen.

"Speaking of Elizabeth," Kate said, suddenly anxious to see her, "I think I'll go see how she's doing."

"She right here," Ross said, grinning from the comfort of his chair. He moved his newspaper and revealed the little bundle cradled in his lap. "She's quite the charmer."

"Oh! Thank you, Ross." Kate sighed in relief and lifted Elizabeth into her arms. Such a familiar fit, warmer now and a bit more weighty.

Jared slipped his arm around her waist. "As I said, Kate: they're irresistible to children and dogs."

"Lunchtime, boys and girls!" Tansy was standing at the door, her spoon held aloft. "Anyone for meatpies and peach cobbler?"

"Meatpies!" A river of children tumbled past Tansy.

"Are their lordships staying for lunch too?"

Ross stood, shaking his head. "Not today, Tansy, but I'll be back one day for those bacon biscuits of yours."

Which sent Tansy giggling all the way down the hallway.

"Running away, gentlemen?" Jared said, his arms now free of Healy.

"All the way to Liverpool," Ross said, folding his newspaper. "On your orders."

"Liverpool?" Kate said, looking first at Jared and then at his two friends. "I have an enormous favor to ask of you both."

Drew dipped a courtly bow. "Anything at all, my lady."

"If you don't mind, Jared. Father Sebastian needs to return to his work in Wicklow and I've insisted that he take the mail packet from Liverpool instead of that leaky launch of his that managed to survive the rocks and the storm."

"If Ross and Drew don't mind traveling with the eccentric old priest, it's fine with me."

"We'll even walk the old fellow up the gangway."

"Thank you, Drew, Ross," Kate said. "Please come back when you can stay longer. I've so much to ask you about so many things."

Drew hooked his elbow in hers and started toward the library door. "Oh, and have we got stories to tell on your husband."

The two men slipped away with Father Sebastian while the children were still eating, avoiding an hour's worth of chaos.

Kate found herself smiling madly through the next two days.

At Jared showing the boys how to tie knots.

At his courageous attempts to read to the girls, who would pile onto him like puppies.

At the nap he took in the middle of the library floor, with Mr. McNair's massive head resting on his stomach.

Three weeks ago she didn't even know the man. Now she loved him to the depths of her soul.

Not because he was impossibly handsome or strong or powerful. But because he was such a good man, honorable and kind and deeply generous.

Though she did love the handsome part, too.

Loved him naked and sliding into their bed with that wicked gleam in his eye.

"Home at last, Kate."

"In our own bed. In Hawkesly Hall," she whispered, as she burrowed into his embrace the following night, surrounded by the fierce heat of him. "I was afraid you'd be all night at your work."

"And miss holding you, love?" He nestled his lips against her ear. "I've learned my lesson."

"You must be a quick study."

"It took me nearly two years to come home to you."

She rolled up onto her elbow, drew her fingertip from his forehead to his lips. "Then how long did it take you to become an earl after you escaped the workhouse?"

He gave a little laugh. "An eternity."

"And how did you meet the queen, let alone become her advisor? You see, I still have lots of questions left over from our courting."

"I saved Her Majesty from a great financial scandal in the first month of her reign."

"I don't remember hearing anything about a scandal."

He touched the tip of her nose. "And you never will. At least not the details."

"So she was grateful to you ever since."

"And to Ross and Drew."

"Is that when you received your earldom?"

"There were another three titles before that. It's a long story, my love, and I'll tell it to you when we have time to spare."

"While you're taking off my drawers."

"With pleasure, my love." He rucked up the hem of her nightgown and slid his hand up her thigh. "Wait. You're not wearing any drawers. See."

Then her amazing husband began his nightly exploration of her most sensitive places with the most tender care. Life with him couldn't possibly be better.

Everyone should be as happy as she and Jared were.

"They really should be married, Jared. Ohhh, I love when you do that."

It took him a moment to let go of her nipple. "Who?"

"Ross and Drew."

He lifted himself on his elbows and gazed down at her. "To each other?"

"You know what I mean." She smoothed his hair off his forehead. "They're such fine husband material."

"Ross hasn't the time and Drew snores."

She laughed. "So do you. And you're the best one of the lot."

"No matchmaking, Kate. They've got enough to do at the moment."

"Like what? What exactly does a spy do for the Home Office?"

He slipped his arms around her, settled his cheek against hers. "For example, a few weeks ago they were investigating a case of gun running."

"That sounds dangerous. Where?"

"The ship was intercepted by customs agents in Portsmouth, the cargo searched and the guns and ammunition were discovered hidden in a shipment of Indian corn."

A tiny chill ran through her. Guns and Indian corn. Obviously bound for somewhere in Ireland. "So what did the agents do then?"

"Contacted me via the Home Office. Then I sent Drew and Ross to investigate the captain and the manifest and other possible clues."

"What happened to the cargo?" All that Indian corn—someone was waiting for it.

Jared curled his fingers in her hair and put his fist to his nose. "Impounded for evidence against the captain and the conspirators."

"Even the Indian corn? Surely there's nothing illegal about importing grain. What if there are hungry children waiting for it to be delivered to their bowls?"

"It's a legal matter, Kate. The corn is impounded by customs and stored in a government warehouse until the investigation is completed as well as any trial that might come as a result."

"How long does that take?"

"A few months, a year. Sometimes longer."

"It'll rot by then. What a waste of food. Imagine how many starving people all that Indian corn would feed if it could be sent to one of the Irish grain depots."

"Wouldn't help now, love. Trevelyan is closing the grain depots for good."

Kate sat up, scooting back against the pillows. "He can't be! That's cruel!" But it was so very much the way of that bastard Trevelyan and his kind.

"According to my source, it's just too expensive for the Home Office to administer. Parliament has been complaining of taxing the English for the troubles in Ireland."

Tears welled in her eyes, hot with sorrow and righteousness because she was striking Trevelyan and Russell and Grey in their evil hearts. Liberating their ill-gotten grain was good and right, and she would continue as long as she could.

"Oh, Jared, imagine all those dear, starving children who won't last the night because of them."

A few weeks ago, Jared hadn't been able to imagine such children at all. Rather, he had no reason to do so, certainly hadn't wanted to. But these were memories of his own that he'd long ago banished.

And now they were back. No longer frightening, but still vastly dangerous.

Unsettled to his core, he gathered Kate into his arms, snuggled her against him like a pair of spoons and slept the night in a deeply restful peace that he didn't quite deserve.

Morning came early in a house full of children.

"They're still in bed!" came a chorus of little voices, just as the counterpane filled up with bony little arms and knees.

His daughters and his sons. Bloody hell.

Kate was already sitting up, thankfully having donned her nightgown for an earlier trip down the hall to the sickroom.

"Out you go, children!" she was saying. "Now. Lord Jared needs his sleep."

He actually needed his robe. But he kept the covers clutched to his chin until the mob was gone and Kate had secured the door behind them.

Feeling as though he had just been raided by a band of

very tiny warriors, Jared fell back against the pillows, exhausted. "Remind me to lock the door tonight."

"I was going to suggest that you wear your night-shirt to bed. But I far prefer my husbands stark naked." Her hips swayed as she came toward the bed, her eyes smokey.

"How many husbands have you got?"

"Just you at the moment. And if you're good, I'll keep you." She was up to something, but he hadn't un-derstood just what she meant to do until she raised the covers, knelt above him and then went to work fondling him.

"Oh, you sweet, sweeeet woman." His penis went from inert to completely engorged in the space of a breath. She kissed and savored him, hummed and wrig-gled and held him until he sat up sharply and pulled her onto his lap.

A shift of her hips and she took his shaft inside her, to the root of him. She climaxed around him, her eyes flashing as he spilled his seed inside her.

A sweaty, hushed moment of stolen pleasure that set him to grinning through the entire morning, and look-ing for Kate's smile around every corner.

He'd moved his office to a small, tall-windowed room off the library. Close to the daily activities, but where his papers were protected from little fingers and sticky treats.

He'd just settled into a long afternoon's reading when he noticed Kate driving a wagon through the gate, and then Elden right behind with another wagon.

Had she been to the village already? The woman

seemed to run from one project to the next, resting only after she'd fallen into bed beside him each night.

Perhaps he could help slow her down a bit. He met the wagons as they stopped at the bottom of the stairs.

"What's this, Kate?"

She looked a little lost for words, gave Elden a weary shrug. "Thanks, Elden."

The man tipped the brim of his cap. "I'll go get Ian to help unload."

Sensing another secret, Jared walked past Kate and lifted the canvas flap. The wagonbed was packed tightly with hampers and wicker baskets and leather cases, trunks and a box of rag dolls.

"Luggage? Was all this left over from the lodge?"

"No." Her shoulders sagged, little spots of pink bloomed on her cheeks. "It's from before."

"Before what?"

"Before you . . . well, before you changed." She caught her lower lip between her teeth, worried it on both sides.

"When was that?"

"Our wedding night." She heaved a sigh and lifted the box of dolls out of the wagon. "And I must admit it was just in time."

He took the box out of her arms and set it on the step. "What are you talking about? What have you got in the wagon?"

She put her fists against her hips in that stubborn way of hers. "You knew I was planning to leave with the children."

"I wouldn't have let you."

"You couldn't have stopped me. The wagons were packed and ready to go at any moment."

He'd married a lunatic. "You could have traveled to the tip of Scotland and hidden out in a rabbit burrow and I would have found you and your tagalongs."

"Ha!" She picked up the box and started up the stairs. "Isn't it a good thing that you didn't have to test your theory."

A very good thing, because the woman was completely unpredictable. "So the wagons are packed with things for the children."

"Clothes and food and shoes and blankets."

He caught her by the shoulders as she tried to pass him. "They're here to stay, Kate. I promise. And so am I."

She dropped her gaze for a moment, then wrapped her arms around his neck and kissed him. "Which makes me the luckiest woman in the entire world."

"And me the luckiest man."

Kate hadn't felt so very guilty about anything in a long time, looking up into her trusting husband's face, holding back still another troubling secret from him.

"I'm sorry about the wagons, Jared. An unpleasant reminder which I plan to be rid of within the next half hour. There's Elden and Ian, now."

He turned his broad back to the two approaching men and kissed her till her knees had turned to honey. "There's more where that came from, wife."

He left her then and disappeared into the house.

Elden came up behind her while Ian went to work carrying a barrel up the stairs.

"You didn't tell him anything, my lady?" The poor man seemed to have aged in the last week.

"I do want to, Elden." Kate slid a leather case and a canvas bag off the wagon bed. "But he wouldn't understand."

And though he didn't know it, he was all tied up in the ramifications.

"When are you leaving for Liverpool?"

"After Jared's asleep tonight. I can't let Father Sebastian stay in that horrid jail cell another day. I've got to get him out somehow."

But what was he doing in Liverpool when he ought to be in Wicklow? Drew and Ross had promised to deliver him safely. That was days ago.

"I wish you'd let me handle this for you, my lady."

"I need you here, Elden. I'll be careful. Hopwood didn't say anything in his note about the League itself being under suspicion. I should be able to spring the good father and be back home by supper tomorrow."

Elden groaned and shook his head. "I don't like the sound of this."

"Neither do I, but I have to take care of it myself. This whole scheme was my idea. If anything goes wrong, I'll take the blame."

But the man only grunted at her and started up the stairs with a battered old trunk.

"With any luck I'll be back home before he ever knows that I've been gone."

And if not, Jared would take good care of their children while she served out her long sentence in some dank old prison.

Chapter 24

Jared woke refreshed and contented, though his bed was empty of his lovely wife and a clock was just striking nine. He stretched and yawned, feeling more at home now than he ever had in his life. Coddled and cared for. Loved.

"Bless you, Kate." She'd let him sleep nearly ten hours after last night's short, but spectacularly torrid bout of lovemaking.

Kate had mentioned something about regretting the tremendously busy day awaiting her and had doubtless risen in the wee hours. She was probably halfway through her list of chores and projects.

He washed and dressed, looking forward to a day of reading up on the estate accounts and meeting with Elden, and his promise to teach the girls to tie knots the way he'd taught the boys.

Hell, his own schedule seemed downright slothful compared to Kate's. But by the time he got to the bottom of the stairs, his schedule had changed irrevocably.

"A message for you, sir." Ian handed him a sealed envelope. "Brought in from the village. Looks to be urgent."

Assuming it needed an immediate answer, Jared had Ian wait while he read it.

"Damnation!" The message needed more than an answer. It needed him, in the flesh.

"Everything all right, sir?"

"No, Ian." Kate wouldn't be at all pleased with him leaving just now. "Would you saddle my horse, please, and bring it around the front. And have you seen Lady Hawkesly?"

"Um . . ." Ian's eyes shifted to the wall and then to the floor. "Well, not this morning, sir. I'll just go get your horse for you."

The kitchen was empty of everyone but the three Miss Darbys, who greeted him with their usual effusion of good mornings, which he had little time to acknowledge just now.

"Do any of you know where I might find Lady Hawkesly?"

"Well . . ." Myrtle sliced a glance at her sisters.

"Myrtle, didn't she say something about the orchard?"

"And checking the progress of those fir seeds she blasted the other day."

This was not what he wanted to hear. "So you're saying that my wife could be anywhere?"

"You know how our lady is, sir," Tansy said as she peered up at him. "Can we help you?"

"I wanted to see her before I left, but I doubt I can spare the time tracking her down."

"You're leaving?" Rosemary hurried to his side.

"Can't be helped. I'll leave a note for Kate in our room, but please assure her that I'll be back as soon as I can. Hopefully before supper."

Jared was packed and on his horse fifteen minutes later, the hurry familiar and suddenly tiresome.

But he had been called to Liverpool by Customs to follow up on the great grain conspiracy.

My Lord Hawkesly,

Holding suspect in Home Office theft case at the Customs House in Liverpool. Awaiting your inquest before remanding suspect into the custody of the Royal Guards.

He had no choice but to look into the problem himself. Drew and Ross had sent a message yesterday that they been called back to Whitehall by Lord Grey, with Drew about to take on a personal assignment for the queen. But the consequence was that the investigation into Grey's missing grain now fell to Jared.

Right in the middle of a wondrous honeymoon with his magnificent wife. The beginning of the kind of marriage that he had only dared dream about and surely didn't deserve.

Retiring permanently to the country was looking very, very attractive.

He arrived in Liverpool during an early evening rain and walked from the train station to the Customs House, where he was redirected to a small building across the street and met by a slightly familiar face.

"Good Lord, if it isn't the earl of Hawkesly!" Lieutenant Nicholls grabbed Jared's hand and shook it with gusto. "I haven't seen you since New Delhi!"

"And you weren't a lieutenant at the time. Congratulations, Nicholls."

"To what do we owe the honor?"

Jared looked around the tidy office, a main room and two smaller, one whose door was barred but standing wide open.

"I'm here on behalf of the Home Office. You're holding a suspect. I'd like to see him as soon as possible." Because his head ached and he wanted to get back home to Kate.

Nicholls gave a laugh. "Actually, you can't see him, Hawkesly. Nobody can."

God he didn't need these parlor games. "Why? Is he dead?"

"Might be." Nicholls leaned back against his desktop and shrugged. "I wouldn't know. He's not here."

Jared hated these little kings in their kingdoms. "Then who's got him, Nicholls? I haven't got all day."

"Nobody's got him. The old fellow has flown."

"Escaped?" So he'd come all this way for nothing. "When did this happen?"

"A few hours ago." Nicholls went to the tea cart and poured a cup of the black stuff. "You wouldn't think an old man like him would have had the craftiness. But damn, if he didn't get himself sprung from his cell. Tea, Hawkesly?"

"No, thank you." Jared hitched his satchel strap higher on his shoulder, not wanting to stay a moment longer than necessary. "How did the suspect get out? Through the window?"

"Walked right out the front door." Nicholls took a slurping sip of his tea.

"In the middle of the day? With a room full of officers? How could that happen?"

Nicholls had the sense to look slightly chagrined. "I don't know, sir. I wasn't here."

"Then have you a report on the incident?"

"Ah! Right here. I was just going to file it away." Nicholls studied the single page. "But as I understand the circumstance, the man was caught in the early hours of yesterday breaking into one of the government's warehouses on the Albert Dock. A guard found him cutting open a sack of Indian corn."

"Not by chance the impounded cargo from the *Pickering*?"

"That's right. So you're on top of all this, Hawkesly?"

So it seemed, but tottering. An odd, unsettling coincidence. "What happened then?"

"Customs interrogated him, but he wouldn't say a word, apparently. So they brought him here to stew for a while, and then sent for you."

Bumbling idiots. What would he have done with an old man anyway? "How did this dangerous prisoner manage to walk out the door unnoticed?"

"He had a partner, a beautiful young woman. She came in a bit after noon claiming to have the old fellow's medicine. Well, it was lunchtime and we were short staffed and from what I hear the woman bewitched the impressionable young Sheridan."

"Bewitched him in what way?"

"Wiles, if you know what I mean. Helpless and charming, so Sheridan left her to visit with the prisoner in the cell. Then she asked for tea for the old man, and then water, and a warm blanket and such, one thing after another. So the fool Sheridan left the cell door open for her, and next thing he knew the pair was nowhere to be seen."

Bloody hell. "Didn't Sheridan go after them?"

"He searched the few blocks around, then gave up. Figured he was just a shabby old priest who muttered a lot and a faithful parishioner sent to spring him. Hardly a threat to anyone."

An elderly priest and a beautiful young woman?

Nicholls was obviously not an investigator, or hadn't a brain in head. The ploy had conspiracy stamped all over it. Too many common threads not to be entangled.

"All right then, Nicholls. I'll be on my way. Notify me through Customs if you ever find the pair."

Determined not to leave Liverpool without gathering at least some new information, Jared shouldered his satchel and crossed the street to the new edifice of the Albert Docks.

He'd watched it being built but hadn't yet seen it completed. A huge rectangle of water and wharf, made entirely of iron and concrete. Impressive.

No wonder both Lord Grey and the government had chosen the dock for their warehouse site. Expensive, but secure.

Jared's credentials gave him entry into the Customs warehouse to inspect the store of impounded Indian corn. The sight of a thousand sacks of grain sitting idle made his chest hurt.

Perhaps he could buy it from Customs, and see that it got to its original destination, because, as Kate had so wisely said, there were sad, starving children waiting for it somewhere.

Lord Grey's warehouse was across the rectangle, huge and meticulously administered, making him wonder how a noticeable quantity of grain could go missing every month for such a long time without a great deal of cleverness and organization.

Not only from Grey's warehouse, but from Lord Russell's in Briston and Trevelyan's in Plymouth.

And what had Drew mentioned about all those relief committee warehouses they'd found here in Liverpool? Jared searched his notes in the fading evening light and found the list of a half dozen of them on a variety of docks.

He walked across the street to the Salthouse Docks, finding an additional three relief committee warehouses, two of them completely empty, but little of interest until he came to the Ladies' Charitable League. One of those on Drew's list.

Though early evening sky was a steely gray, he saw no lights burning anywhere in the building. He would have knocked but noticed that someone had left the rear door open an irresistible inch.

Not wanting to announce his presence, Jared pushed the door open to the vastness of the warehouse, then closed it just as he'd found it. He stood quietly in the hulking dimness, letting his eyes adjust, listening to the building, the cry of the wheeling gulls outside the door.

But the creaky old warehouse seemed to dip and rise with the incoming tide, stiffly shouldering its roof and open rafters, its lofts and the few small rooms, the neatly organized rows of grain sacks.

A haunting voice, a melody of wood and iron.

And a soft, familiar fragrance in the midst of the salt and the creosote.

He wasn't alone here in the pale gray light from the clerestory windows. Probably only a clerk closing up after a long day. But he quieted his pulse, trying to localize the other sounds.

Clunk.

The noise came from somewhere ahead of him, in the front of the building that faced the cobbled streets instead of the wharf behind him.

Then a few soft footfalls. A shifting. Then nothing.

He found a silent floorboard and walked along its center until the first seam, then found another and another, past plump grain sacks and fat barrels until he had made it across the warehouse floor and was standing at an office door.

Banking on the element of surprise, Jared shoved the door open, ready for anything.

But the room appeared unoccupied. It was long and windowless and dimly lit by a single lamp on the table nearest the door. Crates were stacked in a jumble, filing chest drawers hung open, a disorder of papers spread out at the long worktable at the center.

Someone had either just left in a hurry, or he was still there.

He held his silence, listened for the telltale sound of breathing, the rustle of clothing, the scrape of a shoe.

He heard nothing at all, yet felt a presence, the unmistakable sense that someone else was in the room.

"I know you're here." He heard the faintest gasp from the far end of the room, and then a bump. "Come out, please. I just want to ask you a few questions."

An unintelligible, anxious whisper, and then that palpable silence again.

"I'm not going to hurt you. In fact, I apologize for entering the premises without knocking. My name is Hawkesly. I'm with the Home Office, making inquiries of the relief committee warehouses, and your door was open."

He thought he saw a cloaked shape slip between two sets of shelves. Small statured, obviously not too keen about him being there.

"You ought to realize that I'm not leaving here until I talk with you face to face. Do you understand that?"

The figure stepped partially into view, the movement loosening a long sprig of hair from beneath the hood of the cloak.

A woman? Possibly the one who had released the old man from jail. The perfect connection: a priest, a poor relief warehouse and a store of impounded Indian corn.

Not above prompting a response with little threat, Jared said, "I'm investigating a major theft ring, which puts you squarely in the midst of a great deal of trouble, madam. Whether you're a knowledgeable partner in the crime or not. Things will go far better for you if you cooperate."

Silence. And that familiar fragrance again. Tendrils of lavender and lemons.

Kate's scent, doubtless carried on his jacket, his collar, finding him in the dimness, but waiting for him back at Hawkesly Hall.

Impatient to return home in time to slip into bed beside her tonight, he snapped, "Dammit, woman, you'll come here and tell me what you know, or you'll find yourself back in the same cell you visited earlier today."

His shout must have shaken her loose of her obstinacy. She stepped from behind the shelves, shapeless in her large cloak, her head down as she moved toward him.

"A wise decision, madam."

Though there was an unsettling sway in her bearing, and in the shape of her arms as she reached up behind her head and pulled back the obscuring hood.

A glorious cascade of hair tumbled across her shoulders, burnished gold in the pale candlelight, loosely curled and shimmering.

The color of Kate's hair, the same dancing flame and lace, the delicious scent of her caught up in his clothes, in his nostrils.

Familiar and intimate.

The woman raised her nose and then her chin and finally her piercing blue eyes. Until he was looking into the face of the woman he loved beyond his life, who haunted his days and his dreams.

"Kate?" But that made no sense. Not here in Liverpool.

She was at home with their children. She couldn't be here in this obviously suspicious warehouse, embroiled in a political conspiracy against the prime minister and the most powerful members of his cabinet.

Not his Kate.

"Jared, I'm so sorry. . . ." But that was her voice, the lilt and smoke of it. Those were her blue eyes, beseeching him as she came fully into the brightest boundaries of the candle flame.

Kate!

He reached out to her, but the world had shifted, rocked him backward.

"Christ, woman, what are you doing here?"

Kate had wanted to sob in relief when she'd heard Jared's voice from the office door. The man who had become the breadth of her world in such a short time.

He'd come all the way to Liverpool to find her, to protect her. But, no, that couldn't be true. He couldn't have known she was here in the warehouse with the grain unless Elden had confessed it. And that was impossible.

He must have come after one of his criminals.

And he'd found her instead.

Now he was framed against the lamplight, towering above her in his fury, silent, his eyes flinty as winter.

Unforgiving.

"Jared, I'm sorry—"

"Who are you, madam? You look so much like my beloved wife."

He might as well have slapped her. The stinging rebuke of a stranger's distaste. "Jared, please listen to—"

"To more of your lies?" His voice was so intimately condemning, so resonant. He began a slow circle around her, his eyes fixed on hers. "But please, go ahead, tell me anything you wish. I love your stories: falsehood clad in all sorts of disguises. Do start with the reason that you're here in Liverpool, in this warehouse."

The truth would only separate them further. "What I do here has nothing to do with you and me."

"It bloody well does!" His circling made her turn and turn, in order to face him, to follow his eyes. "My God, Kate, I'm here from the Home Office to investigate a massive conspiracy. To find and interrogate a thief. Have I succeeded? Have I found my thief?"

A huge sob caught in her throat, making it difficult to answer, and the truth taste so bitter. But she raised her chin as he stopped his blasted stalking and matched the fury of her gaze to his.

"If you mean have you found the person responsible for the transfer of grain from Lord Grey's warehouse, and Russell's and Trevelyan's to the Ladies' Charitable League's warehouse, then . . . yes, you have."

He reared back as though she'd struck him, took a sharp breath as if just hearing her admit the truth had injured him to the quick, though he must have already known. Then he clamped his hands around her upper arms and pulled her close, a dark fire blazing in his eyes.

"Christ, Kate, do you know what you've set in motion, what you've done? To yourself? To me? To our children?"

"I know exactly what I've done and who I'm doing it

for. I am apportioning justice as best I know how."

His breath bellowed against her cheeks. "By recklessly stealing tons of grain from the three most powerful men in Britain?"

She nodded. "And then giving it to a soup kitchen that keeps thousands of children from starving to death every month." The bright light of righteousness filled her chest. The rightness of her cause.

"Kate, are you listening to yourself? Boasting to me of your crimes. Have you any idea who I am?"

"My husband." Her hardheaded champion.

"Dammit all, I'm Lord Grey's deputy! Do you know what that means?" He growled and held her even closer, the lamplight shadowing his eyes, darkly planing his jaw. "If you were anyone else in the world I would clamp you in handcuffs, parade you across the docks, and toss you into a jail cell. You'd have a short trial and be transported for the next fourteen years of your life. Fourteen years. Hell, Mera would be married, with her own children by the time you were sent home. That's who I am, Kate!"

"And for all that, Jared, all your blustering, I'm not just anyone else in the world. I'm your wife. And you're still my husband." Aching for him and this breach between them, Kate touched her hand to his chest, feeling his heart clattering around beneath her palm. "I love you because I know that you'll do what's right and honorable."

"And what about you, Kate?" He took hold of her hand. "You're supposed to be home with our children."

"I left them safely in your care. How could I have

known you were going to leave too?" And yet a wave of guilt washed over her, with neither of them home to protect them. "Father Sebastian had gotten himself into trouble and—"

"Then the old priest in the prison cell was Father Sebastian?"

"He'd heard Drew and Ross talking about the Indian corn from the *Pickering*. It's stored right outside that door in a warehouse in the Albert Docks."

"Yes, I know. The *Pickering* is my investigation. So is Lord Grey's missing grain. Not to mention the case of my wife the jailbreaker." He turned away from her, flattened his palms against the tabletop and the scattered papers she'd been sorting through. "Hell, the inquest into this whole illegal operation of yours belongs to me."

Her heart sank at the sight of his misery, his head hanging, his wondrously dark hair falling over his forehead. She wanted to touch him but knew he would flinch from her and that would hurt too much.

"I wouldn't have kept the secret from you forever, Jared." After the famine was over and the children grown, when they were both old and sitting comfortably by the hearth. She would have told him then about the justice she had meted out to the wicked death dealers back in '48.

But he didn't seem to be listening, had picked a piece of paper off the table. "What's this?"

"It's nothing. Just a bill of lading." And other evidence against so many people if anyone ever looked closely enough. She started collecting the paper into stacks. "Endless paperwork. Invoices and letters, manifests."

"Corroboration of your crimes." He grabbed her wrist and stopped her, his mouth set in a resolute line. Then he went back to sifting through the piles, tossing pages here and there, until he yanked one back.

"Martin Hopwood," was all he said. Then he raised his frown to her. "My estate manager's signature on a manifest for the *Katie Claire*, dated only last week? What the hell's going on here?"

Kate swallowed, her tongue dry as dust as he watched her mouth and then her eyes. "Martin Hopwood is one of the bravest men I've ever met, with a heart the size of the sun."

"You recruited him to do your dirty work? An old man who should be living out his retirement in peace? Is no one safe from your calculations?"

"Martin helped me start up our grain-running scheme and now eagerly manages the traffic. Who better to keep account of our work than a man who ran an estate for thirty years?"

"Not only that damn fool Hopwood, but the *Katie Claire*? Now you've involved one of my ships?"

"The *Katie Claire* belongs to me, named for me. And far better being used to carry food to innocent children than to lay at anchor and abandoned in Liverpool."

He shook his head at her, raked his fingers through his hair. "Christ, I'm just glad I caught you in time."

"In time for what?" But a cold panic had already settled across her shoulders.

"To pack up all this, for starters." He grabbed an

empty crate from a shelf and started shoving the papers inside.

"Why? What are you doing? I need those."

"No you don't. I'm going to incinerate the lot and anything else incriminating that I find," he said, with a narrow-eyed growl. "And then I'm taking you home."

Kate backed away from him, out of reach around the end of the table, fearing the worst, that he would never understand. "And then what?"

He kept up his paper stuffing. "Then you're going to live out your life safely beside me at Hawkesly Hall."

"No, Jared. I can't."

"Can't?" He stared at her, as though unable to comprehend her words. "What the devil does that mean?"

"I still have work to do." Months of it, years perhaps. So many children to feed.

"Your work is done, Kate. I'm taking you away from this unholy mess while I still can. Consider the Ladies' Charitable League disbanded for good."

"I will not." Tears began to swim in her eyes. "We've just gotten everything running smoothly. The warehouses and the grain transfers and the *Katie Claire*. I won't stop it now."

"Are you mad?" He'd dropped the papers and now rounded the table toward her, a helpless fury gathering in his voice. "You're an inch from being caught."

"But nobody knows what I'm doing here."

"I do." He took his steady steps toward her and still she backed away, fearing his determination. "Ross and Drew know. They don't know that you're the culprit, but, Kate, they soon will."

"How would they, unless you told them?" Surely he wouldn't reveal her secret! He wasn't that kind of man.

"Christ, I don't need to tell them. The prime minister has put the chancellor of the Exchequer on the case. You'll be found out and arrested and it'll be out of my hands. I can't have that"—he slipped his hands behind her head—"because, Kate, I can't lose you."

"You won't. But I can't stop running grain. The children are hungry *now*. They're starving *now*. You held our Elizabeth." She couldn't help the tears streaming down her cheeks, couldn't hide them. "You said yourself that there was nothing to her. Twigs for bones. If she hadn't been left to Father Sebastian she wouldn't have lived another day. Think of how horrible that would have been! Never to know her—"

"Kate, please stop this!" His eyes were glittering and hot, rimmed red in his fury and frustration.

"But you saw how quickly she rallied with just a few sips of Rosemary's gruel. You fed her yourself. Ounce by ounce. I've heard you cooing to her, seen you encouraging her to eat." Kate slipped her fingers through his hair. "Think of the hundreds of babies like Elizabeth, just waiting for a little food from a kind heart. From someone who dares to give a damn."

He stopped and stared at her for a long time, the muscles in his jaw flickering. "Dammit, Kate, if you'd only . . ." But then he stopped, relaxed some, his shoulders easing. "Hell, I should have thought of it before."

"What?"

He sighed as though the world had suddenly righted for him. "Look, if it means so much to you, I'll buy you enough grain every month to supply three soup kitchens."

Three! Two extra kitchens. Think how many thousands would that feed! "Oh, Jared, that's wonderful."

"But it means the end of your conspiracy. We close down your League activities. No more plundering the prime minister's warehouse."

Her tears welled up again; he didn't understand. "As much as I'd like to accept your offer, I can't."

Jared could only stare at his wife, trying to make sense of her plain-faced statement.

"What do you mean, you can't?" He'd just supplied her with all the answers. "I've money enough and ships. And, by God, if it'll extricate you from this mess you've made for yourself—"

"I don't want extricating. I want justice for the innocent lives they've taken and the ones they've yet to take." She wore her pride high on her cheeks.

"Justice?" She bandied the word like a ball, as though it were a simple thing to conceive or carry out. God knows he'd tried in his life.

"I want Trevelyan to pay for his cruelty, for his injustice and inhumanity." She started straightening the piles of papers with her long, capable fingers, putting things back in their places. "I want Lord Grey and the cowardly Lord Russell to feel the price of their evil every month, every day, every hour. I want them to watch the grain slip out of their warehouses as though it were their life's blood. I want them to know it can't be staunched—"

"Are you mad?" He grabbed her hand, turned her toward him. "You can't keep this up forever."

"But I have to try. Until the famine ends. There's too much at stake. If I let you spend your honestly hard-won money to supply the grain instead of stealing it from the three men who have so selfishly, carelessly mismanaged the famine and caused the starvation, then they win. Their egregious sins cost them nothing. That's not right."

"I can't let you, Kate." Though her every word rang with such clarity in his heart. Evil men with evil hearts.

Closing relief depots, withholding the funds that would have saved countless lives, imposing laws that made paupers of hardworking farmers, and broke up families.

And used workhouses to punish and degrade, to steal away hope and joy.

"You know it's the right and good thing to do, Jared."

Do it for Thomas. For the boy who'd never had a chance against Craddock. For the boy he had tried so hard to save.

And the woman who had become his life. She looked like a runaway, not a wife, wild-haired and rumpled, standing guard over her cause.

He had his answer, and something deep inside of him knew it was right and unregrettable.

He picked up one of the *Katie Claire*'s bills of lading, his hands shaking, because this was probably the most foolish step he'd ever taken. "How does it work, Kate? Your little conspiracy?"

Her eyes grew wide, frightened. "Why?"

Surely she didn't really think he would ever turn her

over to the authorities. "Because, Kate, I need to know every nuance of your proceedure. The smallest detail of every warehouse, every person, your schedule, the ports—"

"But why?" She clutched at the front of her cloak, looked terrified, as though he was about to betray her.

"To keep myself out of trouble. Because if I'm caught it means the gallows for me."

"The gallows!" She clamped her fingers over her mouth. "What do you mean? Caught doing what?"

"Oh, my love, things you'd never imagine I was capable of doing." Feeling reckless and desperately in love with the beautiful, wide-eyed woman, Jared tossed aside the bill of lading, slipped his hands inside the warm folds of her cloak, then lifted her up to sit on the table.

"Jared, we haven't settled this problem between us."

"We have. But you forget, my love, I'm a spy." Enjoying her moment of confusion, he opened the cloak clasp at the base of her throat. "And soon to be a pirate in truth."

"You're also a priggish, stone-headed lunatic." But she sighed as he ran his hands slowly over her ribcage and gathered her against him, moaned against his cheek and then sat up. "What do you mean, you're going to be a pirate?"

"It's what you want me to do, isn't it?"

"I said nothing about a pirate."

"Perhaps I need to become a member of your club." He'd conquered the buttons on the front of this particular shirtwaist and had them undone before she noticed, and his hands playing at the linen of her camisole. His uncorseted wife and her lovely nipples which crimped when he fondled them, and made her gasp.

"Ohhhhhh . . . my! A pirate? You've gone completely mad." She sighed, nicely flummoxed, her eyes so blue, her lashes wet. "I don't have a club."

"Ah, the League, then." He covered her delicious sweet mouth with his, made love there with his tongue. "The Ladies' Charitable League. Or do I need to be a lady for that?"

Another long sigh against his mouth. "I prefer you as a lord."

"But obviously not as a master. You haven't the slightest idea how to obey."

She stopped her squirming and glared at him. "If you think this little seduction is going to make me change my mind, you're wrong, husband."

"What if I offer myself up as your own personal double agent in the Home Office?"

She quirked her brow. "What do you mean?"

He took her hand, kissed her fingers. "If you promise never to take a risk that you don't first tell me about. Ever, Kate."

"I'm listening—"

"If you must have your justice done, then I'll help you."

"How?"

"I'm a spy, remember? I pick locks and tamper with evidence, forge signatures and have access to most any piece of information you'd ever need to mask the activities of your little band of thieves."

Her eyes had grown wide with wonder. She took

hold of his jacket and smiled madly up at him. "You'd do that, Jared?"

"For the children, Kate. For you. Because I love you beyond all things. Because you waited for me to come home and love me in spite of my faults."

Kate saw a peace come over her splendid husband, his eyes smiling, his grin lopsided. Her handsome hero, who could love a dozen children all at once, and rescue her from her recklessness, and danced so finely in the moonlight—

"I love you, Jared."

She'd have said more, but the delicious man had enfolded her in his arms and was making the most amazing love to her mouth, whispering his heart and his hopes, telling her of his dreams for the children.

A most amazing man.

Her husband, her pirate, her spy.

Lose yourself in enchanting love stories from Avon Books.
Check out what's coming in December:

HOW TO TREAT A LADY by Karen Hawkins
An Avon Romantic Treasure

Harriet Ward invented a fiance to save her family from ruin, but when the bank wants proof, fate drops a mysterious stranger into her arms, a man she believes has no idea of his own identity. And so she announces that he is her long-awaited betrothed!

A GREEK GOD AT THE LADIES' CLUB by Jenna McKnight
An Avon Contemporary Romance

What if you had created the perfect replica of a gorgeous Greek god, and right before you're about to unveil it to a group of ladies, it comes alive in all its naked glory? What if your creation wanted to reward you by fulfilling your every desire? What if you're tempted to let him . . .

ALMOST PERFECT by Denise Hampton
An Avon Romance

Cassandra wagered a kiss in a card game with rake Lucien Hollier and willingly paid her debt when she lost. Then, desperate for funds, she challenges him again . . . and wins! Taking Lucien's money and fleeing into the night, the surprisingly sweet taste of his kiss still on her lips, Cassie is certain she's seen the last of him . . .

THE DUCHESS DIARIES by Mia Ryan
An Avon Romance

Armed with advice from her late grandmother's diaries, Lady Lara Darling is ready for her first Season. But before she even reaches London, the independent beauty breaks all the rules set forth in the Duchess Diaries when she meets the distractingly handsome Griff Hallsbury.

REL 1103

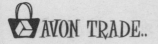